About the author

Miranda took up writing as a hobby when she was a stay-at-home mum and her moods swung dramatically from "all sweetness and light" to "demented mother of three". She has had a number of short stories published in magazines both in Ireland and the UK and wrote a series of "Demented Mother of Three" articles for a local paper when her children were very young. She particularly likes the short story as a genre both as a reader and a writer. She has been a runner-up in more short story competitions than she cares to remember and wonders what that says about her. *Who is Alice?* started out as a short story and just grew. It is her first novel. She returned to her day job as an office manager when her children grew older.

She has three adult children and lives in Galway.

Acknowledgements

I would like to thank Paula Campbell, Ailbhe Hennigan, Sarah Ormston and all at Poolbeg for their assistance and encouragement after *Who is Alice?* was accepted. Many thanks to my editor Gaye Shortland for her endless patience during the editing process.

Thanks also to Mary Madigan for reading the various drafts and making useful suggestions. To Tom Murphy and Lily O'Brien for their encouragement while I was writing the book, particularly towards the end. And lastly to my family, the Murphys and the Mannings, for just being there.

To John, William and Emer

Chapter 1

Nicola just knew that this was going to be an awful day. It had started with yet another row with Jonathan, the man she called her partner and was longing to call her ex. The Taoiseach had dropped dead a few days earlier as he walked from his car into Dublin Castle and, while the country was not in turmoil, there had been nothing else discussed anywhere since. Then the first phone message on her machine was from a deeply distressed woman, who said her name was Alice O'Brien. She said that she had been locked out of her apartment, that the locks had been changed, and that she and her children had nothing except the clothes they stood up in. The call had come after closing time the previous evening so Nicola felt that she was already too late when she dialled the number on the message.

"Alice?" Nicola asked, surprised when a very confident-sounding woman answered.

"No," the voice replied. "I'll get her."

The voice that said a timid hello was the same one as the one on the answering machine.

"This is Nicola McCarthy, the social worker you phoned last night. How can I help you?"

"I'm not sure really. It was my neighbour who suggested I

call, because I have nowhere to turn, and she can't put me up for much longer."

"Have you any idea why the locks were changed?"

"I don't know really."

"Have you missed paying your rent?"

"Oh no – I'm not renting."

"Is there a doorman you could ask about the locks?"

"Yes – I went to him first thing – but all he would say was that he knew nothing about it, but I'm sure he did."

"Why do you think he knew about it?"

"Because he has let me in, in the past, when I lost my keys. But yesterday he said that if my keys didn't work neither would his – but he wouldn't even try. As well as that, he didn't seem a bit surprised. I explained to him that my partner sends me the housekeeping money by bank draft and it arrived yesterday but he still didn't even attempt to let me in."

"Why didn't you phone your partner and get him to come and deal with the situation – or at least put some money in your bank account to tide you over? Where is he anyway?"

"He's in Dublin. I've tried contacting him, but he's not answering my calls."

"Did anything happen? Did you have a row?"

"No, we didn't have a row. But something did happen in a way." The voice was very hesitant now and even less confident.

"What happened?" Nicola encouraged her. "You can tell me. This conversation is completely confidential."

"Well, the Taoiseach died."

"What has that got to do with your situation?" Nicola was curious now as well as puzzled.

"My partner is Jack Madden," came the reply.

"Oh," Nicola said, knowing that this was where the story could easily be complete fiction.

In this job she had heard some very strange stories. It was not uncommon to come across a client who was delusional and certainly, if this woman was in a relationship with the dazzling Jack Madden TD, it was the best-kept secret in the West. Nicola wracked her brains trying to drag out from the dark corners of her memory any rumours she had heard about Jack Madden. She failed. God knows the tabloids and gossip columns wouldn't have let him get away with a mistress. His family had moved to Dublin with him some time fairly early in his political career and it was well known that he visited his constituency here in Galway every week. He held a regular clinic on Mondays in a hotel on Eyre Square and he had a holiday home in Connemara where his family spent most of every summer. No, Jack Madden must be the one TD about whom Nicola couldn't recall hearing anything salacious, even in jest. In fact, the only rumour she could recall was that Mrs Madden had something in common with Imelda Marcos, in that she had a penchant for shoes. And now that the Taoiseach was dead, everybody considered Jack Madden his obvious successor.

"Are you sure you can't get back into the apartment?" Nicola asked, hoping to get some sense of whether this situation was real or not.

"Yesterday, as a last resort, my neighbour suggested getting a locksmith to let me in but when he arrived at around five yesterday the doorman threatened to call the Gardaí. Cassandra had to pay the man, even though he didn't do the work, as I didn't have any money on me – only a couple of hundred in my bank account."

"Do you have any family you could stay with?"

"No. My family have made it very clear that I am not welcome at home unless I come alone. I can't go home with the children. My family were very upset when I took up with Jack and were even more upset when I had the children."

"Would it help if I got in touch with them?" Nicola was grasping at straws. "Sometimes it helps in family situations when a neutral person intervenes." If the woman gave her permission to phone her family it would be one way of establishing the veracity of the story.

"No! Don't do that." Alice's voice was panicky. "My father recently had a stroke and any kind of worry or upset would make his situation worse."

3

Nicola sighed. "Could you come into the office this morning, so we can explore your options?"

The woman on the other end of the line burst into tears.

"I can't!" she wailed. "When I went out this morning to take the children to school my car had disappeared from the car park. Could you come out to me?"

"Well, I'll have a look in my diary and see how I'm fixed." Nicola could hear loud convulsive sobs.

Then a more businesslike voice was on the phone.

"Hello. My name is Cassandra. I'm Alice's neighbour. I know her story sounds far-fetched but I believe it's true. She really needs help."

"How long have you known her?" Nicola asked.

"To be honest we're only on nodding terms, but I've known her to see since she moved in here eleven or twelve years ago."

"And how do you know that what she's saying is true?"

"Because I've seen Jack Madden in the apartment block often enough to know which apartment he stays in."

"How come you didn't get to know Alice better in all that time?"

"Let's say we both have reasons to keep our distance but my feeling is that Jack Madden had Alice completely in his control. I think you should come out. It would be more private and I honestly don't think she knows where the bus stop is."

Looking through her diary, Nicola realised that she had a fairly free morning so against her better judgement she agreed.

"Where do you live?"

"Number 4, Lady Gregory Court, Taylors Hill. Don't talk to the doorman. Use the intercom and I'll buzz you in."

As Nicola drove towards Taylors Hill she had only a vague idea where Lady Gregory Court was. Cassandra had said it was at the bottom of the hill on the right, next door to the rectory, but Nicola was a fairly recent arrival in the city and so wasn't aware that there was a rectory there. But Lady Gregory Court was easy enough to find, or at least the gate was. She got out and pressed 4 on the key pad.

Cassandra's voice was clear. "I'll open the gate. Park in space Number 5 – it's one of my spaces – and then press 4 again when you reach the building. I'm on the second floor. I must emphasise again: don't speak to the doorman."

The gate opened in slow motion and Nicola was astonished at the lush gardens as she drove inside. Despite the fact that it was autumn there wasn't a leaf out of place. The manicured lawn and elegant trees and shrubs gave an indication of the opulence she would meet inside the building. She drove to the car park, tastefully hidden behind the shrubbery, and parked. She headed for the building, conscious as she approached the door that the doorman was already aware of her entry into the grounds.

She pressed 4 and pushed the door in when she heard the buzz. She walked past the doorman without a sideways glance and stepped into the mirrored lift to the strains of a popular classical tune which she could not name. She could feel, rather than see, the doorman's look of annoyance and she was aware as the lift doors drew together gently that he had picked up the phone.

This was a small, classy development. There were two apartments on the second floor. The door to Number 4 was slightly ajar, but Nicola stood outside and knocked. Immediately the door opened wider and a tall elegant woman in her late thirties, with shoulder-length dark hair, appeared. She was vaguely familiar. Nicola wondered if she'd seen her at a fashion show or some such event or perhaps in a wine bar, but she decided she could have been familiar from just passing her in the street. Her clothes were casual but expensive and she had the confident aura of a woman for whom life held very few surprises.

"Alice?"

"No, I'm Cassandra. Come in. Alice is having a shower. We were up late last night, I'm afraid. She's a bit shell-shocked. She doesn't seem capable of making a plan."

"Are you both sure she can't get back into the apartment?"

"Absolutely. The doorman was adamant and quite menacing.

There was no way he was going to allow us to change the locks."

As Cassandra led the way into a medium-sized, beautifully furnished sitting room, Nicola asked: "Is there any way you could look after her for a few days? Because that is the least it will take to get the system in motion."

"Out of the question," was the rather brusque reply.

Nicola hoped her surprise at the response did not show in her expression. She sat down on a luxurious sofa and Cassandra sat beside her.

"I'm sorry," Cassandra said. "How confidential is this situation?"

"Nothing you tell me will leave this room without your express permission."

Cassandra looked Nicola straight in the face and said: "The truth of the matter is I'm an escort. I cancelled my clients last night and today but my business will suffer if I don't keep the rest of my appointments. This business is becoming increasingly competitive and I am not getting any younger."

To illustrate the point she went and opened a door, which was quite close to where Nicola was sitting, revealing a room decorated in such a way that it was clear she was telling the truth. It was not in any way like your average bedroom. Nicola thought it looked like one in a rather tasteful bordello.

As she shut the door again, another one at the far side of the room opened and a woman, Alice no doubt, stood hesitantly in the doorway. She was a blonde, smallish, fragile-looking woman, whose appearance and demeanour made it difficult to tell her age, but Nicola guessed that she was in her late twenties. The fact that she was wearing an ill-fitting track suit made her appear even more vulnerable.

"Come in, Alice," Cassandra said. "This is Nicola, the social worker."

"Oh, hello!" Alice said. "I didn't realise you were here. I needed a shower. I'm sorry to have kept you waiting."

"That's okay," Nicola said with a smile, hoping to lighten the atmosphere.

Alice came into the room and sat nervously on the edge of a chair. Nicola didn't know where to start. The young woman was obviously very stressed and Nicola needed to establish, among other things, how the children were faring.

"Alice, I have to ask you a few more questions so that I can work out the extent of the problem and how I can help," she said gently.

"That's okay," Alice replied softly.

"How many children do you have? And what ages are they?"

"Two, both girls. They're aged eleven and eight."

"Where are they now?"

"At school, even though I hadn't even a clean set of underwear or socks to put on them. I thought it best to behave as normally as possible but we literally have nothing. Everything we own is in that apartment."

"Do you have a job, any money? Credit cards? A bank account?"

"I'm a full-time mother. Jack supports us. I have a bank account which I use for everyday stuff and I have a credit card."

"How did you get a credit card if you have no visible means of support?"

"Jack organised it when we moved in here. I just use it occasionally, normally for a special occasion for the children – birthdays and Christmas. Jack pays it off."

If this woman was delusional she was very convincing.

"When was the last time you heard from Jack?"

"I haven't heard from him since he left here on Tuesday morning. He would usually have been in touch by now, if only to let me know when he is coming and he rarely leaves my calls unanswered except perhaps when he is abroad."

"Do you think he's aware that you're locked out?"

"He should be. I sent him several texts yesterday but my phone was cut off this morning. It's a bill phone and he pays it. I've never even seen the bill. Cassandra thinks he's deliberately avoiding talking to me."

Nicola looked at Cassandra quizzically.

"I don't mean to upset Alice," said Cassandra, "but I believe that a mistress and two children that virtually no-one knows about don't fit into Jack Madden's plans for the future. Other TDs who have strayed have usually come out in the open eventually, but not Jack Madden. My guess is that Alice and the children were never going to be part of his future if there was a possibility of becoming Taoiseach. On the surface his marriage seems to be a good one and I suspect that less than a handful of people, including me and the doorman, know about Alice."

Alice blew her nose loudly and Nicola wasn't sure if she was crying or just had the sniffles.

"You mentioned you don't pay rent, Alice?"

"No, I don't – Jack bought the apartment."

"Did he buy it outright or does he have a mortgage?"

"I think he bought it outright. He's never talked about a mortgage. But . . . maybe he was into buying properties . . . occasionally letters arrived addressed to some company – Tower Enterprises or something like that. He never told me why they were addressed to our apartment so I always assumed it was some private business enterprise of his."

"Then it's possible a company owns the apartment – we'll have to establish that," said Nicola. "Right – can you remember exactly when you moved in, Alice?"

"It's definitely over twelve years ago because it was a few months before Grace was born and she'll be twelve on the 29th of October. Is that important?"

"Yes, because the length of time you've been here is significant if we have to establish a legal right to remain in the apartment. It's complicated but I'll explain it to you soon if the need arises. We have more immediate things to deal with now."

Alice sighed.

"Tell me more about your situation," Nicola encouraged her.

The story that unfolded over the next half hour was bizarre even by Nicola's standards, but the most bizarre aspect of all was the fact that, as Alice recounted the story of her life over the past thirteen years or so, she appeared to think that it was quite normal.

She told them that her relationship with Jack Madden had begun when she was aged seventeen and she went to work for his family as a sort of au pair. She had intended to work for them for a year or more because she was undecided what she wanted to do with her life after her Leaving Certificate. She had hoped to make a decision by the end of the year. The sexual relationship between her and her employer had begun on her eighteenth birthday. Her face practically glowed as she told them and she said that she was delighted when some months later she found that she was pregnant. Jack, she said, was delighted too and suggested that they set up home in Galway, which was his constituency and where he had grown up, and he already spent a lot of time there doing constituency work. "I can have two real homes," he said, beaming at her. His wife, of course, was not informed of this arrangement. Alice went along with it and, judging from the way she told the tale, she was quite happy to do so.

Alice recounted her story as if it was the most normal thing in the world. She was deeply hurt by the fact that her parents were disapproving of her situation and, though she had a brother and sister, only her sister was in regular contact with her now. She did send photos of herself and the children home. They were the first grandchildren in the family, but she knew from her sister that the photos were not framed and put on the mantelpiece like the rest of the family photos. They were kept in an envelope in a drawer and only taken out if an immediate member of the family showed an interest. No – nobody in Alice's home village knew that she was in a relationship with the dashing TD and that she had two children and was living in sin in a posh apartment in Galway.

As the story unfolded it became obvious to Nicola that virtually nothing had occurred by accident. Jack Madden had planned most of it. He had targeted a very young girl when she was at her most romantic and naïve and even now, thirteen years later, stunningly beautiful. He formed the relationship with her entirely on his own terms. He dazzled her with his wealth and, if there was ever a possibility that she would question his commitment to her and the girls, he simply bought her another expensive gift or arranged for them to go on a holiday to a really exotic location . . . and, if he was really feeling generous, he would grace them with his presence for a day or two while they were on holiday and just for that few days they behaved like a real family. And if, by chance, they bumped into an Irish person while on holiday he would pass Alice off as his niece. On one occasion, when a city councillor from Galway walked over to them by the pool in a beautiful hotel in Antibes, they even joked that he was too young to be a great-uncle to the girls. Alice had laughed along with them, going along with the deceit. Jack preferred it that way.

He usually stayed with his second family three nights each week except during the summer when the Dáil was in recess and his other family were holidaying in their second home in Connemara. That was the time that Alice found most difficult because she saw less of Jack. His visits were short and hurried and, even though he tried to say that this made it more romantic, Alice didn't like not having him around. There was also the added complication that she could meet his wife on the streets of Galway but she avoided that by just turning away if she saw her coming. But, in general, she accepted her situation. She had known he was married when she fell in love with him and there was never a question of him leaving his wife.

Apart from the unusual nature of the relationship, Alice described it as a very comfortable way of life. When the girls were babies she had a nanny – an older woman who was very discreet. Jack had chosen her but Alice was quite happy with his choice. She certainly didn't want another nubile young woman coming into Jack's life in the way she had. Jack was marvellous but he wasn't a saint!

Alice lived in a sort of a cocoon in which Jack organised and financed everything. She had been upset when he insisted she put 'Father unknown' on the birth certificates but she supposed she could understand it really. While he really loved having two families and assured her that things would "sort themselves out in the future", it was just not appropriate for it to get out at that time.

He was marvellous and attentive when he was with them and always phoned or texted to let them know his plans. He was generous with money and never asked her to account for how she spent her allowance. She always had a good car which he paid for, taxed, insured and changed every two years. He allowed her as much freedom as she wished. She had girlfriends and he was happy with that so long as she promised him that she would never disclose who the girls' father was and made sure no friends dropped in when he was there. He trusted her and up until today she had never betrayed that trust.

"Grace is getting older now," she whispered, "and beginning to ask questions. So I told her that her dad had died in a drowning accident and his body was never found and that Uncle Jack has stepped into the breach. She seems happy enough with that."

"And you haven't heard from him for two days now?" Nicola eventually asked. The situation was almost too strange to be believed. "This is unusual, you said?"

"Very. He normally gets in touch almost every day – and he has never left an urgent message unanswered."

"What type of urgent situations arose in the past?"

"Like when Orla was rushed into hospital with a burst appendix. He was here within hours and arranged everything for us."

"How do you mean 'arranged'?"

"He got her a private room, the best consultant and so on – I didn't have to worry about a thing."

"And did nobody in the hospital remark on that?"

"Not to me and, if they remarked on it to him, he probably told them I was his niece." Her lower lip quivered again.

"We will have to try and fix you up with accommodation for the next few nights and I will see what I can do in the longer term," Nicola said in an effort to bring the conversation back to the present.

"I have very little money for a hotel, though I suppose I could use the credit card," Alice said thoughtfully. "I'll need clothes as well for me and the children."

Cassandra intervened at this point.

"I could take you to Dunnes," she said, "and then we could try and book you into a hotel. I am fairly free for the rest of the day so I can do the driving."

"I usually shop at Brown Thomas," Alice said.

The other two women looked at each other, both having the feeling that she wouldn't be shopping in BT for much longer.

It was arranged that Cassandra would take Alice shopping, book her into a B&B or hotel near the school and Nicola would go back to the office and see what she could arrange for the longer term.

As she drove back to the Health Centre, Nicola wondered if she was being conned. In her heart she believed Alice, and Cassandra seemed to believe her as well, but the situation was so far-fetched that she wondered if she was being naïve. She was going to have to convince a Community Welfare Officer to pay Alice subsistence within the next few days and she could almost see in advance of that discussion the look of incredulity on the CWO's face. If she was being taken for a ride, it wouldn't be the first time, but that sort of thing went with the territory. People in desperate situations sometimes were less than totally honest but, in this case, if the client wasn't being sincere, Nicola could be left with a lot of egg on her face. As she drove into her parking space she wondered how the case would unfold.

Chapter 2

By the time Alice and Cassandra came to Nicola's office the next day she had some homework done. She had spoken to Alice's local Community Welfare Officer and got a predictable sceptical response but the CWO said Alice should attend one of her clinics over the next few days, bringing relevant documents showing proof of address, bank statements, Child Benefit receipts, PPS number etc, and she would do what she could to help her. But even that was more complicated than Nicola expected. When she spoke to Alice she discovered that she didn't know her PPS number – in fact, she had never heard of one. Jack took care of all the paperwork.

"You must have one!" Nicola said. "You have to have one to claim. You must surely be getting Child Benefit, aren't you?"

"I didn't claim it. Jack said it wasn't necessary. He would look after us."

"We'll have to register you for it so. Everybody in the country is entitled to Child Benefit. And the fact that you don't know your PPS number will undoubtedly delay your application for a Social Welfare payment and Rent Supplement so we'll have to apply for interim emergency help. How much money do you have in the bank now?"

"Just over two hundred euro," Alice said tearfully. "And that will have to pay for the B&B. My credit card wasn't accepted in the shops yesterday. It seems that has been stopped as well."

"Keep it anyway. We'll need it as evidence."

"For what?" Alice sounded panicky.

"To prove that your children are Jack Madden's and that he has a responsibility to provide for them. But that is a long way down the road and we need to look after your more immediate needs now – like where you are going to stay for the next few weeks or months. We'll need proof of your address for starters. Do you have a driving licence?"

"Yes, but it's in the apartment. Everything I own is in the apartment – even Orla's favourite blanket. She couldn't sleep last night." Alice broke down in tears again.

"We need to get into that apartment but we will need an injunction and I'm not sure that we can get that on legal aid, based on your story."

Cassandra, who had been silent up until now, said quietly, "I think I can help."

"How?" the others asked in unison.

"Don't ask. Alice, make a list of what you need from the apartment and I'll see what I can do."

Nicola looked doubtfully at Cassandra and was about to question her further but then thought it best not to know what she was up to. She turned back to Alice.

"Now that your money has run out," she said quietly, "I'll have to get you into a women's refuge."

"But those places are not for the likes of me! I've never been hurt by any man!" Alice's tone was appalled.

"What do you call this?" Nicola said. "I don't mean to offend you, but you have to face up to the fact that you've been abandoned and you're in for a very difficult time. If you don't face up to the reality of it, you will not be able to deal with it."

Fresh sobs convulsed Alice's body and Nicola felt sorry she had been so blunt but she felt the sooner Alice accepted her situation the sooner she would be able to make difficult decisions, like pursuing Jack Madden for maintenance, even if it meant costing him his career.

By the time Alice and Cassandra left, Nicola felt quite frustrated by Alice's attitude, but she was glad in a way that she had such a complicated case to deal with.

She had gone home the night before, stressed out completely, to find that Jonathan had passed out on the sofa. She had looked at him in exasperation. He was gorgeous – no doubt about that. The epithet 'tall, dark and handsome' described him to a tee even if it was a bit of a cliché. But his charm was beginning to pall – for her at least and not without good reason. She'd thought she noticed the sickly sweet smell of dope on the landing as she turned the key but had hoped that it was not from their apartment. The stronger smell in the apartment confirmed her worst fears but it was when she found traces of coke on the coffee table that she nearly blew a fuse.

"What the hell do you think you're doing?" The place was like a bomb site with the remains of his breakfast and lunch on plates on the floor beside the sofa.

"It was only a little line," he whined. "And I had to have a smoke to come down. In any case I deserve it. I've had a bad week."

"I am a social worker with the Health Service Executive!" Nicola shouted. "What do you think it would do to my career if the police found drugs in my apartment?"

"Don't be so neurotic. They won't find anything. Chill out." Jonathan heaved himself into a sitting position, his beautiful brown eyes drowsy with sleep. He was more dishevelled than usual and looked as if he hadn't even washed that day.

"For God's sake, Jonathan! Grow up! You know that that sergeant living on the ground floor already suspects you since he came complaining about the noise at our New Year's Eve party and you went out to him as high as a kite!" She had taken off her jacket and now automatically started to clear up.

"You have nothing to worry about. It's me that uses the stuff. He can't get you for anything."

"Except that it's my apartment and if they carried out a search, it's my name would be in the local paper! I would be fired and I would be unemployable. I want you to flush what you have down the loo and never bring it into the apartment again!"

"You can't be serious. It cost me my last few quid."

"Maybe you should be wiser about the way you spend your money."

"You are so uptight. What's a bit of weed and a few lines of coke between friends?"

"You're my partner. We live together. That, I would have thought, makes us more than friends. I've never been comfortable with your drug-taking even though you think you can control it. Most alcoholics and heroin addicts hold the view that they are in control. I think it's getting out of control. You can't afford it in any case, apart altogether from the fact that it could cost me my job and ultimately my apartment."

Jonathan went through the motions. She didn't follow him to make sure that he had destroyed the stuff and she suspected that he hadn't, but she hadn't the energy for the argument that would be inevitable if she insisted on watching him.

Nicola sighed and tried to shake the thought of Jonathan out of her head. She wondered, and not for the first time, what she had ever seen in him. He was handsome, talented, witty, but she was fed up with his tantrums and she wasn't sure if the relationship was worth the hassle. But that was for another day, and for now she had to concentrate on Alice.

Having received permission from Alice to do so, Nicola went to discuss the case with her manager. He just didn't believe it.

"I've been a member of that party for years, all my adult life in fact. If he were carrying on I'd know about it. You know me. I'm aware of a lot of secrets that people don't know about but this is definitely not true. Your woman is mad or very cunning, and I suspect the former."

Pat Kelly was normally very astute. He was an easygoing man who was not easily phased. He dressed casually even at work and in general exuded that type of impression.

"You haven't met her, Pat. I believe her. Otherwise she has put on a performance worthy of an Oscar."

"Oh, come on, Nicola! I would never have put you down as a woman who sees every woman wronged in some way."

"I'd never have put you down as a member of the old boys' club, where boys will be boys, and so long it's not too open we don't tell!"

"Don't be so snide, Nicola! It doesn't suit you. Help this woman by all means but I don't believe her story."

"If she gives me permission today I'm going to ring him at his Dáil office," Nicola told him quietly.

"That is not a good idea. If it blows up in your face, you're on your own. This could cost you your career but it's not going to cost me mine."

The conversation depressed Nicola. She and Pat had always got on well and, up until now, she'd felt she could trust him with anything. In fact, they had been through many rough situations together in the few years she had been in Galway and she'd always felt that they were of like mind where it mattered.

She dealt with a number of other cases and visited a young father of five children whose wife had died a month earlier of cancer and was again astonished by his excellent coping skills. Despite the fact that this family had been visited by the most horrendous loss, the children were so well looked after that she knew she need have no concerns about them. The biggest question posed here was how this man could retain his not very well-paid job and still look after his children, because his wages wouldn't run to childcare and his extended family were in Cork. She wished Alice O'Brien had half his coping skills.

Chapter 3

When Cassandra and Alice came to Nicola's office the following day Cassandra had good news.

"I got some of the things Alice needed from the apartment – her passport, the children's birth certificates, her driver's licence and some of their favourite clothes and toys. And this." She put a large jewellery case on the desk. "Jack Madden was quite generous when it came to gifts of jewellery."

"How did you do that?" Nicola was amazed.

"I have friends in low places and it comes in handy at times."

They all laughed, probably for the first time since they had met.

"I don't think Alice should come back to the apartment block after this," Cassandra said. "What will I do with the rest of the stuff? I have a boot-load of it."

She had a satisfied smile on her face and Nicola saw Alice smile again, giving her some hope that this child-woman would come through this.

"I might be able to store them in this office, if they're in bags," said Nicola, "and I'll lock the jewellery in the filing cabinet until Alice has a secure place to live. She may need to sell some of it in any case if it's saleable and things get desperate. Alice, don't ever tell anybody that I stored your stuff. We're not supposed to get over-involved in cases – there are boundaries we are not supposed to cross."

"Okay," said Alice doubtfully. "But where do I stay? The B&B will only keep us for two more nights."

"I'll look at the refuges," Nicola said, "but I want to ask you some awkward questions first. Firstly, I would like to phone your sister to see if she can be of any assistance – and also Jack Madden. When I phone Jack it could cause a huge furore and we all have to be ready for that. If he denies that he is the father of your children he may take out an injunction to stop us going near him. But I suspect he will not want to do anything so public and that may be an advantage. We can thank our stars that there is no such thing as a superinjunction in this country."

"My sister is in Botswana with a Third World charity so she can't help. If you have to phone Jack, that's okay. Tell him I love him and that we are okay. I really think that this is only temporary and he will be back to us."

The other two women looked at each other in despair before Cassandra went out to get some more of Alice's property from her car.

"Go give her a hand there, Alice," Nicola said. "I need to think."

She phoned the two refuges, asking if they would have a place for a woman and two girls for the weekend. The response was doubtful. They were both full but, in one, there was a possibility that one of the women was going to return to her home.

"If she does, then you'll have a place," Nicola said, relieved at the possibility.

"If she does, she will be going back to the husband who has ill-treated her and her children for the last seven years, so we are not encouraging her."

"Sorry – I didn't mean to be pushy." A wave of depression swept over Nicola as she put down the phone.

Her next job was to establish Alice's PPS number so she set about doing that as the other two women brought Alice's property into her office, Alice wheeling a girl's bike.

"You've got a very big car!" Nicola laughed as a small hill of black bags containing clothes and toys began to form on her office floor. "I'll put them in that empty filing cabinet for the time being. I'm not sure what I'll do with the bike."

"Grace will be so glad to have it back." Alice smiled. "She would really miss it."

"I might be able to take it home until we find you somewhere more permanent." Nicola had crossed more boundaries in one day than she had in the previous three years and it worried her.

She told Cassandra and Alice about the refuges.

"Have you ever heard of The Coven?" Cassandra asked Nicola.

"Sounds intriguing, but I haven't."

"It's somewhere on the Headford Road. It's reputed to be a large mansion which is run by a woman called Eliza Lynch whose son-in-law walked out on her daughter and their two children and left her near destitute – and this woman vowed to do her best for any other women in that situation. She is very unconventional and there's a long sob story attached but this might be the answer if you can't get Alice into a refuge."

This day was getting more and more surreal. Nicola felt a ray of hope though she was conscious again that this was not correct procedure . . . but if all came to all it might be the only option open to her.

"How does one contact The Coven?" Even the name of it was off the wall.

"In fact it's called Cappagh Hall, I think, but some outraged husband nicknamed it The Coven and it sort of stuck," Cassandra said with a grin. "I think I can get hold of a number for you. But I need to go now. Alice, why don't you go into town and have a bit of lunch and let Nicola get on with her job?"

Alice looked doubtful but meekly left with Cassandra.

Nicola's next job was to call Jack Madden. But first she went to the canteen for lunch. She hoped she would meet someone not in the Social Work Department so that she could take her mind off her case load, at least for the hour. She was lucky. She had just found a seat when Billy, an elderly porter who had been with the HSE since Adam was a boy, sat down next to her.

"You don't mind if I join you?" he smiled as he plonked himself and his very full tray down.

"I don't appear to have an option," she grinned.

He was a lovely man, great with the staff and even better with the clients. He had an empathy that was unusual and could be trusted with anybody's deepest secrets.

"Well, who do you think will be Taoiseach?" he demanded cheerfully.

"Not sure really," Nicola replied. "I'm not into politics and I'm only just getting used to the fact that the other guy has popped his clogs."

"Mother of God! What is the world coming to? The correct way to speak of the deceased is to call him 'the late Taoiseach' – and he didn't 'pop his clogs' as you say – he went to his final reward."

"Sorry," Nicola smiled though she knew from the grin on his face that Billy was only half serious. However, you could never be quite sure with the older generation.

"They say Jack Madden is a cert," Billy went on, taking a hefty mouthful of the shepherd's pie.

"Looks a bit like it alright," Nicola acknowledged. "Though you never know!"

"I'd say it's a cert alright. He's very well liked and he was only beaten by the casting vote of the Chair last time round. It would be nice to have a Taoiseach from the West. They might even finish the Distributor Road in his honour." He paused for another mouthful.

Nicola was beginning to regret that he had sat beside her. She ate her salad thoughtfully while Billy chatted on and when she looked up she noticed that the Community Welfare Officer with whom she had spoken about Alice was there. What's more, she was looking at her and so were the other three people at that table. It was a pity that everybody couldn't be as discreet as Billy. Frowning, she gulped down the end of her coffee, said goodbye to Billy, and went back to her office.

It was Thursday afternoon and, from what Alice had told her, Jack Madden would normally be heading for Galway or maybe be at his Dublin home but she calculated that, with all that was going on, all of the Cabinet would still be in their Dáil offices and, in particular, those who were in the running for Head of Government were unlikely to leave the seat of power.

At two thirty, giving him plenty of time to have had his lunch, she phoned Government Buildings. She got Jack Madden's secretary immediately and was surprised when she was told Jack Madden was available. This was easier than she had expected but she was caught slightly on the hop. She'd expected to have to make several calls before she actually got him.

The familiar smooth voice of Jack Madden slid down the line.

"Good afternoon, Nicola. What can I do for you?"

"It's a professional matter, Mr Madden. I think you may be able to help me."

"I certainly hope so, and you can call me Jack."

"Thank you, Jack. I am a social worker with the HSE. I have a client at present who has informed me that you are the father of her children and that up until two days ago she lived in an apartment on Taylors Hill which you paid for and that you joined her there at some point almost every week. But, since the Taoiseach died, she is having trouble contacting you and she has been locked out of the apartment. Can you tell me, Jack, if all this is true?" Nicola had managed to keep her voice quite steady and professional. She didn't accuse him of anything. She behaved as if she was just clarifying something.

She heard a slow intake of breath, as if he was composing himself.

"Of course it's not," he answered. "Who the hell is this woman anyway? She must be some kind of nut. People who are mentally ill often form a fixation on someone, in particular someone who is famous, and they imagine they have a relationship with them. She is, I presume, a sort of a stalker – though I wasn't aware of her until now. What did you say her name was?"

"Her name is Alice O'Brien." Nicola felt safe naming her but she wouldn't let him know her whereabouts.

"And she says that I am the father of her two daughters? She's mad."

"She may be, Jack, but I never mentioned 'daughters' to you nor did I say there were two. I said 'children' and the fact that you know they are daughters and that there are two of them certainly makes me wonder."

"Don't you get smart with me, Missy! It's more than your job's worth."

"Surely, Jack, you're not threatening me?" Nicola replied, shocked now at the tone the conversation was taking.

"No, I am not threatening you but you should know that some social worker cannot just phone a TD and accuse him of having two illegitimate daughters, without having any proof."

"I haven't accused you of anything. I just asked for clarification and you have clarified two things."

"And what are they, may I ask?"

"That you know Alice O'Brien and that you know she has two daughters."

"Lucky guess! You had better not be spreading rumours around Galway."

"I have no intention of it. That is certainly more than my job is worth. I have a job to do and part of it will be to get a One Parent Family Payment for the client and to establish who the father of the children is and help her follow him for maintenance. It's all quite routine really, though we don't often have a case where the alleged father is so well known."

"When you investigate this further you will be unable to find anything concrete that links me with this woman and her children."

"You seem quite sure of that, Mr Madden. If that is the case you have nothing to worry about." Nicola was beginning to worry that he seemed so sure, though in a way that was not a surprise. The way Alice told it, it seemed that he had arranged things in such a way that there was nothing on paper to link them. This investigation would not be easy.

"I have nothing to hide. But if I find that you are snooping around in my business I will make sure that you are transferred to a little island off the Mayo coast and your career will come to a dead end. You don't get to be a Minister of Government without having some perks."

"Gosh, Jack, that sounds remarkably like a threat again and I don't like it. I will do my job and if you are telling the truth it will be no more than an inconvenience. If however you are not honest with me, my investigation could turn up some very interesting facts which could affect both of our careers, and not least yours."

"Look here, girl. I won't be threatened or intimidated by some jumped-up slip of thing who thinks that because she has been to college for a few years she can bring down a government. I can deal with you in any manner of ways. I have friends in low places. So don't cross me."

"Gosh, Jack, that is the second time someone said that to me today. The other person who said she had friends in low places is a call girl. What does that make you?"

"It makes me a very dangerous adversary, Miss McCarthy." And he put down the phone.

Nicola's hand was trembling as she replaced the receiver and she wondered if she had been wise telling him that she didn't think he was being truthful. She was also regretting that she had mentioned she had spoken to a call girl that day. If Jack Madden had friends in low places, like he claimed, it was unlikely he didn't know what his neighbour in Taylors Hill did for a living and he would almost certainly not be pleased that she was talking to anyone who could make life difficult for him. It was funny that she had heard the same expression twice in one day. The first time it was said it made her laugh and the second it sent a shiver down her spine.

Alice had never been so scared in all her life – not even when her parents had said that they wouldn't have her back in their home

24

with the children. She had known then that Jack loved them and would look after them but now it seemed as if he had just stopped doing that. She couldn't believe that the situation was permanent. She kept looking at her phone, expecting him to have texted to say it was all some big misunderstanding. But the screen remained depressingly blank.

She wandered around the shopping centres in a daze, filling in the time before she picked the girls up from school. She tried not to cry as she saw Jack's face on the front of every newspaper, his other family by his side in some of them. That had never bothered her before. The other family! She'd always felt that they were his Dublin family and she and the girls were the Galway family. But now it seemed Jack had opted to forget her and her girls. No smiling pictures of *them* in the papers! How could there be? Only a handful of people knew of their existence and those people were intensely loyal to Jack. None of her acquaintances knew the full story and even if they had been told they wouldn't have believed it.

The government was clearly in turmoil. It looked as if Jack would be some sort of caretaker Taoiseach at any rate. One of the papers was suggesting that he would be acting-Taoiseach until the next election and that the party would look at the situation in advance of that and consider whether or not it needed a new leader.

In the meantime Alice had to come to terms with what was happening to her and her children and she wasn't sure just how she would do that. Things like PPS numbers were a foreign country to her. She wondered if her mother had one. She had never heard of one but the way Nicola was talking you'd think that they were what made the world go around. She hoped that Nicola would be able to find hers, though maybe if she could get in touch with Jack he might have a very good explanation for his behaviour and she wouldn't need it. It was all very depressing.

The weather was lovely for September. Usually a brisk walk on the prom with its beautiful view of the Clare hills cheered her up, but she didn't want to walk the prom. She always met people she knew there and she was avoiding people she knew at the moment. She just couldn't bring herself to tell people that she was homeless. She told the children that they were just looking for a new place and they seemed to believe that. She didn't mention it to their teachers and she certainly wasn't going to tell other mothers at the school gates. She still hoped that the situation was temporary and that something akin to a miracle would turn up or maybe that she would wake up and it would all have been a nightmare. But in her heart she knew that this wouldn't happen. She was all over the place really and she knew it, but she had no idea how to deal with the situation. Nicola seemed capable enough but she appeared hassled as well and Alice couldn't decide whether or not she herself was the only cause of the hassle.

She really didn't want to go to a refuge. She thought The Coven place sounded even worse but Cassandra said that that was not its real name so maybe it was nice. Alice went into Goya's and ordered a cappuccino and apple crumble. She smiled at a woman in the corner who had children at the school. There was no way she wanted to talk to her, even though the woman had often made friendly overtures towards her. But if she talked to anybody now she was afraid that she would burst into tears and let the cat out of the bag. Imagine the turmoil! Jack Madden had a mistress and two daughters! No one would believe it. They would probably have her certified. No, she couldn't talk to anybody, even her friends, until she had something sorted out.

She noticed when she went to pay that she had only a few notes left in her purse. Crikey! She had paid the B&B for two nights and now her funds were very low indeed. She needed to get dinner for the girls but that would have to be in a restaurant or, at any rate, McDonald's – more expense. What was she going to do if something didn't turn up today?

She wondered which clothes Cassandra had taken from the apartment. She was about to phone Nicola to see if she could check what was there when she remembered that her phone had been cut off. She really needed a change of clothes for the girls and also Orla's blanket but she hadn't even a car to get back to the social worker's office and Cassandra was busy for the rest of the day so she couldn't ask her.

She decided if she walked fast she'd have time to get back to the office and, if Nicola wasn't too busy, she could rummage around in the bags for what she needed for the next few days. She knew that luckily nearly all their clothing was clean as she had a habit of keeping everything up to date. She never wanted to have to be doing housework when Jack came. She made sure it was all done while he was away.

When Alice arrived at the office Nicola was just putting down the phone.

"I'm sorry to interrupt, Nicola, but could I have a look at the things Cassandra brought from the apartment? I could do with some of the clothes, in particular for the girls. Is there anywhere I could rummage through the bags?"

"You're okay, Alice. We'll lock the door and you can sort some things out in a couple of minutes. When do you have to pick the girls up from school?"

"Three thirty. I have a bit of time yet. I could put what we need for the next few days in one black bag and I could take it with me when I go to the school."

It dawned on both of them at the same time that most mothers at the school gate would think it odd if Alice turned up on foot with a black plastic bag. Nicola saw Alice's lower lip quiver and felt truly sorry for her. Everything had become so different for her in the blink of an eye.

"Maybe you should just take what you need for tonight and tomorrow," Nicola said. "When we find you a place I'll bring the rest of your stuff in my car. I might have a Tesco bag here and no one will know what's in it."

Alice's relief was obvious and the tears didn't come though

they had been close. Nicola was astonished as they sorted the clothes. Cassandra was a star. She had taken track suits, underwear, pyjamas and some good clothes. There was enough there to get them by – for the moment anyway.

Alice was relieved, and Nicola noticed that the smile of relief reached her eyes.

"That's something positive anyway," Nicola said. "They'll have their own clothes and some of their toys."

"Yes, but I'm running out of money. I don't know what to do."

"We'll go to your Community Welfare Officer right now – she has a clinic from two today – and see if we can get you an emergency payment. It will be enough to get you by for the week if you're careful – very careful."

Alice looked plain scared as they arrived at the HSE Community Welfare Centre. Nicola could understand how any new applicant would find it intimidating and in this case the applicant, Alice, hadn't known up until yesterday that such a person as a Community Welfare Officer existed.

As Nicola had limited time – she had an appointment with another client at three forty-five – she had rung ahead and asked if they could jump the queue, mentioning also that the children had to be collected from school and there was no one else to do it. The CWO had agreed reluctantly but emphasised that Alice would be treated like everyone else no matter who she thought her partner was.

Nicola and Alice sat and waited for the CWO to emerge from her office. At least fifty per cent of the people in the waiting room seemed to be under huge stress. An African woman with a baby who clearly was ill was sitting opposite them and beside them was an Irishman whose tattooed hands were shaking.

At last the CWO came to her office doorway with a departing client and beckoned to them.

Nicola knew the Community Welfare Officer well. She had

the jaded appearance of a person who had heard it all. She was known to be cranky but fair.

"This is Alice O'Brien," Nicola said. "I'm in the process of sorting out her social welfare payment and accommodation but she needs an emergency payment. She has only fifteen euro left and that will go in McDonald's this evening."

"Alice, you need to complete this form," the woman behind the desk said. "If you have any questions just ask."

She spoke as if she was talking to a child, which in some ways reassured Nicola. She must have believed the story.

Nicola watched as Alice painstakingly completed the form. "Don't put down your Taylors Hill address – put the B&B," she said.

The lower lip started to quiver again. "Why?" It came out as a wail.

"Because it's not your address any longer and we are going to put down eviction as the reason you need the cash."

Alice did as she was told and the other women watched as tears slid from her face onto the paper in front of her. When she had the form completed she handed it across the desk.

"I'm afraid I'm going to have to ask you some questions now, Alice, which you may consider to be intrusive," the CWO said gently.

"Go ahead," Alice said.

"What was your previous address?"

"It was 3, Lady Gregory Court, Taylors Hill."

The CWO began to take notes.

"How long did you live there?"

"Around twelve years."

"Were you renting?"

"No – we owned it – at least my partner did."

"And you lived there with him?"

"Yes – and our two children. But he lives half of every week in Dublin."

"Why did you leave that address?"

"I didn't leave. I was locked out while I collected the children from school a couple of days ago." Alice was trembling now.

"Have you made any attempt to get in?"

"Yes, but the doorman wouldn't let me in and he threatened to call the Guards when my neighbour called a locksmith."

"Have you contacted your partner?"

"I've tried but he won't answer my calls."

"Is he currently employed, your partner?"

"Yes, he's . . . he's . . . a politician."

The CWO glanced at Alice as if she were about to ask a question but then thought better of it. She returned to her note-taking.

"Do you have a job or any other source of income?"

"No – Jack has always paid for everything."

"Any savings?"

"No, I haven't."

The CWO laid down her pen and looked at Alice. "Okay, Alice. I'll give you a cash payment today and I'll set up a weekly payment for you for the next three weeks. That should tide you over until you sort yourself out. If there is any change in your circumstances, such as if your partner resumes supporting you or the children, you must contact me immediately."

"Of course! Do you think he might?" The hope in Alice's tone was pitiful.

"You would know that better than me," the other woman said, not unkindly.

"I don't know what to think. Everything happened so suddenly. I am still hoping to wake up and find that it's a dream. The only positive thing is that things can hardly get worse."

The other women looked at her sympathetically. Both knew that things could and probably would get worse before they got better.

Alice and Nicola left the office together. They parted company at the gates of the Health Centre and Alice, carrying the bag of clothes, trudged slowly towards the grim grey building that was the school. The B&B where she had stayed the night before was a few hundred yards further on.

When Nicola arrived at her apartment that evening she just wanted to have a bath, a nice dinner, perhaps with a glass of wine, and an early night. She was finding this case very stressful. All the time, she was conscious that she was on dangerous ground, whether or not Alice was telling the truth. In fact, she believed that she was on more dangerous ground if Alice was telling the truth than if she was not.

Jonathan looked like he had just woken up.

"Would you start the dinner?" she said. "I am exhausted and I could do with a long soak. You'll find everything in the fridge. I did a shop yesterday on the way home from work." The apartment was like a bomb had hit it but she decided that she wouldn't mention that. If he got dinner she would forgive him anything – put his untidiness down to his artistic temperament.

"There isn't anything I feel like cooking," came the bored reply.

"Go out and get something else so, but you could do a stir fry. The ingredients for that are there and it's quick and easy."

"Actually I can't stay for dinner," he said suddenly. "I have to meet a guy in The Quays for a drink. He may be able to set up an exhibition for me."

"Oh! You didn't say." Nicola was surprised.

"That's because I didn't know until today. Actually, I should be going about now. Couldn't lend me the price of a cab, could you?"

"Why don't you get a bus?"

"At this hour I wouldn't get there on time."

Nicola handed him ten euro, feeling mean and resentful at once. She often lent Jonathan money but she never got it back. He was always broke, waiting for his next big sale which seldom came. As he sauntered towards the door she wondered again what she was doing with him. Any vestige of romance in the relationship was long since dead. He was also not very inclined to look for work but often complained about being broke, criticised what she cooked, and suggested, practically demanded, 'they' get new computer, a larger flat-screen TV, an iPod . . . though they both knew he would not make a contribution to any new purchases.

There must be nicer guys out there, she mused. And what's so bad about being alone anyway? With that thought she ran the bath and decided to microwave a ready meal for one.

Chapter 4

There was a loud ring on Nicola's door at seven thirty the following morning. Jonathan was sound asleep beside her. She hadn't heard him come in and he was oblivious to the world now so she presumed he'd had a lot to drink or smoke or both. She nudged him into wakefulness.

"There's someone at the door," she whispered.

"Nobody for me," he mumbled and turned over.

Nicola went to the window and looked into the front garden of the apartment block. There were two gardaí standing on the front patio.

"It's the Gardaí! Get up! I wonder what they want." She was hoping that Jonathan hadn't been in some sort of trouble the night before. She was always on edge where he was concerned.

Jonathan leapt from the bed as if it were on fire and started rummaging in his locker. "Don't let them in yet!" He produced a pouch of what she knew to be cannabis before she even smelled it.

"I thought you'd got rid of that! Have you anything else?"

"Naw. Used that up yesterday."

Nicola was livid, though now was not the time to have a confrontation.

Jonathan flushed the contents of the pouch down the toilet as she went to the door.

"We have a warrant to search this apartment," one of the gardaí said before Nicola had an opportunity to greet them.

"On what grounds?" she asked, trying to read the document he flashed in front of her.

"There have been complaints of unusual traffic into and out of the apartment, particularly late at night and there is a suspicion of drug-dealing."

"That is completely ridiculous!" Nicola couldn't figure out where the complaints might have come from. It was more than six months since their neighbour had complained to the Gardaí about the noise and might have, on that occasion, smelled the cannabis. The late-night traffic to the apartment was definitely a fabrication. The situation was weird as well as worrying.

"Do I have to let you in, or do I have the option to ask you to come back when we're dressed?"

"I'm afraid not. With a search warrant there is usually an element of surprise. There is no point in giving the resident an opportunity to destroy evidence. So if you would stand aside."

Nicola let the two gardaí, one male and one female, through, hoping that there was no evidence of any drug in the place. She didn't want to be booked for possession. Jonathan dabbled but she knew he was not a dealer and she hoped that he wouldn't have a dealer in the apartment, but she wasn't sure about that.

"What is the procedure?" she asked.

"We just search the premises," was the reply.

Nicola went into the kitchen. Jonathan was there, looking groggy. She put on the kettle.

"I had better get ready for work," she said to him. "They'll probably be finished by the time I'm ready to leave." Her voice was shaking and so was her hand as she put two slices of bread into the toaster.

The gardaí came in and began to open cupboards in the kitchen.

"Do you think you could look in the bathroom and the bedroom first?" Nicola asked.

34

They both looked at her, obviously not understanding why she would make that request.

"I need to get to work. I'm a social worker and it wouldn't be good if I go into work late because the Gardaí were searching my apartment. The fact that you won't find anything might get lost in the telling."

"Okay," said the female garda. "If you would both remain in the kitchen I'll start on the bathroom and my colleague will continue here."

Nicola could hardly breathe as they started their search. She continued getting her breakfast mechanically and when the garda was finished in the bathroom she went in and closed the door, glad not to have to look at either them or Jonathan.

In the shower she made the decision to dump Jonathan. She couldn't go on like this. There was nothing in the relationship for her any longer and she now realised more than ever that he could be quite a liability. She would tell him tonight and hope that he would go over the weekend.

When she emerged from the bathroom Jonathan was still in the kitchen, the gardaí emptying drawers and cupboards around him.

"We've finished in the bedroom," the woman garda said.

Nicola got dressed, applied her make-up and got ready to leave. She hoped they would be finished soon. She didn't want to leave them with Jonathan and she didn't want to be late for work either but it was a small apartment so she was pretty sure that they wouldn't take much longer.

"We're finished," the male garda said when Nicola emerged from the bedroom. "We haven't found anything, so you have nothing to worry about."

She thought his voice sounded sympathetic.

"Surprise, surprise," she replied curtly. "I need to go to work now so if you could please leave before me – I want to talk to my partner."

"Of course! Good morning." Again he seemed almost apologetic.

"Good morning," Nicola said and, closing the door behind them, she went back into the kitchen.

Jonathan said nothing at all.

"I've got to go now," Nicola said, "but I want to talk to you tonight."

"Not tonight, I'm afraid." Jonathan sounded bored again. "I have to go to Dublin today and I thought I might stay the weekend."

"What's so important that you have to go today?"

"Nothing much. I'm just meeting a few friends."

"Well, meet them tomorrow. I need to talk to you tonight, it's important. And could you tidy up here and get a start on the dinner before I get home?"

Jonathan knew by her tone that this was serious. "I suppose I could get the train in the morning, or you could drive me and do some shopping while I meet the guys. We could stay with my folks."

"I don't think so," Nicola replied.

If she played her cards right she would be helping him pack tonight and he could stay with his folks until he met some other gullible woman who fell for the line about being his muse.

She was glad not to bump into any of the neighbours as she went to the car. For some reason the traffic was never so dense on Fridays as other days. She got into work on time and immediately focused on getting Alice sorted out. The refuge confirmed that they wouldn't be able to put her up so as a last resort she contacted Cassandra about the place she'd called The Coven. She would have to inspect it before she considered placing Alice and the girls there.

Cassandra, true to her word, had managed to find a phone number for Cappagh Hall and Nicola phoned immediately and talked to the owner, Eliza Lynch. She seemed very sympathetic and gave Nicola directions to come and meet her.

Driving up to Cappagh Hall was an entirely different experience from driving into Lady Gregory Court. The drive was about a quarter of a mile long with mature trees on either side. It had an old-world feel about it. There were sheep in the meadows on either side and she saw horses grazing in the distance. It was an idyllic setting but she wondered how someone like Alice would manage here without a car and with two school-going children to consider.

The mansion was very old and looked dilapidated from the outside. Eliza Lynch greeted her at the door. She was an unusual person to say the least. She was wearing a flowing dress and flat shoes and she wore her long shiny grey hair in a sort of French roll. She led Nicola into the house and floated into a large kitchen which would not have been inappropriate in a hotel.

She invited Nicola to take a seat at the table and went to put on a coffeemaker. Then she took a seat opposite her.

"Tell me about this person," she said.

"I can't tell you much, I'm afraid. Because of the confidentiality involved in my work I can only talk about her in general terms. I'm here to establish if this place is suitable and to enquire if you have space. If your accommodation is suitable and you have a space and are willing to offer it to her, she will then tell you her name and any other details she feels are appropriate. But in general her story is that she has two little girls aged eleven and eight and her partner has abandoned her suddenly. She now finds herself dependent on welfare after having had quite a comfortable life, financially at least, up until recently."

"It sounds sadly like the situation my own daughter found herself in about ten years ago," the other woman said sadly.

"And did you look after her?"

"Alas, no. We had not approved of her choice of partner and when the relationship broke down she didn't feel able to come home, even though she was alone with twin boys. In fact we didn't find out about her plight until about six months after it happened but she still wouldn't come home. She lives in London and I will always regret that she didn't want us near her at that sad time."

"Oh," Nicola was taken aback. "I heard that you set up this

premises after your daughter was abandoned. I presumed she was your first tenant."

"No." Eliza's eyes filled with tears. "She has never been in this house."

"I'm sorry," was all Nicola could say.

"But we have been able to help many other women in the same situation." Eliza brightened up. "Why don't I show you around? My husband and I retired from conventional farming around the time our daughter left Ireland and we bought this mansion. We have since converted one wing of it into several apartments for the women we help and we run an organic garden which is my husband's hobby and he is quite passionate about it. It all works very well. I'll show you the two vacant apartments. We have three families in the others at present."

As they were chatting, a man about the same age as Eliza, dressed in corduroy trousers and wellingtons but looking every inch a country gentleman, came into the kitchen leaving a trail of mud in his wake.

"This is my husband, Hugo," Eliza said. "As you can see he has been working in the garden. This is Nicola. She is a social worker and is enquiring if we could perhaps accommodate one of her clients."

The man smiled at Nicola. "I won't shake your hand," he said, showing her with a gesture that he was covered in mud. "But you are very welcome and we do have a vacancy at present."

He had an old-fashioned politeness about him which Nicola found endearing.

"Eliza was just about to show me a vacant apartment," she said.

"Your client is welcome to it if she wants it," Hugo assured her and Nicola and Eliza went up the wide staircase towards the accommodation.

"These are our own quarters," Eliza said, waving her hand vaguely to the left. "And here are the apartments for our guests. We have two three-bedroomed ones, both occupied at present, and three two-bed ones. Only one of them is occupied. If your client comes to live here, her girls will have to share a room, but they are very big – unlike modern apartments."

"How can you afford to do this?" Nicola asked.

"It's not difficult. We have no mortgage on the house, we have investments and we make a bit from the garden. When the women are settled they often get rent allowance and that helps with the running costs of the house. The apartments pay for themselves in this way."

"What if a tenant was unable to get rent allowance for some reason?" Nicola held her breath as she waited for the answer.

"That's not a problem. Most of them are in such a distressed state it takes weeks for them to recover sufficiently to even apply for it but when it comes it is often backdated. In any case we can do without it if we have to. Our most important role is to provide support for women who have been abandoned and money is not an issue for us."

Eliza showed Nicola into a spacious apartment on the first floor. It was simply furnished, Shaker style. There were two quite large bedrooms, a bathroom and a kitchen-cum-living-room. It was bright and cheerful with large old-fashioned windows and looked quite cosy. Nicola could see Alice's family settling in here quite nicely.

"The apartment is lovely but could I possibly meet one of the other tenants? It would give me some idea whether my client would be happy here."

"I'll see if Mary is home. She has been with us six months now. She is very friendly. Obviously these apartments are their home so though there are a few ground rules we don't monitor the movements of the tenants at all. I'll knock."

Mary opened the door with a smile. "Hello, Eliza. You caught me napping literally. The baby was awake all night – teething – but he has gone to sleep now so I lay down on the sofa."

"In that case I'm sorry we disturbed you," Eliza said. "This is Nicola McCarthy – she's a social worker with the HSE. She has a client who she feels might benefit from a stay here until she gets back on her feet – rather like yourself."

"Oh, come in and I'll make a cup of tea."

"Not at all," Nicola said. "You get back to sleep. That baby will probably be up all night again tonight, if I know anything about babies, so you'll need all the rest you can get now. I am sorry we disturbed you."

Eliza and Nicola went back downstairs to the kitchen where they continued to talk over coffee.

"How long do the women stay here?" Nicola enquired.

"As long as they need – it varies from three months to about three years. We don't put any pressure on them."

Nicola felt that the place was perfect except for its distance from the school which Alice's children attended.

"What's the public transport like?" she enquired. "I'm worried about getting the girls to school."

"Public transport isn't great. But there's nearly always someone going into town first thing. Four of the other children here go to school so someone usually takes them in the jeep. They love it. They think they're on safari."

"If my client wishes to come here, could I bring her today?"

"Of course – as I say we have two vacant apartments."

"How is that? There's an acute shortage of emergency beds in the city."

"We're not officially part of the system. We usually get our tenants by word of mouth. All of them have recently been deserted by a partner. We don't take conventional families even if they are in crisis. I bet you heard of us from someone outside the social services field."

"Yes, but now that I know about you I might want to place other families here. I had better be off. I'll speak to the client and will probably be returning with her later today. One way or another I'll call you."

As she drove away from the house Nicola wondered how she could have the Lynches checked out by the police without their finding out. She couldn't place an at-risk family here without doing that. After this morning's little episode with the Gardaí she wasn't keen to phone them to do the check but then she remembered a really nice sergeant who had accompanied her on a child-protection issue when she first came to Galway. She phoned him from her mobile immediately and he assured her that he would carry out the check and get back to her as soon as possible.

Feeling reasonably cheerful, considering all that had happened in the previous few days, she drove back to the office.

Alice was due to call immediately after lunch, before she picked up the children from school, and Nicola had started to work on the PPS number when Pat, her manager, came in.

"I won't beat about the bush, Nicola," he said, not taking a seat as he usually did. "I have had a most serious complaint about you."

Nicola was shocked. She was overstepping the mark considering placing Alice in The Coven but she hadn't informed anyone about her intention and she had hoped to get away with it. It was not uncommon for a social worker to find rented accommodation for a client and most people would judge that that was what she had done. She wondered how Pat had found out about it and how she was going to talk her way out of this.

"I can't imagine what it might be about," she lied, closing the file she had been working on.

"One of your clients has complained about a breach of confidentiality. She says that her ex found out where she was living and turned up and created hell for herself and the children last night. The Guards had to be called and she had to take the children to the A&E because she thought her son had a broken arm. Since you were the only one who knew both him and her, she is blaming you."

Nicola was both relieved and surprised. "I can't imagine who you mean, Pat. But you know me well enough to know that I wouldn't do that. Who made the complaint?"

"A woman called Christine O'Neill. She is adamant you must have done and she's very angry. So I hope you have your i's dotted and your t's crossed. A breach of confidentiality such as this could cost you your job."

"I know, Pat, but I haven't done anything. I remember working with her a few years ago and I have done nothing unethical. The woman is mistaken. Has she made a formal complaint?"

"No. But I told her that if she had a complaint she had to follow our procedure and I gave her the form."

"I think she has her wires crossed," Nicola answered but she was perplexed.

Alice was just walking in the office door when the Garda Sergeant rang Nicola back and said that the Lynches had never come to the attention of the Gardaí if you discounted the odd parking ticket which, he assured her, was paid promptly. That was a relief. Alice looked so apprehensive that she was glad to be able to tell her that she had found her a place to stay.

"I can take you there in my car," Nicola said. "We'll put your belongings into the boot now and collect the girls from school. You don't have to worry about anything. They seem to specialise in looking after women in your situation and they can wait until your social welfare and rent allowance are sorted out. They even provide food for the first few weeks if that is necessary."

"Will it be awful?" Alice's voice was small and tired.

"Your situation is very difficult," Nicola replied gently, "so I suppose it will be depressing sometimes but it's a lovely old house and the apartment is perfect. I think you're very lucky that Cassandra told me about this place. It's unique in that you are not expected to pay your way until you can. I think you will like it. It is a very safe place. It will be a new beginning for you and the girls. Let's pack your things and take the girls to their new home."

When Nicola dropped Alice and her family off at Cappagh Hall she promised to call to see them after the weekend. She felt a bit guilty when she saw the fear in Alice's face but a weekend without a social worker was the least of what she would have to face over the next few months or so until she got herself on her feet. In any case Nicola rarely called on people over the weekend unless she felt they were at risk and Alice didn't fall into that category now.

Getting back into her car, she thought about the fact that she had her own new beginning to plan. She was not looking forward to going home. In the car *Drive Time* was full of the political situation. Jack Madden as Tánaiste was now, in theory at least, running the country. The state funeral would be on the following Tuesday and it was anticipated that the leadership election would take place within a month of that. Practically the whole programme was taken up with speculation about the future of the country, the party and the leadership of the party.

They attempted to draw Jack Madden out on the subject but in very sombre tones he said: "I am very busy at present with affairs of state, for which I have so suddenly and unexpectedly become responsible. I don't believe it to be appropriate to discuss my future intentions until after the funeral of the Taoiseach, may he rest in peace, and that is all I have to say on the matter."

"Creep!" thought Nicola. But I am going to forget about him and Alice and deal with my own problems over the weekend. Hopefully I will come into work on Monday ready for anything.

By the time she got home it was six thirty. Jonathan was chopping vegetables but the apartment was as untidy as when she left it that morning. Well, after today, if the apartment was untidy she would have done it by herself and she could live with that.

"What are you cooking?" she asked.

"Stir fry. It's all there is." Jonathan appeared to be sulking.

"Sure what's wrong with that? It's fine. Will I open a bottle of wine?"

"Suit yourself."

"Is there something wrong? Why are you so cranky?"

"I was going to Dublin this evening and you decided that we had to discuss something that couldn't wait until after the weekend. I really don't see why it couldn't have waited. I was really looking forward to the break."

"But you're going tomorrow anyway. What difference does a night make?" Nicola asked, reasonably enough she thought.

"If a night is so unimportant, why couldn't what you want to discuss wait until I came back? That will be in two nights, three at the most!"

Nicola hesitated. There was no point in procrastinating.

"Because I don't want you to come back."

He spun around, obviously incredulous.

"*What?*"

"I think this relationship has run its course. It's over. I don't want you living here any more. Given that you are going to Dublin tomorrow anyway and will be visiting your family, it seems to me to be a practical time for it to end. You can stay with them until you get a place of your own."

"You can't be serious!"

"I am." Nicola was surprised by the certainty in her own voice.

"Where did this come from? We were getting on great. You never said you were unhappy. You gave me no indication that you wanted to end this."

"We haven't been getting on great, as you call it, for ages. You know I'm unhappy about your drug-taking and that I feel vulnerable because you do it here. I was absolutely petrified this morning when the Gardaí came. We haven't had fun in ages. We only visit your friends and you have no interest in mine. You're always broke and complaining about it, as if in some way it's my fault. I am fed up of carrying both of us. Life has to be easier than this."

"Maybe it is, but it can be lonelier too. I seem to recall that you couldn't get enough of me when we met first. You were all over me like a rash. When did that change, I wonder? When you realised that I was not about to become a famous artist?"

His voice was whiney and it irritated her.

"No, when I realised that for you earning a living would have to wait until you became famous, even if it took a lifetime." She was surprised at the coldness of her own voice.

"That's not fair! You know that I really try." He looked at her as if she had dealt him a physical blow.

"You only try to sell your art and you're half-hearted enough about that. You rarely paint anything new these days. All artists subsidise their art with teaching or commercial work but not you. You are waiting for the world to recognise your genius, when even you must know that most geniuses don't get recognised in their own lifetime. I'm fed up of going it alone, of your constant demands and your unwillingness to pull your weight here."

"What do you mean I don't pull my weight?"

"Well, apart from the fact that you make no financial contribution to the upkeep of this apartment, you don't make any other contribution either. There is no question of you having a meal ready at dinnertime even if I have had a particularly hard day. In fact, you don't even ask about my day. The whole country is in turmoil because the Taoiseach has died but you haven't even mentioned it. You must be the only person in the country who hasn't an opinion on it."

"Oh, I have an opinion alright. I can't see what the fuss is about. That Madden guy will hold the fort and will probably be elected as party leader. Where's the big deal? What's it got to do with me? And when do you really have a hard day? You're well able to deal with your job."

Nicola decided not to even try to explain. He was so egocentric that there would be no getting through to him. She just realised that this guy was not for her and she wanted an end to it.

"I don't see the point in having this conversation now," she said quietly. "I have decided that I don't want to live with you any more and, seeing as this is my apartment, I want you to leave."

"Oh, that's lovely! There's many a man who supported a woman just because she wanted to stay at home and mind children, but he'd be the worst rat in the country if he said that it was his house and he wanted her out." He said this as if he had made a clever point.

"We have no children and you make a song and dance if I ask you to make a cup of tea, let alone mind a child!" She could hear the anger in her voice and she didn't want to continue this conversation. He was, understandably perhaps, beyond reasoning.

"So what am I supposed to do? Pack my bags and leave in the morning?"

"Ideally, yes, but I suppose if you can't take everything I could send the rest to your parents' house." She was hoping he would go without much ado.

"My God, you're serious!"

"I am. I can give you cab money and money for the train, if you are short, but I would like you to take your things in the morning. I have a lot on at work and I don't want anything else to worry about at home."

"What kind of woman puts her job before her relationship?"

"There *is* no relationship any more so my job is now my primary concern. In any case, you wouldn't say that to a man. Now can we eat? I'm starved and I want to have an early night."

She helped him serve the meal and they ate in silence. She wondered how they were going to get through the next twelve hours.

"I can help you pack if you like," she said as they got up from the table, hoping he would refuse the offer.

"I'll manage," he responded sullenly but she knew that she would at least have to get his cases out or he wouldn't make a start.

She put the dinner things in the dishwasher and tidied up. Jonathan sat sullenly at the table, saying nothing. She got out his cases.

"If you need any help, give me a shout." She went into their room and got ready for bed. They didn't mention what their sleeping arrangements would be that night but she hoped he would have the cop-on to sleep in the spare room. She turned on the bedroom television and decided she would not leave the room unless he needed her help. It was at times like this that she would have loved a sleeping tablet but she had never needed them before so there were none about. She hadn't even had a glass of wine which might have relaxed her enough to make her sleep.

She flicked through the channels until she found a suitably inane soap and soon felt herself get drowsy.

When she woke in the morning Jonathan was gone.

Chapter 5

Nicola felt positively cheerful as she set out for work on Monday morning. She had spent the weekend putting what remained of Jonathan's belongings in boxes and had rung a courier to collect them on Monday evening. It was like taking a ton weight from her shoulders. By evening all traces of Jonathan would be out of her apartment and out of her life. No longer did she have to worry about who might know about Jonathan's habit – which he never admitted he had. No longer did she have to jolly him along like a child to get him to do even the smallest task. No longer did she have to massage his incredibly fragile ego. She could look after herself first for a change and it was a long time since she had done that. In fact it was a long time since she'd had anybody reliable to look after her so she decided that she was the best person to do it.

She had scarcely sat down at her desk when she got a call from Cassandra.

"Alice's apartment, Number 3, was gutted over the weekend," she said in conspiratorial tones.

"You mean there was a fire?" Nicola was incredulous.

"No, I mean that every stick of furniture, every carpet, every rug was removed – bed linen, personal effects – the lot. Three or four men came on Saturday and put everything in a skip. I tried to get a look into the apartment but they kept the doors closed while they were working. However, I did see some correspondence sticking out of a packing crate one of the men had left in the hall as I passed, so I swiped it, in case it would come in handy in the future. In fact I made several trips to the car that afternoon and took any papers that looked like they might be helpful."

"You're great, Cassandra. What did you get?" Nicola couldn't believe that Cassandra was so quick-thinking.

"I just had a quick look and there is some correspondence addressed to Tower Properties and some stuff for Alice. I thought that if you were free this morning I would bring it in to your office. It might not necessarily be safe here. Obviously the doorman is paid by Jack Madden and I would be surprised if I don't become the prime suspect if they miss anything. They may go through the stuff when they take it off site and maybe notice things missing, between what I took last week and what I took over the weekend. The doorman may put two and two together."

"You make it sound very cloak and dagger," Nicola replied. But she remembered with a shiver her conversation with Jack Madden and she realised that Cassandra might be right. In fact it was obvious that he was capable of practically anything. How would he believe that he could simply eliminate his mistress and children from his life just by detaching himself from them unless he knew that he could get away with it? He must have been fairly certain that nobody would let the cat out of the bag.

She stared at the newspaper she had bought on the way into work. Jack Madden, the family man, was staring at her from a large picture on the front page. The Sunday papers had been full of him as well. There were of course pages about arrangements for the funeral but underneath it all the chattering classes were agog about the next Taoiseach. Some of the papers had done biographical articles over the weekend. There were photographs of his parents, his siblings and of course of his wife and two beautiful children. There were quotes from childhood friends, college classmates, even a woman who claimed that she had been his nanny. It was enough to make Nicola want to reach for the Bailey's. Not a mention at all of the two other beautiful children who he appeared to be able to forget at a moment's notice literally. Nicola wondered how Alice and the children would take the saturation coverage of the weekend newspapers and how they would get through the next week with the funeral and the succession being the top story in every news bulletin. In fact, despite what Jack Madden had said on the day of the Taoiseach's death about not making any decisions until after the funeral, the future leadership of the party was getting as many headlines as the funeral. Alice was in for a long and stressful week and Nicola hoped she would hold up.

Cassandra had agreed to come into the office at eleven and they would go through the correspondence she had taken from the apartment block then.

But at ten o'clock Pat put his head around the door.

"Bad news, I'm afraid. Your client has made a formal complaint. She sounds very serious and very angry."

Nicola's heart sank. There had never been a formal complaint against her before and she didn't even know the procedure.

"What do I do now?" she asked.

"You'll be invited to a meeting with me and the Department Head and the complainant. That will be in about a week's time – as soon as we can arrange a time suitable for everybody."

"And will I be able to continue working or will I be suspended?" Nicola could hear the shake in her voice.

"No, you won't be suspended unless it gets to the next stage."

"That's a relief anyway. This is a mistake and as soon as we meet up Christine will realise that she is in error."

"You must not contact her between now and the day of the meeting." Pat was firm. "And if you bump into her accidentally don't talk to her. This is for your own good more than hers."

"Of course. Should I contact my union?" Suddenly in Nicola's mind this had escalated from something which could be sorted to something which could have serious consequences.

"Contact your union if you wish but, unless you specifically want to, it might be as well to have the meeting with the complainant as informal as possible – initially at least. If this goes further, of course you should have union representation." Pat closed the door gently as he left the room.

To her own surprise Nicola burst into tears but she stopped abruptly when she realised that it was near eleven and she couldn't let Cassandra see her like this.

At eleven on the dot Cassandra glided into the room. Her clothes and jewellery were immaculate. She looked as if she was going to a high-powered business meeting. Not the first time Nicola wondered who her clients were. Judging from Cassandra's lifestyle they must be very wealthy. She sat down with a pleased look on her face and emptied a sizeable Gucci bag onto the desk.

Nicola stared at the desk and giggled. "Couldn't you get any more?" She grinned. "What about her supermarket receipts?"

"Oh, Alice didn't shop in supermarkets much," Cassandra assured her. "She mainly went to McCambridge's and Chez Maurice and of course The Vineyard if she wanted a bottle of wine – no supermarket plonk for Alice and her well-got beau. Even her breakfast cereal was gourmet. But actually I think there are some receipts for her groceries in there as well."

The women laughed as they sorted through the pile of paper on the desk.

"This will come in handy," Nicola said, picking up an ESB bill addressed to a property company. "Tower Properties! They must own the apartment! We can find out who the directors are if need be."

"Yes," Cassandra said. "And here is a letter from the school to Alice, correctly addressed, regarding an increase in the voluntary fees. That's handy. It's proof they lived there. I'm feeling quite pleased with myself. Where do we go from here?"

"You can drop the ESB bill and the other letters addressed to Tower Properties into the mailbox for Number 3.

"Why?" Cassandra was incredulous.

"Because it's an offence to open a person's mail and a company is a legal person. As a social worker I have to be very careful. All the other stuff belongs to Alice, so we can just give it to her."

"I thought you were pleased I got the letters to Tower Properties!"

"I am. But all we need is the name of the company in order to investigate further. So far I haven't behaved illegally though you may have. But you're not an employee of the HSE. So you won't lose your job if you get caught. In fact if you take back the Tower Properties stuff there will be no evidence against you anyway."

"I never knew social workers were so clever," Cassandra grinned.

"We have our moments." Nicola was laughing. "Tell me this? How did you know about The Coven? I have been working in this city for nearly three years now and I never heard of it and I think none of my colleagues know about it either."

"They helped out a friend of mine a while ago. They don't broadcast what they do and I'd say all of their tenants arrive there by recommendation – sort of. They are – how can I say this without sounding priggish – people who wouldn't normally expect to find themselves in the sort of predicament they get into." Cassandra looked embarrassed.

"Cassandra, you don't sound priggish but you do sound a bit naïve."

Cassandra grinned when she realised that this was the first time she had ever been called naïve.

"No, seriously. Don't you know that family violence and abusive relationships cross all social boundaries? You'd be very naïve if you believed that such situations are the sole prerogative of the less well off," Nicola said grimly. "I recently had a client who was married to a doctor. He punched her hard for the first time on the way to the airport for their honeymoon. She stayed with him for six years, despite regular serious assaults and, yes, she went to the hospital frequently with the 'I fell down the stairs and I bumped into a bookcase in the dark' stories. But she left him, in the clothes she stood up in, the day he pushed their four-year-old son so violently that he went flying and needed stitches to his jaw after hitting it off the hearth. No, this problem knows no boundaries."

"God, I never thought of it that way. It's hard to believe."

"You can believe it alright. In fact, middle class and wealthy women usually are more adept at covering it up and often put up with it for longer because they are so ashamed. Until it happens to them I'd say they also believe that it only happens to uneducated poor women who aren't very bright."

"To be honest, I never gave it much thought even when it happened to my friend. I thought it was just her bad luck and probably a very rare occurrence. By the way, when are you going to see Alice again?"

"This afternoon probably," said Nicola. "She'll be delighted with all your help. Though she is still probably in a state of shock and may not appreciate all you have done, initially at least. I have worked on getting her social welfare and when she is settled we will have to decide how to go about getting Jack Madden to support her. That is not going to be easy."

"No, I suppose it's not. Tell her I send my love. I would like to go to see her if she would like but I don't want to go uninvited."

"I will tell her," said Nicola. "I'd say she'd be delighted with your friendship. She will be feeling very alone now. She may feel that she can't tell her friends about her situation and will probably find it difficult to think up a plausible story as to why she no longer lives in Lady Gregory Court. For professional reasons I can't befriend her so I'd say you'd be very welcome."

"Good," said Cassandra. "I'll be glad to befriend her."

Driving out to The Coven late that afternoon Nicola wondered what she would find. She had made some progress getting Alice's social welfare payment sorted and once that was done rent allowance wouldn't be a problem. She had left her visit until late deliberately. She wanted to meet the children and see how they were settling in.

The large front door was wide open and Eliza appeared in the hall before Nicola had a chance to ring the bell.

"Nicola! Hello. You'll be looking for Alice," she said

cheerfully. "She's in the kitchen teaching me to make gingerbread men. She's a marvellous cook."

Eliza led the way into the large kitchen. Alice was there with Grace and Orla. The girls were tucking into gingerbread men as if they had lived in The Coven for all of their short lives. Alice still looked a bit fragile but otherwise she appeared to be coping admirably.

"It's lucky we have such a large kitchen, Nicola," Eliza said, "despite the fact that all the apartments are self-contained."

"Why is that?"

"I run a catering service on an occasional basis. It's sort of a hobby but it helps pay the bills if our other sources of income let us down. Also, most weeks, all the residents have dinner together – usually on Friday. That way we form a sort of community. So Alice and the girls had a baptism of fire on their first night but I think they enjoyed it."

"We sure did!" It was Grace who spoke. "It's really nice here. There are other children to play with and we're allowed make as much noise as we like!"

"Well, not quite," Eliza joked.

"Our other house was full of adults. I think we were the only kids there. Even when Uncle Jack came we had to keep quiet."

The women all looked at each other at the mention of Uncle Jack, and Nicola guessed that Alice had confided in Eliza at some stage over the weekend.

"Can we go out and play with the dog?" Orla was animal mad and of course they couldn't have a pet at Lady Gregory Court.

"Yes, if that is okay with Eliza," Alice said.

"Of course," Eliza said. "He's well used to children and loves the attention."

The two girls skipped out the door as if they hadn't a care in the world.

"I suppose the saturation news-coverage hasn't passed the girls by?" Nicola said to Alice.

"They've seen it all right but it doesn't seem to bother them.

It's an explanation in their minds as to why Jack isn't here but Grace asked me when he would be down again just this morning."

"And what did you say?"

"The truth, in a way. I said I didn't know." Alice smiled weakly.

"Cassandra got some correspondence from your apartment," Nicola said then, anxious to change the subject. "I'm afraid workmen have been in over the weekend and have stripped the apartment bare. Cassandra swiped this stuff from crates outside the door."

The dismay in Alice's face was pitiful to see. Until that moment she had harboured a hope that somehow this was all a mistake and she would be back in her apartment when it was sorted out. It was obvious now that she would never be going back. Her eyes widened and her chin began to quiver. Nicola could have kicked herself. She had been so insensitive. She knew that Jack Madden had detached Alice and her children from his life but she should have realised that Alice had not taken this completely on board.

"Oh, I am sorry, Alice. That was completely insensitive of me."

"Don't be sorry. In a way it is a good thing. I can't kid myself any more. He's not coming back – not unless you drag him kicking and bellowing in any case." She smiled a bit and uttered a very weak laugh.

"I don't see myself dragging anyone anywhere but we *will* follow him for maintenance." Nicola was determined. "It is a fairly routine procedure but if he denies paternity – and I imagine he will – it will take time and could be very messy. That is why we have to fix you up with a welfare payment as soon as possible."

"Don't worry about money too much," Eliza interrupted. "As I told you, we are in a position to support Alice and the girls indefinitely. In any case, Alice might be able to help me out with the catering business. She's an excellent cook. She prepared the starter for dinner on Friday and it went down a treat."

"Jack likes good food. And since we never ate out – except for the occasional lunch – I had to learn to cook. I enjoy it and it became a sort of a hobby."

"It's quite a hobby," Nicola smiled. "And so useful."

"Actually I have a great line in novelty birthday cakes and would always provide the cake when it was a friend's child's birthday. I have, or should I say I had, a pile of recipe books. God knows where they are now."

Alice was grimfaced and somehow she didn't look as fragile as before. Nicola was beginning to feel that she could get her through this and that Alice would emerge stronger for it.

"Let's look through the correspondence in your apartment, together with the documents Cassandra already gave you," Nicola said. "I need birth certificates for all of you, proof of your last address, proof that the children are at school. That will be enough for the moment. I will try and fast-track getting your PPS number and after that things should be easy enough. In the meantime we can get your Community Welfare Officer to continue giving you an emergency payment."

Nicola and Alice made their way up to the apartment. Alice spread out the correspondence and the documents she already had on the table and Nicola took what she needed for her immediate purposes.

"How are you settling in?" asked Nicola then.

"It's very nice," Alice smiled. "The house is beautiful and very comfortable. Having our own apartment is great because we have our privacy and I need that."

"I'm delighted you're happy here," Nicola said. "It is lovely."

"On Saturday night when the girls were in bed I just bawled my eyes out. I couldn't stop. I must have cried for three or four hours solid," Alice said ruefully.

"That's hardly surprising after all that you have been through. But, yes, it was good that you didn't have an audience. How did the children get to school this morning?"

"Eliza drove us in the jeep. I went with them for the first day. They are used to me taking them to school. We took the other children with us. But the jeep has limited capacity so I probably won't go with them again unless I am needed to drive them. I think the girls won't mind. They are taking this in their stride."

"That's great anyway. The fact that the place is so nice helps. Have you been in touch with any of your friends?" She had to establish how isolated Alice felt.

Alice seemed surprised at the question. "Not yet. I will but I'm not ready to explain. And they can't contact me since my mobile got cut off." Her voice trailed off. "And in any case it might not be wise for me to broadcast my situation. If I get in touch with any of my friends and say that we have been deserted they will surely get more curious about who deserted us. It's all so complicated." She looked downcast again.

"It is and I think the less we make public the better until we can find a way of making him live up to his responsibilities. I think if we went public at this point he would go for us with all guns blazing and he might succeed in stopping my investigations. If he isn't sure I'm investigating him he won't do much. He has too much to deal with nationally to bother with me if he thinks I'm some ineffectual 'jumped-up slip of a girl', as he called me the other day when I rang him."

"You never told me you rang him!" Alice was aghast.

"I didn't want to upset you any further. I did and he denied knowing you and suggested that you might be a stalker with a fixation about him. He threatened me and insinuated that he had the power to have me fired. He was quite nasty."

"Oh God," Alice gasped.

"I knew this was not going to be easy so don't worry about me. But we will have to take legal action if he denies that the children are his. In particular if we want him to take a DNA test. So this is going to get worse before it gets better. But don't worry, you have a lot of support and Eliza and Hugo seem great. So you are very safe. This is an opportunity for you to get on with your life and figure out what to do next."

"I do feel safe here," Alice said. "Shattered, but safe."

Chapter 6

Jack Madden had barely time to bless himself in the aftermath of the Taoiseach's death. The funeral had to be arranged and the Cabinet had to be briefed. He was on a constant round of radio and TV interviews both nationally and internationally. The whole world seemed shocked at the suddenness of the death. The Taoiseach had been popular – even at an international level. In Strasbourg and Brussels he was regarded as genial and easygoing and a consummate negotiator, though some of the European media had adopted a more jaundiced view since the country's economic troubles began to emerge. However, they were anxious to have details of the funeral and many wanted to do a profile of this charismatic leader of a small country.

Jack was anxious that the next few days went well. He was a cert for leadership of the party – everybody knew that, but there's many a slip and he could have done without the worry of Alice and this bloody social worker who appeared to be on his case. He had only heard from her once but he was pretty sure she wouldn't give up easily. She was probably some uptight little madam anxious to get on but nobody in the Health Service Executive had briefed her. Surely she knew that the best way to get on was to keep in with the powers that be – in this case himself. She surely didn't think that he would sit there and let her delve into his personal life and not use his influence to see that she got what was coming to her. He had taken the precaution of setting up a few little surprises for her. She would be aware of them by now though probably would have no suspicion as to how they arose.

He was surprised at how much her phone call had rattled him. It hadn't occurred to him until then that Alice would have any contact with Social Services. He wondered how she had found a social worker. He had been quite careful to make sure that she had minimal contact with officialdom. He had supported her well financially and she never claimed any Child Benefit or anything else. She had never worked outside the home so he had presumed that when he was finished with her she would just go back to her family. Oh, he knew that they were not on speaking terms but it would take a very cold family indeed not to take her in if she had nowhere to go. The irony of that thought, given that he had made her and his children homeless, wasn't lost on him but these were very important times for him and the country. There was no time for sentimentality. Hard decisions had to be made. He gritted his teeth. He knew that Alice and the kids would find it hard for a while but sure weren't there unmarried mothers in every townland these days and nobody passed any remarks? Alice's parents never approved of her relationship with him so he presumed they would be pleased to see the end of it. They had probably guessed at the outset that the relationship had no chance of surviving. Jack was a well-known family man and his wife was very well connected politically so he was hardly going to sacrifice all of that for the daughter of some party hack from the arse-end of nowhere. He also presumed that the humiliation of it would prevent them from spilling the beans on him and in any case he reckoned that, if they did, no one would believe them.

But this social worker bitch was another matter – a glitch that he could have done without at this point in time. In retrospect he could see that the speed with which he had to act after the death of the Taoiseach meant that he really hadn't thought things through.

The next few days were crucial and Jack Madden had no intention of letting anything come between him and his goal. He would make himself very prominent at the funeral ceremony and his family would sort of hover. The image he would project would be of a reliable pair of hands to look after the country – temporarily initially but it would be only a formality getting elected as party leader.

The Taoiseach's private secretary arranged everything for him. There were several advisors on tap as well and though Jack had been to several state funerals both at home and abroad and knew what was involved, the fact that this was so close to home made it extremely stressful. He smiled to himself and thought how it might have been convenient if one of the older guys had died in office when he was a rooky and he could have experienced it and observed all the protocols involved from a safe distance. But this way – the first funeral of a serving Taoiseach in the history of the state – he would be in the limelight most of the time, as would the whole Cabinet, and he had to be careful not to put a foot wrong. Not that it was really an issue. He just wished that he hadn't this worry about Alice. He had a niggling regret at having to consign her to the past. Such a sweet little thing! Always loving, always welcoming. She never made any demands. That was the attraction. She was gorgeous and so accommodating. Left to her own devices she wouldn't have followed him.

Damn that social worker! But he hadn't time to think of her now. He had to meet a journalist from Dublin Radio who was known to have a nose for politics so he would be asking awkward questions about the future. Jack would have to be careful not to be seen to be dancing on the Taoiseach's grave, while giving an indication of his capabilities as a politician.

He went into the bathroom adjoining the Taoiseach's office, which he was occupying temporarily. He had brought some of his clothes in so that he could go straight from the office to any engagement that might come up suddenly in the course of these few days. He toyed with the idea of having a shower before doing the interview. He felt a bit clammy and it worried him that this might not be due solely to the warm weather. He was more rattled than he was prepared to admit even to himself.

The interview went well and Jack was happy with the way he put himself across. Those days spent at Carr Communications had paid off. He had lunch with his private secretary as there were a few details he had to iron out. He took a call from David Cameron and surprisingly from Angela Merkel. It was looking okay but he would be glad when the funeral was over on Wednesday and he could get on with his campaign for party leadership.

When he came back from lunch there was a message from Nicola McCarthy on his desk. She was requesting that he ring her at a Galway number. Well, the bitch could wait! He was not about to let her know that she had rattled him by ringing her back straight away. She could wait until after the funeral and if she called again he would leave it a further week, and maybe even set up another surprise, before he returned her call.

Nicola wasn't surprised that Jack Madden hadn't returned her most recent call. She'd made it to let him know that she was still around and that Alice had support. She decided that she would not try and get in touch with him again until after the funeral. He was on every news bulletin, every programme about the late Taoiseach's life. He was all over the place. She felt sorry for Alice. It was inevitable that there would be blanket coverage of the funeral and it was likely that Jack's wife would be in the picture. He would make sure of that to copper-fasten his image of a stable family man. The funeral would be the start of his PR exercise in the lead-up to the leadership election and ultimately the general election which was due within twelve months.

She was glad to be heading for home and bought herself a gourmet lasagne and a rhubarb crumble at KC Blake's Pantry by way of celebration. She was looking forward to having the apartment to herself and decided that she would work on her social life in a few days when she had sorted out all her personal stuff. She was glad to be rid of Jonathan but they had been together for quite a while and she knew that she would miss him on occasion. She hoped she would deal with that well and that when it arose her head would rule her heart.

After a satisfactory meal and a long bath she got on the internet and booked herself into a spa for a pampering weekend as a first step in her move to look after herself. The phone didn't ring all evening and it was only as she prepared to go to bed that she thought to look at the machine. There were several messages: three from Jonathan and one from a friend in Cork she hadn't seen for about a year. She listened to Jonathan requesting earnestly that maybe they should have a chat about "us" and asking her to call him. He almost succeeded in keeping the whinge out of his voice but not quite and she was glad that the courier had come as requested and that now the last of Jonathan's property was en route to his parents' home in Glenageary. It was nearly eleven so she decided not to ring her friend in Cork but resolved that she would do it immediately she got home from work the following day.

Chapter 7

Rising the following morning Nicola felt a bit uneasy. She had Alice sorted, in so far as that was possible, so she couldn't at first figure out why she felt edgy. Then it came back to her. The complaint! She had been so busy that she had not given it any thought but, now that the immediate problem of Alice's accommodation was sorted, she began to wonder how it had come about. She knew that she hadn't breached confidentiality. And she wondered if there could be something she had not foreseen behind the complaint. Then it crossed her mind that Jack Madden had put the woman up to it but she dismissed her fears as ludicrous. This is Ireland, not Mafia country, she scolded herself and put it out of her mind.

She rang Alice early just to say that she wouldn't be seeing her that day nor the next probably and to ensure that things were still going smoothly.

"We're okay," Alice said. "Eliza has fixed me up with a mobile and I was even able to retain my old number so that I can now be contacted by any one of my old friends that might want to get in touch . . ."

Her voice trailed off and Nicola knew that she was still, at the back of her mind, hoping that Jack might make an appearance. Nicola decided that she should bring her back to reality.

"Do the children have the day off tomorrow?" she asked.

"No, but the school is taking them to a Mass for the Taoiseach, at the time of the funeral Mass."

"That's good at least. The last thing you need is them at home with the funeral being shown on the television. You will have to be ready for a hard time tomorrow, Alice. It is very likely he will be very much to the forefront and so will his wife. You'll virtually not be able to avoid it."

"Luckily I'll be out for the actual funeral as well. The animal sanctuary has asked Hugo to rehome a neglected pony and Eliza and Hugo have suggested that I go with them to pick him up. The only time the people at the sanctuary could fit them in is around noon tomorrow, so I won't even be in the house. Do you think they thought of that when they invited me?"

"It sounds very like it to me. They're great and it looks like the sanctuary staff have no interest in politics either – which makes them a very rare breed!" Nicola laughed. Life had a way of cheering you up sometimes. Who would have thought that outside the city of Galway a lovely couple had given up a lot of their home and most of their time to helping women in trouble and that virtually nobody in officialdom knew about them? "Best of luck tomorrow, Alice, and give me a ring on Thursday. I should have your social welfare sorted by then and we can then arrange your rent allowance and you'll be an independent woman."

"For the first time in my life." Alice gave a nervous laugh and Nicola knew that she didn't want to be an independent woman. She wanted to be provided for by Jack Madden, but that wouldn't happen and both women knew it.

As she put down the phone Pat put his head around the door.

"How are you today?"

She couldn't figure out if he really wanted to know or if he was just being polite. She had been quite shocked initially when he told her that there was a complaint against her but she was even more shocked when she realised that he might not be behind her completely.

"I'm fine. Any more news about the complaint?" She hoped

that he would not realise how much it bothered her now that she had nothing more pressing on her mind.

"The meeting is set for next Monday. Is that okay?"

"Would it make a difference if it wasn't? I thought I had no option but to fall in with the arrangement. Morning or afternoon?" She thought how funny it was that she could come to work with one problem on her mind and before the first hour was over a completely different thing was taking up her thoughts.

"Morning," Pat replied pleasantly enough. "Pencil it in."

"I will. I just hope that this meeting will be the end of the affair – that it will all be sorted out on the day." She looked carefully at Pat. She wondered whether there was more to this than met the eye and if perhaps Pat knew more than he was saying.

"Hopefully it will go well. I'm sure it will be grand," he assured her with a smile and closed the door.

The rest of the day was pretty routine and she was relieved that it was well within her capability and not too taxing. She was about to leave the office when her phone rang. It was Cassandra.

"Hi, Cassandra! What good news do you have for me now? How much information have you managed to glean from the apartment block? Or is this a mere social call?" Truthfully, she didn't expect it to be a social call. She wasn't on calling terms with call girls, though having met this one face to face she could see how she might very well become her friend. She liked Cassandra from the little she knew of her and, unlike many other girls with the same profession, she felt Cassandra was in control of her own life and she would leave it when it suited her.

"Actually, it is a social call – sort of. I was wondering if we could meet for a glass of wine tonight? I'd like to have a chat."

She sounded a bit hesitant, not the confident Cassandra Nicola had met in recent days.

"Of course. It will be good for both of us. Why don't we meet at that new place in Lower Salthill and we could walk the prom afterwards?"

"That sounds good. How about seven thirty? I have another appointment at nine thirty."

Nicola laughed.

"Why are you laughing?" Cassandra asked, puzzled.

"It just seems odd to me that you can so casually fit me in between customers," Nicola replied. "Sorry, I hope that doesn't sound crass."

"Not really. I know that my way of life is strange to you but it pays well and is a means to an end for me."

"I know, Cassandra. I'll see you at seven thirty and we'll have that chat. See you then."

Nicola hung up and headed for home.

She pondered on why Cassandra might want to see her. It was strange and indeed she wondered if she had been wise to agree to meet this woman who she had met through a client in a semi-social context. But the last few days had been so strange, she had agreed to meet Cassandra before it hit her that it might not be that wise.

When she got home she had a quick shower and then chose what to wear carefully, smiling to herself. I am about to go for a glass of wine with a call girl and I am worrying how I look! But Cassandra was so elegant that she didn't want to look like a frump beside her.

Cassandra was already seated when Nicola walked into the wine bar. She was elegance personified in understated casual clothes, with more than a hint of class. Despite taking time over her own outfit, Nicola felt gauche but she decided to ignore that.

"Well, Cassandra, I was surprised to hear from you," she said after they greeted each other and she sat down. "Is it about Alice? Did you go to see her?"

"No, actually, I didn't and, no, it isn't." Cassandra looked Nicola straight in the eyes. "It's about me."

Nicola was startled. "Oh? What's the matter?"

"I need to talk to someone and I wasn't sure if I could talk to you in the office. It might be regarded as a social-work issue but it might be more of a counsellor issue."

Nicola didn't know what to make of this and she felt slightly nervous. Call girls often had strange contacts and she was wondering what was going to come next.

"Actually as a social worker at the HSE I deal with child welfare cases, so unless you have a child you wouldn't come within my remit. I am a trained counsellor, but I don't officially counsel anyone, though the ability to do it comes in handy in my work. It would be better if we regarded this as a social outing. Why don't you just talk to me as a friend and I will see if I can help."

Cassandra looked relieved. "I don't know where to start," she said.

"Try the beginning," Nicola said with a grin, "and if this is a very long story you had better start now because you have less than two hours. Will we get a glass of wine? I didn't bring my car."

"Neither did I. Why don't we order a bottle? It might act as a conversational lubricant." Cassandra raised her hand to attract the attention of the waiter.

She choose a Pinot Grigio and asked Nicola if that was okay. She seemed quite knowledgeable so Nicola bowed to her superior expertise. The waiter poured the wine, Cassandra tasted it and nodded to the waiter to fill both glasses.

After he departed she took a sip of her wine and then leaned towards Nicola and said, "I have a dilemma I have never had before. Not for a long time anyway and this time it is very complicated."

"I'm intrigued."

"I'm in love." Cassandra smiled sheepishly.

Nicola was startled. "That's good, isn't it? Or is it?"

"Not really. He doesn't love me, except as a friend, and he's married."

Nicola had seen it all before. "The age-old problem. How come you fell for a married guy, particularly if he was unlikely to love you back?" She wasn't sure if she was overstepping the mark by asking this.

"He is a client. And I know that this sounds awful, but his wife is ill. He just needs a relationship where he can forget his problems. It's not that he is selfish or anything. If he was, he'd have left her a long time ago. But he really loves her. She has had MS for a number of years so their life is quite hard. Their children are teenagers and he tries not to lay anything on them in terms of looking after their mother or doing many extra chores – so all of it falls to him. About once a fortnight he comes to see me. We do have sex, it is a factor, but that is not what's important for him. He just wants to have dinner with a woman and have a carefree conversation. He is clearly devoted to his wife. In a strange and weird way, I sort of envy her – MS and all." Cassandra paused.

"Wow, that's quite a story! Does he know? That you love him, I mean?"

"God, no! What do you take me for? He likes me, I know that, but I'd say he views me as quite a clinical person who does what she does for a purpose and that suits him. I'd say he'd run a mile if I said I loved him. What am I to do?" She looked as if she was on the verge of tears.

"Have you told anybody else? Is he from Galway?"

"No and no. He's from Sligo and comes here for a few hours once or twice a month."

"Well, it's a problem alright and not one I can see an easy answer to. I never considered you might fall in love with a client, though obviously it can happen. If it's any consolation you're the third woman in the last week that has been hit with lousy luck with men."

"Who's the second after Alice?"

"Me. I have just finished a relationship I should have got shut of long before now."

"You! Well, you may think that call girls aren't supposed to fall in love but surely social workers aren't supposed to fall for bad guys!" Cassandra was grinning.

"So between the two of us we've exploded a few myths over the past few days!" Nicola laughed. "But how do you think I can help with your problem?"

"I don't know really. I just felt I had to talk to someone. It seems so mad. I have quite a few friends in Galway but no-one knows what I do for a living. It's quite interesting how you can get by without telling people you know quite well anything about your work. They know I'm some sort of consultant – they just don't know what kind!"

"Well, you came to the right place. We might be able to help each other. I just dumped Jonathan over the weekend and I haven't started to miss him yet. I know I've done the right thing but I am dreading being on the single scene again. And, while what I'm feeling now is relief, I am sensible enough to know that I'll begin to miss him if I don't replace him soon. As you know, it always looks easier to get a new man when you're involved than it actually is when you're not. The last time I think I was about eighteen months between boyfriends. Incidentally, have you ever been in love before?"

"Of course I have, but it's been a while – a long while. This seems so hopeless – ridiculous even." Cassandra gave Nicola a sheepish look.

"It's not ridiculous but it does seem hopeless. It can't survive unless his wife dies." Nicola shot the other woman a look.

"Oh, don't say that! I certainly wouldn't wish her dead. I love him and if I'm honest I think I would like her as well if we met. He talks about her a bit sometimes, not in a maudlin sort of way, but she sounds like a great person, in particular when you consider what she is going through. I feel sort of guilty about her sometimes, though I've no need to. As I said, it is quite obvious that he still loves her deeply and his little trysts with me are just something to keep him sane as he goes through this particularly difficult patch. She doesn't know about me but, if she did, she just might take the view that I am in some way lightening the load for both of them."

"It's unlikely but you never can tell." Nicola was thoughtful. "Look, I'm glad you told me. One good thing that came out of the Alice affair is that we met and can cry on each other's shoulders from time to time as the need arises. What do you think?"

"Great," Cassandra agreed. "It looks like we might both need it."

"I know this sounds mad," Nicola said thoughtfully, "but I've booked myself into a spa – Inchydoney – for a few days, so why don't you come along with me? It would be more fun with a friend. I can barely afford it but I'm sure that I'm going to be significantly more solvent now that I no longer live with that leech. How about it?"

Cassandra laughed. "Why not? It sounds like fun. When did you book it for? I'll need to check my calendar."

"The weekend after next. There is a meeting I'm dreading that week and I am hoping to unwind after it."

"I think I'm free that weekend."

"Will I book it for you so?"

"No, I'll book it myself. The prostitute and the social worker wouldn't look good together in the Hotel Register!" Cassandra said with a grin. "Though, it would make a good title for a book, wouldn't it? *The Prostitute and the Social Worker*."

Both women laughed heartily and were still grinning as they walked home in opposite directions.

Chapter 8

Nicola decided not to watch the blanket coverage of the funeral. She'd had her fill of men and, though she had liked the late Taoiseach at a distance, she had seen and heard so much bad stuff about men in the last few days she felt she couldn't trust herself to look at the funeral with any great sympathy. She had experienced this sort of feeling towards men before, usually when dealing with a particularly harrowing story, so she knew that the feeling would pass and her equilibrium would be restored. In any case she knew there would be so much coverage that she would catch enough glimpses flicking the channels to get a general idea, and her colleagues at work would fill her in if she felt the need for more detail.

When she went into the office next day she decided to take out Christine O'Neill's file. It was so long since she had dealt with her that she had forgotten some of the detail and she needed to refresh her memory.

As she read, the story came flooding back. Christine had been brought to her attention by a neighbour who was concerned about her. The neighbour had heard awful screaming in the night and the children crying. She could hear a man shouting, calling Christine a slut and a tramp, but the neighbour had never

71

been aware that a man was living there. Nicola had asked the neighbour to call her again on a morning immediately after such an occurrence and she would visit.

When she made her first visit at nine thirty one morning what she saw had shocked her. Initially when she knocked there was no answer. Nicola persisted and eventually the door opened slowly. Inside a little girl of about six was standing on a chair in order to be able to open the latch.

"Is your mam in?" Nicola asked.

"She is but she's in bed. She's sick." The little girl looked scared.

"Could you ask her to come down?" Nicola said as gently as she could. "I might be able to do some shopping for her or get her medicine or something."

"I'll ask her but I don't think we have any money." Her lower lip quivered but she didn't cry.

"Ask your mam to come down," Nicola said again.

The little girl went upstairs and Nicola could hear voices.

After a short while the girl came down again and said that her mother was too ill.

"Who are you anyway?" she asked.

"Someone who can help your mam, if she'll let me. Would you take this up to her?" She scribbled a short note, hoping that the mother could read. She wrote that she was a social worker and would like to talk to her. She knew that that would get a response. Sadly social workers were seen as a threat by some people in need because they had a reputation for taking children away. She held her breath and within minutes the girl came back followed by her mother.

The woman that stood at the bottom of the stairs looked even more scared than the child and Nicola knew that she had done the right thing by insisting on seeing her. The story was somewhat unusual. It emerged that Christine was a lone parent whose ex-partner was employed and would in some ways be regarded as a pillar of society. When he left her for another woman she came back to live in Galway because she thought she would have a better support system but her family were not wealthy and several of them had problems of their own, so she was effectively alone. She was encouraged by the Department of Social Protection to follow her ex for maintenance but every time either they or she made contact with him he just visited her late at night and assaulted her – teaching her a lesson. That way he hoped she would not contact him again. Last night's attack had been particularly violent. He had been married about a year and had only just discovered that his wife had a fertility problem. Christine's contact had rubbed salt into the wound. His wife did not know of her existence and certainly didn't know about the children. Christine had a black eye, a gash on the side of her face which looked as if it needed stitches and a severe bruise on her shin. Nicola didn't ask if she had other injuries.

Nicola had moved quickly. She arranged for the local authority to transfer Christine to a different house, she contacted the Department of Social Protection and informed them about the situation and insisted that they never ask Christine to seek maintenance again and after that Christine's life had gone from strength to strength. Nobody was ever sure if her ex visited Galway again but if he did he hadn't found Christine and she no longer lived in fear.

Nicola was mystified as to why Christine had accused her of breach of confidentiality. Looking at the file confirmed her memory that she didn't know who Christine's ex was and had never known him. She had a feeling he was in the army though she didn't know why she felt that. So clearly she couldn't have breached confidentiality in this way. She was confident that the meeting would prove this to all concerned and, if it was a case that Christine's ex had found her, she felt she would have no trouble proving that it was not she who had told him where she was. The meeting was a few days away and Nicola decided, as a precaution, to check with A&E about the time Christine and her children had been admitted on the night of the alleged assault and also to check with the Guards about when the call came in to them. She was about to pick up the phone when it rang.

"The apartment is up for sale," Cassandra's voice was urgent. "I don't know if this is significant in the context of Alice's rights."

"I don't know either," Nicola answered. "I'll make a few enquiries off the record. Thanks for letting me know. I'll talk to you later."

Séamus the senior solicitor in Legal Aid had fancied Nicola since they had met in college.

"Are you still with that arty-farty ne'er do well?" he asked her when she rang him.

"Actually I'm not, but that's not why I rang." Nicola couldn't keep the laughter from her voice.

"Well, there's hope for me so. But what can I do for you, apart from take you out to dinner?"

"We'll let the remark about dinner go as this is a professional consultation. Can I rely on your confidentiality?"

"That goes without saying. It's like the seal of the confessional. They don't call me 'The Priest' for nothing."

"Good." Nicola was hesitant now. "Because this story is so far-fetched I can hardly believe it myself. I'm not going to name names because the client doesn't know I've rung but I was hoping you could give me some advice as to how to proceed and if my client has any rights."

"Fire away, ask the expert." Séamus was only half joking.

Nicola took a deep breath and began. Séamus listened without interrupting.

"What do you think?" she asked when she had finished.

"I think this is like the plot of a Jeffrey Archer novel. It seems quite sinister. It is very complicated. Off the top of my head, your client might have squatters' rights which is also called adverse possession if we could prove that she did not have the permission of the owner to remain in the apartment."

"But she had – the 'important person' actually moved her in and stayed with her several times a week."

"Yes, but if a company actually owned the apartment and you

74

believe it was owned by Tower Properties, she may never have officially got permission from them to reside there."

"But I suspect that the company is owned by the 'important person'." Nicola was doubtful.

"That would be beside the point. A company is a separate legal entity and, if there is no evidence from the company documentation that a decision was made to allow your client to live in the apartment, we may be able to establish rights for her. But, you should get your client in here quickly because if the apartment is up for sale we need to move fast so that we can put a stop to it. Can you bring her in this afternoon? It's quite urgent because getting documentation together might take a few days – a week even and an apartment in that area could be snapped up by then. It's much sought after and there are still a lot of people with money in this city – not that they ever have need of our services. We only watch them at a distance."

"Okay – are you there all day? I might try and get her now if you're free. She may not be that free after lunch because her children have to be picked up from school."

"Yes, as it happens. I could see you any time. Get back to me with a time as soon as you contact your client. In the meantime I'll make some preliminary enquiries."

"Thanks, Séamus. I owe you one."

"No, you don't. This is my job. But if you'd come out to dinner with me I'd be delighted."

"You don't give up, do you?" Nicola laughed. Having someone actually interested in her was a change. "I'll consider it when all this is over, but don't hold your breath."

"No, but I will remain optimistic."

When Séamus hung up Nicola rang Alice immediately.

"I didn't expect to hear from you for a while," Alice said. "I thought you'd be concentrating on other clients." Her tone indicated that she knew all was not well.

"So did I. But I need to talk to you. Can I come out?"

"Well, I was going out with Eliza and Hugo. The pony, remember? What's so urgent?"

"I'll explain when I see you. I may need you to come back into town with me. I have set up a meeting for you but I need to explain the reasons first."

"Oh, God!" was all Alice said.

Alice was in tears when Nicola had finished explaining that the apartment was up for sale and that they might have to move fast in order to prevent it. Eliza tried to comfort her but she too was clearly worried.

"I need you to come into town with me and we can go to Legal Aid together and after this first visit they will deal with you directly," Nicola told her. "I just thought I would go as moral support in the first instance. I might be able to help you with documentation and stuff."

"What is Legal Aid?"

"It's an organisation that helps people who have low or no income to deal with legal issues that affect them. It sometimes helps people who are homeless or in danger of becoming homeless achieve their rights with regard to their housing."

"But I'm not . . ." Alice's voice broke into a sob as she realised that she was indeed homeless or would have been had it not been for Eliza.

Séamus had already done some homework when the two women arrived into his office.

Alice considered his unruly red hair, John Lennon glasses and very casual attire made him a pretty untypical solicitor but he was friendly and confident and she felt comfortable with him.

"I've got advice on the situation," he said. "Obviously I didn't name names because I didn't have them but it seems that we could seek an interim injunction preventing the sale of the apartment on the grounds that it has been your home for the past twelve years. Is it a full twelve years by the way?"

"Yes," Alice replied. It must have been the third time she had answered that question since the eviction.

"Good, because if we succeed in getting the injunction, we

would then have to go about seeking adverse possession for you. If we succeed in that, and it's a big if, you would own the property."

"I had hoped that we could leave it a month or two, until the political situation calms down," said Nicola. "You see, Alice's ex is Jack Madden."

She noticed the fleeting look of surprise on Séamus's face.

"I didn't want him to know just yet that we would be following him for anything," she went on, "but I suppose that's out of the question now."

"I'm afraid it is. With an injunction, time is of the essence. I will have to work on this straight away." Séamus looked at Alice. "If it turns out to be Tower Properties, as you think, I will then have to go to the company's office to see who the directors of it are and try and get discovery of all company documentation. Do I have your permission to engage a barrister and establish ownership of the apartment?"

Alice had started to cry again. "But I have no money to pay a barrister!" she wailed.

"Don't worry about that. I know a number of sympathetic barristers. To work on a case such as this would be reward enough for them and, who knows, if we are successful we might even get costs."

"Is there anything I can do?" Nicola asked.

"I'm not sure – but I will get back to you," Séamus replied. "Alice, I think you will need to try and get any documentation that proves you lived in that apartment for twelve years. The more official the better! Letters from the school, letters from the hospital when you were having children, their birth certs, anything that would contribute to the evidence that you lived there for a whole twelve years. If you were living there less than twelve years, even by a day, we don't have a case."

"Most of that was still in the apartment when we were locked out!" Alice wailed.

"But we got some of it back and I'm sure we could get some duplicates from the hospital and doctors you attended if needs be." Nicola was trying to reassure Alice though in her heart she knew how difficult it could be to get doctors to provide that sort of information several years on.

"One good thing about this is that you missed the coverage of the funeral," Nicola said to Alice as they left the office. She was trying to lighten the situation.

"I would have missed it anyway. Eliza and Hugo were going to take me to pick up the pony."

"Oh, yes. I forgot. Okay – I think the first thing you should do is go through all of the documentation Cassandra took from the apartment and see what you have. When you've done that, phone me." Nicola was already working out in her head how they would go about getting as much official documentation as they could. Until Alice did her bit Nicola could do no more.

They drove back to The Coven in silence and when Nicola dropped Alice off she walked towards the house with her shoulders hunched and Nicola suspected that she had started to cry again.

Nicola stopped at a garage for a sandwich on the way back to her office and ate it in the car, feeling very depressed.

She decided to work on the Christine O'Neill case and try and prepare for the interview the following week. She phoned A&E at the hospital. She was well known there because she was often called upon in cases of domestic violence if there was a child-care issue or if a client of hers had been injured. Without telling the staff nurse why she wanted to know, she asked at what time Christine O'Neill and her children had been admitted on the 25th of October and what, if any, were their injuries. She could hear the nurse tapping into the computer.

"I can't see it here," the nurse said. "I had better check the paper files. Each patient will have a paper record as well and sometimes on a busy night they don't all get put into the computer. This could take some time. Can I call you back?"

"All right," Nicola replied. "Thanks."

The next call she made was to the Gardaí and she was almost expecting the reply.

"There is no record of Christine O'Neill making a complaint on that night. No squad car went to her house." The sergeant was sure.

Nicola was afraid to feel relieved. She knew that the Gardaí didn't record every single call. She was extremely puzzled. She had always got on well with Christine and always regarded her intervention in her life as having had a good outcome. So why would she lie?

She was not surprised when the staff nurse rang and said that there was no record of Christine or her children anywhere in the A&E on the night in question, or at any time in the recent past.

Nicola phoned Pat and told him.

"Can we call off the meeting?" she asked, expecting that to be only a formality.

"Oh, no! It must go ahead now. She has made a serious allegation and it must be dealt with through the normal disciplinary channels. The fact that you got this information obviously helps your case but we must go ahead. And don't, in any circumstances, approach the client."

"You've already told me not to do that!" Nicola was exasperated. She could have done without this extra hassle, though she was really curious as to why Christine might accuse her of breach of confidentiality.

Alice rang her back within the hour.

"The oldest piece of official documentation I can find is Grace's birth certificate. It clearly says that the address is 3, Lady Gregory Court. But she was twelve on the 29th of October, so we're a few weeks short." Her voice was panicky.

"Do you have the card you get from your doctor or gynaecologist with the record of your prenatal visits?"

"No, I don't think I kept those – even if I did I don't have them now. Is there anything else I could use?"

"A bank statement. You said you have a bank account. What address is on that?" Nicola tried to keep the anxiety out of her voice.

"Lady Gregory Court, of course."

79

"When did you open the account?"

"I opened my first bank account when I went to work for Jack and his wife."

"Do you remember what address you used then? It was hardly Galway seeing as you were living in Dublin."

"No, I used Jack's address and then, when I moved here, I changed it."

"You should ring the bank and ask them to send you a letter stating when the account was opened and when you changed the address on it. They should have a record of that. If you have any trouble with that we can ask your legal team to help us. If you can think of any other documentation or come across anything else which might be useful get back to me. I'll keep you informed of what is going on or Séamus will ring you if he needs to. Try not to worry."

Putting down the phone Nicola realised that they could be in trouble. She knew getting an injunction was not easily done and applicants had to have their i's dotted and their t's crossed, not to mention coming to the court with 'clean hands' – that is, free from any unfair conduct in regard to their claim – but at least they were safe enough on that score.

Pat put his head around the door.

"Feeling better about the complaint?" He seemed positively chirpy.

"Yes, but I can't believe she did it. I liked her and I thought she was pleased with the way things turned out for her when she was one of my clients. I really am surprised. If she was someone whose case had gone badly I would understand, or if she really had been assaulted and had to go to A&E I could understand that she might have thought, in her confusion, that I could have told her ex where she was. But this is very strange. She appears to have made it up."

"Are you sure you asked about the right date?"

"I did – twice! Do you still think I could have done it?" Why was it that every man she had contact with this week was turning out to be severely lacking in one department or another?

"I never said I thought you could have done it. In fact I didn't think at any stage that you could have done it – but you know the procedure. We have to take every complaint seriously and follow a transparent procedure." He smiled, clearly believing that he had explained himself sufficiently.

"Go away. I've more serious things on my mind at present and I have to work on them."

"Hardly that woman who believes that Jack Madden is the father of her children?" A resigned look crossed his face.

"Yes, as it happens. But things have become complicated and the apartment she was living in is up for sale." She was sorry she said it the minute it was out of her mouth. Suddenly she didn't trust anybody.

"And what does that mean? You've found her another place, haven't you? I hope you haven't harassed Jack Madden further at this difficult time."

"Yes, on both counts. I have found her another place and I haven't gone near Jack Madden since I called him the day she turned up in my office. It's just a jolt for her, that's all."

"Well, you watch your step. If you do anything rash I'm not going down with you." It was the second time he'd told her he wouldn't support her in this case and Nicola didn't like it.

"Get a grip, Pat," she said.

She decided that she wouldn't tell him anything else about the case. At that point she was so depressed with the system she just didn't care what happened to her. She decided that she would work on this case as hard as she could and, if it rattled a few cages, so what? There and then she decided that if she got through this with her job intact she would take a career break and maybe look at going into a different field. If the case led her into trouble with her superiors, the decision would be made for her. One way or another she hoped that by this time next year she wouldn't be working in this office, not knowing who to trust.

Chapter 9

The following Monday Nicola arrived at her office bright and early. She had her meeting with Christine O'Neill on that day but more importantly she was going to the Circuit Court with Alice in Ennis on the following day, Tuesday, seeking the injunction preventing the sale of the apartment. She had never felt so uptight in her life. She was reasonably confident about the meeting with Christine O'Neill but the injunction was another matter altogether. She wasn't sure of the procedure but that wasn't her responsibility because Alice would be ably represented by the legal team.

Séamus had been a tower of strength, organising everything in double-quick time. She was only going for moral support and Cassandra was going as a witness. But she had this morning's meeting to get over first and then she would go out to The Coven to talk to Alice. She knew that Alice was absolutely dreading the proceeding but Séamus and the barrister he had engaged, Gerard Murphy, were confident they could get the injunction. The real problem would arise after that – getting title to the property through adverse possession. They felt she had a good case but private property being such a big deal in Ireland, being specifically protected in the Constitution, they were not completely confident they would succeed. Going up against Jack Madden wouldn't do either of their careers any good at all, though they both assured Alice and Nicola that they had no ambition to be Attorney General in the near future and, besides, who knew what would happen if there was a change of government?

At nine thirty Pat put his head around the door.

"Ready?" he enquired.

"As ready as I'll ever be," Nicola replied with a grim smile.

Christine looked nervous when she came into the room. She was with her sister whom she had brought along for moral support. Christine looked shabby and lacking in confidence. She was wearing jeans and a fleece that had seen better days. She had changed her hair colour from blonde to jet black since Nicola had last seen her and at first she wasn't sure it was her. The sister was brasher and looked like she was ready for a fight. She had a piercing in her nose and a small tattoo of a heart on her neck. She looked Nicola straight in the eye when she came into the room.

Pat opened the proceedings by introducing everybody. The sister's name was Gemma. They all nodded to each other.

"Christine, would you like to tell us the nature of your complaint?" Pat then said gently.

"Well, last week my ex-partner came to my house and threatened me."

"What do you mean he threatened you? Did he have a weapon? Was he in the house?"

"He didn't have a weapon but he was in the house. My son let him in. He didn't recognise him at first. He started shouting that he wanted the kids and that I was an unfit mother. I was really scared." Her voice was shaking as she spoke.

"Is this the son who had to have the X-ray on the night because you suspected he had broken his arm?" asked Nicola.

"Yes. He is thirteen now and he tried to stand in front of me when his father went for me. His father pushed him out of the way and he landed funny on his arm and I took him to A&E."

"Were you injured yourself?" Pat asked. "Or the other children?"

"No. Only Jason. I shouted that I would phone the Guards and I had my mobile in my hand so he left." Christine seemed to know that the story sounded lame because she didn't elaborate.

"Why would you think I could have told him where you were, Christine, given that I was the one who arranged for you to get transferred in order that he wouldn't know where you were and couldn't visit you again and assault you again? I remember well the first day I met you and you were seriously injured by this man. Why would I tell him your whereabouts?" She was trying to sound calm and conciliatory.

"I know it could only be you. You are the only one who knows him. Anyway you never liked me."

"You must remember as well that I have never met him. I'm not sure you ever even told me his name." Nicola paused, expecting Christine to react, but there was no response. "I'm wondering why you came up with this story. I have checked with A&E and you didn't go there on the night in question nor did you make a complaint to the Gardaí. Why are you doing this, Christine?"

Gemma spoke up. "Are you calling my sister a liar? If she said she went to A&E, she did. Who are you to say different? She probably just got her dates mixed up." She was aggressive and much more confident than Christine.

"I'm not calling her a liar but I know that for some reason she is not telling the truth now. I don't know why. She came into this office and said she had been threatened the previous night. It is unlikely that she got her dates mixed up, as you say, so soon after the event." Nicola paused, thinking that Christine would offer an explanation, but she didn't. "I don't know what happened that night but the two things that Christine said which could be proven are untrue so it would be very difficult for anybody to believe the rest of it. If her accusation is true I could lose my job so that is why I am so anxious to find out why she is doing this."

Christine burst into tears. "I didn't mean it! I just want to go home!" She sobbed great convulsive sobs.

At this point Pat intervened. "Christine, you are not in trouble. Just tell us again what happened on the night before you made the complaint."

"Didn't she tell you already?" demanded the sister. "That gobshite came to her house shouting the odds and threatening to take the children from her and pushing her and the children about. Isn't that the point? What are you going to do about it? And, anyway, I don't believe that A&E told your one over there that Jason never went there. Isn't that service private as well or should she make a complaint against them too?"

Christine looked at her sister and smiled slowly. Nicola could see her confidence coming back.

"Christine, you know the first day I met you I took you to A&E because you were so badly beaten up?" Nicola said. "Your ex had done that several times before. I don't believe that he was anywhere near your house last week because, if he was, you would have been injured and anybody in your house who tried to protect you would also have been injured. What is happening here?" She tried to make her voice sympathetic. "Why are you accusing me of letting him know where you were? You know it could cost me my job."

"You might find out what it is like for us then, you stuck-up bitch!" said Gemma.

"Would you just shut up?" Nicola said angrily. She was surprised at herself. She prided herself on being restrained but this woman was making things worse.

Her outburst clearly shocked both the other women but Gemma recovered quickly.

"You can't speak to me like that," she said, looking at Pat for confirmation.

Pat looked from one to the other of them. Then he calmly asked, "Christine, do you still wish to make the complaint or do you wish to withdraw it? You can walk away from this now and there will be no consequences for anybody. If you wish to proceed you will have to produce some proof that your ex was present in your house on the night in question and that you visited the hospital with your child as a result and that he was X-rayed. It would be helpful if you could also identify the Guard you say you spoke to since they are telling us that you didn't make a complaint." His voice was gentle but firm.

Christine started to cry again. Her sister was silent.

"I want to withdraw the complaint," Christine said through her tears.

"You lot are all the same!" Gemma said. "All in league with one another. The Guards, the hospital, the community welfare!" She was very angry but less confident now.

"My advice to you is to take your sister home and not to make another complaint against anyone unless you can prove it," said Pat. "Now Nicola and I have to get back to our work. Good morning to you."

"I'll show you to the door," Nicola said. She felt sorry for Christine though she was mystified as to why she would make up something like this.

"We know our way out. We don't need your help," Gemma said and Nicola and Pat watched as the two women turned and left.

"I wonder what that was about?" Pat mused after the door closed.

"So do I."

"Probably thought we'd pay them off to shut them up."

"Or someone paid them off to try and shut me up," Nicola said. She was sorry she spoke as soon as the words were out of her mouth.

"You're paranoid," Pat said dismissively.

Just because I'm paranoid doesn't mean there isn't someone out to get me, Nicola thought to herself but she didn't say it. She wondered again if Jack Madden could have had anything to do with it, given that he had threatened her.

Nicola went to The Coven immediately after lunch. Alice was there looking fearful. Nicola felt so sorry for her. There was no preparation for the morning necessary. The legal team said that they would be doing most of the talking. All that would be needed was that Alice would say she had been living in Number 3, Lady Gregory Court, for the past twelve years and that she could provide written evidence to prove that. The fact that Cassandra, as a neighbour, was willing to verify that would be helpful.

Hugo picked Alice's children up from school so that the women would have an opportunity to discuss anything that was bothering them and Nicola assured Alice, yet again, that she would go to Ennis with her and that Cassandra would be there as well. Séamus would accompany the barrister, saying that though he occasionally had to inform clients that they might have squatters' rights he had never before had to follow a case up and actually seek those rights for them.

Alice was clearly nervous and Nicola was concerned to see that Eliza seemed to be preoccupied. They were in the sitting room of the main house at Eliza's invitation. She would not be accompanying them the following day to the court. There was no need and, in any case, she had a medical appointment.

Alice had all her documentation ready. She'd got a letter from her bank stating clearly that her address twelve years ago was 3, Lady Gregory Court. She had ample evidence that she had lived there without a break for the subsequent twelve years.

They rang Séamus and he seemed happy that all was in order. He had established who the directors of the company were – Jack Madden was one, of course – and had made them aware of the impending proceedings.

Nicola wondered what Jack Madden thought about that. She hadn't spoken to him since that first day and while he was, no doubt, aware that she had tried to get in touch with him once since then, she was now glad that she hadn't succeeded in talking to him. The less he knew about what she was up to in relation to Alice the better. He would in all probability send legal representation to the court and, unless a stray hack got hold of information about the hearing and who the respondent was, it was likely that the injunction would be granted, or not, without the general public being any the wiser. She knew this and she knew that Jack Madden knew this so she had presumed that she wouldn't hear from him, and she had been right.

Alice was relieved that she wouldn't have to come face to face with Jack at this early stage. She still felt very vulnerable.

"I don't know how I'd feel if I saw him." Her voice was low and shaky. "I have only just about come to terms with the fact that he has dumped me and the girls without so much as a backward glance. And you know something?"

"What?" asked Nicola, dreading the answer.

"He never said goodbye."

And with that she burst into tears and Nicola held her till her tears subsided.

Just then Eliza came in carrying a tray of tea and scones.

"What's this? We can't have this. If you don't stop I'll start crying myself and I don't want to do that now."

Nicola stared at her. Her voice was shaky as well and she noticed for the first time that day that Eliza appeared to be a bit pale.

"God, Eliza, that would never do." She got up and took the tray from Eliza and put it on the coffee table. "Alice, everything will be fine. Séamus is very confident."

"I know," Alice said, taking the cup of tea that Nicola had poured for her. "But I'm nervous and I feel so lucky that you two are there."

"And Cassandra," Nicola reminded her. "She's going to be your chief independent witness tomorrow. She'll be coming to Ennis with us."

"Of course! How could I forget Cassandra? Wasn't it she who took me in and pointed me in the right direction when Jack left?" Alice smiled wanly.

Nicola again noticed the strained look on Eliza's face and she had a feeling that it was not only the court case that was bothering her.

Chapter 10

Just as she was leaving the apartment the following morning Nicola got a call from Cassandra.

"Could you pick me up on your way to pick Alice up?" Her voice was low.

"Of course. Something wrong with your car?"

"I went out for some muesli this morning and as I pulled into the car park at Centra my brakes failed. I'm a bit shaken." Cassandra sounded far from her calm confident self.

"My God! Are you all right?"

"Yes, I was going very slowly but I hit another car which was parked and there was all the aggravation about that. I got my car towed away and so am dependent on Shank's mare for the moment."

"I'm sorry to hear that. You must have got an awful fright. Are you sure you'll be all right?" Nicola knew that Alice's case would be weaker if Cassandra didn't turn up.

"Of course I'll be alright. It would take more than a small prang to put me off helping Alice get what's her due and neither Jack Madden nor anyone else will stop me." Her voice was harder now and more determined.

"What do you mean? Do you think he had something to do with the accident?"

"What indeed?" Cassandra said mysteriously. "I had my car serviced last week. It's quite a new car anyway but last week it was in perfect nick. I think that the garage report today will be very interesting indeed."

Nicola felt cold. She knew that Jack Madden was nasty. He had threatened her job but it had never occurred to her that he might threaten anybody's life. Cassandra had no such doubts.

"Look, today the most important thing is that we all turn up at the court and do our bit," Cassandra said. "We can worry about my car and why its brakes failed when that is over. Listen, it might be wise for you not to come into Lady Gregory Court. I'll meet you at the traffic lights. When will you be here?" She sounded so calm now that she might as well have been arranging to meet Nicola to walk the prom.

"I'll be there in ten minutes," Nicola replied. She locked all the doors and windows as she left her own apartment and, driving slowly down the road, she checked the brakes of her own car a few times, before she speeded up a bit and headed for town.

"We won't tell Alice what happened," Cassandra said as she got into Nicola's car. "We'll just say that I couldn't start the car or something. Let's not give her anything else to worry about."

"You're right," Nicola replied. "I'm dead nervous myself. Alice must be beside herself."

However, Alice seemed calm enough when they arrived at The Coven. In a pale pink linen suit she was the picture of innocence. Nicola thought that if she had advised Alice how to dress for the day she would have advised something like this. But she doubted that Alice had done it deliberately.

Eliza, who again looked strained, came outside to see them off, assuring them that she and Hugo would look after everything – meaning they would pick up the girls from school and get them a snack etc, assuming Alice hadn't returned by then.

Cassandra suggested turning on Ryan Tubridy on the radio

and Nicola thought that a good idea – his light-hearted version of the day's events would prove a suitable accompaniment to the trip. Eventually they switched off the radio and Nicola rooted out a Van Morris CD which they listened to in virtual silence until they reached the courthouse in Ennis.

Séamus met them and said that they were second in the order of business, so if they wanted to get a quick cup of coffee in an adjacent café he would come and find them when the time came.

Alice started to shiver. "I thought that when they called us for ten thirty that would be the time they would hear the case!" she wailed.

"Oh God, I should have explained," Séamus apologised. "They call everybody for ten thirty and it isn't until the day of the court people find out the order in which they will be called. Sorry, Alice, I should have warned you."

"That's alright." She smiled wanly. "I think I can rise to a latte if they make such a thing here."

Séamus grinned, relieved. "I'll come and get you when they're winding up the first case," he assured them.

An hour of strained conversation followed. The quality of the lattes (bad) was discussed, as was the décor of the café (vile). The women were almost relieved when they saw Séamus approach. But Alice's hand was shaking as she rooted in her purse for the money.

The women followed Séamus into the small courtroom. There were a few people in the public gallery, waiting for their cases to be called.

"We'll sit in the body of the court near your barrister," Séamus said to Alice. "That way you can go to give evidence if required without walking the length of the court."

Alice nodded meekly.

"Where will we sit?" Nicola whispered.

"Well, Cassandra should sit as near to Alice as possible as she may also be called and you might as well sit beside her."

"*Alice O'Brien versus Tower Properties,*" the Court Clerk announced.

"What is being sought in this case?" The judge sounded grumpy.

"An injunction, Judge." Alice's barrister, Gerard Murphy, was on his feet immediately. He was a dapper, smallish, very young man. "My client Alice O'Brien is seeking an injunction preventing the sale by Tower Properties of 3 Lady Gregory Court, Taylors Hill, Galway, on the basis that it has been her family home for the past twelve years."

"Well, if it's the family home, of course it can't be sold without her written consent but," the judge continued in a droll tone, "I doubt she is married to Tower Properties."

The judged had cracked a joke and the legal eagles smiled dutifully.

"No, Judge. She is not married but she lived with her partner and two children there until she was evicted a number of weeks ago. She thought her partner owned the property and that he had bought it in order to provide her and her children with a secure home. She has been made homeless by the eviction. She was, in fact, locked out of the apartment when she was collecting her children from school."

"And what did her partner do about that? Did he just stand idly by?" The judge had a theatrical air about him but was clearly intrigued by the story.

"My client thinks that her partner arranged the eviction. He is a director of Tower Properties but it is the company that owns the apartment."

"Oh, and who is the lady's partner and why would he arrange to have her evicted so suddenly?"

"John Madden," the barrister said without hesitation and suddenly you could hear a pin drop in the courtroom.

Nicola held her breath. She was pretty sure that there would be a clatter of newshounds within minutes, but no one moved.

"We had better swear the lady in," said the judge. "I will need to hear the story from her own mouth."

Alice's voice could barely be heard as she took the oath.

"Ms O'Brien, could you please speak louder than that when you are giving evidence?" the judge said, not unkindly. "There is no need to be nervous. I only need to find out the facts in order to see if an injunction is warranted. Now, would you tell me in your own words why you think you are entitled to stop the sale of this property?"

Alice coughed. "I have lived with Jack Madden at 3 Lady Gregory Court for the past twelve years. During all those years he spent roughly half the week in Galway and half the week in Dublin. I regard it as my home."

Alice was speaking slowly and clearly and her barrister was delighted.

"When he was in Galway he stayed with me. He is the father of both my children and he supported us completely up until recently."

"Would you tell the judge how you came to be homeless?" Gerard Murphy asked gently.

"I just went to the school to collect the girls as usual and when I came back the locks had been changed in the apartment and I couldn't get in. My neighbour called a locksmith for me but when he arrived the doorman of the apartment block said he would call the Gardaí if we opened the door so he left. I tried to contact Jack but he didn't answer my calls. I stayed with my neighbour that night and when I came out of her apartment next morning, my car was gone. My neighbour put me in touch with a social worker and I have since then been living on a social welfare payment and have found alternative accommodation – but it is not permanent. I hope to be able to go back to my home in Taylors Hill."

"Do you want to question this lady?" the judge asked the barrister for Tower Properties.

"Yes, Judge. Ms O'Brien, you say you lived with Jack Madden. Everybody knows he is married and lives in Dublin. How can you have lived with him?"

"I already explained. His constituency is Galway and he lives in Dublin for part of the week and Galway for the rest. I lived with him for about the same length of time each week as he lived with his wife." Alice's voice was certain.

"What an unusual set-up! Did you not think that strange?" The barrister's voice was sneering. He turned to the judge. "Judge, my client, Tower Properties, will maintain that Jack Madden did indeed visit this young lady at Lady Gregory Court. She was an ex-employee of his and he was sympathetic to her predicament. The apartment had been bought by the company, along with other properties, as an investment and for Mr Madden's occasional use, and Mr Madden allowed her to stay there until she found her feet. However, she abused his generosity and never made any attempt to get a proper job or find alternative accommodation. Since she had Jack Madden's permission to reside there, initially at least, she does not have a case for adverse possession. I understand she is seeking an interim injunction to stop the sale of the property so that she can gain re-entry and then seek to establish adverse possession."

Alice was crying before the man stopped talking and her own barrister interrupted.

"Judge, since the apartment is owned by a company and there is no record in the company documents that my client, Ms O'Brien, was to be allowed to live there I would maintain that she lived there for the requisite period without the permission of the legal owner, i.e. Tower Properties."

"And do you have proof she lived there for that long?" the judge asked.

"Yes, we have documents addressed to her at her home and her neighbour is also in court and can give evidence that my client lived there for twelve years."

"That will not be necessary. Just show me the documentary evidence." The judge seemed anxious to sort the situation out quickly.

The barrister handed a wedge of documents to the Court Clerk. The judge glanced at them in a rather cursory way.

"There appears at least to be a case to be heard. I am going to grant the injunction until such time as the substantive issue is dealt with by another court. I would advise Ms O'Brien's legal team to seek a date as expeditiously as possible. However, Ms

O'Brien, the fact that I have granted the injunction does not mean necessarily that you will be successful in your bid to gain title to the property by adverse possession. Adverse possession is a very complicated legal issue and is an exceedingly rare occurrence. So the outcome is by no means certain. However, you may have some rights under other legislation and I presume your counsel will investigate this. One way or another there appears to be a case to be answered. You may step down."

"Thank you," Alice said.

Gerard Murphy was smiling when he approached Alice and her friends outside. "That went well!" he said.

"What happens next?" Alice asked fearfully.

"I will seek a court date, preferably in Ennis, for the hearing. We have most of our evidence in place so there isn't much work to be done. I think we have a good case, though I have more work to do to try and copper-fasten it. I'm surprised that the judge granted us the injunction so quickly. He's an arch conservative and of the old school. I wouldn't have thought he would have much sympathy for single parents. However, I also think he would take a very dim view of a TD having an extra-marital affair. That probably went in our favour in the end."

Nicola felt like laughing. "It was almost easy," she said.

"Yes," Cassandra agreed. "I'm so glad I didn't have to give evidence."

"You won't be so lucky next time," Séamus said. "I think all the witnesses will be cross-examined – maybe even you, Nicola."

"But I would have thought I am not involved really?"

"Didn't you say that Jack Madden threatened your job when you asked him if it was true that he was the father of Alice's children?"

"Yes, but I can't prove that. We don't record our phone calls at the Health Service Executive."

"Yes, but you could still be asked about that conversation. Do you take notes?"

"Sometimes but I didn't on that occasion. It all seemed a bit unreal. I have a record in my diary of all the calls I made that day but not necessarily their content." Nicola could have kicked herself that she hadn't taken notes but the conversation had been so dramatic she remembered every syllable.

"That will probably be sufficient – it will have to be," Gerard replied. "Don't worry about it. I believe we have a good case. I'll be in touch. I'm afraid I have to dash."

With a wave, he got into his car and sped away.

The three women stood in the car park with Séamus, still sort of shocked. Nicola started to laugh, then Alice and then Cassandra. They laughed until tears were running down their faces.

Séamus stared at them, wondering what to do.

Nicola noticed the bemused look on his face and tried to pull herself together.

"Don't worry, Séamus – it's just tension," she said through her laughter. "We'll get over it. Ladies, we've frightened him. Get a grip!"

The other two eventually stopped laughing and apologised to Séamus.

"Don't worry," Séamus assured them. "In my job I come across all sorts, though this is pretty unusual for me as well."

As he walked to his car Séamus wondered if it was his imagination that Gerard Murphy seemed to be slightly less confident than he had been before the hearing.

The women got into Nicola's car and when she started up the engine Van Morrison was singing "Days Like This".

Chapter 11

The women were in high spirits when they got back to The Coven.
They knew that the war wasn't over yet but it was clear that they
had won the first battle. They didn't phone ahead because they
wanted to tell Eliza and Hugo the news face to face. But Eliza wasn't
yet back from the doctor and Hugo had gone to pick up the girls
from school. The place seemed oddly desolate. The other residents
were about their own business. There was no one to be seen.

Bemused, they didn't quite know what to do until Alice
suggested making tea in her apartment. The three women walked
up the stairs. There was not sound in the whole house.

While the kettle boiled Nicola thought to put on the TV.

"Oh, God!" groaned Alice. "I hope it's not on the news."

"Not at all," Cassandra assured her. "Sure wouldn't we have
seen the camera? There was no journalist of note there, though
I suppose there could have been a stringer from one of the
nationals, but in any case there wasn't a camera."

"Yes, it almost seemed too easy," Alice replied.

"Yes, but I think that was the easy bit," said Cassandra. "It's
when you go for adverse possession that things could get nasty,
in particular if the media get hold of it. And the judge did say it
isn't a foregone conclusion."

"I'd say that Jack Madden won't want any publicity," Nicola interjected. "That might work in our favour in the end. He is unlikely to turn up at court at this critical point in his career. Though the media could still get hold of it and God knows what the consequences of that would be for him."

"Or for me," Alice said in a timid voice.

"Alice," said Cassandra gently, "I think the worst has happened to you. Things can only get better from here on in."

"I hope you're right," Alice said doubtfully. "But I hope for the girls' sake that there's not too much publicity."

"We're home!" Hugo's voice came from downstairs.

The three women went to meet him and the girls.

Grace and Orla raced up the stairs and hugged their mother.

"We missed you!" Grace said as if she really meant it, even though she didn't know where her mother had been that morning.

"I missed you as well," Alice said, puzzled by this sudden rush of affection. "But I'm back now. Why don't we have a drink and some scones?"

"Have it in the main kitchen," Hugo suggested. "Eliza will be home soon and we're both anxious to hear your news."

There was an odd atmosphere in the kitchen as they ate their snack, an air of expectancy. As soon as the girls were finished they raced out to find the dog and Hugo turned to the women.

"It went well, I take it," he said.

"Yes, Alice was granted the injunction," said Cassandra. "But she has to apply for adverse possession at the earliest possible opportunity, and that, apparently, will be the hard part. What time is Eliza due? I thought she'd be back before now."

"Soon now. Her appointment was for two thirty."

When Eliza's car eventually swept into the drive the three women and Hugo went to the steps to greet her. There was something about the way she got out of the car that made them realise that all was not well. All four of them paused and then Hugo walked towards her with his arms outstretched. She collapsed into his arms and silently began to weep. The three women stood there, not knowing what to say.

Nicola was the first to regain her voice. "We should go."

She and Cassandra left without another word, afraid to think about what had transpired at Eliza's appointment.

About an hour later Nicola had a phone call from Alice.

"You and Cassandra are invited to The Coven for dinner tonight. Eliza insists. Hugo and I are cooking. You can bring dessert if you like."

"Are you sure it's okay? It looked as if Eliza got bad news."

"She hasn't told me what it is but I gather though it's bad it's not completely awful. She insists that she wants us all to have dinner together. She will tell you her news herself and she wants to know all about our day."

"Okay. I'll phone Cassandra and hope she's free this evening."

"Oh, and Eliza said that if you bring a bottle of wine you can stay over! So bring a change of clothes so that you can go to work from here."

"Sounds great," said Nicola.

"See you then."

Nicola then rang Cassandra, who was very surprised to get the invitation.

"Yes, I am free tonight," she said. "I deliberately didn't make any appointments because I didn't know how I would feel after the court. I'll call into Goya and get a tiramisu if I can or maybe Death by Chocolate – that ought to cheer us up."

"Not Death by Chocolate. We don't know what Eliza's news is."

"Oh, God, you're right. How crass of me!"

"I'll call for you at eight thirty. I suppose I had better not call to the door. I'll pick you up at the traffic lights again. Did I say we're invited to stay?"

"You didn't but that might be nice. I hope that what Eliza has to say isn't too bad."

Nicola could hear the doubt in Cassandra's voice. "I suppose it can't be too bad – otherwise they wouldn't have invited us."

"I suppose not," Cassandra said.

Nicola couldn't believe it but since she had met Cassandra she was always more careful about what she wore, in particular if she was going to meet up with her. So she rifled in her wardrobe, wondering what would be sufficiently casual but stylish for the forthcoming event.

Event! Is that what you'd call this evening, she thought. She didn't know what to call it really. It wasn't going to be a celebration now and she hoped it wouldn't turn out to be a sort of Last Supper. She was not sure how to approach it but she decided that an 'event' was indeed the best way to describe it. She took off the carefully chosen suit which she had worn to the court. Her wardrobe wasn't exactly replete – living with a scrounger had seen to that. She resolved straight away to buy herself some new clothes before she went to Inchydoney – even if she had to use her credit card – it wouldn't take long to pay off now that she was feeding, entertaining and clothing only one. Yes, she needed some new clothes.

She had a long soak in a bubble bath one of her clients had given her when she had helped her with the procedure for being allocated a local authority house. She hadn't wanted to take it, being conscious of how little the woman could afford it, but she didn't want to offend and the look of pure pleasure on the woman's face when she accepted it indicated to her that she had made the right decision. She felt refreshed if no less apprehensive when she got out of the bath and again surveyed her scant wardrobe. Eventually she settled on simple linen-look trousers and a matching top, deciding that it looked appropriate no matter how this evening turned out. She then packed her overnight things and an outfit for the following day and turned on the news.

Things were beginning to settle down on the political front at least. Another major developer had gone to the wall, leaving a half-built office block in a prime site in Dublin. She could almost hear other developers, like vultures, flying in for the kill. One of them could certainly pick that up for a good price if they were solvent. Their ruthlessness never failed to amaze her. Anyway it was a relief that the whole news bulletin was not taken up with

Jack Madden and there was not a whisper about the proceedings in the Circuit Court in Ennis that day.

Suddenly she felt extremely tired but it was too late to have a nap. If she went to bed now she would be very reluctant to get up again and tonight of all nights she had to go to The Coven. Idly she flicked through a magazine while she waited until it was time to pick Cassandra up.

Cassandra was standing at the traffic lights when Nicola pulled up. She was wearing a really elegant knit trouser suit. Nicola didn't allow herself to be envious. They were in a different league in every sense of the expression and there were a lot of things about Cassandra's life that Nicola certainly didn't envy.

"You look fabulous," she said as Cassandra opened the passenger door. "Your style always appears so effortless."

"Effortless it certainly is not. It took me many years and a lot of thought and advice to get as far as this style-wise. But I like clothes and in my line of work it is important to be well presented, in particular if a client wants to take me to a dinner or a corporate event." She spoke as if she were a PR executive.

"And does that happen often?" Nicola was curious and knew that Cassandra would soon tell her to mind her own business if she overstepped the mark, so she felt safe enough asking the question.

"A bit, particularly if the client is from out of town. Obviously if they are local they take their wives. I also have to be fairly up to date in current affairs so as to make an interesting dinner companion and so that nobody will suspect that I am being paid for my presence."

"Wow, I never thought of it like that!"

"Like what?" enquired Cassandra with a wry smile. "That a call girl has to be a companion as well as a sex slave?"

There was only a hint of mirth in her voice and Nicola decided to bring this conversation to an end. "In any case you look gorgeous, as usual. Maybe we could go shopping together some time and you can give me a few tips."

"That would be fun," Cassandra answered. "You know, because nobody that I socialise with knows what I do for a living, I'm always on my guard. It would be nice to go shopping with someone who knows exactly who and what I am and is comfortable with that."

Nicola wasn't sure about the comfortable bit but she accepted Cassandra's position and didn't consider it her place to pass judgement.

"Great," she smiled. "You can be my stylist."

When they parked their car at The Coven Alice was waiting for them at the large front door. She looked as frail as she had looked when she'd first arrived. The new confidence she had exhibited earlier in the day had evaporated completely.

"Do you know Eliza's news?" Nicola asked apprehensively.

"I have made an educated guess," was the reply. "Come in. Hugo is pouring the wine and Eliza is getting ready."

"How is Hugo?" asked Cassandra.

"He's a rock," Alice replied.

"Every woman should have a Hugo," Nicola said with feeling.

The three women smiled as they went into the large kitchen.

"Can we do anything, Hugo?" Nicola asked though she could see that the table was already set for five. Clearly this dinner was going to be an all-adult affair and no other residents of The Coven were invited.

Nicola had wondered about the other residents from time to time since Alice had come to live in The Coven. They weren't much in evidence, though that could be explained by the fact that the edifice was large and other than the weekly communal dinner they probably lived quite separate lives. She wondered though if Alice wasn't a sort of favourite with Eliza and Hugo or perhaps it was just that at the beginning of everybody's tenancy they were given special attention. She decided that this was most likely the case.

"No, thank you, my dear, I think myself and Alice have it all organised."

Eliza appeared at the door of the kitchen, more composed

than earlier. Hugo went over to her, kissed her gently on the forehead and handed her a glass of wine. The other women didn't speak.

She looked more fragile than Nicola had ever seen her but there was a resolute air about her that Nicola was relieved to see. She wondered how soon she would tell them what her diagnosis was. She couldn't stand the suspense for much longer.

Hugo told them to sit at the table while Alice went to bring out the starter.

"I believe you had a good outcome in Ennis," Eliza said.

"Yes, we got the injunction," said Nicola. She looked apprehensively at Eliza. "Tell us your news – please."

Eliza looked from one of them to the other.

"It appears I have breast cancer. The doctor thinks I will need a full mastectomy, but he says that the prognosis is still quite good. With chemotherapy I should be as right as rain in about a year. I will, of course, have to visit an oncologist to confirm the diagnosis and to find out exactly what has to be done and when, but in a nutshell that is what the doctor said to me."

Her words hung in the air for a few moments and no one spoke.

Alice was the first to break the silence. "Is there anything we can do for you?"

Eliza looked at her. "Sweet Alice," she said. "Over the next few months I expect I will need the company of friends. I don't want all of this to fall on poor old Hugo. He has broad shoulders but he will need a break from looking after me – emotionally, at any rate. I would be delighted if you would just be my friends, a sort of shoulder to cry on if I need it."

"Of course we will." Alice was speaking for all of them.

It occurred to Nicola that in a few short weeks her life had become intimately entwined with three women that she had never laid eyes on until the day after Alice's first phone call. She knew that it was inappropriate for her to befriend a client and others connected with her case but this was different and it felt right.

"And now," said Eliza, "we'll have no more talk of illness. Tell me about your day."

While of course they were all delighted with what had gone on in the court that morning, somehow their news had lost its shine.

"It was all over in a few minutes really," said Cassandra. "We just went in and the legal team asked for an injunction to prevent the sale of 3 Lady Gregory Court. The judge asked why and when he was given the reason he just asked Alice to tell him in her own words why she thought she was entitled to prevent the sale of the property. I'd say that Alice was only giving evidence for a few minutes. The legal team for Tower Properties maintained that Jack Madden only visited Alice because she was an ex-employee for whom he had sympathy and that he gave her the apartment for free. The judge said that he thought there was a case to be answered in relation to the sale and granted the injunction. It was all over just like that."

"That sounds wonderful," Eliza said enthusiastically.

"Yes," agreed Hugo but he had a distracted air of someone who has other things on his mind, which of course he had.

"What next?" Eliza asked.

"Well, we will have to go to court again to try and establish my entitlement to the property," Alice replied, amazed that Eliza could still be interested after the news she'd had that day, "on the basis that I lived there for twelve years without the permission of the owner."

"But surely that is where you have a huge problem," Eliza said, puzzled. "You had Jack Madden's permission."

"Yes, but in fact that apartment is owned by a company," Nicola explained. "Alice's solicitor got hold of the Memorandum and Articles of Association of the company along with minutes of AGMs etc. There was no evidence in the minutes that she was given permission to live there. It only says that it was bought as an investment and for the occasional use of Jack Madden. Because a company is a separate legal person, there should be some record of the directors agreeing to allow her to be there."

"And there isn't, of course," Hugo said.

"No. It's looking very good for me at the moment, though the judge said it is very complicated which is a bit worrying." Alice said. "If I didn't have to go through another court case I would be delighted but it will be a small price to pay if I get ownership of the apartment."

"It will indeed," Eliza said. "Now shouldn't we eat or else the food will be cold?"

"I've invited Nicola and Cassandra to stay the night," Hugo said. He appeared glad of the company.

"That's a good idea," Eliza said.

"Thank you," said Cassandra. "That way we won't be up too late." As she spoke she thought it was likely that, though they might get a reasonably early night, it was likely that Eliza at least wouldn't sleep.

Life certainly had a habit of giving with one hand and taking away with the other.

Chapter 12

The day of Nicola and Cassandra's departure for Inchydoney was bitterly cold. The November winds did their worst and initially the rain was coming down in torrents. They could feel the wind push against the car – they had taken Nicola's – as they drove between Ennis and Limerick but they were in high spirits and chatted animatedly, planning their break. They had abandoned the idea of booking separately and had managed to alter Nicola's booking, so they would be sharing a deluxe twin room. They had already chosen the treatments they would have.

"This is going to put such a hole in my bank account," Nicola laughed. "But I think I deserve it. I have never done anything like this before. But I'm sick of being sensible, watching my money in case I might need some for a rainy day!"

"Yes, there's such a thing as too sensible, though it's nothing I've ever been accused of," Cassandra agreed.

"What I never took into account was that with Jonathan every day was a rainy day. I am so much better off without him. Financially, I notice it already and he's only gone a little more than a fortnight. And there's a great feeling of freedom which I didn't expect. I don't even feel lonely."

"You know, I can't remember when I last had a boyfriend," Cassandra mused. "The job makes it practically impossible."

"I suppose so," Nicola agreed. She didn't know how else to answer that statement.

"It's quite the conversation-stopper, you know."

"What exactly?" asked Nicola, startled.

"The truthful answer to 'What do you do for a living?'" Cassandra said with a grin.

"I suppose so! So what do you usually answer?"

"I told you before – I say I'm a consultant! They usually presume that I'm in interior design or perhaps a fashion consultant and you'd be surprised how many people don't ask you to expand, especially men. A consultant has a good ring to it and they usually think they have you sussed."

"How do you manage friendships?"

"With great difficulty! If they come to my apartment I have to keep my work room locked. Try explaining a locked room to people who want to be your friend or maybe more."

"How do you explain it?"

"I say that I am storing furniture for a friend or relation and that the room is so packed I just want to close the door on it."

"And do they believe that?" Nicola was plain curious but it was Cassandra who had started this topic so she felt she could ask the questions.

"It satisfies most of them, though one person did smell a rat and got quite nasty when I wouldn't show him the room. As I said, I don't really do relationships."

"When was your last relationship – apart from the one you have with the client you like?" Nicola asked tentatively.

"Sadly, that is not really a relationship. The last relationship that I thought could develop into something more was about five years ago."

"Wow, that's a long time! What happened?"

"I realised that I could never tell him about my way of life and I couldn't have a long-term relationship based on a lie. He didn't seem too put out when I finished with him. I think he suspected that I was married or something but he never said anything. I was sad to finish it but I don't think he would have been interested in me if he knew the truth." Cassandra fell silent.

"And do you want a long-term relationship?"

"Who doesn't! And unlike you I often feel lonely. Achingly so!"

"Where are your family?" Nicola asked. "Have you any siblings? Are your parents alive?"

"I'm from Limerick originally and I was an only child. My mother and father were devoted to each other but my mother died about ten years ago and unfortunately my father has Alzheimer's and is in a nursing home near Ennis."

"That's difficult. I have a sister and a brother and even though I don't often see them I feel they would be there for me if I needed them. Both my parents are still alive. So I visit them occasionally."

The journey to Cork took them about four hours – three to the city and another to West Cork and Inchydoney. Neither had ever been there before so they weren't quite prepared for the narrow country roads leading from Clonakilty. Despite this and the weather, the beauty of the place took their breath away and when they could see the white horses of the Atlantic they knew they were nearly there.

The weather still wasn't doing them any favours and while walking from the car park to the hotel they were nearly blown away. But inside they relaxed and quickly checked in and went to their room, which was suitably opulent. Then they freshened up before going down to a latish lunch.

"Do you know what I was thinking?" Nicola said as they headed down for their first therapy session. "Should we look for Eliza's daughter? I'd say that Eliza would be delighted if she came to see her."

"I don't know, Nicola." Cassandra was very doubtful. "That smacks a bit of interference."

"I spend most of my working life interfering. It just seems

awful that Eliza is going through every woman's nightmare and her only child doesn't know about it."

"But she knows where her mother is and she never gets in contact."

"She could be ashamed or just not know how to start the ball rolling. The fact that her parents were right and her partner was a waste of space makes it all the more difficult. But if we nudged her in the right direction she might be willing to try and mend fences. I'd say that Eliza and Hugo would welcome her with open arms, especially now."

"You could be right but how would we go about it?"

They went into the scented therapy room, removed their bath robes and allowed the therapists to pamper them, massaging them with scented oils whose effects were magical. They pondered the situation while the therapists did their work and afterwards continued the conversation while they were getting dressed.

"If we could find out who her friends were in Galway it's likely that she's in touch with at least one of them. They might give us her address." Nicola was thinking aloud. "We could go and see her. It would be terrible to tell her that her mother had cancer over the phone but if we went to see her she might listen."

"Steady on, Nicola!" Things were moving too fast for Cassandra. "That is quite a big step. Are you proposing that the two of us – two total strangers – turn up on her doorstep and tell her that her mother is seriously ill? She'll love that!"

"Of course she won't but she might be glad we did it. I just think that if my mother was ill and no one told me I would be full of regrets and I think my mother would also be hurt."

"Okay, okay, but where do we start?" Cassandra said, resigned to the fact that Nicola would not be deterred.

"I think I might know. I have a friend who was a mature student for yonks. He was involved in the students union to the extent that people thought he was paid by the college and he knows everyone. I could ask him if he ever heard of her. He's still around on the arty scene."

"Or we could just ask Hugo if he remembers any of her friends. And, if so, does he know their whereabouts. If he thinks it's a good idea he would cooperate." Cassandra had a way of finding the most direct way of solving a problem.

"Okay. We'll think about it. But, you know, if we do too much planning while we're here it will defeat the purpose of this trip: a bit of pampering for two very stressed individuals! I think it's time we both relaxed and let the therapists do their bit, don't you agree?"

"I certainly do. Relax we will."

Dressing for dinner that evening, Nicola took particular care. Conscious as always of her friend's glamour, she didn't want to be Ugly Betty. She had chosen the clothes for the trip with care and had even gone and bought a new dress especially for dinner. She had decided not to depend on the 'little black number' on this occasion. She was glad she had made an effort. Cassandra looked stunning in a chic classically cut purple dress which was just perfect for dining with a female friend – not frumpy but not sexy enough to say that she was looking for attention from the male of the species. Nicola wore a plain cerise wool dress which accentuated her figure – which she believed to be her best asset – and suited her colouring to a tee.

They were startled as they crossed the dining room when a man dropped his glass as they passed his table. They saw the red liquid seep slowly over the white linen tablecloth, forming a pretty soft-edged abstract design on it. The man appeared to be totally flustered and his wife puzzled. A waiter guided Nicola and Cassandra to their table and as they sat down a manager arrived on the scene. He removed the wine-stained cloth from the couple's table and replaced it in the blink of an eye. The man looked totally miserable and his wife was whispering to him urgently as if trying to make sense of the occurrence.

The waiter took Nicola and Cassandra's order before gliding to the bar to get their aperitifs.

"I wonder what that was all about?" Nicola mused. "He seemed inordinately fussed about such a trivial accident."

"It wasn't the spilt wine that caused the fuss. It was what caused him to drop the glass," Cassandra said glumly.

"And what was that?"

"Me."

"Why would seeing you cause him to drop . . ." Nicola's voice trailed off as she realised what the situation might be.

"He was a client. A few times, a few years ago. I think he's from Dublin but came to Galway regularly on business at the time."

"Ignore him. If he feels uncomfortable, that's his problem. If he's in the habit of sleeping with – women who are not his wife – he can expect to occasionally meet up with his conquests. If he has any brains he will cop on that you are unlikely to saunter over to him wanting to take a trip down memory lane."

"I'm hardly a conquest. He paid me."

"To some men, all women are conquests. They have an inflated sense of their importance in the scheme of things." Nicola grinned.

Just then the waiter arrived with their drinks.

"Cheers!" Nicola said, raising her glass to Cassandra. "Here's to a lovely break!"

"Yes, cheers to us!"

Nicola noticed that the man and his wife left the dining room pretty quickly. She felt sorry for him – she didn't believe in judging people, because you never knew their circumstances – but she felt more sorry for his wife who was probably blissfully unaware of her husband's philandering.

The meal was to die for, the reputation of the restaurant well deserved, the ambiance perfect. They were truly glad they had chosen to take this break.

"Do you know Eliza's daughter's name?" Nicola asked Cassandra as they ate their starters.

"No. She has never mentioned her to me at all – I only know that she exists from local gossip."

"She did tell me about her but her eyes welled up with tears so I didn't probe. Hugo has never spoken to me about her. I hope he won't think we are nosey when we suggest trying to find her." Nicola was beginning to have second thoughts.

"That's a risk we have to take and anyway I will blame you since by your own admission you make a living out of prying into other people's lives." Cassandra had a quirky sense of humour which she only displayed on occasions.

They both laughed.

The following morning was blustery but dry. They ordered their breakfast in their room, choosing smoked salmon, scrambled eggs from a local farm, freshly squeezed orange juice and Earl Grey tea from the breakfast menu. After breakfast they donned their winter woollies and took a bracing walk on the beach.

The wind was biting and the white horses on the sea added a slightly stormy edge to the atmosphere. They walked as briskly as conditions would allow.

"Oh, God!" Nicola groaned suddenly.

"What? You look like you've seen a ghost."

"Not exactly! But did you notice that couple who just passed us walking hand in hand."

"I could hardly have missed them. They are the only other lunatics on the beach and they look so much in love. I wondered if they were married."

"They are. But not to each other. She's my friend's sister-in-law. I hope she didn't recognise me!"

"I'd say that she hopes even harder that you didn't recognise *her*!" Cassandra couldn't help laughing.

"You're right," Nicola replied. "Fingers crossed they're not staying at the hotel. That would be another couple whose gaze we cannot meet in the dining room."

"Yes, but like my client they have more to lose than we have so we'll just ignore them."

Nicola agreed that Cassandra had a point.

Returning to the hotel, they noticed that the glass-dropper from the night before and his wife were checking out.

"That's one down anyway," Nicola said with a grin. "This place is a bit of a den of iniquity, isn't it?"

"And that's without adding the Prostitute and the Social

Worker to the mix. God only knows the nature of *their* relationship and what they're up to!"

They were giggling like idiots as they ordered hot chocolate before they repaired to the spa for further pampering treatments.

"This is the life," Nicola said. "I don't know how we'll return to normal after this."

"It won't be too difficult. The need to earn a living will raise its ugly head. Still, we have another full day of this before we have to get back to reality. I, for one, intend to make the most of it."

They left early on the morning of the fourth day, intending to round off the trip with lunch at the g hotel on the east side of Galway before returning to reality. They played the Beatles' White Album on the car stereo on the way back and sang along to it. Nicola couldn't believe how comfortable she felt with this woman she had only met a few weeks previously and she wondered to herself if the friendship would continue. She felt uncertain about it and wondered how things would pan out when all this excitement with Alice died down.

At one o'clock they decided to turn on the news, just in time to hear the annoluncer proclaim that the new Taoiseach was Jack Madden.

"Gosh, I had forgotten that today was the day of the election!" Nicola gasped.

"Me too. I wonder how Alice will take this."

"Shh! He's speaking."

They heard Jack Madden's cultured tones waft over the airwaves.

"I am humbled to be put in this position by my party and I intend to do my level best to ensure that they and the country do not regret it. I will be leading the country at a very difficult time – at least until the next election, which I hope will not be for some time yet. At times like these it is easy to get carried away with the need to make decisions which will try to take the country out of the recession in which we find ourselves. It is tempting to make cuts at the easy targets but I intend to look carefully at all the possible options in the hope that decisions I and the government make will be such that savings are made by astute decision-making and not by cutting pay or increasing taxes on the lower paid. I intend to build on the work of my predecessor, the Lord have mercy on his soul, and ensure that this country remains a good country in which to live where everybody gets a fair opportunity to achieve a decent standard of living, despite our current economic problems."

"Thank you, Taoiseach," said the announcer and she went on to the next news item.

"Doesn't that just make you want to puke?" Nicola said as they switched on the Beatles again.

By the time they got to the g the place was buzzing. Around them they were aware that there was no other topic of conversation but Jack Madden. There were people clapping each other on the back, saying wasn't it great to have a Galway Taoiseach. No one seemed displeased at the news.

They had a light lunch of paté and brown bread and headed for home to get ready for the return to work the next day. In fact Cassandra had a client that evening and Nicola had a full schedule lined up for the rest of the week.

When she got back to her apartment Nicola unpacked before listening to her answering machine. The advantage and indeed the disadvantage of mobile phones was that people could get you no matter where you were. But Nicola had left her work phone in the apartment and her personal one had not been very active during the trip.

The only message on her machine was from Séamus, asking if they could have dinner sometime the following weekend. She grinned, pleased but not excited that he was still interested. She was considering her response and decided not to ring him immediately.

Chapter 13

The following day at lunchtime Nicola noticed a missed call from The Coven on her mobile.

"Nicola, could you call me as soon as you can?" Eliza's voice was shaky. "Grace is missing."

Nicola's heart lurched. My God, she thought. Could Jack Madden have something to do with this?

Her hand was shaking as she dialled the landline of The Coven. Eliza answered immediately as if she was sitting by the phone.

"How long is Grace missing?" Nicola asked without even saying hello.

"Since yesterday afternoon." Eliza sounded distraught.

"What exactly happened?"

"As you know, she went on the school tour to Dublin and they were to visit the Dáil," Eliza said.

Nicola had forgotten about the tour. She and Alice had discussed it and decided that since the whole class was going and Grace was really keen to go, it would be difficult to explain to her why it wasn't a good idea. So Alice had agreed.

"The teacher said that the Dáil was last on their list after the National Gallery and the Museum. She was counting the

115

children as they were about to leave the Dáil and she was one short – Grace. Her friend said she had gone to try and find her Uncle Jack who worked there. Her friend had offered to go with her but she refused. She said she wanted to speak to him about a family matter. That was about five o'clock and their bus home was at six. They couldn't find her so the other students came home and one teacher remained in Dublin to continue the search and help the Gardaí."

"God, he'd never be so evil as to do anything to her," Nicola mused aloud.

"I hope not, but the Dáil was searched, high up and low down, to no avail. There doesn't seem to have been any reports about it in the media. I'd say that Jack arranged for a news blackout. But the Gardaí are looking and Alice and Hugo went to Dublin last night."

Nicola's mind was in a whirl. She could hear Eliza's mobile ringing in the background. "You'd better answer that," she suggested.

"Oh, it's Alice!" Eliza gasped.

Nicola was on tenterhooks. She heard Eliza shriek and hoped it was for a good reason.

"Nicola, they've found her!" Eliza said after a few minutes. "She's safe and well but a bit upset. Alice says they're on their way home. They should be here by about eight."

"Would you mind if I came over then, Eliza? I feel sort of responsible."

"Of course you can. But don't feel responsible. The child was involved in a normal school activity. What remains to be seen is how she disappeared so completely while in the care of her teachers."

"How is Orla taking this?"

"To be honest we haven't been truthful with her. She doesn't know that Grace was missing. We just said she had to stay in Dublin last night and that Alice and Hugo were going to keep her company. She seemed to believe us."

"At least she's not upset. I wonder what exactly happened to Grace."

"We'll just have to wait and see. See you around eight," Eliza said and hung up.

Nicola was in turmoil. There were a lot of unanswered questions here. She decided not to phone Cassandra. There was no point. Her afternoon appointment was deferred so she went home. She pulled on a pair of old cords, her warmest winter woollies and did what she always did when she was upset. She walked to Silver Strand. As soon as she turned off the Barna Road she was in the country. She walked briskly, wondering exactly what was behind Grace's disappearance. There must have been some involvement on the part of Jack Madden.

She stared down the narrow country road, taking in the bare branches of the few trees – even in the depths of winter this place calmed her down. The road changed with every season. In winter it had a bleak beauty while in spring and summer it burst into colour with a profusion of wild flowers which looked like they had come straight out of a Monet painting.

The tide was out when she got to the beach. Even though there was a light drizzle she could still see the Clare hills in the distance. She paced back and forth, throwing a stick for a stray dog which seemed bent on befriending her.

I have taken in enough strays in my day and I have just got rid of the latest one, she thought with a grim smile and she threw the stick again as far as she could and walked briskly away.

Back at her apartment she was on edge. It wasn't quite five o'clock. She had three hours to wait before she could go to The Coven. She looked in her fridge. Very little to tempt her there! She decided to go shopping. At least it would occupy her until eight. She changed her clothes for the third time that day and went out.

The supermarket was not that busy but she found it hard to focus. She picked up some fruit, a few small cartons of tomato soup – always a handy snack – and three microwave meals for one. Until then it hadn't quite hit her that she was alone in the world for the first time in years. She cheered up when she remembered that Séamus had invited her out for dinner and she decided to accept the invitation.

It was only six thirty when she got back to her apartment so she made herself a light snack of soup and a salad sandwich and sat down and watched television.

On the dot of eight she was ringing the bell at The Coven.

Eliza came to the door and ushered her in. They were all in the kitchen – Alice, Grace, Orla and Hugo – sitting around the table, having just finished dinner.

"Hi, everyone," Nicola smiled and sat down.

She looked around at the others. For the first time she thought Alice looked her age. Her face was drawn and she noticed lines around her eyes that she had never seen before. Grace looked as if she wasn't sure how to behave. Orla seemed unconcerned. Eliza and Hugo just looked relieved.

Eliza poured coffee for Nicola, Hugo and Alice, then said: "Orla and I are going to watch *The Little Mermaid* in Alice's apartment. I promised her we would watch it tonight. Come along, Orla!" It was an obvious ploy to get the little girl out of the way but Orla was delighted. Taking her by the hand, Eliza led her away.

"Well! Tell me about this big adventure," Nicola said to Grace as soon as Orla and Eliza had left the room. "Where exactly have you been, young lady?" She had kept her tone light but to her horror the girl burst into tears.

"Oh, Grace, I'm sorry," Nicola said gently. "I just need to know what happened. You're not in trouble. Would you rather we spoke about it in your apartment?"

"No," sniffed Grace. "Sure Mum and Hugo know most of it anyway."

"Okay. Why don't you tell me the story of what happened after you left the school group?"

"Well," Grace said, "after we had been in the Dáil Chamber – Uncle Jack wasn't there – I thought I saw him in one of the corridors so I left the group. I told my friend Sarah that I had seen my uncle and that I wanted to talk to him."

"What happened next?"

"I went in the direction that I saw him walking and at the end

118

of a long corridor I could hear his voice inside a closed door. I opened the door and he was inside with several other men. One was a man who called to us sometimes when we were in Lady Gregory Court – the one called Mick, who used to deliver things to him, and I think he once came to bring my birthday present when Uncle Jack couldn't come. There was a woman in the room as well."

"What happened next?" Nicola prompted.

"Uncle Jack looked really surprised. And not in a good way, I think."

Nicola felt really sorry for the child.

"I said, 'Hi Uncle Jack!' He just looked at me strangely and said 'Hello, little girl.' He had never called me that before. It was as if he didn't know me but I knew of course he did. Then he excused himself and whispered something to Mick. Uncle Jack took my hand and led me out of the room and Mick followed us out. When we were out of the room Uncle Jack asked me why I was there and who I was with. I said: 'I'm here on a school tour. I wanted to talk to you. I really miss you and you missed my birthday.' I thought he would be delighted to see me the way he was when he came to Lady Gregory Court but he wasn't a bit pleased. 'Take her back to her school group,' he said to Mick, 'and then come back to the office pronto.' I started to cry – great big sobs – I surprised myself. Uncle Jack got really annoyed. 'But I just want to talk to you,' I said. 'When are you coming to see us again? You just vanished and nobody talks about you. I miss you.' But Uncle Jack just turned away. 'Take her someplace until she calms down and then get her back to her tour,' he said to Mick and he walked away – back into the room."

"And did he try and get you back to the tour?" Nicola asked.

"No. I started to bawl. 'I'm not going home until he talks to me!' I shouted and Mick just caught me by the arm and pulled me down a back staircase and out into the car park."

"Were you scared?" Hugo wondered.

"Yes, I was. Mick put me in a car and sat there with me until I stopped crying. Then he phoned Uncle Jack. I could hear Uncle

Jack yelling at him down the phone. They were both very upset at this stage. Mick started up the car and told me to duck down as we passed the gate man and drove out. I was really scared by this time so I did what I was told."

"I can't believe this," Nicola said. "And you drove out of the Dáil without anybody stopping you?"

"Yes. We drove a long time and then he pulled into the drive of a house and we went in. There was a woman in the house and Mick put me in the sitting room, switched on the television and told me not to worry, that everything would be alright. I could hear him talking to the woman in the kitchen. She kept saying that she wanted nothing to do with it. Whatever 'it' was! I heard him saying she must. Then she came into the room and said everything would be all right."

"And did you believe her?" Nicola asked.

"Sort of and she was very nice so I began to feel better. She said she would look after me and that she would see that I got home safely. I asked her if I could phone home to say that I was safe and she said that Mick had already done that. I asked if she could phone the teachers who had the school group and she said Mick had already done that as well."

"So you thought we knew you were safe," Alice said.

"Yes, I did. She cooked me a microwave dinner – lasagne – not as good as yours, Mum – and we both ate in front of the television. I think Mick went out because I never saw him after that."

"Where did you sleep?" Nicola asked.

"When bedtime came the woman – she said her name was Joanne – showed me a twin room and said that if I was lonely she would sleep in the room with me. She was very nice really but I said I would be okay. She gave me a pyjamas that were so big I only wore the top. I'd say she had no children. Though she was nice, she seemed anxious and worried. In the morning she came in to call me. I was awake for ages before that but I didn't know what to do so I just stayed in bed. I wasn't scared any more but I really wanted to get home. I got up then. I had no clean clothes or anything but I washed and got dressed and Joanne made me hot chocolate and toast. She even asked me did I want a fry! *Yuck!* Then she said she would take me to town and that I could go home soon. I was so happy I nearly started crying again but she was so kind I held back the tears so that she wouldn't be upset."

"You were very brave," Hugo said. "So what happened then?"

"When we got to town she parked the car and then we walked about a mile and she stopped outside a Garda station. She bent down and looked really sad and said, 'I'm really sorry about all of this. I think it is likely that your mum will be looking for you by now. Go into the Garda station and tell them who you are and where you are from and they will tell your mum.' I couldn't understand because she'd told me Mick had already let Mum know where I was. I was scared again then. I asked her to come in with me but she said 'No. Go.' And she turned around and walked away really fast."

The adults in the room just stared at Grace.

"Mum, I'm really sorry! Did I do something really bad?"

"No, love," Alice said with great certainty. "You weren't to know that Uncle Jack had more important things on his mind. He should have just told you that and taken you back to the group. But I'm so glad to have you back safe and sound."

"Do you know something?" Grace asked, as if she had just thought of it.

"What?" asked Alice.

"Our teacher said that the Dáil Chamber is the place where they make all the laws about how children have to be educated and have seat belts in the car and all sorts of important things like that," she said in a tone of puzzlement.

"That's right," Hugo said.

"Well, there were only a few people there, about three men and one woman and the guy in the chair who was called the Cathaoirleach. One of the men was reading long boring stuff out of a paper and the others looked like they were ready to fall asleep. Do you think they were bored? I found it pretty boring."

The adults in the room started to laugh.

"Out of the mouths of babes . . ." said Hugo with an amused grin.

"I'd like to go to bed now," Grace said, relieved.

"That's the first time I've ever heard you say that," Alice said with a laugh and she gave Grace a bear hug before they walked up the stairs hand in hand.

"Mum? Will you come into school with me tomorrow?" Grace said as they ascended the stairs.

"Of course I will," Alice replied.

When Alice and Eliza came downstairs again Nicola asked Alice if she would like her to accompany them to the school next morning.

"No, thanks." Alice was quite certain. "If the last few weeks have taught me anything it's that I'm alone and that in future I have to learn to deal with difficult situations I may encounter by myself."

"But you're not alone," Eliza said in dismay. "You have us."

"Of course, of course," Alice said. "I know I have you, but I must learn to stand on my own two feet. I really appreciate what you have done for me but this is something I can do alone and I need to get used to that."

"I think Alice is right," Nicola said and Alice shot her a grateful look. "We just want you to know that we are here if you need us."

"Thanks, Nicola." Alice was relieved. "Of course I know that you are all there for me and the girls and I will need your love, help and friendship for some time to come, but I must start to be independent."

As Nicola drove away from The Coven she wondered what, if any, implications Grace's little adventure would have. The fact that Jack Madden managed to spirit her away from the Dáil without anybody realising what had happened – except for this guy called Mick and the woman who aided and abetted him –

was worrying. A child had gone missing from the Dáil for about sixteen hours and there was not a whiff of it in the media? She couldn't help wondering if children running into the private quarters of the Dáil was such a common occurrence that nobody took any notice of it. She thought not. She considered whether questions should be asked and if so by whom. These thoughts were still whirring around in her mind as she got ready for bed. She decided that she and Alice should get together soon and discuss the implications of Grace's escapade. It was the oddest situation she had ever come across since she had become a social worker and she didn't like it.

Chapter 14

Driving into work the next day Nicola realised that no one had told Cassandra about Grace's disappearance but, realising that strictly speaking as the social worker for the family she probably shouldn't inform anyone outside the family about it, she put it out of her head. It was inevitable that Cassandra would hear about it sooner or later but it wouldn't be from her.

The office was unusually quiet and she found time to look at and reply to all of her emails during the morning. She did the background work for a case conference before breaking for lunch. It was then she remembered Séamus's invitation and quickly phoned him to accept it before she changed her mind.

"That's great," he said. "Where would you like to go?"

"You choose," she grinned. "It's so long since I've had a dinner date I've almost forgotten where to go."

"There's a new place in Dominic Street and I hear it's nice," Séamus said, not even trying to conceal his enthusiasm.

"Sounds great to me! Should we meet there?"

"No, I'll get a cab and pick you up. Friday okay for you?"

"Yes, fine."

"Okay. Friday at eight for eight thirty. I'll book it and I'll text you if there's any change in the time."

"See you then." Nicola hung up, pleased that she was about to go on a first date. It seemed an age since she had done anything romantic.

"You look lovely," Séamus said, kissing Nicola lightly on the cheek when she opened the door.

"Thank you. You scrub up well yourself." Then she groaned. "I can't believe I said that!"

"Never mind. Often clichés are the most sincere form of flattery."

They were both laughing as they got into the cab.

The restaurant was small and quite full despite the early hour. They were guided to their seat by a waiter who knew Séamus and they got VIP treatment for the duration of their really excellent meal.

"This is lovely," Nicola said. "I didn't even know it was here. The food is great and the service is pretty good too."

"I may not know people in high places, but the head chef is a friend of mine. I told him that I would be with a special friend so he pulled out all the stops."

"I'm flattered. He certainly made the evening very special."

"That was the company," Séamus grinned.

They strolled up to Quay Street, hand in hand, and Nicola was happy at how comfortable it felt. She really liked Séamus, not in a sparks-and-fireworks sort of way but in a way that made her feel safe and secure. It was a nice feeling, having just come out of a relationship where she had never felt secure – not only about the man but also about the mad behaviour which could have landed her in serious trouble. Her relationship with Jonathan had involved sparks and fireworks but not the good kind. Yes, she knew that she would have no such worries with Séamus and that thought pleased her.

The music was good in Neachtains so they stayed till about twelve before getting a cab to Nicola's apartment. She invited Séamus in but he declined and asked if he could see her again.

They agreed that they would meet up again over the weekend

and she left it to Séamus to call her. She was anxious that they didn't rush into things. She needed breathing space after the fiasco with Jonathan and Séamus seemed to understand that completely. He kissed her goodnight and she got out of the cab.

Nicola decided to spend the weekend giving her apartment a spring clean. She went to the supermarket first thing on Saturday morning and got an array of cleaning materials which she used vigorously with excellent results. The thought that she might be cleaning Jonathan out of her life as well as her apartment crossed her mind. By the time the weekend was over she had several bags for the charity shop and several bags for the bin and her apartment had a whole new shiny glow.

She and Séamus had lunch together in Salthill on the Sunday and walked the prom afterwards. All in all it was a good weekend.

There were a few things that needed to be sorted on the Monday. Nicola had only just got into the office when she got a call from Alice.

"I really need to talk to you," she said urgently. "I don't know what I should do about Grace. I am getting advice from all sides here but I want to talk to you since it is your job to know what to do."

Nicola gave a weak laugh. "This is not exactly the type of situation that occurs every week but come into the office this morning and we can chat."

"I'd rather meet for lunch," Alice said. "Somehow I'd feel less needy if we could pretend that this is a social conversation."

"Grand. I'll meet you in the café at the Museum at one."

Alice was certainly coming along nicely, Nicola thought as she hung up, given that only a month or so ago she was completely cosseted and protected, and in a way imprisoned, by Jack Madden and had never really had to stand on her own two feet. Now she was starting to realise that that life was over and her future and that of her girls would be very different. In the space of little over a month she had grown out of all recognition, but Nicola had witnessed that type of situation before. When faced with enormous misfortune, sometimes involving death or serious injury, it was surprising how well people coped. She hoped that while inevitably the next few months and maybe even years would be very difficult, the change in Alice's life would eventually be for the best.

Alice looked tired when they met for lunch. She was dressed smartly but she had worry lines etched around her mouth and eyes. Life on her own was obviously proving very difficult for her and this was only the beginning.

"How did things go at the school after Grace's disappearance?" Nicola asked.

"I had to see the principal and also the teacher in charge of the school tour. I thought it best to apologise for Grace's behaviour because, of course, she was in the wrong and they were not to know our circumstances."

"What was the response to that?"

"Well, the principal said that this was a very serious matter and that the teachers had been really worried, and could I explain why Grace had done this – it was so out of character."

"What did you say?" Nicola was curious.

"Well, I was pondering if I should mention that, while I was very irritated that Grace went off like that, I was not impressed by the level of supervision in that it was possible for her to leave the group and for nobody to miss her until it was too late – but I thought better of it."

"I'd say you were wise in the circumstances."

Alice seemed relieved that Nicola thought she had made the right decision.

"Before I had a chance to answer the principal," she continued, "the teacher, Mrs Cooper, said that Grace had said that Jack Madden was her uncle and that she had gone to talk to him. She stated it in a tone that said she believed the child was away with the fairies so I had to think on the hoof."

"God! What did you say?"

"I said that he was not her uncle but that he was a relation. That we had been quite close but that there had been a falling-out with our branch of the family and that Grace missed his occasional visits. And since she was not privy to the falling-out it was natural enough that she would want to see him, though it hadn't occurred to me that she might take the opportunity while visiting the Dáil."

"What did they say to that?" Nicola couldn't get over how resourceful Alice had been. In fact all that she had said to the principal was true but it gave no flavour of what was really going on.

"The principal seemed happy with that explanation, and so was Mrs Cooper. I requested that they wouldn't disclose this to anyone because Jack is so recently elected as Taoiseach and I would like the discussion to be kept confidential."

"That was sensible."

"The principal agreed and I hope Mrs Cooper doesn't belong to some weird peripheral political party that might smell a rat and dig a bit because you wouldn't know what that could throw up. That's the last thing I need now. A whole lot of media attention while things are still so raw."

"I know but that was a very good explanation. It serves the purpose," Nicola reassured her. She also hoped that the story wouldn't get into the hands of the media but, on the face of it, it appeared to be too trivial. Now the real story – that was a different matter!

"I'm glad you think I did the right thing. What do you think I should do about Mick taking Grace out of the Dáil and keeping her overnight?"

"If the Gardaí don't show any great interest I think you should do nothing. I think that you would be better not doing anything to attract attention to yourself or the girls until after the court case about the apartment. If that goes well we'll start looking for the rest of your entitlements."

"But what if the Gardaí do ask questions?" Tones of the old Alice had crept into her voice.

"Say you don't know who the guy who took her was or why he would have acted that way. Be sure that Grace doesn't let it slip that she knows him – though I don't know what explanation you can give her for that. But I don't think that any questions will be asked. I'd say that they have already asked Grace gently about what happened. They would have had to in the days that are in it."

"Would they?"

"Of course, even though it's pretty certain that nothing happened to her they would have to make sure. But I'd say that's the end of it."

"Why do you think so?"

"I'm not sure really but I think it was no accident that Grace was missing for sixteen hours and not a whisper of it hit the media. I'd say Jack or one of his handlers arranged a media blackout."

"Oh God! I was so worried I never thought of it that way. But now that you say it, it is strange. I'll leave well alone. I feel quite relieved. Hey, know what? I'd love to walk the prom before I pick up the girls from school. Just to restore a touch of normality to my life."

"There's a wind today that would skin a brass monkey but that coat looks pretty cosy. I'll walk out the Claddagh with you and then I'll have to go back to work and leave you to the elements."

Nicola, knowing there was something quite unreal about the whole situation, was glad that Alice could show such a normal front to the outside world when inside she must be in turmoil.

It was several days before Nicola was able to give Alice's case much thought again, though she remained slightly nervous that Jack Madden might try and contact her or Alice.

Oddly enough her next contact with The Coven was from Hugo. He phoned her on her mobile one evening and asked if they could discuss Alice. He asked if he could come and see her or could they meet in town as he didn't want Alice to know that he was worried about her. They agreed to meet in a pub in

Newcastle within the hour and Nicola decided to broach the subject of Eliza and their daughter if the occasion arose.

Hugo was waiting for her when she went into the pub. He seemed anxious. He had a soda water in front of him and asked what he could get her.

"I'll have a camomile tea if they have it," she smiled. "Life's no fun any more. You have to plan any trip out with military precision if you want to drink alcohol so it's just easier not to drink at all. It must be good for sales of tea and soda water, whatever about alcohol."

Hugo smiled, though she noticed that the smile didn't reach his eyes.

"What's bothering you?" she asked as soon as he had ordered the tea for her.

"Well, I'm uneasy because I saw someone prowling around in the back paddock two days ago and again this morning."

"Did you speak to him?"

"It was a woman and, no, I didn't speak to her."

"What do you mean by prowling?"

"Well, she wasn't walking briskly. She seemed to be more loitering and she didn't appear to be looking for something, like a dog, either."

"Maybe she was just communing with nature. Why does it concern you?"

"I doubt she was communing with nature. It was bitterly cold. After Grace's little escapade I just thought that maybe Jack Madden is up to something."

"I don't think so. I don't think he'll do anything odd at this time. However, when we get a court date I hope that he won't then try any intimidation. We never told you but Cassandra's brakes were tampered with before the court hearing and I'm pretty sure he was behind that. And I also suspect he paid a client of mine to make a false accusation against me that could have ended my career."

Hugo was aghast. "Oh, surely he wouldn't have gone that far!"

"It's hard to believe, yes. But we're pretty sure it was him. We have to remember that this is a man ruthless enough to pitch his partner and children out on the streets when they turned out to be a liability. And, also, he threatened me when I first phoned him." She looked at Hugo and sighed. "I'm really sorry to have to tell you all this, Hugo. I hope to God none of it impacts on you and Eliza."

"Nicola," he reached out and patted her hand, "Eliza and I know we are taking risks sheltering women who are seeking escape from abusive partners. So don't feel guilty about it."

"Thank you, Hugo, but I can't help feeling somewhat responsible."

He sipped his soda water, looking thoughtful. "I'm wondering now if I should hire some security."

"Well, as I said, I don't think anything will happen just now. Keep an eye on things and if you see anything you think is really suspicious you should inform the Gardaí, though if it has anything to do with Jack Madden we know he has at least a few friends in the Garda. And, Hugo, don't tell Alice about what I've just told you and maybe it would be wise not to tell Eliza either. They both have enough to be worrying about."

"You're right. Eliza's surgery is on Friday and she will be in for at least ten days after that. I know she's dreading it."

"Go home and look after her. These days before the surgery are the worst."

Hugo smiled. "You're right," he said.

"Hugo . . . on another matter . . ." Nicola took a deep breath.

"Yes?"

"You can tell me to mind my own business if you like but I was wondering if you think it would be all right if I tried to trace your daughter and tell her about Eliza."

Hugo's face just dropped. She knew she had really touched a nerve and was immediately sorry she had said anything.

"Oh, God, Hugo! I'm sorry. I just thought that if my mother was going through what Eliza is going through I really would want to know. I was thinking if you knew the names of any of her friends I could try and trace her through them. We need not tell Eliza at all unless it turns out well. What do you think?"

Hugo's voice was not quite steady when he spoke. "That is very kind of you. But Lizzie was so angry with us I don't know how you would be received. Did you know that we don't even know the names of her children?"

"I was aware that ties were completely cut but time often makes a difference. But I'm sorry – I shouldn't have brought this up at this time. Try and forget I said it and look after Eliza and yourself."

"No," Hugo said. "If she wants to mend fences I have no doubt that Eliza would be absolutely thrilled – but you're right, we shouldn't mention it to her until we see if you can trace Lizzie and talk to her."

"Do you have a starting point?"

"I do know the name and last known address of her best friend when she was in Galway. I will email them to you. And, if you don't mind, don't mention it again until you know the outcome."

"Thanks, Hugo. I understand. Give my best to Eliza. I will call to her in the hospital when she's a few days over the surgery."

Lizzie's friend's name and address arrived by email an hour later. Nicola rang Cassandra and left a message on her machine. She didn't know where to start with this.

Séamus phoned just to say hello and she felt a warm glow when she heard his voice. They chatted for about an hour and made arrangements to go to the cinema later in the week. She felt more content than she had in years as she got ready for bed.

Chapter 15

Driving into work next morning Nicola was composing a letter to Lizzie's friend Deirdre Daly in her head. She really needed to hit the right note. If she was too brusque, Deirdre would tell Lizzie that someone from Galway was looking for her on behalf of her parents and Lizzie would give instructions that that person was not to be assisted in finding her. She was also considering just looking her up in the phone directory and, if she could find her, just ringing her. She wished Cassandra would get in touch – she was much more used to clandestine meetings and arrangements so she might have some useful advice to give.

They had not really discussed how they would work this if they managed to get Lizzie's address from her friend. Would they both go to London and when would that be? When they got there what would they say and how would they react if, when they arrived at the door, Lizzie wouldn't speak to them. It was all so complicated that Nicola was beginning to regret that she had started the ball rolling at all but now that she had mentioned it to Hugo and he had agreed there was no going back.

It was lunchtime before Cassandra rang her. She had been away overnight at some corporate event and had not got back to

Galway till noon. She was in a hurry as she had another engagement in the afternoon.

Nicola quickly explained about her meeting with Hugo – the bit where she asked him about contacting Lizzie – not the reason they had met in the first place.

Cassandra was excited. "That's great news! When do you intend getting in touch with the friend. Did you say her name is Deirdre?"

"I'm not sure really how to start. Is there any chance you could come over to my place this evening and we could discuss the possibilities? Or are you busy?"

Nicola saw no irony in the question but Cassandra laughed.

"No. I'm free as it happens."

"Great. Come over around seven. I'll order a Chinese and we can discuss what we should do."

"See you then."

By the time Cassandra arrived at her apartment Nicola had already searched online for a phone number for Deirdre Daly but could find none that coincided with her address. There was nothing for it but to write a letter. The two women discussed in great detail what to write and after much soul-searching and debate the letter was drafted.

Dear Deirdre,

We are writing to you on behalf of Eliza and Hugo Lynch. We are very anxious to trace their daughter Lizzie and we understand that you may know her whereabouts in London. We have important family news to tell her and to be truthful we are hoping to persuade her to come and see her parents. We appreciate that she has, in the past, made it clear that she did not wish to have contact with her parents but we would like, in the light of the news we need to tell her, to give her the option to change her mind.

We would be very grateful if you could see your way to letting us have her address without letting her know that we are going to call. We appreciate that this is a strange request but we feel that if she knew we were coming she might just disappear. She may be willing to speak to us if she meets us face to face even though, obviously, she would still have the option not to do so.

We appreciate that this out of the blue and would welcome an opportunity to speak with you on the phone. We would very much welcome an early response because we are hoping to go over to London next week.

Kind regards,

Nicola McCarthy: Mobile: 087/6336372; email: N.V.McCarthy@iol.ie

Cassandra Grey: Mobile: 089/5664391; email: Cassandra99@eirnet.ie

They read and re-read the letter several times, changing a word here, a sentence there. In the end Cassandra insisted that they had done enough and they printed it up and put it in an envelope.

"I hope she answers quickly," Nicola said. "I think it would be good if Lizzie came to see her mother soon. If it works it could significantly aid her recovery."

"We'll just have to wait and see," Cassandra said solemnly.

Both women knew that they were treading on dangerous ground and were very apprehensive about the possible outcome.

The doorbell rang at around eight thirty. The Chinese had arrived. They hadn't ordered wine but Nicola found a bottle at the bottom of a press which she suspected Jonathan had stashed for a rainy day. It was a Chablis – not exactly vintage but it would do the trick.

"You can stay in the spare room," Nicola said to Cassandra. "Otherwise you would have to get a cab and come back in the morning for your car."

"Yes, I'll stay," Cassandra said. "It's easier."

As they ate their meal they planned their possible trip to London. They would both try and arrange to take the following Friday off work and fly from Galway to Luton on the morning flight, go to see Lizzie that day and come back on the first flight the next day. If Nicola couldn't get the Friday off they would just go on the Saturday. They looked up the flights on the internet and had a look at lastminute.com to see what hotels might be suitable, though they couldn't really make any choices about location until they found out where Lizzie lived, if indeed they did find out.

Chapter 16

Cassandra and Nicola travelled to London on the early morning flight. They arrived at eight thirty and almost immediately got the Tube to Marble Arch. There was only one flight from Galway a day so they would arrive early enough to browse around the shops. There was also plenty of time to locate where Lizzie lived in case it wasn't easy to find.

Her friend had been surprisingly co-operative.

"Just so long as you don't tell her who gave you her address," she said apprehensively. "She'll never forgive me if she isn't happy to see you."

"Thank you so much," Nicola said. "It is very important."

"I guessed that. Total strangers wouldn't try and contact her with family news unless it was serious. I know if it was me I'd want to know – but please, please, please, don't tell her it was me!"

"Of course we won't," Nicola reassured her and delightedly took down the address and phone number though she had no intention of phoning in advance. The element of surprise was essential in this case. Lizzie was to be given no opportunity to refuse to see them.

"I love London," Cassandra said when they were on the way into the city.

"Me too! Or rather I used to until my last trip." Nicola sounded grumpy.

"Why so?"

"Well, Jonathan had rather romantically decided to bring me here for my twenty-fifth birthday. I was delighted. But the weekend was a disaster. I should have dumped him then and saved myself a whole lot of bother."

"Why was it such a disaster?" Cassandra could think of nothing nicer than to be in London with the man you love, in particular if it was a birthday treat.

"Well, though it was a birthday trip for me, he had arranged to call to a number of small galleries who had in the past expressed an interest in his paintings."

"Killing two birds with the one stone," Cassandra chimed in. "What was wrong with that?"

"Nothing, except that none of the galleries was in a position to offer him exhibition space at that time so by the afternoon of the first day he was in foul humour and not in the least interested in showing me a good time."

"Oh. That must have been disappointing."

"It was miserable and we could have been anywhere. Except that I could have got home fairly easily if we were in Ireland. I really should have known then that he was a selfish bastard but when you're in love you can get over things like that – the first few times at least."

"Women are dead tolerant when they are in love – too much so," Cassandra mused. "Not that I have any recent experience myself but when you look at all of us – Alice, you, me and probably Lizzie – we have all been badly treated by men we loved and we let them away with it."

"Not any more. It's time we started to look after ourselves and each other and if we're lucky enough to meet a good man on the way that will be an extra bonus."

"I wouldn't hold my breath," Cassandra said doubtfully.

"The optimistic social worker in me has to believe that most men are nice people, otherwise I wouldn't be able to do my job!"

They were both laughing as they came out of the Tube station.

Right in the centre of London by ten thirty, the women wondered what they should do next. They decided to browse around the shops until lunchtime, have lunch and then book into their hotel. Lizzie lived in Wimbledon and her friend had told them that she worked as a PA to an executive in a public relations company and that her children were school-going. She told them that Lizzie worked a short day and picked up the children from school and would probably be at home from around four thirty. The plan was to reconnoitre the place after lunch and then go back around teatime when they were fairly sure that Lizzie and her family would be at home. It all seemed quite simple really – so why were they both feeling extremely anxious, Nicola wondered.

Now that they were in London the enormity of the situation hit them. If Lizzie shut the door in their faces they would have to face Hugo, already under enormous strain, with the news that his daughter did not want to see him or her mother, no matter what the circumstance. She shuddered at the thought.

They strolled around Oxford Street. It was a bitter November day but the Christmas decorations had been erected and there was a festive air. They looked in Hamley's even though neither of them had a child.

"Do you think we should bring the children a present?" Cassandra wondered.

"Given we only have a general idea of their ages and have no clue of their interests I don't think that would be practical," Nicola answered doubtfully. "Maybe we can bring Lizzie a box of chocolates or something."

"A bit of a cliché, don't you think?"

"Do you have a better idea? A Highland Malt perhaps or a bottle of poitín?"

"No. Sorry."

The social worker in Nicola took over. "Think about it this way. We don't know her. We don't know her children. We don't know how we will be received. There is no ideal gift for this situation. Chocolates it will have to be."

"You're right. We can buy them when we get to Wimbledon."

But Nicola couldn't resist a cute little wooden toy for her niece.

"This is something I couldn't get in Galway. I've started on my Christmas shopping in November! How sad is that? One down – about twenty to go!"

They had a leisurely lunch and got the Tube to Wimbledon. The journey took about forty-five minutes. Cassandra regaled Nicola with a tale about an American client who had taken her to Wimbledon several years before. She was delighted to be there but he was only interested in entertaining some corporate clients so she spent the day of the final helping him ply the client with champagne and strawberries and she hardly saw the tennis – except for the part when the winner was presented with the trophy. The only consolation was that she was paid handsomely for her efforts.

"I always wanted to be a good tennis player," Nicola said.

"And are you?"

"No, but I did my best, encouraged by the fact that many of the top players at the time were left-handed and so am I."

"I never noticed. Do you still play?"

"Sadly, no!"

"What put an end to your tennis career?"

"I was playing with the best player in the club and I missed a shot that cost us the match and me a boyfriend."

"Why would that cost you a boyfriend?"

"He was my tennis partner and when we came off the court one of his friends was commiserating with him and remarked that I had played well. He was furious with me for missing the shot and he said to his friend: 'She looks good but she can't hit the ball.'"

"Not very gallant!"

"Somehow, so far I'm not good at achieving gallant when it comes to boyfriends – but better luck next time!"

"Hopefully," Cassandra agreed but as they walked towards their hotel neither of them held much hope that Nicola's luck with men might change.

Having booked into their hotel and freshened up, the women armed themselves with a map and began their search. It was not

difficult. Before too long they had located the PR company
where Lizzie worked, the school her children attended and also
the street where she resided in a flat in a large Georgian house
which gave no impression of undue opulence despite the posh
address. It was a quiet tree-lined street which had an old-
fashioned atmosphere of genteel poverty, being quite shabby
without being dilapidated.

They were walking back to their hotel when they saw a
woman who could only be Lizzie walking along the street with
two boys – identical twins – who looked about nine years old.

"Look at that!" gasped Cassandra. "She's the absolute image
of Hugo. Let's go and speak to her."

"No," Nicola whispered. "No. We'll stick to the plan. We'll
wait until she has gone home and has had time to settle in and
then we will knock at the door. If we accost her now she could
just refuse to speak to us and walk away. It would almost
certainly upset her. It is bound to be a bit of a shock. No. She is
more likely to speak to us if we call to the house."

"You're right, as usual," Cassandra agreed. "We'll wait. It
will probably pay off."

They went back to the hotel, had tea and scones in the bar
and at six thirty left and headed for Lizzie's flat. They were both
extremely nervous.

They pressed the bell which said Lynch and the door was
opened by one of the boys.

"Who is it, Simon?" they heard Lizzie's voice call from upstairs.

"Two women," he answered. "They want to talk to you."

"What about?" Lizzie appeared, coming down the stairs, a
spatula in her hand. The resemblance to Hugo was uncanny.

Initially Nicola was lost for words.

"We're from Galway," she said eventually.

"Oh." They saw a shadow cross Lizzie's face. "Simon, would
you go up and set the table and then help your brother tidy your
room."

Nicola was relieved. This probably meant that she was not
going to throw them out – not immediately at any rate.

"Is there any chance we could come in?" she asked. "It's a bit cold out here."

"I suppose so, but I'm cooking dinner so I haven't a lot of time." She held the door open and admitted them to the communal hallway.

"We're sorry to have disturbed you," said Cassandra, "and we appreciate that this is an intrusion but we wouldn't have done it if it were not important."

"I guessed that," Lizzie answered. "Are my parents okay?"

Nicola looked at Cassandra. "Well, not exactly," she answered.

Lizzie drew in her breath sharply.

"Your mum has breast cancer," Cassandra said. "She had a mastectomy a few days ago and the prognosis is very good but we thought you would want to know. Your father is well and is a tower of strength."

"I don't know what to say." Lizzie sounded dismal. Tears started to flow slowly, gently, down her beautiful face.

"That's understandable. We befriended your parents a few weeks ago for reasons which are too complicated to go into now, but Eliza was diagnosed very soon after that," Nicola explained. "We know that she would really love contact with you and your children and I thought that if my mother was undergoing a mastectomy I would want to know about it. So we set about finding you."

"I behaved so badly. I was so angry with them. I am so ashamed. I don't feel I could face them." The tears were still flowing.

"Your feelings are completely understandable, but believe me your parents would welcome you with open arms." Cassandra's tone was warm and reassuring.

"They don't talk about you unless they are asked but it's easy to see that they love and miss you very much. They would just love to see you," Nicola added.

"I feel so badly. I never even sent them a photo of the boys." Lizzie was becoming more distressed.

"We all make mistakes in our relationships and they probably feel they were not completely in the right either," Nicola assured her. "It's possible they would say that they contributed to the problem, though they never told us exactly what it was. What is quite clear to us though is that they love you and would love to have contact with you."

"I don't know! I don't know!" Lizzie practically wailed.

"Lizzie, this has been quite a shock for you," said Nicola. "If you like we could go away. You and the boys could have dinner and we could come back later this evening when they are settled for the night and discuss it again. What do you think?"

"I think that's a good idea," Lizzie said. "I can stop snivelling and get my act together. Come back about eight. The boys usually get a DVD on a Friday – it's a sort of treat – so they can watch that while we talk. Is that convenient for you?"

"Of course it is. Our hotel is only down the road. When we come back we can chat and see where we can go from here. In the meantime don't worry about your mother. She will be all right but we knew you would want to know."

"Yes. Thank you for coming. See you at eight."

Nicola was walking on air as they left the building. "That was easier than I had hoped. I'd say she will come and see Eliza."

"I hope you're right. It's hard to know. She doesn't look as if she's had it easy. I'd say she's not exactly rolling in money."

"No, but she does seem interested in re-establishing contact with her parents. That's the most important thing."

They strolled down the street, deciding not to return to their hotel but to look for somewhere they could get something to eat. They found a pizzeria and went in and ordered pizza because it was quick and uncomplicated and they could be back at Lizzie's flat at eight without having to rush.

At exactly eight o'clock they rang Lizzie's bell at the Georgian house for the second time that evening. She opened the door herself and appeared quite composed, considering the news she had received that day. She led them upstairs and into a large sitting room with a high ceiling and indicated that they should sit down on a large comfy sofa. The two boys were dressed for bed. She introduced them as Simon and Mike.

"They insisted on being introduced to you but they have

promised that they will go their room and watch a DVD now."

"That sounds like a plan," Nicola agreed. "We're very happy to meet you, Simon and Mike."

"Gosh, we haven't even introduced ourselves to you, Lizzie!" Cassandra said. "I am Cassandra Grey and this is Nicola McCarthy."

Happy to have been part of the excitement the boys said goodnight and went into their room.

The three women sat in an awkward silence.

"Where do we begin?" Nicola said, anxious to break the stalemate.

"Tell me about my mother," Lizzie said, her voice trembling with anxiety.

Nicola took on the social-worker role and spoke calmly. "She was diagnosed with breast cancer about a fortnight ago and had surgery a week ago. I went in to see her last night and Cassandra went the night before. We both thought she looked well and she is very positive."

"When do you think she'll be out of hospital?" Lizzie asked.

"Probably on Monday or Tuesday," Cassandra answered. "I asked Hugo the night I went to see her. She is doing very well and probably won't be starting chemotherapy until after Christmas."

"Is that normal?" Lizzie asked.

"As normal as a situation like this can be, I believe," Nicola answered. "The patient usually needs a bit of time to recover from the operation before the chemo which can be quite hard in itself."

"So I've heard. What do you think I should do?"

"That is very much up to you. We know she would love contact with you, as would Hugo," Cassandra said. "How you go about it, I suppose, depends on your circumstances here."

"I don't think it would be a good idea for me to ring her at this stage," Lizzie said. "That would be too emotional. I'd like to go and see her. I might be able to go and see her next weekend. Do you think that's a good idea?"

"Oh, yes!" Nicola was pleased that Lizzie had not opted to make a phone call. After such a long silence that would have been too easy to mess up. "We could pick you up at the airport if you like. Will you bring the boys?"

"No, not this time, I think. It would take too much arranging. In any case, since I haven't seen my parents since before the boys were born it might just be difficult for all of us. But hopefully there will be a next time."

"Who will look after them? Their father?" Nicola asked, immediately kicking herself for taking the social-worker role.

Lizzie gave a hollow laugh. "No. He left us a week before they were born and I haven't laid eyes on him since. It's as if he has disappeared off the face of the earth. But I have very good friends two doors down from here so they can go there."

"When will you know for definite if you can come?" Cassandra asked.

"I'll have to clear it at work. I may need a day off but I could phone you on Monday evening if that's okay."

"Great!" Nicola and Cassandra spoke together and all three laughed.

"We will tell Hugo you are coming and he can decide if Eliza should be told before you arrive or if it should be a surprise," Cassandra said.

Lizzie was uncertain about this. "God, I hope the shock doesn't kill her."

"It won't," Nicola assured her. "The fact that you are back in contact will definitely assist in her recovery. She will be delighted and by next Friday she will definitely be out of hospital and well on the road to recovery, if a bit sore."

"Should I book into a hotel?" Lizzie asked.

The other two women laughed out loud.

"You have obviously never seen The Coven," Cassandra said between giggles. "It's a mansion."

"No space problems then," Lizzie agreed but inside she was very apprehensive. Space was not the only reason she had considered staying at a hotel.

Nicola guessed exactly what she was thinking and felt sad for her.

Chapter 17

On the Monday evening immediately after the trip to London, Hugo phoned Nicola to tell her that he had met the woman who was prowling in the grounds and approached her. It turned out that she was an amateur ornithologist and had thought she had seen some rare bird on their land so she had returned several times in the hope of seeing it again. A hope that was not fulfilled as it turned out.

"Do you believe her?" Nicola asked him.

"Yes. If she isn't telling the truth she's a very effective spy. She seemed a bit batty to me really but her story is convincing. Sorry if I worried you, Nicola. As if you hadn't enough on your mind!"

"Never mind, Hugo. To be honest I didn't give it much thought. However, I have something to tell you as well."

"What is that?"

He listened wordlessly as she told him the story of the trip to London and the outcome. There was silence when she was finished.

"Are you still there, Hugo?"

"Yes, Nicola. There is a God!" He sounded shell-shocked.

"Gosh, Hugo," Nicola laughed, "I didn't think you of all people ever doubted that."

"I did, but not any more. I am totally shocked, but pleasantly so."

"I know," Nicola said gently. "Have a think about it over the next few days and decide how best we should arrange the visit. Cassandra, Alice and I will be of whatever assistance we can in picking Lizzie up and you can decide when and if you will tell Eliza about the impending visit."

"Thank you, Nicola. I really don't know what to say."

"Don't say anything for the moment."

Nicola was close to tears when she put down the phone.

About an hour after that call Nicola's landline rang again. It was Lizzie.

"I got Friday off and I have booked the late afternoon flight from Luton to Galway, coming back on Sunday," she said without any preamble.

"That was quick. I can see you are a woman who acts fast when she knows what she wants to do."

"I did it before I thought about it too much and lost my courage. I can't wait now to see my parents but I am scared."

"Don't be scared. I only know them a few weeks but I know enough to be sure that seeing you on Friday will make up for the absence of ten years and whatever came between you in the past has faded out of existence." She had no doubts about that.

"I hope so," Lizzie replied. "Will I get a cab from the airport?"

"Not at all. I'll pick you up. I'll discuss with Hugo how he thinks we should play this. I have no doubt that Eliza will be delighted to see you but we don't want to give her too much of a shock."

"God, I'm scared," Lizzie said again, her voice trembling.

"Don't be. It will all be grand. We just need to plan it well. I'll see you on Friday and don't worry."

Nicola's mind was in a whirl when she hung up.

There were only a few days in which to arrange this visit so Nicola called a summit. Eliza was to be discharged from hospital on Tuesday afternoon so Nicola arranged to meet Cassandra,

Alice and Hugo for lunch at the Westwood Hotel close to the hospital that day.

It wasn't the best time to meet, as it turned out. Hugo had a distracted air, Alice was still worried about Grace, Cassandra was rushing to meet a client and Nicola had a case conference regarding a very dysfunctional family that afternoon. To say that they had other things on their minds was an understatement.

Quickly they decided that they would not tell Eliza that Lizzie was coming. They would arrange a small dinner party on Friday, to which Cassandra and Nicola would be invited. They agreed that having others around for the homecoming would diffuse any possible tension. Alice would cook. It would make a change, cooking for eight, since when she was with Jack Madden she never cooked for more than four at a time. She said she looked forward to the challenge and it would be practice for the future. The others didn't know quite what to make of that remark but they hadn't time to be considering it at that point so they let it go. Nicola would pick Lizzie up and bring her to The Coven. They would have dinner and Nicola, Cassandra and Alice would leave at about nine so that Eliza, Hugo and Lizzie could make up for lost time. They would explain the dinner party to Eliza as a sort of welcome-home. Neither Nicola nor Cassandra would visit Eliza between then and Friday and Hugo's main job would be to ensure that Eliza was well rested and got plenty of sleep.

Alice also said that she would get a room ready in Eliza and Hugo's quarters without Eliza noticing. Essentially she would be the mistress of ceremonies for the evening. In truth she was glad of a distraction from the worry of Grace's escapade and she was delighted that she could do something for Eliza and Hugo since so far the giving had all been in the other direction. They had completed their plan and eaten their lunch in about forty minutes and they all left hurriedly and went in four different directions.

Lizzie looked absolutely petrified as she came out the door into Arrivals at Galway Airport. She looked around her apprehensively and only managed a wan smile when she recognised Nicola.

"I forgot that things are so small in Galway," she said with an air of unreality. "I don't think I have ever been in this airport before."

"Well, it's no Heathrow but it is a great boon to us Galwegians," Nicola said cheerfully. "It's a small airport but it covers quite a few routes to the UK and one or two to France and who knows what might happen in the future?"

"Who knows, indeed," Lizzie said glumly and Nicola knew that she was not referring to the development of the airport.

"Get in and don't worry," Nicola said briskly, opening the door of the car. "Everything will be fine. Hugo is delighted and so will Eliza be when she sees you."

"I certainly hope so. I couldn't deal with it if this goes wrong."

"Of course it won't," Nicola assured her though she knew that there were no guarantees when it came to families even if, in this case, it seemed that all would be well.

As they swept up the drive of The Coven, Nicola watched as Lizzie craned her neck to take everything in.

"It's so different to the farm we had but it's beautiful," she said.

"It's lovely inside and beautifully restored. Your parents have great vision. And they are very kind. They have helped quite a few women in trouble."

"And I wouldn't let them help me. I didn't even let them know I needed it." Lizzie sighed.

"I think they understand that. But I am in no doubt that they would have helped you in every way possible if you had made contact. That is why I am so sure that this meeting will be grand. You have nothing to worry about."

"I hope you're right," Lizzie replied as they drew up to the door.

"I'll take your bag," Nicola said as they got out.

The front door opened and Hugo came out alone. He embraced his daughter as if he would never let her go.

"We haven't told your mother yet," he said as he forced himself to step back. "She will be delighted."

For the first time since Lizzie had planned this trip she let go of her doubts and let herself believe that that would be the case.

Eliza had her back to the door when Hugo, Lizzie and Nicola came into the dining room. Cassandra had just said something that made her laugh. Cassandra had started to talk again when she looked over Eliza's shoulder and saw Lizzie. Suddenly she couldn't continue what she was saying.

Eliza looked behind her to see what had caused Cassandra to stop dead in her tracks. She looked across the room and initially was silent. Everybody held their breath. Then with a gleeful shriek Eliza shot across the room, grabbing Lizzie in a tight embrace.

"Be careful, be careful!" Hugo said. "Don't hurt yourself." He was referring to the soreness Eliza had suffered since the operation.

"I don't care, I don't care!" Eliza practically sang and the onlookers thought she would squeeze the life out of Lizzie.

They were all in tears when she finally did let her go.

Alice, appearing just then from the kitchen, was the first to speak. "Anyone for sherry?" she asked. She had decided unilaterally that champagne would be too cheesy for this occasion and since nobody at all had taken any interest in the menu for the meal she had made all the decisions herself.

Alice poured the sherry and Eliza sat down at the table, still holding her daughter's hand as if her life depended on it. There was so much to talk about. Nicola was sort of sorry that they couldn't leave at that stage but there was no point in regretting that now. They all sat down around the elegantly prepared table. Suddenly there was a hum of conversation. Lizzie was asked about the flight as if they were used to her dropping by. Apparently the plane bounced all the way from Luton to Galway but she was so apprehensive about the weekend that the turbulent flight didn't bother her. Eliza asked about the children and Lizzie showed her the photographs she had brought – only about ten as she didn't want to bombard her mother with information.

Alice glided in from the kitchen, placing mushroom and truffle paté before them. Nicola and Cassandra had never tasted her cooking before and were really impressed.

"Gosh, Alice, this is beautiful. Surely you didn't make it yourself?" Nicola gasped.

"I did." Alice was pleased with herself. "I am a woman of many hidden talents."

"Obviously," Cassandra agreed. "You said before that you learned to cook out of necessity."

"That's true. Being the ex-concubine of a Very Important Person has its advantages and I fully intend to take advantage of this talent but tonight is not the night for us to discuss that. Raise your glasses to Lizzie! And to Eliza and Hugo – without them I don't know where I'd be!"

They all raised their glasses and Hugo got up and got a bottle of Burgundy from the wine rack.

Alice served pork steak stuffed with walnuts for the main course because Hugo had told her that pork steak was Lizzie's all-time favourite dinner when she was a child.

"I can't believe you remembered that," Lizzie said, her eyes welling up.

"I have only one child," Hugo replied. "And everything about you is important."

Alice looked wistful when he said that – conscious that she would not get the same reception if she were to return home.

Noticing the sadness in Alice's eyes, Cassandra broke in: "Gosh, Hugo, it's a case of blessed art thou amongst women. In all the times I've been here I never actually was aware that you are the only male in The Coven. It's any man's dream."

Amid the laughter, Hugo replied. "Without the two most important women to me, my life would be meaningless. Not that I don't appreciate having you all around. But in any case Mary in apartment three has two small boys, but they are all so independent we hardly see them."

The dessert was a chocolate roulade which Alice had doused liberally with brandy. She had contemplated doing a Queen of Puddings because she knew that too was one of Lizzie's favourites but she decided that that would be going a bit too far.

"Wow!" Nicola said. "Alice, you will have to give me some lessons. I'd love to be able to cook like that."

"Anyone can do it," Alice replied. "It just takes practice and a very serious reason for not eating out – ever. I haven't been practising much since I came to The Coven. I had other fish to fry – if you'll pardon the expression. This was a good opportunity to polish up my skill – such as it is. Yes, it was lovely cooking for such a group. I'm glad you enjoyed it."

"We certainly did," Hugo said. "I'd like to propose a toast to Alice. To Alice!"

They all raised their glasses.

"To Alice!"

Chapter 18

Alice, Nicola and Cassandra had agreed that they would leave Eliza and Hugo to their own devices over the weekend. They were to be left alone with Lizzie. They had a lot to talk about and a lot of catching up to do.

This gave Alice the chance to turn her attention to her own daughter. She had decided that she should explain to Grace at least some of the reasons why Jack had reacted like he did when she turned up at his office.

Grace had been so upset by what had happened to her in the Dáil.

"I couldn't believe it, Mum," she said. "Uncle Jack pretended he didn't know me at first."

"I know, love. He isn't accepting any calls from me either." Alice felt that Grace might feel better if she knew that she wasn't the only one being ignored.

She felt Grace deserved an explanation. Of course she couldn't tell her the whole story but she could let her know what to expect next. With Christmas coming up, Grace deserved to know that Jack would not be visiting this year and that there would be no presents from him.

So Alice explained to Grace that the relationship between

153

them and Uncle Jack had broken down and that it was unlikely he would be a significant part of their lives in the future. She knew however that, strictly speaking, this was not true and that Jack Madden would have to remain in their lives for the rest of his life but not in the way that he had been up until this.

"Did you have a row or something?" Grace was trying to grasp the situation.

"No," Alice replied carefully. "But now that he is Taoiseach he won't have time for us and his family in Dublin will be much more by his side."

"I miss him," Grace said.

"I don't," Orla chimed in. "He brought us nice things but he never talked to us – not the way Hugo does. I like Hugo better."

Alice smiled to herself. Life can be so simple when you are a child. But she was aware that Hugo might not be a permanent part of their lives either, though for very different reasons.

"You're right," Alice said to Orla. "Hugo is a much nicer person but he isn't part of our family either so we can't expect him to be around for us all the time, though I think he would make a better effort than Uncle Jack."

"But you were always so happy when Uncle Jack came to see us," Grace said.

"I was, but that was because I thought he loved me more than he actually did," Alice replied sadly.

"I thought he loved you," Orla chimed in again. "But he never showed any interest in me and Grace really."

Looking back on it now, Alice could see that Orla was right. Funny that the younger of the girls had spotted something that neither her mother nor her sister had.

"You may be right. I don't think he loved any of us that well. We just made his stays in Galway more interesting," Alice agreed.

"In what way?" Grace queried.

"We were sort of like a second family. His Galway family."

"But couldn't we still be that?" Grace asked.

"No. Now that he is Taoiseach, he will be under the spotlight and two families aren't really the done thing."

Grace didn't seem satisfied.

"Grace," said Alice, "we are on our own now. I think we make a great team. Sometime after Christmas – probably near the summer – we will move out of The Coven and into our own place and we will be independent."

"I'm not sure I want to be independent, whatever that means." It was Orla again. "I like it here. I don't want to move out."

"I like it here as well," Alice said. "But the time will come when we are able to stand on our own two feet and then we will leave this apartment and someone else who needs it as badly as we did will get it."

"But what about Hugo and Eliza?" Grace demanded.

"What about them?" Alice asked.

"Will they disappear from our lives just like Uncle Jack?"

"I don't think so. I hope they will always be friends. You can ask them about it when Lizzie goes back to London. We won't disturb them today."

"Okay." Grace seemed reasonably satisfied with the conversation and they decided they would make crumpets for tea.

Nicola's landline rang at eleven o'clock. She was still in bed.

"Hello," she said sleepily.

"Rise and shine!"

Did Séamus always have to be so chirpy?

"I can't shine at this time on a Saturday morning. What kind of a day is it?"

"Cold."

"It's always cold in November. I haven't opened the blinds. Is it raining?"

"No. I have an idea for tomorrow. Can I come over?"

"I suppose so," Nicola replied, still not quite awake.

"Wow, your enthusiasm is really flattering."

"Sorry. When do you want to come over?"

She felt guilty. The last few weeks had been so hectic that she didn't know if she was on her head or her heels but she did know that the time she had spent with Séamus had been calm and relaxing, so she was very grateful to him for that.

"Have you eaten?"

"No. You woke me up."

"Oh, yes. Sorry. I'll be over in half an hour and I'll bring breakfast. Is that okay?"

"Grand," Nicola said. "And sorry if I sound grumpy. I am a morning grouch."

"I wouldn't mind getting used to that," he said cheerfully and he hung up.

Nicola scrambled out of bed and into the shower. She was about to put on a track suit when she decided to go for the more smart-casual look instead. Track suits really shouldn't be worn anywhere other than in the gym, no matter how glamorous, and hers weren't really very glamorous.

She put on her slim-line needle-cord jeans and a purple wool sweater she had bought in the Blarney Woollen Mills and looked at herself in the mirror.

Not bad for an overworked, underpaid social worker, she thought, and she carefully smoothed on her lipstick to make the picture complete. She was tidying away her pyjamas when there was a ring at the door.

"What makes you so full of energy?" she smiled as she opened the door to Séamus who had a full bag of shopping.

"Breakfast for the lady!" he grinned and he busied himself finding the cups, bowls and plates to serve the food, all of which he admitted buying at the nearest supermarket.

"Not bad," Nicola smiled as she tucked into muesli, topped with fresh raspberries – from Israel – followed by crispy fresh rolls and smoked trout from the Corrib. They topped it off with some sort of exotic coffee with which Nicola was not familiar but which Séamus assured her was the only coffee worth drinking. She was not convinced but she drank it gratefully anyway. Jonathan rarely made her as much as a cup of instant, let alone presented her with a full breakfast when he hadn't even spent the night. This was a life she could really come to enjoy.

"What's your idea for tomorrow?" Nicola asked. "Always presuming I'm free!"

"Oh gosh, are you?"

"Tell me what the idea is first and then I'll decide if I am or not."

"Tomorrow is Trail Sunday and I thought we might go and walk the Great Western Greenway."

"Sounds a bit intimidating. What is it?"

"It's a walking and cycling trail which has been created by Mayo County Council along the old railway line between Newport and Mulraney. What do you think?"

"Sounds nice – if we get the weather."

"We'd have to bring rain gear because if it rains we won't be anywhere near a road for a long distance so we would have to keep going."

"How long is it?"

"Eighteen kilometres, but the forecast is good."

"You're on. I will have to root out my rain gear. I haven't used it since I was in college."

"I remember it – bright red and a bit bulky. You sort of looked like a beach ball in the middle of winter."

"You had better watch yourself or I could change my mind!" Nicola laughed.

But he was right and she marvelled at how he could deliver an insult in such a flattering way. In any case she had no other gear and she hadn't time to buy some, so if it rained tomorrow she would again become the bright red beach ball of her poverty-stricken college days. Secretly she was pleased that he remembered her rain gear from so many years ago.

"You had better go home before I clatter you! I will bring the picnic tomorrow."

Nicola's phone rang again. It was Cassandra.

"How are you getting to The Coven to pick up your car? I was thinking we could share a taxi."

"I've a better idea – hang on a second," Nicola answered and she covered the mouthpiece and asked Séamus if he could pick Cassandra up and take both of them out to The Coven to pick up their cars, which they had left there the evening before.

"Of course," he replied.

"Séamus and I will pick you up in about ten minutes," she told Cassandra.

"Can I take it that Séamus stayed with you last night?" Cassandra was all ears.

"No, you cannot. You are such a busybody!" Nicola laughed and put down the phone.

The following day was bright and briskly cold as they set off in Séamus's ancient Volkswagen Beetle.

"I'm hoping to do it up and it could become a collector's item."

"You'll have quite a job to do on the body. It's covered in rust. I thought these things weren't supposed to rust?"

"It's over twenty years old and I think its other owner used to go camping on sea shores so that would test any paintwork," he replied cheerfully.

"Well, so long as it gets us there," Nicola said and they put a Leonard Cohen tape into the ancient tape deck.

The Great Western Greenway turned out to be a long easy walk. Not too much up hill and down dale. The flora was still pretty green, despite the lateness of the season. They walked at a fairly even pace and stopped for lunch at the 12-kilometre point. It was quite cold but they were well wrapped up. Nicola's main concern was that it would rain because, despite what she had said, she didn't really want to look like a red beach ball. She resolved there and then to buy some more up-to-date rain gear if they planned to do more walking.

She had packed a large flask of soup despite the weight and Séamus had put the rest of the lunch in his backpack. There were quite a few people on the trail but not so many that they interfered with their enjoyment of the day. The sun shone over Clew Bay and they even attempted, unsuccessfully, to count the 365 islands.

By the time they got back to the car they were exhausted. The drive home was quiet, mainly because Nicola fell asleep in the passenger seat.

"God, I feel awful," she said when she woke up. "I'm not much company, am I?"

"You're the only company I want," he replied and she knew that he meant it.

They stopped off at a supermarket and got two microwave lasagnes and a bottle of Chianti Classico so that the mood would be totally Italian, and went back to Nicola's apartment.

They watched a DVD and Séamus was about to ring for a cab when Nicola said: "I was thinking you could stay the night. If you want to, that is."

"Of course I do," Séamus replied and he did.

When Cassandra had got back from The Coven that Saturday morning, she'd decided that she would visit her father the following day. With all the happy-families stuff going on with the Lynches she just felt that she needed to see him. She rang the nursing home and spoke to the Matron.

"He'll be delighted to see you," the Matron said warmly.

"Only because he thinks I'm my mother," was Cassandra's reply but she wasn't sad. Her father had Alzheimer's and had forgotten her completely. "Matron, we can plan for Christmas as well if you are working tomorrow. I can come and help out again this year."

"I'll be here. You were a great help over the last few years. It really makes a difference to the quality of Christmas for the residents that you come."

"Thank you for those kind words, but actually I enjoy it and it is a nice way for me to spend Christmas. So see you tomorrow – I should be there at about one. Don't bother to get lunch for me – I'll eat on the way."

Cassandra had one client in the afternoon and planned an early night. The last few weeks had been all go even by her standards and she wasn't as young as she used to be. She wanted to be full of energy and good cheer for her visit to her father because, even though the nursing home was very nice, she found it a bit depressing.

After her client left she had a leisurely bath and chose her clothes for the next day. She decided on wool trousers with soft lines and a long cardigan which matched it exactly. Low heels and an elegant blouse which was not too snazzy, more homely, completed the outfit. She dressed carefully for these visits. She didn't want to appear too brassy but not too dowdy either. She always chatted with the women and had a word for the men as well. Her father always brightened up when he saw her but often had little to say after she sat down. She was in bed by eleven.

It was a two-hour drive to the nursing home and she didn't want to rush. She called into an open shopping centre on the way and bought her father a new dressing gown. She had noticed on her last visit that his was shabby.

It was good day for driving. It was Sunday. She wondered if they took her father to Mass any more. When he'd been in the full of his health he was a daily Mass-goer – the irony of such a conventionally religious man having a prostitute for a daughter was not lost on her. She knew he wouldn't have liked it but he would never know now. She had been really at a low ebb, financially as well as emotionally, when she started and it seemed like the only option at the time. She had been working as a PA to an accountant for a number of years when his company was closed down because of inappropriate use of client funds. She was not consciously involved in this illegal behaviour, so no legal action was taken against her but this was her only work experience and without a reference she was practically unemployable. She did have a degree in History and Archaeology but that didn't qualify her for anything unless she did a Higher Diploma in Education and she felt she wouldn't be a good teacher so she didn't go down that route. At any rate she was hoping to be able to give up her current way of life shortly. She had nearly enough saved to pay off her apartment and after that she wouldn't need the same level of earnings to support herself. It crossed her mind she would like to work in a clothes shop – haute couture perhaps – or alternatively she considered a career in interior design. She could act as a sort of colour consultant for people who wished to decorate and who didn't have much of an eye. Over the years she had heard many women say that they had no eye for colour and, judging from the way they threw colours together, be it on themselves or in their homes, it was quite obvious they were right.

As she drove up the drive to the nursing home she noticed once again that they never let the garden get out of shape – even in the depths of winter when it must have been difficult to get a gardener to keep it up. She drew up to the door and when she rang it was answered almost immediately by a young nurse she didn't recognise.

"I'm here to see Oliver Grey," she said.

"Oh, yes. You must be Cassandra. Matron told me you were coming. I told him that you would be here soon and he was delighted. He is in the conservatory. He likes it there even in winter."

Cassandra thanked the nurse and made her way to the conservatory.

"Hi, Dad," she said as she spotted her father sitting in his favourite chair looking out on the grounds.

"Cassie, my darling," the old man's face lit up. "Where have you been all this time? Have you been shopping again? You'll have me bankrupt."

Cassandra took out the dressing gown she had bought.

"I bought you this, Dad," she said.

"That's lovely. I'll forgive your extravagance," he said, smiling broadly.

"How have you been?" Cassandra couldn't help feeling sad. It was lovely her dad was glad to see her but he had absolutely no recollection of ever having a child.

"Grand," he replied. "Why wouldn't I be? You were ages away and you know how I miss you."

It was clear that yet again he thought he was talking to his wife who had been dead ten years. Cassandra believed that the shock of losing his soul mate so suddenly had brought on the Alzheimer's. He had been quite young, sixty, when the symptoms had started to show and his deterioration had been quite rapid. The doctors couldn't explain it. They just said every case was different.

Luckily he'd had quite enough savings to be accommodated in this very nice nursing home and on the advice of his doctors she had arranged for him to be made a Ward of Court. That way she was able to look after his finances and pay for his care. She hadn't had the heart to sell his house though she realised that she would have to do that sooner or later. It was deteriorating by the month and the insurance no longer covered an empty house. She hadn't rented it out – she couldn't bear the thought of strangers living in it, though inevitably that was going to happen in the not-too-distant future.

"Would you like a game of chess?" she asked him but he wasn't interested. She wasn't sure if he still had the capacity but the last time she had been there they'd had a few games of draughts.

"There you are, Cassandra." The Matron had come back from her lunch.

"Hello, Matron. Dad looks well and happy."

"He is grand or at least as well as can be expected. How was your trip?"

"Uneventful, thank goodness." Cassandra replied. "How are things here?"

"Fine. We lost your friend Mrs Murphy since you were last here. It was sudden in the end."

"Oh, I'm sorry to hear that. She used to love when I did her nails at Christmas before her family came to collect her."

"That's right. She hadn't been feeling well and when we called the doctor he said she had pneumonia and gave her an antibiotic. When we went into her room to check on her a few hours later she had died. It gave us quite shock but that can happen with older people sometimes."

"Her family must be devastated – so close to Christmas as well."

"Nice woman, Mrs Murphy," said Cassandra's father. "She always read the paper to me."

Cassandra was always astonished at her father's rare moments of lucidity, which manifested themselves at the oddest of times.

"She was a nice woman," she agreed.

She and the Matron chatted for a while. They arranged that as usual she would come down on Christmas Eve and help out at the nursing home. Her father was not well enough to be taken out to Galway so for a number of years Cassandra had been coming down, booking into a local hotel and coming to the nursing home on Christmas Eve to help with the decorations and to help with packing and general titivating for the people who were going to their families for the big day. She also helped enthusiastically with the preparations for those that would remain. She spent the night at the hotel and returned on Christmas morning to help with serving the meals and keeping the patients amused.

"Bye, Dad," she said as she eventually got up to go.

"Bye, Cassie, love. Don't be long now," he replied, still thinking he was speaking to his wife though Cassandra made a point of calling him 'Dad'.

Cassandra was always a bit down driving home from such visits but she was glad that she had found such a nice place for her father to spend his final days.

Eliza, Hugo and Lizzie spent the weekend making up for lost time. They talked and cried and reminisced and regretted lost opportunities and by the end of the weekend they had said everything there was to say. They had all said sorry so many times and they all knew at the end of it that they were together again as a family and there would never again be a rift.

Lizzie set up Skype for her parents and for the first time they spoke to and saw their grandsons. The boys were so excited. They had always wanted grandparents like their friends at school but never thought they would actually get to know theirs.

Hugo and Eliza, who could just about do a set of accounts on an Excel sheet, write emails and book the odd flight if they followed the steps carefully, were not exactly computer whizzes so they hadn't even been aware that you could speak to people and see them in real time. They were as excited as the children.

Afterwards they made Lizzie agree to come for Christmas and of course to bring the boys and they were to have their first real family Christmas for more than ten years.

"Of course we'll come. The boys will love it but I won't tell them for a while because they would be so excited that by the time Christmas arrives we would all be exhausted."

"That's fine with us," Hugo assured her. "So long as ye come!"

"We'll come all right. I'm so glad Nicola and Cassandra found me," Lizzie said again and again.

"Not half as glad as we are," Hugo replied, being careful not to mention that he had any part in it.

Hugo and Eliza went with Lizzie to the airport and they thought their hearts would explode with joy as she said she was really looking forward to Christmas. They had a group hug in the tiny Departure area which lasted so long that Lizzie was called over the intercom and was last to get onto the small twin-prop plane.

When they were driving back to The Coven they realised that the cancer had been forgotten for the whole weekend.

Chapter 19

Something changed in Alice when Grace went missing. Overnight she became more grown-up, harder, more practical. Not that she had lost her lovely nature. She just concealed it a bit more. The day after Lizzie went back to London, Alice took the children to school and then asked Hugo and Eliza if she could talk to them in the large kitchen.

This was so unlike Alice that Hugo and Eliza were concerned. Was there something worrying her? Did she wish to leave The Coven? But it was nothing like that. She had a proposition for them. Two actually!

"You have been so kind to me," she said when they were both sitting down. "I wouldn't know how to start thanking you."

"Don't think of it," Eliza said. "It's something we wanted to do and having you and the girls has been such a joy."

"Thank you," replied Alice. "But I have had an idea, which I hope you will agree to. I want to do all of the cooking for you until after Eliza has finished her chemotherapy."

"We can't let you do that. You have your own family to look after and I can cook – a bit!" Hugo smiled.

"And I won't be a complete invalid," Eliza chimed in, though she was still quite sore following the surgery. "I know that the

165

chemo is tiring in most cases but I hear that that it not necessarily always the case. I don't want to feel sort of redundant."

"You'll never be redundant, Eliza," Alice laughed. "Sure wouldn't this place grind to a halt without you? I have a selfish reason for asking this as well as a practical one."

"What is that?" Hugo asked puzzled.

"I am considering setting up a catering business when all the legalities with Jack are over. That's if it turns out that I own the apartment."

"Sounds like a good idea," Hugo mused.

"I agree." Eliza was very positive.

"I know that I'm a good cook but I'm a bit out of practice now – so I was thinking if I did all the cooking every day for five people – you two, my girls and myself – I could get back in practice. It would mean I would be experimenting a bit with recipes and proportions and probably doing slightly more exotic things than we would normally do for everyday but it would be a good way to get into the groove."

"I think it's a great idea," Eliza said. "And I can help out."

"That would be lovely if you feel up to it," Alice replied, pleased. "But that is only part of my plan."

"What other surprises have you in store?" Hugo asked.

"Well, over the last week, I have been making enquiries and the manager of that trendy new hotel on the Moycullen Road that is doing so well was very positive when I put my proposal to him."

"What was the proposal?"

"I offered to provide home-made Christmas cake, Christmas pudding, Yule Log and mince pies in the run-up to Christmas and over the Christmas period." Alice was very excited at the prospect. "It will mean a lot of hard work and I will need to use this kitchen, but cakes are my speciality and I think I could earn a nice little nest-egg between now and January. I could get some nice Christmas presents for the girls, seeing as it is highly unlikely that *Uncle Jack* will come up with the goods this year."

"You're an amazing young woman," Eliza said, full of admiration. "Of course you can use this kitchen."

"Of course, I will pay the extra electricity and any other costs incurred."

"Don't be silly," Hugo smiled but he knew that Alice was determined. "We can let you have the start-up money as well."

"No need," Alice said proudly. "I negotiated an advance of a few hundred and with that I will be able to get started. They have also said that they will pay me on delivery so after the first week or two I should be up and running with my own money. Oh, but can I use the jeep for deliveries?"

"It will be our pleasure," Hugo replied. "And seeing you will be doing all of the cooking here I will take the girls to school every day so you can get a head-start."

"You could earn quite a bit," Eliza said.

"Yes, if I can manage the volume it should be good. They are going to do a themed Christmas – 'Christmas at Granny's'. Hence the demand for home-made Christmas cakes."

"Aren't you clever? What gave you the idea?"

"I saw the 'Christmas at Granny's' theme on their website and I guessed that they were going to use commercial products so I just went in and said that no self-respecting granny ever produced a bought cake for their grandchildren and that I could provide home-made fare and I quoted them a price. 'Home-made Christmas cake and pudding! That would give us the edge alright!' The whizz-kid manager was mightily impressed. He nearly creased his pinstriped suit as he hunched over his calculator doing the sums. Dead serious! Not a smile out of him!"

"Sweet little Alice has suddenly become an entrepreneur," Hugo laughed.

"I have, and I also suggested that they should carry the theme to their afternoon teas so that for the whole of the month of December they will be serving Christmas Cake and Yule log in the bar and tea room along with tea, coffee and Irish coffee." Alice sounded almost smug but not quite.

"You have thought of everything." Eliza's admiration was plain to be seen.

"I hope so. But I had better check with Nicola how that type of income would affect my One Parent Family Payment and Rent Allowance."

"Good idea," Hugo said. "You'll probably need to keep accounts but I can help you with that and we can run it by our accountant if needs be."

"That would be great," Alice replied. "Now, can I start my new job by making us a fresh cup of coffee?"

Chapter 20

December was always a busy month for Cassandra. There were corporate events and out-of-town businessmen who wanted to have a pretty woman on their arm when they attended Christmas parties. This year was no exception. Cassandra examined her vast wardrobe at the beginning of the month. She was saving harder than she had been. The glamour of the job was beginning to pall and she just hoped that she could get out sooner rather than later. Her wardrobe was very varied but some of her clothes needed to be cleaned or perked up in advance of their next outing.

She had a number of events already in her diary but the most intriguing by far was a meeting with a man from Dublin who ran a stud farm in Kildare and a Wine Merchant's in Exchequer Street. He said he had a proposition for her. Don't they all, she thought resignedly. She hoped that this one wouldn't be too weird. She wondered why he had not contacted someone closer to home as her website made it clear that she was based in Galway and that she charged by the hour and that included travel and overnight.

She phoned him when she received his email. She always liked to hear the sound of their voices because it gave her some indication of what type of a person they were and she felt that sometimes but not always she could detect if the assignation might be dangerous. She also preferred to meet them on neutral ground and then decide whether she would take them back to her apartment. She had a lone-worker phone-security system. She logged in with the service and informed them when she expected the assignment to be finished and if she did not log out the company would phone her. If she didn't reply they would call the police and ask them to investigate. She didn't know if it was usual for a lady of the night to have such a service and she didn't tell them her profession. They presumed that she was a counsellor and she did not disabuse them of the notion.

The client had emailed her a photograph so she recognised him instantly when she arrived at the lobby of the Westbury. Her image was on her website.

"Cassandra!" His voice was strong and distinguished. He had a lovely accent.

She felt immediately at ease.

He shook her hand firmly and immediately handed her an envelope. She knew instinctively that it included a cash payment for a full day and she didn't check it.

He ordered a sparkling water for himself and a dry white wine for Cassandra. He was in no way familiar though several people in the hotel saluted him in passing. Clearly he was well-known on the Dublin scene. She was interested. She knew that this was going to be different and hoped it wouldn't be 'weird different'.

"I'm not often summoned across the country by strange men saying that they have a proposition for me," she smiled as she sipped her wine.

"I thought it would be good to have someone who didn't know my friends and that my friends and business associates wouldn't know either."

"Correct me if I'm wrong but I imagine even if you had gone for a woman from Dublin not many in your social circle would admit to knowing a call girl."

"Touché," he grinned.

"What's this proposition?" She was curious now but he seemed in no hurry to tell her what he was proposing.

"Have you ever been to Paris?"

"Of course I have. I'm thirty-eight and this is the noughties. Cheap travel and no great moral code!"

"Of course! Stupid question! Are you free to spend a few days with me there this month?"

"That depends on which few days, how much you are willing to pay and what exactly you want."

"The 11th to the 15th December and I will pay you by the hour – and all of your expenses of course."

"That sounds okay but why would you want to bring a companion from Ireland when surely there is a plentiful supply of women of my profession in Paris. An hourly rate will cost you an arm and a leg."

"I can afford it. And, yes, there are plenty of Frenchwomen available but I have a reason for wanting an Irishwoman with me on this occasion."

"Why?"

"You're very curious."

"It's a security thing. I want to know what exactly I'm letting myself in for before I commit myself to spending a week with anyone anywhere – let alone spending a week in a foreign city with a man I have only just met for whom money seems to be no object."

"Of course! How crass of me."

"Yes. You think that just because I'm a call girl I should accept any proposition, without being clear on what exactly it is, just because I'm being paid. Well, I don't work like that."

"Sorry. The situation is that I am going to Paris on business for four days. I will be caught up in meetings during the day but I would like to have someone to attend functions with me at night."

"That's understandable but again I can't see why you wouldn't just find someone in Paris."

"Well, the truth is I'm gay. That's not normally a problem but

I want to do business with a very large winery in Burgundy which has an outlet in Paris."

Cassandra was perplexed. "So why, if you're gay, would you need a female companion?"

"Because the guy who owns the winery is also gay and I am pretty sure he is interested in me."

"I take it that you are not interested?"

"No, but I think if I have a female partner he won't be offended by my lack of interest. He may have twigged that I'm gay but if I turn up in Paris with a woman he'll think he was mistaken. To be honest I am worried about not being able to do the deal if he feels I have rebuffed him."

"Okay, but if I'm to do this I will need your real name. I have a security system in Galway but that won't work in Paris. I want to look you up on the internet and verify that you are who you say you are."

He looked a bit concerned about this. He seemed to think about it for a while.

"I have no interest in exposing you as a customer," she assured him. "But I have to be sure that I am safe with you and knowing who you are would give me that security."

She explained that she would put his name in an envelope in her safe-deposit box at the bank which would only be opened by the bank if she disappeared.

"That way you would only be exposed if anything happened to me."

"Okay." He sounded doubtful.

"To be honest, I have not accepted this assignment and I don't intend to until I have checked you out, so as far as you are concerned there is no decision to be made. If you don't want to tell me who you are, I won't go to Paris with you."

"Okay," he said again.

She could tell that he was not happy but she knew she would have been mad not to take precautions. She was very much aware of what could happen to a woman in her profession if she went with the wrong man.

"If you tell me your name and address and if I am happy with what I find out about you in my research, I will go to Paris with you on the dates specified. You have my word."

"And if not?" he asked anxiously.

"You'll have to find someone else."

"My name is James Madden," he said.

Cassandra held her breath. She wondered if he were related to Jack Madden. That would certainly make a difference as to whether she would go or not. If he was, say, Jack Madden's brother, the agenda for this visit could be anything. She kept her voice calm.

"Any relation of our new Taoiseach?"

"God, no. Can't stand the man. I think if I was related to him I'd disown him."

"That's an unusual reaction. He's very popular."

"He pretends to be broadminded and inclusive but he's not. But the main reason I don't like him is that recently he was involved in a car accident in which he crashed into a friend of mine. He apparently behaved like a complete imbecile – effing and blinding and threatening to destroy him. And all over an accident where nobody was injured even though both the cars were write-offs. Apparently it was like a scene out of a movie that could have been entitled *Road Rage*. His chauffeur apparently had to calm him down and stop him from starting an all-out brawl. It's coloured my view of his ability to conduct even the most peripheral of relationships. I don't like the fact that a guy who can't negotiate a situation like that in a civil manner is running the country. God knows what kind of bother he could get us into."

"Not that keen on him myself," Cassandra rejoined without expanding. She was thinking that she didn't exactly admire the way in which he conducted relationships either. "When did this happen?"

"A few weeks ago. I don't exactly remember when."

Cassandra smiled. Something must have been rattling Jack Madden and she was pretty sure she knew what it was.

"Where did you say your business is situated?" she asked.

"Madden's Wine Cellar, in Exchequer Street."

"I know it. I considered joining the Wine Club there once."

James had a slightly anxious look as she got up to leave.

"I'll do my research," she said, "and I'll get back to you within forty-eight hours. If I don't find anything that worries me, we have a date!"

He smiled a little when she said that and she headed for Heuston to get the train back to Galway.

She hoped that the trip would work out. It would be like a holiday. Spending a few days in a beautiful city, where all she had to do would be turn up and look elegant and behave as if she and her companion were an item, was almost too good to be true.

Nicola was always busy in December. It was an emotive time for families who had problems. There were visits to be arranged between parents who were separated, and decisions to be made about how the children would spend Christmas Day. The financial aspect was often very complicated – helping the clients explain to their children that they might not get exactly what they wanted and then helping the parents provide as good a Christmas as possible for their children.

People who were going to be alone at Christmas had to be considered as had clients who have suffered a bereavement during the year, and people in hospital.

Though not a churchgoer herself Nicola found that the churches of most faiths really pulled out the stops when it came to Christmas. They took the issue of community seriously and if she was able to link in a client with a church group it often made Christmas easier. The Vincent de Paul, of course, were excellent, providing much-needed food and toys and other Christmas essentials for those in need.

With increasing multiculturalism Nicola found also that those cultures who did not celebrate Christmas found themselves a bit isolated when it appeared that the whole country was *en fête*. She linked people in with people of similar beliefs and usually it worked out okay.

She had herself to think of as well. This would be the first year in ages that she hadn't had a partner. She would probably go home. Her mother was always asking her to go home for Christmas but Jonathan didn't ever want to be part of their family Christmas. He found all the reminiscing boring. In fact, he found any occasion which wasn't all about him boring. He insisted it would be 'more romantic' with just the two of them together. For some reason there was never a possibility of their going to his parents. They were probably as bored with his egocentricity as everyone else, she thought grimly. She and Jonathan had never really had a good Christmas together so going home to Mammy this year seemed almost like a good idea and she hoped that Séamus would still be waiting in the wings when she got back. She wondered vaguely what he was doing for Christmas. They hadn't discussed it.

She hoped that she would have time to drop out to The Coven and see what was what a few times in December. Alice was still a client, in theory at least, so that could be the excuse.

Chapter 21

Cassandra went to Paris with James Madden on the 11th of December as arranged. It was the strangest assignment she had ever taken on. He was the perfect gentleman. They stayed in a beautiful hotel near the Elysée Palace and she was free every day. She wrapped up warm and spent the days walking around the city centre. She visited the Musée de l'Orangerie which been created by the architect Camille Lefèvre in collaboration with the painter Claude Monet to house paintings by the artist. The Musée had been closed for extensive renovation the last time she had visited so this opportunity to visit it was a real treat. It was superb. She spent two days browsing through the works of Monet, Picasso, Renoir, Matisse, Cézanne and others. She then made her way to the Cimetière du Père-Lachaise where Oscar Wilde and Jim Morrison are buried – among other very famous names. She had very mixed feelings about the glass barrier erected around Oscar Wilde's grave to protect it from lipstick kisses but she supposed she could see the purpose of it.

She got particular pleasure out of the elegant Christmas lights in the city. But it was the window of Printemps in the Rue Lafayette which really enchanted her. It reminded her of the Switzers window in Dublin when she was a child and her parents took her every Christmas so see the fantasy world created within. The window in Printemps was similar, with Santa's workshop, a scene from *Snow White* and a beautiful Sleeping Beauty. There was a tiny passageway outside the window cordoned off for children so that they could walk past the window and see everything while their parents walked behind them outside the cordon. She stood for quite some time just watching the wonder on the faces of the children and, not for the first time, regretted that she might not have children of her own.

In the evenings she dined with James and his business associates or attended wine tastings. They paid particular attention to the ullage, they peered at the meniscus, while they eulogised the nose and commented on the legs to the extent that Cassandra began to believe that she was in a physiology lesson. But the company was interesting enough and she liked wine in any case though she wouldn't have regarded herself as an expert.

She did a little bit of Christmas shopping. She bought a very elegant scarf for her dad though he seldom went out but, like herself, liked elegant clothes and she got some beautiful Christmas tree decorations for Alice – a sort of start-up pack for her apartment since Cassandra knew that she had lost everything in that line in the eviction.

On the evening before they left, she and James and his business associates went to the Opéra, which rounded off the stay beautifully. She caught the wine merchant eyeing her up several times. James was right – he did fancy him – so Cassandra played her part and behaved like a particularly affectionate lover which she considered to be part of her job.

By the time they headed for the airport she felt beautifully relaxed. James got her a dry white wine in the executive lounge as they waited for their flight. He was very good company and she was enjoying herself thoroughly until Jack Madden came into the lounge surrounded by his entourage. Cassandra could feel the colour drain from her face. It was the first time she had seen him since Alice had been evicted – and more importantly since her car was tampered with. He saw her instantly and paused momentarily before sitting down at a table as far as possible from hers and ordering a large Irish.

"There's your friendly neighbourhood Taoiseach," James said with a grin.

"Neighbourhood he may be but I'm not so sure about the friendly," Cassandra returned, hoping that he wouldn't be on the same flight.

"I suppose he has the government jet," James said and Cassandra relaxed again, realising that James was probably right.

But the gloss was gone from the trip and when they got back to Dublin Cassandra was glad to be able to catch a connecting flight to Galway and get back to her own apartment.

She had only a few clients before Christmas and James had paid her so handsomely that she decided not to take on any more.

Alice was trying with all her might not to be frazzled. There was no end to the demand for her Christmas 'fayre' at the hotel and she was at the same time trying to prepare for Christmas at The Coven and give the girls quality time because this would be their first Christmas without Jack and she wanted them to enjoy it. Nicola and Cassandra had been full of admiration when she told them about her business venture but the work was hard, she was permanently tired, and there were times when she wondered if she had bitten off more than she could chew.

On the 8th of December she took the girls Christmas shopping, continuing a tradition which her own mother had established when she and her brother and sister were children. The atmosphere was wonderful, the street lights spectacular and both girls noticed their mother went out of her way to put €15 into a collection box of a group of students who were singing carols in aid of the homeless. As well as presents for everyone at The Coven, they bought craft books because Orla was particularly anxious to make Christmas decorations this year – she had learned how to make some tree decorations at school. Alice considered this a good idea – in particular because they had none left from Lady

Gregory Court, so they bought the materials for those and other decorations they found in the books.

After that, Alice made it her business to have delivered her orders before collecting the girls from school and then she devoted the evenings to them. The girls worked with huge enthusiasm on the decorations and on several days Alice let them invite friends so that they could all do the decorations together which made it even more fun. The visitors usually took home some of the handiwork but that was also part of the fun. By the time the girls were ready for bed every evening that month so was Alice. The girls didn't seem to notice how tired she was but Hugo and Eliza did and helped out as much as they could, given their own circumstances. They were determined that Alice's first Christmas without Jack Madden would be one to remember for all the right reasons.

Alice had written a letter to her parents, telling them that her relationship with Jack was over and that she was now living in temporary accommodation until she found a place of her own. She didn't go into detail because she didn't want to burden them with the truth and she put in a photograph of the three of them which had been taken in the street on the day they went Christmas shopping. She sent them a Christmas cake by courier though her mother was a great baker and had probably already made a few for herself and other family members.

Hugo and Eliza were beside themselves with excitement at the prospect of meeting their grandchildren for the first time. Lizzie and the boys were expected on the 23rd of December and they would be staying until the 29th. It would be a great family Christmas. They invited Alice and the girls to Christmas dinner because they were the only tenants who would be remaining in The Coven for Christmas.

"We can't intrude," Alice said, conscious that this would be their first Christmas with their grandchildren but Eliza wouldn't hear of her and the girls having Christmas dinner in their apartment.

"It won't be an intrusion," she insisted. "The boys will probably get bored of the adult company and will be glad of the girls to show off to. I'm not sure what they're getting for Christmas but I guarantee you boys love to show off so the girls can be their audience. In any case, how could we hope to keep them apart?"

"You know, I'd been wondering about that," said Alice. "Well, I'll help with the dinner so."

"We'll be glad of your help," Hugo said. "We are so out of practice these last few weeks we're not sure where we keep the pots and pans any more!"

"I'll bring a trifle," Alice said. "It's my grandmother's recipe and it has to be eaten to be believed. I haven't met a person yet who didn't find it scrumptious."

"That's settled then," said Eliza.

Nicola was really looking forward to the break, though she and Séamus wouldn't be spending the actual day together. They were each going back to their families and had arranged that they would return to Galway before the New Year and spend their first New Year's Eve together. She was still very comfortable with Séamus and she knew that he was very happy with her. After Jonathan, comfortable was what she wanted. She'd had enough of excitement and passion (though there was a fair share of passion in Séamus as well!). She was glad to see the back of the excitement because towards the end most of it was unpleasant.

On the 22nd of December she and Cassandra made their way once again to The Coven and were greeted at the door by Hugo. Alice had prepared a wonderful dinner, aided and abetted by Hugo. They both thought that Alice looked tired and maybe a bit stressed though she participated enthusiastically in the evening.

When carol singers came to the door they all went to listen to them and they joined in with enthusiasm. The girls were delighted with this so they put on a Christmas CD and they all belted out such favourites as "Deck the Halls" and "Jingle Bells" until it was time for the girls to go to bed and Cassandra and Nicola to go home.

Chapter 22

Cassandra headed down to Clare early on Christmas Eve morning. She liked to get there early because the nursing home was usually very busy. The people who were not going anywhere for Christmas usually had visitors that day and the Matron was very pleased that Cassandra was willing to muck in. Cassandra paid particular attention to the ones who appeared to her to be lonely. There was a woman who had never had a visitor since she came to the home so Cassandra usually spent time with her on Christmas Eve and brought her a small gift for Christmas morning as well. She did her hair and her nails and in general made a bit of a fuss of her so that she would not feel excluded. She helped the ones who were going to family for the celebration with their packing and she made sure that those who were going on Christmas morning were well wrapped up against the cold. Her father smiled at her every time he saw her as if it was the most natural thing in the world for him to be there among a group of people neither of them knew well and that she should be helping to look after the others. Cassandra believed that this might have been because at home her mother was always inviting people in if she felt they were lonely and there was many a Christmas when they had someone not that well known to any of them at the table for dinner.

Christmas Eve was busier than Christmas Day because there were more people there. After some had left in the afternoon she helped serve the tea and turned on a suitable CD in the recreation room for those who did not wish to watch television in the lounge. She found working with these elderly people forced her to slow down. She was away from the rat race and she liked it. The fact that she was so near her beloved father was the icing on the cake.

Christmas Day was bright and cold. Cassandra arrived at the nursing home at eight thirty and things were already buzzing. She went to her father's room and saw that he had already showered and was struggling with his clothes so she helped him.

"Thank you, my love," he said and again she knew he thought she was her mother.

"Happy Christmas, Dad," she said as she gave him the scarf she had bought in Paris. "I got this in Paris. I thought you would like it."

"*Trés gentile*," he said with a mischievous grin.

Cassandra laughed delightedly at his remembering his smattering of French.

The local priest was coming to say Mass in the recreation room so she arranged the chairs for the residents and staff. There were only ten, excluding herself. She helped the residents to their places. After that the Church of Ireland clergyman came and gave a blessing. Cassandra couldn't figure out if any of the residents were of his persuasion but they all seemed pleased to see him. She chatted to the men while they were devouring coffee and mince pies provided by Matron.

The day passed quietly with the Christmas dinner, served at two o'clock, being the highlight. Cassandra went back to her hotel at about nine, having had a sherry with the Matron, and promised to return the next day to help the residents who had been away for a few days to settle in. She had spent her Christmases like this for several years and found it extremely relaxing.

By contrast, Christmas at The Coven was a madhouse. The boys were boisterous to say the least and this made the girls equally high-spirited. Eliza insisted they all go to Mass at ten o'clock even though she knew that this was probably not customary for Lizzie and the boys. She was right. The boys stared around them in awe. They were not sure how to behave but they watched Grace and Orla and sort of followed their example. When they got back to The Coven they opened their presents. Santa had left the presents for all the children under the large tree in the hall and everybody else left their presents nearby. It was a culture shock for both families who were used to having relatively small gatherings at Christmas though Lizzie usually invited friends in on St Stephen's Day – or Boxing Day as she had come to call it. Christmas Day was just her and the boys.

Everything was labelled and Orla, who had been in a state of high excitement since she got up, acted as the distributor because she was the youngest. They opened Santa's gifts first as the children couldn't contain themselves. Alice was pretty sure that Grace no longer believed but she played along with the fantasy and showed no signs that this might be the case. The boys got games for their DSs and a box of Lego Creator each. Orla got Sylvanian Families and also a Creative Design Kit while Grace was ecstatic about her iPod touch. Then the girls were given gifts from Hugo, Eliza, Lizzie and the boys and the twins got gifts from Alice and the girls in return and from their grandparents. The icing on the cake was the DVDs Cassandra had left under the tree for each of the children and the Cadbury's selection packs from Nicola.

The adults then exchanged gifts and eventually it was time to sit down to dinner. Alice and Hugo served the dinner with Eliza helping with the dessert. The meal was wonderful and the dessert, when it eventually arrived, superb. As well as the trifle, Alice had made a fresh fruit salad and home-made ice cream in case none of the children wanted the trifle or the pudding. She was right. Only Grace had dessert and she went for the ice cream. They were full after the main course and anxious to get at their new toys so they left the table early while the adults remained over a leisurely dessert and ample cups of freshly ground coffee.

After lunch they wrapped up warm and went for a long walk in the woods. Alice really liked Lizzie, and Hugo and Eliza were delighted with the way the day was going.

When they got back to The Coven Alice and the girls went back to their apartment to watch a Christmas movie together.

It was only after the girls had flopped into bed exhausted that Alice began to contemplate the prospect that she had managed to put to the back of her mind all day. She hadn't told anyone but she had received an email from her sister, home from Botswana for the Christmas break, saying that she and their mother would be coming to Galway for the Sales and asking could they come and visit.

Alone on the sofa she began to fret. She looked around the apartment, glad it was so nice. She was determined to put on a brave face. If everything worked out okay she would soon have her own home and she would be able to get on with her life. She didn't want to explain anything to her mother – not at this point in any case. It was so complicated she knew her mother would worry. Her mother had always been devoted to her family but Alice understood that what she had done in having a relationship with a man whom the whole family had looked up to had been a bridge too far. But she felt sure that her mother would be able to patch up the relationship now that Jack was out of the picture. She was less sure about her father. To him, Jack would almost certainly be a fallen hero who had taken advantage of his little girl but she felt that he wouldn't necessarily absolve her of blame either. She felt that he might be harder to win round. She wondered if he was staying at home because he didn't want to see her or whether it was because of the state of his health. She knew he'd had a stroke but had virtually no information about how bad it was or what the prognosis was. She would email her sister before Thursday, the day they were to come, and ask her a few questions so that she would be better prepared.

Chapter 23

Alice barely slept on Wednesday night and didn't tell the girls until Thursday that their aunt and their granny would be coming to visit that day. She prepared a beef casserole for lunch with Christmas pudding and brandy butter for dessert in deference to the season. She had given her sister Niamh instructions on how to get to The Coven and told her to look at the bells and press the one with her name on it. Niamh thought they would get there around twelve thirty.

By a quarter past twelve she was on tenterhooks. She understood completely why some people take to the sherry! She could have done with access to some drug which would stop her hands shaking and she dropped the cutlery on the floor when she was setting the table. Grace jumped at the clatter and then wordlessly picked up the cutlery, washed it and finished setting the table without being asked.

At twelve thirty-five the bell rang and Alice and the girls went down to the front door.

Alice looked at her mother wordlessly. Margaret O'Brien had aged. Her hair was completely grey now and Alice somehow hadn't expected that. They stood at the open door looking at each other and then Alice stepped forward and hugged her mother and was pleased to note that the hug was reciprocated, if a bit tentatively. Tears came and she wiped them on her sleeve.

The girls stared at their grandmother as if they didn't believe she was real.

Orla gave a small cough and Alice laughed. "That's her way of saying I'm ignoring her," she said. "Mam, Niamh, this is Grace and this is Orla."

The girls smiled but didn't say anything. They had picked up on the fact that this was a strange situation for their mother and probably for their grandmother and aunt as well.

Niamh was the first to speak. "Well, girls, I think I'll be your favourite aunt from now on," she said.

"That's easy," agreed Orla. "Because we haven't got another one. And you can be our favourite grandmother," she said, turning to Margaret. "We don't have another one of those either."

"That will be lovely," Margaret said. "Now can I give my two granddaughters a hug?"

Though the ice was broken there was still some tension in the atmosphere.

They all went up the stairs to the apartment and Alice's mother looked around.

"You have a nice place," she said.

"Yes. We've been lucky."

They sat down in the living room, the atmosphere still not in any way relaxed until Orla, unable to contain her excitement, blurted out: "We're delighted ye came! We're the only people we know who didn't have a granny or granddad. Some of our friends have only one of each but some even have two."

Margaret looked completely taken aback and then she laughed.

"Well, now you have one of each even though you haven't met your granddad yet. I'd like you to call me 'Nana'."

"That's fine with us," Orla replied. "It's nicer than 'Granny', isn't it?"

This time everybody laughed.

"And it's lovely to have an auntie too, especially one in Africa," Grace put in diplomatically, with a shy glance at Niamh.

"And it's lovely for us to have you," Niamh responded.

"How have you been?" Alice asked her mother. "Niamh told me that Dad hasn't been well. How is he?"

"He had a minor stroke last summer but he's recovering well and is expected to make a full recovery, or close to it at least."

While the girls chatted to Margaret, Niamh helped Alice serve the lunch and the atmosphere gradually became less strained.

The visit went reasonably well. Alice didn't relax completely though the girls seemed totally at ease and towards the end their nana was listening to them sing songs from their nativity play and admiring their Christmas presents and saying that they must visit her and their granddad down on the farm.

"Come on, Mam," Niamh said eventually, "we'd better go. Aren't we getting you a new winter coat?"

"The sales in Anthony Ryan's are always good value," Alice said. "Or you could try Nestor's."

"Right," said Niamh. "We'll be off so."

"Mam," Alice said when they were at the door, "I'm so delighted you came. I really would love to have you and Dad back in my life if that is possible."

"I'd say it is," Margaret replied with a sort of sad smile. "But one step at a time."

"You can set the pace," Alice said. "And Niamh, thanks! Come again if you are in Galway before you go back to Africa."

"Great! I'll email you," said Niamh with a grin.

As Margaret turned to say goodbye to the girls, Grace and then Orla reached up and kissed her on the cheek as she bent to hug them.

"We're delighted you came," Grace said.

"Yes," said Orla. "An aunt and a grandmother we didn't know we had. Soon we'll be like any other family. Could you bring Granddad the next time?"

Alice held her breath.

"I'm not sure he's well enough to travel yet but you could come to see him," her nana said and that seemed to satisfy her.

Alice shut the front door of The Coven happy that, while the visit had been a bit strained, it was the first step on the road to repairing the rift between her and her parents. The two girls bounded up the stairs, satisfied in themselves that their nana and granddad and aunt would become a permanent fixture in their lives.

Chapter 24

Alice's hands were shaking as she read out the document to Eliza and Hugo in the kitchen of The Coven. It was the 7th of January and the household was just getting back to normal after Christmas. The other tenants had returned to their apartments, Lizzie and the boys had gone back to London and Alice was tying up loose ends following her foray into the world of business. Eliza, however, was getting ready for her first session of chemotherapy that day.

"*Tower Properties v. Alice O'Brien. Set for hearing at Ennis Court on 14th February.*"

The irony of the date was not lost on any of them. Eliza and Hugo stared at Alice. She was trying not to cry but shades of the fragile little girl were very close to the surface.

"You should ring Nicola," Hugo said, conscious that he should be trying to provide a calm environment for Eliza for what undoubtedly was going to be an unpleasant, if beneficial, experience. Eliza just looked dumbstruck but her own impending ordeal was probably playing on her mind.

"You're right," Alice said. "I got such a shock I just had to tell someone."

"Of course," Eliza said calmly. "I'm glad you came to us. I'm sure Nicola will be in contact with the solicitor and she will know the procedure from here."

"Oh, God, Eliza! I just remembered your chemo is today! I'm so sorry for burdening you with this." Alice was close to tears.

"It's no burden. In fact it's good to take my mind off what is before me."

"I'll ring Nicola and I'll let you know what happened when you get back," said Alice. "How long will it take today?"

"I think about four hours," Eliza replied. "Hugo is bringing in a book of short stories and if I am allowed to turn the pages I will read them myself. If not, Hugo has said he will read them to me. They are my favourites – Seán Ó'Faoláin."

"I'll ring Nicola now. Should I do lunch? Do you think you'll be home by then?"

"Probably not," Hugo said. "In any case you may be busy if there are any preparations to be done. I'll try and pick the children up from school but if I am late I'll text you."

"Thanks so much, Hugo. Best of luck, Eliza – see you later." She gave Eliza a quick hug and turned away.

They looked at her drooping shoulders as she trudged up the stairs to her apartment.

The date of the court case was news to Nicola. Not being a party to the legal proceedings she had not been notified, though she knew she might be called as a witness. She wondered if Séamus knew yet but he was at a meeting when she rang him. She rang Cassandra to let her know the date well in advance so that she could arrange to be free on the day, though of course Gerard Murphy would eventually be notifying her.

Alice had sounded panicky so Nicola had said she'd meet her for lunch at the café in the Museum.

"We've several weeks to prepare for this and the legal people will know exactly what to do," she said, trying to be reassuring as they waited for their soup. Alice had a drawn look that Nicola had only seen rarely on her face before. "This is what we've been waiting for. This will be the start of the next phase of your life."

"If it goes well," Alice said glumly.

"No matter what way it goes, you will be finishing a bad chapter of your life. And haven't you made progress already in setting up your own business and making a nice little profit in the process?"

Nicola's upbeat tone did little to cheer Alice up. She played around with her spoon and had eaten very little of her soup.

"I suppose I had better tell my CWO about my earnings. Hugo helped me with the accounts. I don't think I have earned enough to affect my benefits yet but if I continue – and I intend to – I will probably do that soon enough."

"Good idea," Nicola agreed. "You must inform them of any extra earnings even if they are small."

They were about to pay their bill when Hugo texted to say that he had been delayed at the hospital and wouldn't be able to pick up the girls.

"I have to go," Alice said. "Hugo can't make it to pick up the girls. Can you come out later to discuss the court case?"

"I'm not free today. Better to wait till tomorrow in any case. We'll have more information. I want to talk to Séamus and he'll probably be in touch with the barrister."

"I suppose so," Alice agreed and she got up and headed for the school to pick the girls up on the first day of their new term.

Her heart flipped when the girls came charging out of the school, all news and laughter. She loved them so much. She was well over the fact that Jack didn't want to have anything more to do with her but every time she looked at her girls she couldn't believe that he could turn his back on them – but he had.

They got a bus home and were quite tired when they got there because The Coven was about a mile from the nearest bus stop. Alice made them hot chocolate and they collapsed on the sofa. She said they could watch television for an hour and went downstairs to start dinner. She was sautéing the vegetables when she heard the jeep draw up. She went to the door to greet Eliza and Hugo.

Hugo got out first and Eliza followed. She looked better than Alice expected and seemed quite perky.

"How did it go?"

"Not bad at all. But I believe that it may get worse. Today's session was grand. I think I'll lie down now but I'm fine – a bit tired, that's all." Eliza seemed quite happy in herself.

"Will I come up with you?" Hugo asked.

"No, I'll be fine and you could do with a break from looking after me." Eliza brushed her hand affectionately on his arm and went up the stairs.

"Come and have a nice cup of camomile," Alice said to Hugo. "I've a few scones baked as well."

"Do you want me to turn into a complete wimp?" Hugo laughed as they made their way to the kitchen. "Any chance of real tea? I'd love one of your scones though."

"Coming up," Alice smiled and she busied herself preparing the tea. "Now tell me, how did it go – really?"

"Actually it was as Eliza said," Hugo said as he sat down at the table. "She had to sit on the chair fairly still while they put various drips into her arm. But it was fine."

"That's good anyway." Alice was glad for Eliza. Every time she looked at Hugo she envied Eliza her luck.

"How did your day go?"

"Well, nothing happened really. Nicola didn't know what the next step was and Séamus wasn't available. She's to get back to me tomorrow."

"This is good, Alice," Hugo said gently. "When this is over, you can begin again."

"That's what Nicola said." Alice sighed as if she didn't believe it.

Chapter 25

Garda Declan Cotter was on desk duty on the 9th of January when he got a call from the Serious Crimes Division in Dublin.

"A special investigation has shown that Hugo Lynch, whose address is Cappagh Hall, is purchasing, downloading and exchanging the most vile child pornography on his computer. It will have to be seized without delay."

"On whose instructions?" Garda Cotter asked.

"Mine," was the reply.

"And who are you?"

"I'm Detective Sergeant Matt O'Sullivan."

The gruff response surprised Declan Cotter. Nor had he ever heard of a Detective Sergeant Matt O'Sullivan.

"I'll have to check this out with my superiors," he replied and hung up.

There was something odd about the call but he couldn't put a finger on it. He was aware of where Cappagh Hall was but the occupants had never come to the attention of the Gardaí as far as he was aware. He reported the phone call to the Duty Sergeant.

"Ring up the Serious Crimes Division and see if there is a Detective Sergeant Matt O'Sullivan," the more senior man advised. "It's a bit odd all right."

It was a while before Garda Cotter got a chance to attempt to verify the authenticity of the call but when eventually he got through to the Special Crimes Division there was no Detective Matt O'Sullivan there.

"What will I do now?" he asked his superior.

"Ignore it. Your instincts were right. This is someone who wants to make trouble for Hugo Lynch – God only knows why. If by any chance it's genuine they will come back."

Both men returned to their work stations, slightly ill at ease and wondering what this was all about.

About a week later Chief Superintendent Tom McEvoy, of the Garda Station in Dominick Street, Galway, got a personal call from Jack Madden the Taoiseach.

"Good morning, Taoiseach," he said, hardly able to keep the surprise from his voice. "What can I do for you?"

"Well, Superintendent, a week ago a report was made to your station about an individual, namely Hugo Lynch, who was downloading child porn to his computer and nothing was done about it. I am astonished."

"That's correct, Taoiseach. The report came from a source we couldn't verify so we didn't follow it up. It's a very serious accusation and we have no evidence."

"Well, I'm telling you now that this is no vague accusation and I want that computer confiscated within twenty-four hours and the man arrested."

"We cannot arrest the man until after the computer is checked out, Taoiseach. Is this part of Operation Turquoise?"

"No, it's not! This is new information and I, as Taoiseach, am telling you to act on it."

"This is very unusual."

"I know it is." Jack Madden couldn't keep the irritation out of his voice. "But it warrants immediate investigation. What do you think it would do to the image of the Gardaí in Galway if it emerged that this man who harbours vulnerable women and children is a rampant pervert and you did nothing about it? Do it without further delay. Do you know that ramshackle mansion he occupies with his menagerie is colloquially called The Coven and that could mean anything."

The Superintendent put down the phone feeling very uncomfortable indeed.

A few days later Hugo was taking Eliza into the hospital for her treatment and Alice asked if she could come along. She needed to talk to Nicola so had arranged to call to her office that morning. They were coming down the steps of The Coven when a Garda car drove up and three gardaí got out.

"We have a warrant to search this house and remove any computers which may be here." It was the female garda who spoke, flashing a sheet of paper before them without actually giving them the opportunity to read it.

"This is ridiculous," was all Hugo could think to say. "On what grounds?"

Eliza and Alice were silent. This was a huge shock.

"There is evidence that someone in this house is downloading child pornography from the internet."

Hugo laughed. "Well, that is not happening. I'm the only adult male here and I have no interest in that sort of stuff."

"This is not a laughing matter and we must do the search now."

"But I'm the only man in the building!" Hugo was nonplussed.

"Exactly," said the garda with some menace and she asked him to open the front door.

"I'll take Eliza to the hospital," Alice said. "Don't worry. By the time we get back this misunderstanding will be sorted."

Hugo walked up the steps and opened the front door and the two women drove off. They were in no doubt that nothing would be found but they were shocked by the accusation and worried about the effect it would have on Hugo.

At the hospital, Alice settled Eliza in and saw that she was comfortable.

"I'll ring Nicola and tell her what has happened," she said.

"She may have some idea what the procedure is in cases like this."

Nicola was out visiting a client when Alice rang so she left a message on her voice mail: "Ring me as soon as you get this. It's urgent."

Alice and Eliza were reading as the chemicals were being fed into Eliza's body when Nicola returned the call.

"I'll take it outside," Alice said to Eliza, conscious that she was within earshot of several other patients.

Outside she quickly told Nicola what had happened.

"Jack Madden is a complete creep!" Nicola exploded when she heard the news.

"Why do you say that?" Alice said, shocked. "What has it to do with Jack?"

Nicola paused. She and Cassandra still hadn't told Alice or Eliza about how someone had tampered with Cassandra's brake cables and apparently had tried to get Nicola fired. And Hugo had kept what she'd told him the night they met in Newcastle to himself. She and Cassandra agreed that, as Jack Madden didn't succeed in incapacitating them for the first court case, he wouldn't try anything nasty again . . . until the next one was imminent.

It was time to tell Alice.

"Alice, I'm sorry – this is going to be a bit of a shock for you but you need to know." Taking a deep breath, she told Alice what had happened to her and Cassandra.

Alice was dumbstruck. When Nicola rang off she felt faint and had to hold on to a chair for support. A nurse spotted her and brought her into the nurses' station and gave her a cup of tea. It was not unusual for a relative of a patient in the chemotherapy section to find the going tough and the nurse presumed that this was the case on this occasion.

When eventually Alice was together enough to go back to Eliza, the older woman looked at her anxiously and asked, "Everything okay?"

"I felt a bit faint when I went out into the corridor. It must have been the hospital smell or something. Some help I am!"

"You poor thing! I think I'd feel faint myself except for the fact that I am sitting down anyway. So what did Nicola say?"

"Her attitude is the same as ours. There's no way they will find anything and we shouldn't worry." She had decided that it was not the appropriate time to tell Eliza what Nicola had told her.

"That's okay then," Eliza said and went back to her book.

When Alice and Eliza arrived back at The Coven Hugo was sitting at the kitchen table looking dismal.

"They took the laptop and all our discs and USBs," he said miserably.

"Never mind," Eliza said, trying to be cheerful. "They won't find anything on them."

"But I was then asked were there any other computers in the building and I had to knock at the doors of the apartments and ask the women if they had a computer." His voice was low and barely audible.

"Oh God . . ." Alice felt so guilty for having brought this misery to this wonderful couple. "Were there any other computers?"

"Mary has one and needs it for her studies. She persuaded them to look at her USB on the spot and let her keep it, but she gave me a very odd look when she handed over the laptop."

"Don't worry about that." Alice was taking charge again. "Go into the sitting room and I'll bring you in a cup of tea. I have a nice lasagne in the freezer and we can have it for lunch."

She texted Nicola and asked if she could meet up with herself and Cassandra as soon as possible. They arranged for the following evening in Nicola's apartment.

"I'll bring the food," Alice said. She had plenty things in the freezer – after all, she had been practising.

Chapter 26

The following morning Eliza woke up with pains in her bones. She knew that this was the beginning of the side effects and that hair loss would probably follow soon. She couldn't stop herself crying. Hugo was just miserable.

Alice drove all the children to school. When she got back she looked in on Hugo and Eliza and it was clear that they wanted to be left alone. She called to Mary's apartment just to gauge her reaction to the events of the day before and found her fairly upbeat.

"They let me keep my memory stick," she said, "so I can continue my work at the college. Hugo looked really upset though."

"He is," Alice replied. "But they won't find anything."

"Of course they won't," Mary replied and Alice was happy that she appeared to mean it.

That evening Alice cooked a casserole in her apartment and brought half of it downstairs to Hugo and Eliza.

"I'm going to Nicola's this evening because I missed my appointment with her yesterday. Cassandra will be there as well. The girls are under strict instructions to go to bed at half eight and not to disturb you except there is a real emergency."

"That's grand," Eliza said. "Thanks for the dinner, Alice. It smells delicious."

Alice smiled at the compliment. "Hugo," she said, "would you look in on the girls at nine to make sure they're in bed? I haven't locked the door."

"Of course," was the reply and they all knew why she had made this request.

When Alice pulled into Nicola's apartment block Cassandra's car was already there. She took the food she had brought out of the jeep – a bowl of tomato soup, a quiche, the ingredients for a side salad and a French stick she had picked up on the way – and buzzed the bell. She felt drained and worried a bit about how she'd hold up for the next few weeks.

Nicola and Cassandra each gave her a warm hug and they all headed for the kitchen. Alice swung into action, putting the meal together. Cassandra told her in more detail about the things that had happened to her and Nicola in the run-up to the first court case. Alice was stunned.

"And you never mentioned it to me!" she gasped as she mixed a tasty dressing with the absentmindedness of an experienced chef.

"We didn't want to distress you further," Nicola replied. "And after the case was over it was obvious he hadn't succeeded in scuppering it so we just presumed he wouldn't try anything else for a while. And, of course, we had no real proof. Just part gut instinct and part logic."

"We'll have to think about the possibility of something untoward happening again," Cassandra mused.

"So do you think he was trying to damage me by discrediting Hugo?" Alice said.

"Yes – you brought your children to live with a pervert." Nicola's tone was grim. "Or alternatively he might be hoping that you might believe the accusation and leave, thereby removing an integral part of your support system."

"God, I can't believe this." Alice was taking the quiche out of the microwave. "Hugo knows, you say? We had better tell Eliza. Should I move out, do ye think? Eliza and Hugo have enough worries without this." There was a tone of panic in her voice.

She felt so secure at The Coven. She knew she'd have to move out eventually and even had plans to do so – but not now. Not before the court case. Not before she knew for certain if she had an apartment or not.

"I think we should tell Eliza tomorrow – she needs to know now," Nicola said.

"You're right," Cassandra agreed. "I'd say we should all be careful over the next few weeks."

"But we should clear it with Hugo first."

They ate their beautifully presented meal in near silence and they might as well have been eating sawdust for all the pleasure they got out of it.

"*Desperate Housewives* is on the TV. Why don't we watch it?" Nicola suggested as she cleared the table.

The other women burst out laughing.

"And not a housewife among us – desperate or otherwise!" Cassandra laughed.

They sat together on Nicola's three-seater couch, taking comfort from the physical closeness, and sipped their coffees.

Surprisingly they laughed a lot at Gabrielle's self-absorption, Susan's neuroses and Bree's obsession with perfection. They felt much more cheerful when the show was over.

"I'll call over to The Coven at around eleven tomorrow, Alice," said Nicola. "It will be an official visit for me and we will talk to Hugo and Eliza about who we think is behind this latest event."

"Thanks, Nicola. I feel awful. Responsible somehow!"

"You're not responsible," Nicola assured her, "but, as Cassandra said, we should all be careful from now on. Be aware of anyone or anything unusual."

"My God, it's like something out of a B movie!" Cassandra said.

"You have to be particularly careful, Cassandra, seeing as you work alone," Nicola said, choosing her words carefully. As far as she knew Alice didn't know what Cassandra did for a living and she didn't want to let that particular cat out of the bag unless Cassandra agreed.

Cassandra flashed her a grateful smile and she knew she had done the right thing.

"Don't worry about me," Cassandra said. "I'm always careful."

"Good," Nicola said but she was worried.

When Alice got back to The Coven, Eliza had already gone to bed and Hugo was reading in the large sitting room.

"Nicola's coming to see the three of us tomorrow morning," Alice said. "She'll be here around eleven."

"That'll be grand," Hugo said. The confiscation of his laptop didn't seem to be bothering him too much, at least on the surface.

Alice was weary as she let herself into her apartment. She looked in on the girls, kissed their sleeping faces, got into her own bed and wept bitter tears.

Chapter 27

Nicola arrived at The Coven to find Alice, Eliza and Hugo waiting for her in the kitchen.

"I have something to tell you," she said grimly.

"What's so serious?" Eliza asked, feeling that she'd had more than enough to deal with over the last few weeks.

Nicola looked at Hugo. "I believe Jack Madden might be behind the confiscation of your computer."

"The thought already occurred to me," Hugo responded. "But I've nothing to hide."

"So long as they don't plant anything." Nicola was still uneasy.

"Why would you say that?" Eliza queried.

"Because, at this stage I don't trust anybody," Nicola replied and she began to recount in detail what had happened to her and Cassandra before the court case.

Alice looked on dismally, wondering where it would all end.

Chief Superintendent Tom McEvoy had had a bad feeling in his gut since he got the instruction from the Taoiseach to seize Hugo Lynch's computer. He was not a political man but put a hurley in his hand and he came into his own. He was active in the local

GAA to the extent it could have been regarded as his religion but unlike many other people in the club he had no interest in or connections with any political party. That is not to say that there wasn't a lot of political gossip going on in the club bar on occasion – not that its purveyors would consider it to be gossip. 'Informed political debate,' was the order of the day. However, Tom McEvoy didn't like the Taoiseach. He knew he was one of the most popular politicians in the West, maybe even in the country, but he didn't trust him. He was too good to be true. Nobody was as perfect as Jack Madden purported to be. Everybody has at least one skeleton in his cupboard and Jack Madden was unlikely to be an exception to that rule. Tom had heard vague rumours – the kind that are so vague and unsubstantiated that they could be true. But he had to admit that the rumours were not widespread and did not often come into conversation.

He didn't like getting instructions based on anonymous tip-offs no matter what the source. In particular, there had never been a whiff of impropriety about Hugo Lynch despite his rather unusual living arrangements. Not even a speeding fine as far as he was aware. He felt the fact that the Taoiseach had passed this on to him and instructed him to act on it was an abuse of his power so he decided to speed things up. When Hugo's computer was delivered to him he rang a friend of his, Dónal Carey, in the Serious Crimes Squad in Dublin.

"Dónal, Tom McEvoy here. Can you do me a favour?"

"That very much depends on what it is. But fire ahead."

"I have been instructed to confiscate a computer from a man who I believe has nothing to hide. I have also been instructed to arrest him after we find child porn on his hard drive, but I believe that someone is trying to get at him."

"What do you want me to do?"

"Well, I was thinking of fast-tracking it to you today and asking you to have it examined immediately under your supervision."

"This is very cloak and dagger," his friend said. "What do you expect me to find?"

"Nothing! That's the point. I think this guy is being singled out but I haven't figured out why yet. In any case I want to send the computer for your attention and I want you to deal with it directly. I half-suspect that whoever instigated this could be planning to plant stuff on it."

"And you say you got the instruction from high up. How high?"

"Don't ask. I don't want to tell you who in case I get in trouble for this. It's as well that you know nothing."

"It's a good job I know and trust you so well. I wouldn't do this for anyone else."

"Thanks. If you find nothing have it sent back to me by the end of the week. If you find something, of course, it will have to be dealt with by the Serious Crime boys in the normal way."

"You don't ask for much!"

The remark was light-hearted and Tom McEvoy was glad he had a friend he could trust. "I owe you one!" he laughed.

"You owe me several and I will come and collect the next time I am in Galway," his friend replied and put down the phone.

Eliza had several doses of chemotherapy each week and it was really taking its toll. But for the fact she had read up on it and sort of knew what to expect, she would have thought she was going to die of exhaustion. The nausea and her hair loss added to her woes and when she looked in the mirror she hardly recognised herself, so old and drawn did she look. Everybody rallied round but they could feel that she was starting to get depressed.

"Even my eyelashes are falling out!" she wailed. She had the most gorgeous deep blue eyes which her unusually long lashes enhanced beautifully.

Alice was in her apartment when the Garda car drew up outside. She could see it from her apartment window. The garda, who looked quite senior, knocked on the main front door. Alice decided not to answer it. If he wanted to speak to anyone other than Hugo or Eliza he should look at the bell panel and ring the appropriate bell.

She knew Eliza and Hugo were due home from the hospital any minute and had prepared a light lunch in case they hadn't eaten, even though it was after three. They were picking up the girls at the school on the way back. Just as Alice was about to move away from the window the jeep swept into the drive.

The girls got out and ran to the front door. Eliza was moving slowly since the chemo had started to affect her bones and Hugo had to help her out of the car. He looked at the garda and hoped that the fact that it was such an obviously senior guy didn't mean bad news.

"Good afternoon," he said, ever the gentleman. He opened the front door. "Go up and see your mum," he said to the girls. "Please come in, Garda."

In the sitting room Eliza sank down on the sofa and just wished she could sleep.

"I am Chief Superintendent Tom McEvoy," the garda said when he and Hugo were also seated.

"I am Hugo Lynch and this is my wife Eliza – but I suppose you know that."

"Yes, sir. We confiscated two laptops from this premises earlier in the week on a tip-off. We found nothing and I am here to return the property. I have the two laptops in the car."

"Thank you, Garda," Hugo said amiably. "It will be good to have ours back. We use it a bit, both for business and to speak to our grandchildren on Skype. Mary will be pleased as well. You can leave hers with us. She is out at present, I think."

"I am at a loss to know why somebody would make up an accusation against you. You must have annoyed somebody very badly and that somebody must have connections at the very highest level."

The garda was speaking as if he were thinking out loud. It struck Hugo that, strictly speaking, he shouldn't have said that to a member of the public.

"Garda, I can't think how that could have occurred. We don't know people in high places. But I am glad to have my computer back. Would you like a cup of tea?"

"No, thank you, sir. Your wife looks tired. You should attend to her."

"Yes, I should."

"I hope you'll feel better soon, Mrs Lynch," said the garda and Eliza managed to muster a smile.

The two men went outside. Tom McEvoy went to his car, took out the laptops and handed them to Hugo.

"What did you say your name was again?" Hugo didn't quite know why he asked.

"Chief Superintendent Tom McEvoy. Call me any time."

"I hope I won't have the need but it's good to know that you would be available should anything else untoward happen."

"Good day, Mr Lynch."

"Good day, Chief Superintendent."

When Hugo came back into the room Eliza was asleep and Alice was coming down the stairs with lunch.

"I'll put on the kettle," Alice said.

"Thank you, Alice. I could do with a strong cup of real tea. I am so relieved to have my computer back and that they found nothing."

"Yes," Alice replied. "Even though we knew that you had nothing to hide, it was still a worry. Particularly after what Nicola said about the possibility of planting evidence."

"Yes, but in general the Garda are a trustworthy bunch, thank God," Hugo said and he sat on the sofa and held the hand of his sleeping wife.

Chapter 28

Jack Madden was decidedly disgruntled. When Hugo Lynch's computer was confiscated he was in Strasbourg. It wasn't an ideal time but he couldn't exactly have given his timetable or announced his plans to Chief Superintendent McEvoy and instructed him to confiscate the thing at a time when he was in the country. Initially he didn't worry much about it. When he got home he would immediately contact his friend in the Serious Crime Division and ensure that something unsavoury was found on the hard drive. He thanked God (or someone up there) that the Garda was like any bureaucracy and that in general they moved with all the alacrity of a geriatric sloth. He hadn't bargained for a Superintendent who had a very refined sense of right and wrong and who didn't automatically think that, because an instruction came from the Taoiseach, it was in order. It had never occurred to him that anyone would speed up the enquiry. Indeed, it wasn't until he got back from Strasbourg that he found out that the computer was back in Galway and that nothing had been found. He was spitting nails.

His intention had been that when Hugo was arrested there would be a question-mark over the safety of the women and children and that they would have to be moved to other quarters. Alice and the girls, along with the other occupants, would have to move and hopefully would just go back to live with her parents and forget this business about the apartment. Even if Alice stayed in contact with Hugo and Eliza Lynch (he had taken to calling them The Odd Couple in his head) they would have a major worry of their own and wouldn't be in much of a position to support her.

Apart from being annoyed, he couldn't figure it out. How the hell did the computer get examined within a few days of its confiscation? There was something going on and it made him uneasy.

Meanwhile the court case was coming up and, along with his wish to avoid publicity, Jack Madden was anxious for it to go his way. He presumed that nobody would believe Alice that he was the father of her children but the matter of the apartment could be tricky. He certainly did not want Alice getting such a valuable asset. Who did she think she was? Hadn't she got enough already from him? The past twelve years had been materially very good for her and unless she was completely naïve she must have known that it was not a permanent arrangement. But then again it was her child-like innocence and trust that had made her so attractive in the first place. Jack Madden's thoughts flitted momentarily to the first day that Alice had come to work as his au pair.

But he was a man not prone to sentimentality and he had a few surprises in store for Alice's other friends. But the outcome was by no means a foregone conclusion. His legal team was not optimistic about the chances of Tower Properties holding on to the apartment. He got some comfort from the fact that the judge had said the situation was complicated but his reference to rights under more recent legislation had rattled him. While they were still looking for a loophole, they were promising nothing and they hadn't worked out yet if it was possible for the case to be heard in his absence, thereby hopefully avoiding publicity unless some eagle-eyed hack from the *Clare Champion* was in court.

Of course, he hadn't told Rosemary about the case. Indeed she didn't even know that Tower Properties Ltd., a company of which she was a director, owned a property on Taylors Hill. If it got out the tabloids might start digging and the opposition would have a field day. That social worker hadn't tried to contact him for months and rather than being happy about that he felt she had something up her sleeve. He didn't know what but it was like waiting for the second shoe to drop.

To top it all, some gobshite of a developer had got on the phone to him that morning and threatened to report him to the Tribunals if he didn't at least try and use his influence with one of the major banks not to force a liquidation. Apparently back in the nineties this guy had given Jack a hefty sum of money in exchange for a vote on the rezoning of land when he was a County Councillor. Jack had absolutely no recollection of it but of course that was not the type of payment that went through the books so he couldn't be one hundred per cent certain that it never happened; in fact, it probably did, even if it couldn't be proved. But mud sticks in these situations and what was to stop someone who could prove that he took money from coming out of the woodwork? It never failed to amaze Jack Madden how nasty people could be, even people he had helped significantly.

There was no end to the worry. There were even rumblings of discontent within the party. Just rumblings! No immediate talk of a heave but if he didn't play his cards right these rumblings could escalate into a full-blown vote of no confidence so he had to be sure not to put a foot wrong there either. If he could go into the next election, which would probably be within the next twelve months, as leader, he'd be home and dry.

On the bright side Rosemary had been wonderful in all of this. He knew he had chosen well when he had decided to marry her. She was a very beautiful young woman, of good political pedigree, who was more than willing to play the part of the politician's wife. She had worked as an air stewardess so was well used to dealing with difficult situations and she had moved in all the right circles. The fact that she spoke French and German fluently was no burden and she also spoke Irish with the fluency of a native speaker which made her a very good canvasser in the Gaeltacht when election time came around. Rosemary had given up her job when she became pregnant with their first child, Caoimhe, and had never had any regrets as far as he could tell.

Her job for nearly twenty years was as a wife and mother and he really respected her for that. Yes, she was a great woman and, yes, he loved her dearly – not in the hearts and flowers way he had once loved Alice or in the volcanic-eruption way he had loved the Spanish MEP, Francesca Olazabal – more in the way you'd love a family retainer – with a comfortable affection where he always knew where he stood.

Yes, Rosemary was really great! After the late Taoiseach's death there were comings and goings to their house in Monkstown at all hours of the day and night. Rosemary served up all that was required, whether it was just a cup of tea or a four-course dinner. She did it with elegance and aplomb. Of course she had staff in the kitchen but she always served the guests herself and was a most gracious hostess. A real touch of class was Rosemary and she wanted to be the Taoiseach's wife just as much as Jack Madden wanted to be Taoiseach so all worked well on the home front. If he could get over the few hiccups about which Rosemary knew nothing, all would be well.

Alice was trying unsuccessfully not to worry about the impending case but there was one thing to be cheerful about. She had put a proposition to the whizz-kid hotel manager when he rang her to arrange for her to pick up her last cheque and again he was impressed. She had proposed to provide the desserts for all of their special-occasion catering – not the run-of-the-mill stuff but weddings, corporate events and other special occasions. That way the hotel could get a reputation for these events and she would not be working full time. She could arrange her work fairly easily around her family commitments – at least until this whole uncertainty about their future was sorted out.

"When could you start?" Whizz Kid asked her.

"How about immediately?" she replied, hoping in her heart that he wouldn't have any special occasion in the near future.

"Great, I can give you a trial run. We have a corporate function on Thursday night and you could provide 200 mixed desserts for that. I can judge from the reaction if it is worth continuing."

"What type of people will be attending?"

"Internal auditors. A stodgy bunch but they like their food and can be very picky about each course. They are not the easiest to please. Can you do it?"

"Of course I can," Alice replied.

After the call she raced upstairs and looked up the few recipe books she had bought since the eviction. She would provide about ten different desserts and suggest that the hotel use dessert trolleys. She knew that they probably wouldn't be too happy to do this but it was the simplest if she was to provide such a variety. Two hundred wasn't too bad and if she picked the desserts carefully she could prepare at least half of them a day or two in advance. She chose the desserts, mixing the traditional and the modern. She weighed up whether apple pie would be too traditional or lemon pots too far out and in the end she decided to include both. She included her granny's sherry trifle which was like no other, a blackberry mousse which she had cooked for the first time over the Christmas period and a delicious chocolate sorbet which always went down well – with Jack Madden in any case, so she crossed her fingers that it would go down well with these auditors as well. It didn't take her long to decide on the ten desserts. She took a few risks choosing bread and butter pudding for the traditionalists and a chocolate crème brulé for the more adventurous. She decided not to try anything she hadn't made before and she knew that she could produce all of the desserts to standard. Also by deciding on ten different ones, she had only to make twenty of each, thus the proportions would not be too intimidating.

She was not used to large numbers but she was going to do this. She had the future to think of and Nicola had been right – no matter what the result of this case she would be in a new phase of her life and that would almost definitely involve earning a living to provide for herself and her girls. Thank God for Eliza's enormous kitchen, she thought to herself. She was still cooking for everybody and intended to continue to do it for some time to come, because after her chemotherapy Eliza would have to undergo radiotherapy and this could mean that she would be very tired until well after the treatment was completed. Eliza was definitely feeling the strain and Alice wanted to help ease that as much as she could.

She borrowed the jeep from Hugo the next day and drove all the children into school. She then went to McCambridge's and bought the more unusual ingredients for her desserts and then to The Vineyard to get some special liqueurs. She had a significant slush fund left after her work before Christmas and she knew she could make another tidy profit from this venture if it worked. The only thing that concerned her was that she was on a sort of a trial. If these desserts weren't perfect it was unlikely she would be asked to do it again – but that's business, she said to herself, and Alice the entrepreneur was once again about to set out her stall.

Eliza and Hugo watched Alice wide-eyed. She worked diligently and with great organisation. This was the first time she had to work to such a short time-line. On the Thursday she delivered all the desserts at two o'clock. She borrowed cool boxes from Eliza's kitchen and left instructions with the hotel staff on how to keep the desserts up to standard and the best way to serve them. Afterwards she collected the girls from school herself.

"You are an amazing young woman," Hugo said to her as they sipped hot chocolate in the large kitchen.

"Where there's a will there's a way," Alice said grimly. "Let's hope that they like them now."

"Of course they will," Hugo replied. "How could they not?"

"You are so kind, Hugo. You know I couldn't have done this without you and Eliza."

"Mum, can you help me with my reading?" Orla called. "I really find it very hard today."

Alice suspected that she was just looking for attention from her mother who had been somewhat distracted of late, so she went upstairs with her daughter and they settled down on the sofa to read the required piece. Orla snuggled into Alice as she read the piece perfectly and Alice hoped that soon she would not be so worried and would be able to pay the children the quality of attention that they so deserved.

Chapter 29

Alice's new venture into business was a welcome distraction, not to mention a good little earner. The first group for whom Alice had made the desserts – the picky bunch of internal auditors – had been fulsome in their praise and indicated that their conference would be held at this hotel the following year "if only for the desserts," according to the very happy hotel manager.

"One of them described your blackberry mousse as orgasmic which I thought was a bit gross." But he couldn't have been more pleased.

"Well, if the quality of the rest of your service is as good as my desserts," Alice grinned, "you deserve the business."

He laughed out loud. "God, you're so modest!" He handed her a cheque. "But, seriously, do you think you could do starters as well?"

"Not just now," she replied. "I have another commitment which is quite time-consuming. I may consider it in a month or two." She was delighted to be asked but there was no way she could commit to such an undertaking at this time.

Nicola was busy but not with Alice's case. In fact there was nothing she could do about Alice except provide her with emotional support when that was needed. Her main function as a social worker was to look after the welfare of the children but in this case she was well aware that the best way to do that was to look after the emotional welfare of the mother. There was no doubt that the children were being very well cared for by their mother but if Alice became too stressed that would show and the children would undoubtedly be upset. She was relieved to see that Alice was holding up well under the stress and demands of her new business.

"You must be very proud of yourself," she said to Alice one day over lunch. "You've come such a long way since October."

"I'd be proud if I wasn't so scared. I just wish this was all over and then I will be able to be proud."

"It will be soon, Alice. You're doing exceptionally well in the circumstances."

"I know, but that doesn't stop me from being scared," Alice said and they both sipped their coffee thoughtfully.

As soon as Nicola returned to her office she rang Séamus.

"Any news about the case?" she enquired.

"Not much really. It looks as if Jack Madden may be subpoenaed by our side."

"God, poor Alice! I don't know how she will take that."

"Don't tell her until we're sure. We'll have to have at least one meeting with the barrister in advance of the hearing. It may be time enough to tell her then."

"I suppose so," Nicola agreed.

"You and Cassandra will definitely be called as witnesses by our side which also means ye may be cross-examined by the other side and they will attempt to discredit you both, so be ready for that."

"I have been in court a few times but usually just to give a report. While in some cases it was a bit adversarial, it didn't feel as bad as I think this will be."

"Well, I'd say that your experience will stand to you. I think we should meet up on the 7th of February. We should be able to make last-minute arrangements then."

"Okay – you arrange it and when it is confirmed I will tell the others."

Nicola put down the phone, feeling most apprehensive.

Nicola and Alice arrived together for the meeting with the barrister, Cassandra arriving a few minutes later. Séamus was also in the office.

Gerard Murphy, welcomed them and explained what they could expect the following week. He was dressed in a pinstriped suit, which though typical of the type of attire worn by his colleagues didn't in any way make him look older, and the women were once again struck by his apparent youth.

"It is likely that you will all be asked to take the stand," he explained. "Alice will probably be asked most questions and Cassandra will be asked to confirm that Alice was resident at the Lady Gregory Court for twelve years. Nicola, you may be asked about your conversation with Jack Madden."

"What exactly will I be asked?" Alice enquired.

"Well, I will ask you questions about your residence in Lady Gregory Court. I can give you a tentative list of questions but I may be forced to diverge from them a bit. Then, of course, the opposition will get a chance to cross-examine and you may find that difficult. They will try and trip you up and discredit you."

"Oh God!" Alice moaned.

"Don't worry about it." The lawyer was positively cheerful. "Just tell the truth. I feel we have a very good case and I have subpoenaed Jack Madden."

Alice's jaw dropped. "What does that mean?" she whispered.

"It means he will be there and I will cross-examine him."

"Gosh, I sort of thought that he would let his legal team appear for him again this time," Alice murmured.

"Probably he would prefer to do that but if he just swore an affidavit I would have no opportunity to question him and I think it is better that he is there."

"I had hoped to avoid publicity in this case," Nicola said. "I think if there is no publicity I have a better chance of getting support for Alice's children after this is all over. I would be able to use my knowledge of his relationship as a sort of lever or a bargaining tool."

"I can't be sure that there will be no publicity but this is the most boring type of court – no smoking gun or dripping knife. And, as these cases go, there is very little in dispute: she did occupy the house as if it was her own for twelve years and she hadn't as far as we can ascertain the permission of the owner. It is good that it is not a piece of land with a history, but a fairly modern apartment in a fairly anonymous location. There is no history of ownership here. This apartment had not been in anybody's family for generations. But the judge is right and even in a case where it appears simple, legal complications can pop up that we weren't expecting."

"So you're saying there will be no publicity?" Cassandra butted in.

"I'd be hoping so. I don't think that Jack Madden will exactly seek it and unless an eagle-eyed court clerk realises in advance that the Jack Madden in question, or John Madden as he will be referred to in court, is the Taoiseach and tips off the papers, this could be over and done within an hour or two. Even though every court case, with the exception of family law, is a public hearing, the truth is that it is rare for anyone other than the interested parties to attend cases such as this."

Nicola was probably the only one in the room to notice that the idea of publicity did not appeal to Cassandra either but she knew her friend was willing to take the risk to ensure that Alice and her children got what they were entitled to.

Chapter 30

That evening Cassandra rang Eliza and offered to take her shopping for wigs and headgear the next day. Eliza was delighted. They set out the following morning with strict instructions from Hugo not to tire Eliza out too much. They were in high spirits. Cassandra knew exactly where to go. They found some excellent real-hair wigs exactly like Eliza's hair and had them styled appropriately. They also found a really elegant turban which Eliza could wear when she didn't have time to style her wig or if she simply didn't feel like putting it on and then they went to the beautician's counter at Brown Thomas for false eyelashes.

"I never thought of that," Eliza gasped. "It's a really great idea."

"They'll do the trick until your own grow back and I will show you how to apply them. We can do some work on your eyebrows as well and you will feel your usual glamorous self."

"I'm not sure about 'glamorous' but it will certainly be a great improvement." Eliza was delighted and she bought herself a very elegant dress for good measure.

When they got back to The Coven they showed Hugo their purchases and Cassandra said to Eliza that she would do her nails and in about fifteen minutes she had Eliza's finger and toenails buffed, polished and varnished.

"I rarely have felt so pampered," Eliza said. "My nails have never been so elegant."

"Well, it's about time you got pampered a bit and for the next few weeks you won't be damaging your nails with housework so this is an ideal opportunity to get them done."

"Thank you so much, Cassandra. I really enjoyed this morning."

Cassandra was glad that she could be of service.

Cassandra was meeting the man she was in love with, Luke, that evening. He would be coming to her apartment as usual and she had arranged to have dinner delivered from Les Jumelles. They had on occasion dined there because she really liked it but it was a bit risky for him because it was so central and it was more likely he could accidentally bump into someone he knew. So Cassandra chose the safer option of dining *chez elle*. She hadn't seen him for quite a while because his wife's condition had deteriorated a bit and he had felt honour bound not to try and get away while things were so difficult for her. But in recent weeks she was much improved so she had actually encouraged him to take a break and he had contacted Cassandra. Dinner had been delivered and was being kept warm in the oven when there was a light tap on her door. She hadn't heard the bell so she was a bit surprised but the doorman must have let Luke into the building.

Cassandra opened the door wide and was horrified to discover that her visitor was not Luke. She felt a fist hit her face with such force that she fell backwards to the floor. She tried to get up but was kicked in her abdomen so hard that she was completely breathless. She also realised with horror that she had not logged onto her security system. With Luke she was never nervous and she had not bargained for this.

"Well, well. If it isn't Miss Smarty Pants!" The leering sneering voice came out of the haze but she recognised it. "I didn't realise it was you when I was asked to do this special job, but it's certainly a bonus."

Cassandra groaned. The pain in her face was excruciating and she felt a few of her teeth were loose. If she got another blow to her face she felt sure her teeth would come out. But that was not the only reason she groaned. She had recognised the assailant. She had met him in a bar a few years earlier with a view to his becoming a client but he had made her so nervous, telling her what he wanted to do to her and what he liked from his women, that she decided to leave. He was undoubtedly very annoyed and sent her several abusive emails and texts for several months after that. She had escaped because she had a taxi on call that she could just get into when she left the bar.

She rolled over onto her back and attempted to get up but he put his foot on her abdomen and kept her down.

"What do you want?" she gasped.

"You have enemies in very high places and I was asked to take on this job as a sideline from my normal line of work which is knocking off undesirables for other undesirables." He was smug.

Cassandra's heart lurched. She didn't know what exactly he meant but even in her dazed state she could guess. She tried to move again but her assailant knelt down beside her and expertly looped a sort of pliable plastic rope around her throat.

"I could have decided to just shoot you," he said, showing her a small handgun with a silencer, "but I think it would be more fun using this." He took a long-bladed sharp knife from a sheath strapped to his leg.

Cassandra tried to scream but the noose was too tight and no sound came out. He had her completely immobilised.

"I think I will do this nice and slow. How about some light scarring to the face? That would ensure that you wouldn't ever work again."

Cassandra shuddered.

"Not that you will be working anyway because you'll be dead. But I think it might be fun to watch the blood trickling into your mouth and eyes." He held the knife close to her cheek and Cassandra froze.

"I thought about having sex with you after I tie you up but I wouldn't touch a slut like you – particularly a stuck-up one. Who the hell do you think you are, not letting me have one when I was offering to pay you?"

Cassandra was crying silently. She could do nothing else.

"Imagine you, a paid slut, deciding that you were too good for me. Well, I wouldn't have you even if you paid me! But I am being paid handsomely for this and I have been given carte blanche about how I go about it – but even still I wouldn't touch you – not in that way anyway."

He moved away a little as if he was thinking about what to do next.

"Yes, this will be nice and slow and when I'm finished I might eat that very nice dinner I can smell. Were you preparing it for your next client?"

She saw that he was wearing latex gloves like a doctor or a vet would. She wondered how long it would take. She hoped that she would fall into unconsciousness. For the first time in years she prayed. She didn't know who she was praying to but all the prayers of her childhood came flooding back to her.

He came towards her again and held the knife to her throat.

She struggled. He pulled the cord around her neck so tight that she was gasping for breath. She thought she was going to die but just as she thought she was blacking out he let it go. She knew that he wanted to kill her slowly and that if she continued to just lie there that is exactly what he would do. He came closer to her again and kicked her in the stomach just because he could. She gasped in pain but didn't react. She didn't cry out. In any case it was likely she wouldn't be heard even if she did. Since Alice had left her apartment there was no one on her floor. She decided then she would fight. It was better to die fighting than to lie there compliantly and let him kill her slowly.

The next time he bent down over her she was ready. She waited until he was sufficiently close to her and kneed him in the groin. Her strength came from rage. The blow wasn't as effective as she would have liked but he yelled and fell back momentarily. It gave her the opportunity to get to her feet. She still had the rope around her neck but her hands were free. So she loosened the rope and yelled for help at the top of her voice. She had little hope of help but she knew that the fact that she shouted would perhaps make him nervous. She was right. He punched her hard in the face again and she fell back.

As she was falling she heard a knock on the door.

Luke! She had forgotten about him.

"*Help!*" she roared with all her strength. "*Please help me!*"

Her assailant was furious. He looked around to see if there was an escape route and with that the door burst open and Luke exploded into the room. He took one look around him and grabbed the still dazed thug and punched him hard before kneeing him in the groin – the second time that evening for the recipient but this time it had the desired effect and he fell to the floor.

"My God, who is that and where is the doorman?" Luke asked Cassandra.

"He said he was paid to kill me," Cassandra whimpered. "I don't know where the doorman is. Isn't he downstairs?" She was still groggy from the punches.

"No, not a sign – but I used the code you gave me and came up unannounced."

"He has a gun. I think it's in his pocket. Find it and then phone the Gardaí."

Just as Luke found the gun the thug came around, got unsteadily to his feet and just stumbled out the door.

"We'll let him go," Luke said. "I'll call an ambulance for you and then the Gardaí. They may catch up with him later."

The ambulance came in double-quick time – not so the Gardaí. So Luke turned off the oven and locked up and was about to follow the ambulance to the hospital in his own car when the Gardaí finally turned up. Luke explained what had happened and the Gardaí said that they would follow them to the hospital and take statements.

Luke arrived at the hospital to find that the medical team was extremely concerned about Cassandra. First examination showed that she had several loose teeth, a broken cheekbone, several cracked ribs, severe bruising to her neck, her stomach and her legs and they couldn't be sure that there was no internal damage.

"I really don't want to involve you in this," Cassandra said to Luke, speaking with great difficulty.

"I'm involved whether you like it or not," Luke said.

"There are things I can't explain," she said. "What time is it?"

It seemed like a life-time since she had been happily preparing for her meeting with Luke.

"Eight thirty."

"Good," Cassandra replied. "I want you to ring Nicola McCarthy and tell her that I am in the hospital and ask her to come and see me as soon as she can. I think you should go home then."

"But I can't go home and leave you in this state!"

"You must," she said, grimacing with pain. "You have other responsibilities. Nicola will come and we will decide what we should do next. Some time I may be able to explain all of this to you but not yet. Please ring Nicola."

Luke did what she asked and reluctantly left her in the care of the medical staff.

Nicola was there within thirty minutes. She was horrified when she saw Cassandra's bruised face. The A&E was very busy but Cassandra got excellent treatment. In between tests and questions Cassandra explained to Nicola what had happened.

"You must come and stay with me," Nicola insisted.

"Absolutely not," Cassandra said, barely able to pronounce the words due to facial swelling. "It's far too dangerous and we don't know where he will strike next."

"In any case," a nurse said brightly, "she isn't going anywhere tonight. We must keep her in for observation. After such a beating she could have internal bleeding and she will probably be kept in for twenty-four or even forty-eight hours."

"That gives us time to figure out what is best to do in the circumstances," Nicola mused. "That is presuming they don't find anything more sinister when they do the other tests on you."

"Be careful yourself and watch your back," Cassandra said as Nicola left.

Chapter 31

Nicola rang Séamus but he was on the train from Dublin and wouldn't be in for at least an hour. She rang Hugo. She needed someone with a clear head and he was the best she could think of.

"Why don't you come out and we can have a chat?" Hugo said, even without her having to explain about Cassandra. He knew instinctively that if she was ringing him at night it must be something serious.

"To be honest, I don't want to bump into Alice," Nicola replied.

"If you wait until around nine she will have put the girls to bed and generally she remains in her apartment after that. Eliza is about to go to the bed as well so it will be just the two of us."

"Okay," Nicola agreed.

She went down to the Prom in her car and looked out over the bay in the direction of Ballyvaughan. It was a clear night and she could make out the lights of the village which was near the Clare coast. She was scared and cold and was looking forward to sitting in the kitchen of The Coven.

She arrived to find Hugo making two cups of hot chocolate and buttering some of Alice's scones. They sat at the kitchen table and she gratefully began to sip the hot drink.

"Right – tell me what's the matter," Hugo said, expecting that it would be serious – but he hadn't expected the story which Nicola told him that night.

"This is the work of Jack Madden, without a doubt," Nicola concluded.

"I know," Hugo agreed, not sure what to do next.

"What worries me is that none of us is safe now. When he hears that Cassandra is still alive I think he may try and go after one or all of the rest of us. He seems to be desperate to scupper the court case and incapacitating the witnesses is probably his only option."

"You're right," Hugo replied. "But I have an idea."

"I'm glad you do because I have no idea where to go from here."

"I'll ring Chief Superintendent Tom McEvoy and ask his assistance. He knew that there was something odd about my computer being confiscated and I know that made him uncomfortable. I think he would help us if we asked."

"I hope so."

"In the meantime you can stay in the vacant apartment tonight and we can make more definite decisions tomorrow. Think up a feasible story for Alice in the morning. I don't think she could deal with the truth at this point." Hugo was grim.

"Right. When do you think you can get hold of the Super?"

"I'll keep trying until I get him. I presume that Cassandra is safe in the hospital?"

"Unless this country has gone to the dogs altogether, I think she is."

Chief Superintendent Tom McEvoy was about to leave the station to go home when he got the call from Hugo Lynch. Somehow he wasn't surprised.

"I'm on my way home," he said. "I'll call out. Your house is on my way."

"That's very kind of you," said Hugo.

"All in a day's work," Tom McEvoy said and they both knew that strictly speaking it wasn't.

Hugo felt like he'd been making tea or hot chocolate all evening. He had just brewed up again when the Chief Superintendent's car drew up outside. He was a large broad man with an air of authority and confidence and that was just what Hugo needed at that time.

Hugo began tentatively. "I really don't know how to say this but I had the feeling that you weren't happy to have confiscated my computer last week and I am guessing you got the instruction from a very unusual source."

"Yes," the Chief Superintendent answered.

"Am I right in guessing it came from the Taoiseach's office?" Nicola enquired, knowing the answer before she heard the reply.

"Not his office. He rang me himself. I smelled a rat immediately but I couldn't refuse the Taoiseach. How did you know?"

"Can you assure us that this conversation is confidential?" Nicola asked.

"Of course," the Chief Superintendent replied and so Nicola told him the whole story.

"The most recent thing," she concluded, "is that we believe that he took out a contract on Cassandra Grey, Alice's former neighbour. The thug who attacked her told her that he was going to kill her and that she had enemies in very high places. He broke her cheekbone, several of her ribs, throttled her, knocked out some of her teeth and she has severe bruising to her abdomen and legs. He is an appalling sadist and obviously enjoyed his job. Fortunately he was interrupted. But he got away."

"When is the case coming up?" the Super enquired.

"On Monday. I'm not sure any of us is safe between now and then." Nicola was terrified at this point.

"I was thinking that Nicola and Cassandra could stay here until after Monday," Hugo said.

"But that would put you and Eliza in danger," Nicola said, "and so far he doesn't seem to have aimed anything at you – except for the computer business, of course."

"I think I can arrange security around the clock here until after the court case," said Tom. "It would be cheaper and more effective than arranging security for all of you at different locations. And if you like, Nicola, I will go with you now to your apartment and you can pick up as much as you need for the next few days."

"That would be excellent." Hugo was relieved. "Ideally we would like the security to appear low key. We would like that the children and the other tenants are not aware of it."

"I think we can arrange that. You will see it but passers-by who are unaware of it in all probability won't notice it."

"It's a good job we have a vacant apartment," Hugo said.

"I will call to the hospital tomorrow to assure Cassandra that all is well," the Chief Superintendent said. "In any case I have a valid reason to call to discuss the assault with her. It will take me till tomorrow to arrange the security but I should have it in place by about 10 a.m. I don't think anything else will happen between now and then. Jack Madden will not realise that his murder attempt has failed until the morning and unless he is really on the ball he wouldn't have an opportunity to arrange anything else."

For a few minutes the three of them sat in silence, taking in the enormity of the situation. Here they were calmly discussing the fact that the leader of the country appeared to have tried to murder one of their friends – perhaps twice.

It was three nights before the court date.

Tom McEvoy visited Cassandra early the following morning. Because he was a garda the hospital allowed him in even though they had not completed their tests on the patient. He was horrified at what he saw. The woman looked as if she had been in a head-on car crash. Her face was completely swollen and was purple in colour. He could also see the ligature mark on her neck.

"Hugo Lynch has invited you and Nicola McCarthy to stay at his home for as long as is required and I have arranged security for the house," he said in a whisper.

"That's very kind of Hugo but I can't put him through that. They may try again."

"You have no option but to stay with them or in here. I can't guarantee your safety if you don't."

"But I have nothing except the clothes I came here in. I haven't my phone, my purse – anything of a personal nature," Cassandra's diction was still not clear.

"I can arrange for two female gardaí in plain clothes to go to your apartment and get all that you require. If you give them the code they'll go in and if they are stopped they'll say that they are your sisters. We'll have them under surveillance all the time. We can arrange any repairs to secure the place as well, if that turns out to be necessary."

"Do you know what I do for a living?" Cassandra asked, afraid that if he knew he might be less willing to offer her this protection.

"I have a good idea. It's not for me to judge. My job is to keep you and the others involved in this situation safe." He kept his voice low as he spoke. He didn't need some nosey nurse getting wind of what was going on and going to the papers. Nicola had explained to him her plans for after the case – if it was successful – for getting Alice what was due to her and the girls. She didn't want anything to happen that might give Jack Madden any advance warning about what was to come.

"They are letting me home today," Cassandra said. "They think that there is no really serious damage done but I'm to have complete bed rest for the next week."

"Well, take their advice and you should make a good recovery."

"I'm going to court on Monday. I don't care if it kills me and God knows it may. That creep is not going to get away with what he did to Alice and those girls."

"I understand your feelings. We will try and make the journey to Ennis as comfortable as possible. I'll be going myself as an observer. It's a public hearing."

"What do you think that will do to your career if Jack Madden sees you?"

"I don't think he knows me to see and I will be in civvies but in any case I am willing to take my chances."

Cassandra smiled even though it hurt her face.

Nicola went to work from The Coven the next day. They told Alice that Cassandra had been assaulted in the street the evening before and that she would be coming to stay at The Coven while she recovered. They would all go to Ennis together. She didn't know as yet just how serious the assault had been and they decided not to tell her who they thought was behind it.

The day was as normal as could have been expected. Alice didn't seem to notice the unmarked cars that were around the area during the day.

Hugo, Eliza and Alice were shocked when they saw Cassandra. Tom McEvoy had picked her up at the hospital and the nurses had given her instructions not to get out of bed except to use the bathroom for the next four days. They all knew that she would ignore that instruction. But she did gratefully accept their help. Alice had to liquidise all her food since it was nigh impossible for Cassandra to chew anything due to her facial fracture.

Chapter 32

The Coven was a hive of activity on the 14th of February. Nicola, who was sharing an apartment with Cassandra, was woken by her mobile phone at seven. Her heart lurched. Who could be ringing her so early? She had an unspoken agreement with friends and relations that they didn't ring each other before eight or after midnight unless it was really urgent.

It was a blocked number and when she answered it she was treated to a pretty tuneless rendition of "I Just Called to Say I Love You".

"You clown!" she laughed. "You nearly gave me a heart attack."

"God, I knew my singing was bad but I expected a better reception than that! Should I try 'All You Need is Love'?" Séamus was completely unabashed.

"I actually forgot what day it is. It was a lovely thought. But I have been so preoccupied that I didn't even get you a card."

"Never mind! We can have dinner tonight if this case goes alright. What time are ye setting out?"

"About half past eight, I think. The Chief Superintendent is taking us."

"He's a brave man. I'd say that will be enough to grind his career to a halt."

"That doesn't seem to bother him. To be honest, Cassandra and I feel very safe with him and Alice doesn't know who he is at all. So it's a fairly good arrangement."

"I suppose so. And it's probably best that none of you use your own car."

"Yes – especially after what happened to Cassandra the last time."

"How is Cassandra this morning?"

"I haven't spoken to her yet. You woke me up, remember! I had better go. See you down there."

"Okay. See you. And I meant it, you know."

"You meant what?"

"That I just called to say I love you."

"Clown," Nicola replied and ended the call smiling.

Cassandra still looked awful. Her face was purple. She looked frail but thankfully her diction had improved.

"I wonder could we go for an adjournment?" Nicola mused.

"Not on your life," Cassandra said through swollen lips. "This is our opportunity to nail Jack Madden and I won't wait a moment longer than is necessary. I'd say Alice wouldn't want to adjourn either. After all, this is her life!"

"I suppose you're right. Do you need help dressing?"

"If you could help me into the shower and maybe drying off, I'd be glad. Every time I move my torso it hurts. Talking isn't exactly fun either but you can't help me with that."

When Cassandra and Nicola arrived down to the kitchen Hugo was there making porridge.

"Alice is getting breakfast for the girls and then I will take them to school," he informed them while serving up two piping hot bowls of porridge, along with generous servings of blueberries.

"Thanks, Hugo," Nicola said. "We're very grateful. We'd better try to stay out of view of the girls. They may twig that something is up if they see us both here so early in the morning, particularly with Cassandra in the state she is in."

229

"Yes, I'll leave with them at about quarter past eight. Tom should be here around then and hopefully all of you will be ready to roll."

Cassandra carefully tasted the porridge. It was delicious and just the right consistency for someone who couldn't chew.

"Are you alright, Cassandra?" Hugo enquired. "Are you sure you can do this today?"

"I'm fine. I can do it," Cassandra replied with a weak grin. "I may just collapse into my bed when it is all over but I'll be able to hold out until then."

"You're very brave," was all Hugo could say and Nicola agreed with him silently.

Hugo left them to their own devices when the time came to take the girls to school and they watched through the window as the two girls skipped beside him to the jeep. He was a treasure – both women knew it and were so happy that he was there for all of them at this time.

They noticed that a black people-carrier passed Hugo in the drive and they held their breath until they saw Tom McEvoy emerge. Just as they were about to open the front door to him Alice came down the stairs in the same pink suit she had worn at the last court hearing. Nicola again thought how appropriate it was but Alice had lost her child-like innocence in the last few months and now she looked like a woman and a mother who had serious worries for the future of her children.

Tom McEvoy had borrowed his sister's people-carrier. It had the dual advantage that it was not recognisable as his to any gardaí or court officials in Ennis that might know him but also he could put down the seats to form a sort of bed for Cassandra so that she could lie down during the journey, thereby taking the strain off her fractured ribs. He even had a rug to put over her in case she was tired and wanted to sleep. Alice and Nicola sat in the other seats and they began their journey.

Whether it was the presence of a man or whether they knew that this was a far more serious and far-reaching case than the first, nobody suggested putting on a CD. They listened to

Morning Ireland in virtual silence and after the nine o'clock news Tom tuned into Lyric FM without consulting the women.

They turned into the car park in the courthouse to find it almost full – much busier than the first time they were there.

"No ministerial cars, as far as I can see," Nicola said quietly. "He mustn't be here yet."

"That's not really an indication of anything. I'm not using my own car," Tom replied. "He'd be mad to drive in here in a state car. My guess is that he will be in an anonymous car belonging to one of his minions and he is hoping that this case will not attract media attention – and he just might get away with it."

"I'd say he came in that clapped-out Toyota over there," Cassandra said and they all laughed, despite how much it pained Cassandra to do so.

"Something has attracted media attention," Nicola said as she was getting out of the car. "Look at the cluster of people at the doorway. At least one of them has a microphone and I think I recognise a guy from the *Irish Times*."

"Oh, God," Alice murmured.

"Ignore them," Tom said. "There may be a murder or something being tried today. Walk straight by them. We don't want them to take an interest in us."

Cassandra leaned heavily on the arm of the Superintendent as they walked up the steps into the foyer of the courthouse and immediately Alice's counsel was at her side.

"We were on first, but I requested an adjournment till this afternoon. The other side have intimated that they might be willing to settle. I need the three of you to come with me immediately." He looked at Tom and asked, "Who are you?"

"Just a friend," Tom replied.

"You can go wherever you like but the women must follow me."

In a gallant gesture he offered Cassandra his arm. She took it gratefully and they walked slowly down the stairway into the basement where Gerard Murphy opened the door of one of several meeting rooms.

Séamus was already in the room as was Jack Madden and his legal team. It was a characterless room. There was an oblong table and eight chairs, like in a conference room. Gerard indicated to them where to sit, putting Alice as far away as was physically possible from Jack Madden. Alice was beside herself with anxiety. Nicola and Cassandra were also nervous at this turn of events. They didn't expect to have to deal with the situation in this way.

"Let's get this over with," Jack Madden snarled as Alice's barrister was about to make the introductions. "I think we all know who everybody is."

"Mr Madden, for the benefit of your legal team I wish to make the introductions since they have not met two of my witnesses before today," Gerard Murphy said calmly and he proceeded to introduce the women.

"I think we all know that you have a very weak case for title to the disputed apartment on Taylors Hill," the Counsel for Jack Madden said.

"On the contrary," Gerard said calmly. "I don't think we would be in this room if you didn't think we have a pretty good case. Besides, there are the principles of natural justice to consider. What are you offering us?"

"An order to end this farcical situation as soon as possible. Mr Madden, in his generosity, is offering €100,000 to this woman and that will be the end of it."

Alice held her breath. Nicola was dismayed and Cassandra was just plain angry.

"That is a ridiculous offer," Gerard Murphy said in a voice which was bordering on aggressive. "Your client had an ongoing relationship with my client for about thirteen years. He put her up in the apartment, which she presumed would be her home for life and they had two children together."

"That is a barefaced lie," Jack Madden said in the tone of a person who expected to be believed. "I took pity on Alice O'Brien when she was pregnant and alone because she was an employee and this is how she repays me!"

Gerard Murphy threw him a scathing look and continued.

"He then put her and *their* children out on the street rendering them homeless and you expect her to walk away from this with just €100,000. That's not going to happen."

"You have absolutely no proof of any of these allegations." Jack Madden's counsel was incensed.

"Oh, but I have. I have a neighbour, Cassandra Grey, who saw Jack Madden in that apartment block nearly every week for the relevant period and she is willing to testify that he spent several nights a week in the disputed apartment."

"Nobody will believe that whore," Jack Madden snarled.

Nicola groaned inwardly and Alice gasped audibly.

"I will thank you not to refer to my witness in such disrespectful terms," Gerard Murphy said.

"Still," Jack Madden's barrister said, "she's hardly a person whose word could be trusted. It's not exactly an edifying way to earn a living."

"No more unedifying than yours!" Cassandra spoke sharply. "Going into all sorts of contortions defending the indefensible and taking money from all sorts of renegades just because they can pay you big bucks, no matter what the rights and wrongs of the case!"

Everybody in the room stared at Cassandra. She may have been bruised and battered but she was in no way cowed.

"I will be under oath and my word will be believed," she continued, looking straight at Jack Madden as she spoke. "I am very familiar with Jack Madden's lifestyle over the past thirteen years."

"Now," Gerard Murphy continued, "are you willing to up the offer or will we go into court this afternoon?"

Alice held her breath. The idea of waiting for two hours in Ennis Courthouse until her case was heard appalled her.

"€200,000 is our final offer," the other man said.

"We'll take our chances," Gerard Murphy said and he snapped his briefcase shut and turned towards the door.

Alice's heart sank. She would have accepted the €200,000. It wasn't the value of the apartment but she would have managed.

She wished Gerard had asked her what she would have settled for before they came into the room but it was too late now.

The women were standing up when Jack Madden spoke.

"I haven't time for this aggravation. The case could go on for days and I have affairs of state to think of," he said. "I will arrange for her to get title to the apartment and will spend the rest of my life regretting a very expensive mistake."

"That's more like it!" Gerard Murphy said. "You can send me the relevant documentation within the next fortnight and if I don't receive it by the 28th of this month I will seek another court date as a matter of urgency. But for today I will tell the Court Clerk that the matter is settled."

He stood back and let the three women leave the room ahead of him.

Tom McEvoy was sitting on a seat in the waiting area when they came out. He stood up and offered Cassandra his arm wordlessly and they walked towards the stairs.

Gerard Murphy had a big smile on his face as he walked up the stairs into the main foyer of the courthouse. The journalists were still hanging around, looking as if they were not quite sure why they were there.

"We'll have to wait until the 28th before we can set the wheels in motion to transfer title of the property to you," he said to Alice with a smile.

"What if he changes his mind?" she asked uncertainly.

"I don't think he will. If this case had gone into court today the press would have had a field day, no matter what the outcome. It would have been the end of him. He won't take that risk."

"That's a relief," Alice said as she and Nicola gingerly helped Cassandra into the car.

"You got a bit of a surprise, I'd say, when he called me a whore," Cassandra said to Alice when they were in the car.

"Yes, but who am I to judge?"

"Well, it's not every day you discover your next-door neighbour is a prostitute."

"Maybe, but that was what I was in a way except that I didn't know it. Jack had no real affection for me and the girls, otherwise he wouldn't have dumped us so easily. Effectively he was keeping me in the apartment and supporting me and the girls for sex. He was paying me for sex."

Nicola was astonished that Alice could say that without a quiver in her voice. This was a totally different woman to the one who had rung her less than six months earlier. She had come a long way.

When they got to The Coven Hugo had taken out several of Alice's legendary lamb casseroles and was defrosting them. He had picked up the girls from school. They rushed at Alice and hugged her.

"Where were you?" Grace demanded. "And why are you dressed up?"

"I was just looking after some business and I needed to look extra smart," Alice grinned.

"And is the business looked after?" Grace asked, clearly not sure of the meaning of the phrase.

"Yes," Alice smiled. "There's a bit more to do but it went very well."

"We love you, Mum," Grace said and Alice burst into tears.

"Now, now," Eliza said, "there'll be no tears on this great day. Hugo, crack open the champagne!"

Hugo obliged, while Nicola organised sparkling non-alcoholic wine for the girls and Tom McEvoy who had to deliver his sister's car back to her intact. The meal was jovial and the girls enjoyed it thoroughly and raised their glasses when Eliza proposed a toast to Alice even though they certainly weren't clear on why she was being toasted.

"Chief Superintendent, you have been very kind," Hugo said when he got him in a quiet corner later. "Are you usually this attentive to people who have been suspected of scurrilous crimes?" He was referring to the confiscation of his computer.

"When Jack Madden himself phoned me to tell me to confiscate your computer, I smelled a rat. As you know, I never quite trusted the man."

"Well, I think I was lucky that you were on the case."

"Yes. I arranged for it to be fast-tracked under the supervision of a friend for exactly that reason. I'm not a person to be slagging off my colleagues but like in every profession there are a few bad apples."

"I must thank you most sincerely for that," Hugo said.

"Not at all! Justice was done and that's my job."

Tom McEvoy left soon after that and he was sorry to go. He was dreading going home to his wife. They had done nothing but argue and fight recently. This situation was a welcome distraction and going home meant he had to face up to his problems again.

"What's next?" Alice asked Nicola after the Chief Superintendent was gone.

"We all relax for a few days and then we take the next step."

"What's that?" Alice asked.

"Well, I think the most immediate step is for the girls to go up and do their homework and then we should all relax for the evening."

Nicola didn't want to discuss her next move in front of the girls, given that they had no clue that their father had denied in Ennis Courthouse that they were his and that he had made them homeless. The girls were not aware that they had a father and this was not the right time in their lives to tell them.

"Right, girls!" said Alice. "You heard what Nicola said. Homework for you!"

"And to think we thought that Nicola was our friend!" Orla said with mock disdain but she bounded up the stairs to the apartment as if she hadn't a care in the world.

It was agreed that Cassandra and maybe Nicola would remain in the vacant apartment in The Coven, at least until Cassandra had recovered from her injuries.

"I don't think we are in any further danger from Madden," Nicola said, "but, just in case, it is probably best."

"I'm certain of it," Hugo said, "and Tom has said he will leave lightweight security on the place for a further week or two."

Alice's jaw dropped. This was the first she knew about the security.

"The more I hear about this the more it shocks me," she said.

"You don't know the half of it," said Nicola. "But I think the fact that we got what we wanted is great and I wouldn't be surprised if the presence of the media in the courthouse didn't strengthen our hand a bit. I wonder why they were there? There didn't seem to be anything exciting going on, if you discount our case. They must have got wind of it somehow, but I can't imagine how. They must have been disappointed when nothing happened." She wondered if Jack Madden had managed to get out of the courthouse without attracting their attention.

Alice sighed as if she couldn't figure out how she landed in this situation but she had such support from the people in the room that she was fairly confident she could do what was required to get her life back on track.

Cassandra said she was going to bed and refused offers of help. She was glad to have a place to stay where she felt safe. She hadn't said to anyone that she might not go back to Lady Gregory Court but that's what she was thinking. She didn't know what she was going to do but the assault had shaken her to the core and she was considering not returning to her old way of life.

Nicola was glad that Séamus had arranged a night out for them and she was looking forward to it. She would come back to The Coven that night and stay there for a few days at any rate.

Hugo and Eliza were just delighted that they had been able to help Alice and the girls and as far as they were concerned they could remain on in The Coven for as long as they needed. They had become quite attached to them.

Chapter 33

Nicola stayed in The Coven for a week and then went back to her apartment. She told the others that she felt quite safe there and in any case Séamus had offered to stay over, so what with her Knight in Shining Armour she couldn't be safer.

Cassandra was not so lucky. Her face turned a bilious shade of yellow. She was still in pain and her doctor advised her to take it easy for at least three weeks. The hearing had taken more out of her than the others, partly because she was in such bad shape and in a lot of pain, but also because she knew in her heart that the man who had arranged the assault on her was Jack Madden and he was likely to get away with it. She got the shivers every time she thought about her assailant. Only for Luke she would have been murdered.

She hadn't heard from Luke since as her work phone was still at the apartment and he didn't know where she was. She hoped that he hadn't much of a problem explaining to his wife the significant bruising to his knuckles and also a small gash on his left cheek. She realised during the week that followed that she had hardly thought about the dreadful situation she had put him in. She dearly hoped that the event had not caused him too much aggravation. She loved him and would die rather than cause a problem between him and his wife – particularly given that her feelings didn't appear to be reciprocated.

Eliza was attending the University Hospital for radiotherapy five days per week. She found it tiring but manageable and Hugo was a tower of strength. Alice took Eliza when Hugo wasn't free. In general it was going well but they all knew that it would take some months for Eliza to recover fully. In the meantime Alice continued to do all the cooking for The Coven, including for Cassandra who freely admitted she couldn't boil an egg. Alice also found time to continue to do the desserts for the hotel and was considering taking on the starters after Easter if all continued to go well.

Exactly fourteen days after the court hearing Alice got a call from her barrister.

"He has sent me the documentation." he said. "The apartment will be legally yours very soon."

"That's wonderful! What do we do now?"

"Come in to my office and we can discuss your next step."

"Can Nicola come with me? I think she has a plan."

"Of course. See you tomorrow at eleven."

Alice flipped her phone closed and told Hugo, Eliza and Cassandra the news. They were delighted. By this time Cassandra was beginning to look more like her old self and the pain had abated.

Alice dialled Nicola's number and told her the news.

"Can you come with me to the barrister's office?" Alice asked anxiously.

"Of course," Nicola said. "It's part of my job. See you tomorrow."

Gerard Murphy was positively gleeful when he greeted them.

"I love winning," he grinned.

"So do I," said Alice. "Especially since it is so important to me."

"I was wondering if the presence of the media in the

courthouse was a factor," Nicola remarked. "He gave in quite easily in the end."

"It could have been," Gerard said. "Because, truthfully, when I researched the case thoroughly I found that it could have gone against us on several counts."

"Wow! You never told us," Alice said.

"Well, these things are never black and white and I didn't want to worry you, but I wasn't as confident as I pretended."

"I'm still wondering why the media were there," Nicola mused. "Obviously they didn't spot Jack Madden as there was nothing of note in the papers the following day."

"Maybe somebody tipped them off that something *could* be about to happen," Gerard said with a strange smile.

The two women stared at him but neither of them dared to ask him what exactly he meant by that.

"What do you want to do next?" Gerard asked Alice.

Alice looked from one to the other of them. "I don't know."

"I've had a plan for some time," said Nicola, "and you can tell me if it is daft or not."

"Go ahead."

"We are now in possession of information which is potentially explosive. We can't prove any of it yet and there is probably no point in going down that route at this point in time."

"Go on," Gerard said.

"I propose to ring up Jack Madden and ask him for maintenance for Alice and the girls. He won't like it but I suspect that since we have got this far without him getting any adverse publicity he will want to keep it that way. That gives us a very strong hand."

"What do you mean?" Alice sounded anxious.

"I mean I may only have to ask him for it and threaten to expose him and I suspect he will agree unless we make absolutely horrendous demands."

"I think it may work," the barrister said.

"I was thinking that once I get him to come to a meeting we can have Alice and you there so that the thing is all legal. He can bring a legal team if he likes but again I suspect he may not."

"Oh God," Alice sighed. "I was hoping never to have to be in the same room as him again!"

"I think it is necessary this last time," Gerard said.

"I'll try and get hold of him in the next few days," Nicola said. "I can keep an eye on the TV to find out his whereabouts. However, I imagine if I leave enough messages he won't leave them unanswered. He is in a vulnerable position and he'd be very stupid if he didn't realise it."

"Great," Gerard said. "In the meantime I will ask Séamus to get on with the work of transferring title of the apartment to Alice."

"I'd say you have no chance of becoming Attorney General under this regime," Nicola grinned at him.

"Never mind that," he grinned. "I have my eye on the European Court of Human Rights!"

Jack Madden was available the third time Nicola called him.

"Good afternoon, Ms McCarthy. What can I do for you?" His tone was polite, formal and cold.

"Good afternoon, Taoiseach." Nicola was equally formal. "I wish to speak to you about the issue of maintenance for Alice O'Brien's children."

"There is no issue, if you'll pardon the pun," the Taoiseach answered. "I rather stupidly allowed a young pregnant girl stay in one of my apartments and I have paid dearly for that mistake. She has done very well indeed out of it. There is nothing further to discuss."

"But, Taoiseach, I believe there is. I don't believe anyone will believe that you ensconced your au pair in a luxury apartment entirely out of the goodness of your heart."

"Don't you be smart with me!"

Shades of the aggressive man to whom she had spoken previously were emerging.

"I am not being smart, Taoiseach. I believe that Alice O'Brien's children are also yours. If this is the case she is entitled to maintenance for them, thereby saving the taxpayer a One Parent

Family Payment and getting justice for the children." She threw in the reference to the taxpayer for a giggle – his speeches were littered with references to "saving the taxpayer" and "good value for the taxpayer".

"I have told you before that those children are not mine."

"Taoiseach, I have told you before that I don't believe you and if we were to follow you through the courts there would be at least a case to answer. If you do not wish to go the court route, involving DNA tests and the like, I am asking you to meet with me, Alice and her legal advisor and we can come to an arrangement."

"Are you trying to blackmail me?" The Taoiseach's voice had become low and menacing.

"Absolutely not, Taoiseach! I am telling you what I intend to do if you are not willing to come to an agreed settlement on this matter. And before you answer, don't dream of threatening my job again. That type of behaviour is unworthy of a Taoiseach."

She held her breath and heard him draw in a large lungful before he spoke again.

"When do you want to meet?" he practically growled.

"Any time within the next fortnight."

"That is not convenient. I will be busy for the next month."

"This will only take an hour or two and we will meet you either in Galway or in Dublin, whichever is more convenient for you. But it must be within the next fortnight."

"Why is it so urgent?" he hissed.

"Because I believe you are stalling and there is no valid reason you can't meet us on such an important matter – for your children at any rate."

Again the sharp intake of breath nearly sucked her down the phone. She waited.

"I can meet you on Saturday week in Galway – in the apartment in Lady Gregory Court," he said.

"Absolutely not," Nicola said for the second time in as many minutes. "We will meet in my apartment. Alice would feel safer there. I have no doubt you know where it is."

"I can find out," he replied. "We'll meet at three o'clock."

"Feel free to bring a legal advisor if you wish. Alice will have one and we intend drawing up an agreement that will be legally binding."

With that she put down the phone.

Then she sat and stared at the phone for at least five minutes until it rang again, causing her to jump.

"There's a client of yours in reception," the receptionist said.

"Thanks. You can tell her to come in," Nicola said and she gathered her thoughts together so that she would be ready to deal with an entirely different case.

The following week Nicola and Alice met with Gerard Murphy again. He was absolutely delighted to be involved in this case though it hadn't been easy and he'd had quite a few sleepless nights. At one point he was very concerned that he might fail to get the apartment for Alice. He knew that he could never boast about it to his friends – not while this Taoiseach was in power at any rate – but even the cloak-and-dagger element of it appealed to him.

They agreed that they wanted a down payment of €25,000 for pain and suffering caused to Alice and the children by his making them homeless and €300 per week maintenance for the children. They decided that they would not ask for anything for Alice since she would soon have her own livelihood and she was adamant that she didn't want him to feel that he had rendered her incapable of earning her own living. The barrister said they would ask for a €75,000 down payment as a starting point and €500 per week and see where it went from there.

The two women looked at this young man who was about six years younger than either of them, clearly not long out of King's Inn, and hoped he knew what he was doing.

Chapter 34

Cassandra had come to a decision. Even though her physical wounds were healing she felt emotionally drained. She had always known that she was in a dangerous business but she had been so careful and not taken any risks. She had never been assaulted before and even though she knew that Jack Madden had arranged it, from what the assailant had said to her, she felt that she would never feel secure in that apartment again.

She confided in Hugo and Eliza one March morning as they took a walk in the grounds together. Seeing as everybody else involved in Alice's case knew about her way of life she felt it was only fair to tell Hugo and Eliza. If they were surprised they did not show it and they certainly weren't judgemental.

"You can stay with us as long as you wish," Eliza said. "And if we need the apartment for another distressed woman you can stay in our quarters. God knows we have enough room."

"I don't deserve this," Cassandra almost cried.

"Of course you do," said Hugo. "You have been such a good friend to Alice and to us, helping reunite us with Lizzie."

Hugo was so warm that Cassandra knew that he meant it.

"I don't want to say this to Alice at present," she said, "but I'm actually afraid to go back to the apartment. I would really like to get some more of my things out of it but I don't think I can."

"Why don't you want to say it to Alice?" asked Hugo, puzzled.

"In case she opts to go back and live there once title is passed to her."

"I doubt that she has any plans at present," Eliza said, "but I feel that she won't go back there either. While there may have been happy memories, all of her life there was a lie. I wouldn't be surprised if she wants a new start."

"Perhaps," Cassandra agreed. "What do you suggest I do?"

"Why don't you discuss it with Nicola?" Eliza suggested. "You two have become close lately and she will probably have some good ideas about where you should go from here."

And that is exactly what Cassandra did.

Nicola fully understood Cassandra's reluctance to go back to the apartment.

"It's great that Eliza and Hugo have room," she said. "You're under no pressure to make a decision yet and in time you may feel differently."

"But I would really like to get some more of my clothes, my laptop and maybe some of my cosmetics and stuff," Cassandra said.

"If you like you can give me the key and a list of what you want and I can get them for you. I'll ask Séamus to come with me and we can bring a few suitcases full. Séamus knows about your way of life now so I wouldn't be giving away any secrets."

"What did he say when you told him?" Cassandra asked anxiously.

"Do you want the truth?"

"Yes."

"The truth is that the whole situation is so bizarre he honestly hasn't said a word about you in all of this. Remember in his line of work he comes across all sorts of people. He always knew that there were prostitutes around but a Taoiseach who may be willing to kill to stay in power – well, that's a whole different ball game altogether."

"I never thought about it like that," Cassandra laughed. "I'm small news compared to that."

Séamus agreed readily to accompany Nicola to collect some of Cassandra's property, and they went in Nicola's car on the following Saturday afternoon. Neither said it but they didn't want to complicate Séamus's life by giving Jack Madden any information about him, in the form of his car registration, from which anybody with connections could glean a name. They were pretty sure that their visit would be reported to him. On the other hand, they were equally sure, now that he had agreed to settle, that he wouldn't wish to bring attention to himself by arranging any further surprises for them.

But they did get a surprise when they went into Cassandra's apartment and it wasn't a pleasant one. They opened the door with the key and were met with a scene of complete disarray. The apartment had been vandalised completely. The curtains were shredded, Cassandra's clothing was torn up and daubed with make-up. The words 'slut', 'whore' and 'bitch' were written in spray paint and lipstick on the walls and mirrors. Her jewellery was strewn around the apartment. Oddly, quite valuable property was still there but the objective was not to steal but to terrorise. There was a note left on the dining-room table.

"You slut! I know where you live and you won't be so lucky the next time I come to get you. I was paid the last time but the next time will be just for fun. Your so called boyfriend won't be much help. He won't catch me by surprise this time. I will find out who he is and will get to him first."

Nicola got such a shock she had to sit down.

"What will we do?" she asked Séamus who was also visibly shaken.

"We will salvage what we can and take it with us. And we

will phone Chief Superintendent Tom McEvoy even before we go to The Coven. This guy's a psychopath. Have you got Tom's mobile number?"

"No, but I think Hugo has it. Whoever did this got into the apartment with a key. He must have been let in or at the very least the doorman turned a blind eye." Nicola felt very unsafe.

"Yes. Let's just pack up and go."

Séamus was already putting stuff into two suitcases. He found Cassandra's laptop and two mobile phones. He packed them as well in case she needed them, though the screen of the laptop was destroyed and it looked as if it had liquid poured over it. He put it in anyway just in case.

They took what they could and the note and left within fifteen minutes, locking the door behind them. They left by the main door and didn't even look in the direction of the doorman's desk.

They got into the car and Nicola called Hugo and got Tom McEvoy's mobile number. He was at home when they rang him.

"Just get out of there," he said. "You'll have to tell Cassandra but assure her that we will protect her. I will go and see her after the weekend. If she gave you the keys of her car take it as well. I'm sure Hugo can keep it under a tarpaulin or something at The Coven. And watch your back!"

Nicola was in shock as she followed the Super's instructions.

Séamus drove Cassandra's car and they made their way to The Coven. When they arrived they told Hugo what had happened. He suggested they should have a meeting in Cassandra's apartment and decide what to do. They were pretty sure that Jack Madden was not behind this but, since he had been behind the first assault, that might be the way they could pinpoint who exactly the guy was who was making these threats.

But they had to tell Cassandra first.

Cassandra didn't react at all at first when she heard the news. She just listened.

"What can I do?" she wondered.

"The Super says do nothing," Nicola answered. "He will provide protection."

"There may be no danger at present," Hugo said. "This guy is just angry that he was beaten at his own game. Who was the guy that intervened?"

"Oh, God!" Cassandra remembered Luke. "He is a client but a very nice one. He has problems of his own. I hope that monster doesn't find out who he is."

"He probably won't," Hugo said. "This thug is bluffing. His ego is hurt. After all, your client knocked him to the ground and saved your life."

"I haven't even thanked him!" Cassandra wailed.

"I'm sure in the circumstances he'll understand," said Séamus, speaking for the first time since they had come into the apartment.

"God, I don't know what to do," Cassandra said slowly and Nicola realised she had never seen her so unsure.

"We'll do nothing yet," Hugo said. "You are not alone and we can all help out. We just need to decide how best to deal with this and I'm sure Tom McEvoy will help us. You're safe here, now that we have security."

"Gosh, Hugo, I'd say you never expected this when you took me in a few days ago!"

"Cassandra, my dear, I never know what to expect and that way you don't get too many surprises."

"Do you mind staying with me tonight?" Nicola asked Séamus as they drove away from The Coven. "I can't believe it but I am scared."

"Of course I will," he assured her and they continued to her apartment in silence.

Chapter 35

The meeting with Jack Madden was arranged for the Saturday afternoon following the incident in Cassandra's apartment. In the meantime, in so far as it was possible, they all behaved as if nothing was wrong. Eliza went for her radiotherapy. Nicola went to work. The girls went to school and Alice even worked on a contract with the hotel for a function on the Friday.

The girls bounded out of the school that Friday, after Alice had delivered her order, to inform her that they would be participating in the Macnas Parade on Saint Patrick's Day. They were to be dancing *síogs* and they needed costumes by the next week.

Cassandra lay low and let her wounds heal. She was really scared. Any fears she had about returning to her apartment were confirmed by what Nicola and Séamus told her about the condition of it. She had made up her mind never to go back there again. She wasn't sure what she would do but she was giving up her way of life and moving on. Where exactly she wasn't sure but she had enough money to keep herself for at least a year so she had some time to make up her mind.

As the Saturday loomed everybody was on tenterhooks except for the young cheerful barrister who might not really have understood the enormity of what was happening to his client and therefore was less intimidated by the situation than those who did. Also the fact that they had succeeded in getting the apartment had added to his confidence.

On Saturday Alice got up early. She had promised the girls that they would go into town to find suitable material for *síog* costumes for the parade. The girls were hugely excited.

"Alice," Hugo said, "couldn't you leave that until after the weekend?" He was concerned that she might be overstressed.

"Hugo, this will take my mind off what I have to do this afternoon. It is a distraction. And the girls will make sure I get it alright."

"I suppose you're right," he agreed and he lent her the car to go into town.

The girls skipped along beside their mother as she headed for Hickey's fabrics and they picked out some shimmery green voile for the dresses and some Vilene to stiffen the wings. The girls were practising their dance as they pranced along beside her and Alice was pleased that they had no idea how stressed she was or that they were providing her with a welcome distraction from what would probably be the most important meeting of her life.

She bought them burgers in Supermac's for their lunch, a rare treat, and then they headed back to The Coven. The girls were ecstatic. The adults were amused at their high spirits and Hugo took them out to look at the spring lettuce and onions and the rhubarb, to see when they might be ready to take to the Saturday market.

Eliza went to Alice's apartment with her to help her choose an outfit and just to give her moral support in advance of her big meeting. Alice choose a simple trousers and a wool jacket and boots and she looked every bit the sophisticated young woman she had become during the last few months.

"You look great," Eliza said. "Knock him dead – not literally of course."

Alice laughed. "It's certainly a temptation," she said. "There have been times during the last few months when I wished he was dead but at present he is more use to me alive. I shudder to think that he may have been willing to kill in order to stop me getting what is my due."

"Well, so far he hasn't killed anyone that we know of and I don't think he would now. Too many people know the story. It would be too much of a risk. And who knows, maybe he wouldn't have gone that far really."

"I hope you're right. If I'm not home by half five send out a posse." She was laughing as she spoke but they both knew she was dealing with a very ruthless man and the fact that her existence might interfere with the progress of his career path made him very dangerous indeed.

When Alice arrived at Nicola's apartment Gerard Murphy was there ahead of her. Nicola was dressed less casually than she would normally be in her own apartment on a Saturday afternoon and Gerard was wearing a three-piece suit as if he was going to court. He had a briefcase which contained a laptop and writing materials.

Alice sniffed when she came in the door – the pungent odour of cleaning fluids was in the air. Nicola noticed and laughed.

"I had to do something to take my mind off the meeting. My apartment has been bleached to within an inch of its life!"

"We could always asphyxiate him with bleach fumes if he doesn't give us what we want," Gerard said and they all laughed.

Jack Madden pressed the bell at three on the dot. All three occupants of the apartment jumped even though they were expecting it. Nicola opened the door and Jack Madden and another man walked in. Alice recognised him as the man who had occasionally called to the apartment – Mick, the man who had spirited Grace away from the Dáil the day she had tried to talk to her Uncle Jack.

"Let's get this over with," Jack Madden said, without greeting any of them or introducing his companion. "I'm in a hurry."

"That may be," Gerard said, "but this matter is of great importance to my client and we will not be rushed."

Jack Madden looked slightly crestfallen. "What exactly are you looking for?" he asked, addressing nobody in particular.

"My client is looking for a down payment of €75,000 for the trauma which you caused her by evicting her and her daughters, *your* daughters, without notice, knowing that they had nowhere to go. And she also requires €700 per week maintenance for her daughters."

"That is preposterous!" said Jack. "I haven't got that sort of money and, even if I had, there is no way I would pay it to this gold-digger. I have already handed over an expensive apartment to which she has no right whatsoever. And that should be the end of it."

"Mr Madden, I will thank you to refer to my client in respectful terms and count yourself lucky that she is not looking for maintenance for herself."

"There is no way I would ever pay maintenance to her. She is a lazy young one who never did a day's work in her life, even when I was paying her to be an au pair. She can maintain herself."

"As it happens she can and is willing to do so, but her children, *your* children, are entitled to have a stay-at-home mother like the children of your marriage. As it happens, Ms O'Brien will be working from home so you are lucky that she is not claiming more."

"There will be no down payment and I will pay €150 per week maintenance for the children."

"Mr Madden, if you continue in this vein this matter will go into the family court as soon as I can get a date and I think we would easily get what we are requesting and maybe more. So unless you want that to happen you will have to meet our requirements."

"Okay. €10,000 down payment and €250 per week for maintenance."

"Derisory, Mr Madden! I will seek a date for the Family Court."

"Okay! €30,000 initial payment and maintenance of €325 per week."

"Done! Now that wasn't so painful, was it? I will type up the agreement immediately and you and Ms O'Brien can sign it. How do you propose to pay?"

"By bank draft, every calendar month – I'll send it to Lady Gregory Court, seeing as she owns it now," Jack Madden practically snarled.

"Initially I think it would be best if you sent the bank drafts to my office and I will forward them to Ms O'Brien. If they are late – even by one day – I will immediately initiate court proceedings. Is that clear?"

"Yes." Jack Madden glared at the younger man.

Gerard was typing furiously with two fingers but, as there were only about five lines in the agreement, it didn't take long. Jack Madden signed it as did Alice and it was witnessed by Nicola and Jack Madden's companion Mick whose full name turned out to be Michael Dillon.

"The first payment is due on next Friday – that is the €30,000 and the first month's maintenance," the barrister said.

Jack Madden began to walk out without another word.

"Jack!"

Everybody was startled to hear Alice's voice. She had not opened her mouth up until this point.

"I have nothing to say to you," the man snarled and continued walking.

"Well, I have something to say to you," Alice replied.

She moved swiftly and stood in front of the door in such a way that he would have had to push her out of the way in order to open it. He stopped stock still and looked at her in amazement.

"I have been through a lot since you evicted me and our children from the apartment I thought was my home for life. I have met many good people and made new friends. All of them have been subjected to your little tricks. We can't prove that any of the things that happened to them were at your behest but we know that they were. Several local gardaí are suspicious of you, several members of the legal profession and several of my friends know the whole story, so I am telling you now that if anything happens to any of us the others will follow you. And you had better call off that thug you sent to Cassandra Grey. If he lays a hand on her we will set the ball rolling to bring you down. At the very least all I have to do is turn up at your doorstep in Monkstown with our daughters. I'm sure you wouldn't want me to open that particular can of worms at this crucial time. So just put an end to your dirty tricks or I personally will see to it that your career is over. If anything happens to me or the girls there are other people who will do it."

"I don't know what you're talking about," he blustered.

"Yes, you do." She stepped aside and let him leave the room. It was the first time any of them had seen Jack Madden flustered.

"That was quite a speech for Alice in Wonderland," Nicola grinned.

"I have had to come into the real world," Alice said. "But I have to say, that from now on I'm hoping to enjoy it."

Chapter 36

Alice spent the Sunday afternoon after "The Meeting" making the fairy costumes for the girls. Her own sewing machine had got lost in the eviction but luckily Eliza had one that she could borrow.

She had told Eliza, Hugo and Cassandra what had happened at the meeting when she got back to The Coven on the Saturday but she just didn't want to talk about it after that. She knew that now that the issue of maintenance and the ownership of the apartment were settled she would have to start making decisions about her future, but just for that weekend she didn't want to think about it any more. Eliza was not surprised when she disappeared upstairs to her apartment with the sewing machine and the girls in tow.

It didn't take her long to make the costumes. She had a nice pattern, she made appropriate modifications and the girls were willing models.

Late on Sunday afternoon just before teatime she brought them downstairs to show off her handiwork. The girls floated into the kitchen and curtsied with great grace.

"Well, look at you!" Eliza gasped. "You are going to be the most elegant *síogs* in the parade!"

"Do you think?" Grace asked, delighted. "Would you like to see us dance?"

"I don't think you have much of an option," Alice grinned apologetically.

"We'd love to see you," said Hugo. "But why don't we call Cassandra down as well. If she's up to it I'd say she'd love to see you dance. And then we can all have tea. I'm sure Eliza and I can rustle up something."

Eliza put on *Riverdance* while Alice went upstairs to call Cassandra.

She knocked gently on the door. "Cassandra? We are all having tea downstairs, and the girls want to do their dance for us. Are you up to a bit of clapping and cheering?"

"Be there in a sec," Cassandra replied.

Alice had the impression she might have roused her from sleep but the damage was done and she couldn't do anything about it.

By the time Cassandra came into the large kitchen the girls were in full flight.

"If I say so myself, as the proud mum, you're just perfect." Alice's heart was nearly bursting with pride.

"You certainly are," Cassandra agreed. "And I'm not even related so you can be sure that it's the truth."

Everybody laughed and Alice felt that Cassandra was beginning to come back to herself.

"Is it just the two of you dancing?" Hugo enquired.

"No, there are ten. So you'll have to look hard so that you don't miss us as we dance by." Grace had it all planned.

"Grace, maybe Hugo and Eliza and Cassandra have other plans for Saint Patrick's Day!" Alice said.

"We wouldn't miss the parade for the world," Eliza said. "I haven't been to it for years. But this year we have a special interest. Haven't we?"

"If you mean us," Grace said, "you have. We'd really love you to be there."

"We will," Cassandra and Hugo said in unison and the girls were happy.

Chapter 37

The following day Alice and Cassandra woke and without knowing it they had the exact same thought: I'm going to sell the apartment.

For both of them it was a new start and they lay in their beds planning how they would go about it, wondering how much they would get and what they would do next.

It was a very strange time for both of them. Six months earlier neither had any idea that they would be in this position. They hardly knew each other. They had what they thought was a secure way of life and they didn't anticipate any changes but the sudden death of an individual neither of them had even met – the Taoiseach – had changed both their lives irrevocably.

The girls came bounding in to Alice and she got up to get their breakfast and take them to school.

Cassandra remained on in bed for a while. Her bruises were almost gone. She no longer had pain in her ribs and she didn't need to see the doctor for a further week. She felt more like her old self. But she was horrified at the effect that the vandalising of her home had had on her. It was nearly as bad as the assault. She wondered if she should ask the Gardaí to investigate or if she should just leave it and write it down to experience. She made a decision not to make a decision, and turned over and went back to sleep for another hour.

When she woke up she was ready for decision-making. She decided that she would not go back to the apartment but she would get some work done on it before she sold it. She was sure that Nicola and Séamus hadn't told her the full extent of the damage. She had a gut feeling that it was a lot worse than either of them described but she had not pushed them for details because at the time she felt so vulnerable she wasn't sure that she could take the truth. If her gut feeling was right she couldn't sell it in its current condition.

On the positive side they had rescued her work phone. She would take down her website when she got an opportunity. The only reason she wanted her work phone was that she wanted to contact Luke to let him know that she was alright and that she was so grateful for what he had done. She guessed he was wondering what had happened to her and she was anxious to allay his fears. Sure enough when she turned on her phone there were several missed messages from him. There were also many messages from other clients but she just sent a reply to them saying that she was no longer working.

She got her breakfast and contemplated what she would do next. She put Luke's number in her personal phone and decided to wait until lunchtime before she rang him. She pottered around her apartment and made a plan. She had some savings and she could do a Jack Madden on the apartment, i.e. send in men with a skip. After that she could send in painters and when that was done she might go in and decide if she should furnish it before she put it up for sale.

That was the easy bit. The really difficult part was: what would she do with the rest of her life? She had no real qualifications – apart from her degree which on its own qualified her for nothing. She would have to retrain. She laughed to herself as she pictured Jack Madden assuring people on *Prime Time* that he had plans to deal with the unemployment crisis and part of it was retraining those who had become recently unemployed. He would never have imagined his erstwhile next-door neighbour as one of the first takers.

She went downstairs and found Hugo and Eliza in the kitchen.

"How are you this morning?" Eliza asked.

"I'm fine," Cassandra said and was surprised to note that she actually meant it. "How are things with you? Do you have radiotherapy today?"

"Yes, we're on our way now. It should only take about half an hour." Eliza was feeling permanently tired but she knew that this was one of the side effects of radiotherapy and though it wasn't pleasant she accepted it, hoping that it wouldn't last long.

"Can I cadge a lift as far as the hospital? I'm going into town. It's about time I went back into the outside world. I don't want to use my own car yet."

"Of course," said Hugo. "Glad you're feeling up to it. How will you get home?"

"I'll probably get a cab," she replied. "To be honest I'm not sure what I'm going to do in town but I feel the need to just get out there and not let what that creep did to me stop me."

She sounded a bit uncertain for Cassandra but in the circumstances neither Hugo nor Eliza was surprised.

"Good for you," Eliza said. "You are right. This is the first day of the rest of your life." She groaned. "I can't believe that I came out with that awful cliché!" She laughed and Cassandra laughed heartily.

They parted in the hospital car park and Cassandra walked slowly into town, down past the university, past the cathedral, over the bridge, past the courthouse and the Town Hall Theatre. Oddly, as she walked past these iconic buildings it was as if she was seeing them for the first time. She marvelled at the beautiful display of daffodils in the university grounds, immaculately kept. There was a funeral at the cathedral and the traffic jam around it made Cassandra glad she hadn't brought her car. She was glad that Alice's case had been heard in Ennis and wondered idly what the local courthouse was like inside. And the theatre – she noticed for the first time what an attractive building it was. As luck would have it, when she turned into Frances Street the first business premises she came to was an Estate Agent.

There's no time like the present, she said to herself and she went in the door.

The walls were covered in pictures and descriptions of houses for sale and houses that had been sold. She looked at the prices and locations and could not get a realistic handle on how much she could expect to get for her apartment. Until this morning the thought of selling had never occurred to her so she hadn't kept an eye on property prices over the recent years – but you couldn't miss the tales of doom and gloom on the news. Prices were going down, plummeting in fact, and she had no idea what to expect so she decided to ask for help.

The perky receptionist asked her to wait for an auctioneer to be free and then she ushered her into a plush office, indicating that the property market hadn't quite collapsed yet. She told a man who looked inordinately young to be doing this job what she wanted.

"And you say the apartment is in Lady Gregory Court?" he asked.

"Yes," Cassandra said.

"Nice apartments! Great location!"

"Yes," Cassandra said, mildly irritated that he was telling her the obvious. "What do you think I could get for it?"

"Well, one sold there recently for €600,000 but prices are dropping by the day. We are saying publicly that the market has bottomed out but I don't believe it. If you put it on the market today you might get €400,000 but you might not. My advice to you is to put it up right away."

"I can't do that. It was broken into and vandalised so I have to get it decorated to remove all traces of that. I don't think any prospective buyer would be happy to buy an apartment in a gated community where the gates provide no protection if the burglar is determined enough."

The auctioneer looked at her. "I suppose so but, as you say, when you redecorate there will be no trace of that and it should sell for a good price. Prices at that location haven't decreased as much as in other areas."

"Thank you for your time," Cassandra said and she left the office.

She was happy walking up the street. She was still not sure how much she would get for her apartment but she had paid €150,000 for it thirteen years earlier and the mortgage was nearly paid so unless there was a complete collapse in the market she would make a tidy profit and she could at least buy a house or an apartment in a less fashionable area and have quite a bit left over. Given that she had no clue how she was going to earn her living for the rest of her life, that thought gave her some comfort. She went into Brown Thomas and bought herself a Dolce & Gabbana bag by way of celebration. She regarded the purchase as a sort of last hoorah to her old way of life. She had a feeling that in the future she was more likely to be selling expensive bags for an employer than buying them. She then went to Vina Mara and had an excellent lunch in lovely surroundings.

As she ate she thought about Luke. If he was at lunch he might be free to talk. She called his number and braced herself. She was not sure what she would say.

"Hello," came Luke's voice.

"Hi. This is Cassandra."

"Wow! Am I glad to hear from you! I didn't recognise the number." He seemed genuinely pleased to hear her voice and she was relieved.

"I don't use the number you have for me any more. It's a long story. Can you talk?"

"Yes, but I am on my way to a meeting so I can't stay long. How are you? I was so worried."

"You had no need to be. Do you realise that you probably saved my life? I saw that you left several messages on my phone but I actually didn't get that back after the attack until recently and to be honest I hadn't the courage to switch it on until this morning."

"That's understandable in the circumstances," he said. "Was it a punter who attacked you? If you wish I will give evidence against him."

"You are so kind. No, it wasn't a punter. It's a very complicated story and I don't feel I can tell you all of it because the privacy of other people is involved. I probably won't take any action but I am ringing you to tell you that I am giving up work – that sort of work anyway and I felt you, of all people, deserved an explanation."

"Gosh. I don't know what to say. Could we meet up one more time?"

"Of course we can but I can't bring you to my new place – because it isn't mine in any case – but why don't you ring me when you can arrange to get away and we can decide then?"

"Grand," Luke said. "I'm not sure when yet but I will be in touch soon."

"That's great, Luke," Cassandra said. "I know that it isn't always easy to get away but there is no hurry. We have all the time in the world."

As she ended the call she wished that they would be spending more time together.

Chapter 38

Alice was also mulling over her decision. She had a plan which she hadn't really articulated but she had been hatching it for quite some time. She had been afraid to tell anyone about it because it was partly dependent on the outcome of the court case and whether she could get maintenance from Jack Madden. Now, however, she was in a position to push ahead – but not this week. She had a function for the hotel which had to be ready for Wednesday night and Thursday was Saint Patrick's Day – and the children had the day after that off so she was planning on having a nice family weekend where she could pay them lots of attention. She couldn't get over how good they had been during the past few months. Their little lives had been turned upside down and they had not complained once, not even when they were in the B&B and they must have thought that was strange – not to mention cramped. When she was still in a relationship with Jack, any time they were on holiday or staying away from home for whatever reason they had stayed in hotels and they had a room to themselves. In the B&B they had all slept in the same room and the girls had to share a double bed. They had behaved as if this type of thing happened every day. They hadn't even complained when they came to The Coven which was so far away from the school that they had significantly less contact with their school friends. She would have liked them to have more contact with their friends. She was looking forward to buying her new place where her girls would have a more normal life and she could get on with setting up her business.

She was working away in the large kitchen when Eliza came home from the hospital that day.

"I was thinking," Eliza said, "couldn't the girls invite some of their school friends and their parents if they wish to a sort of a party here after the parade? The end of the parade is always a bit of an anticlimax for the children."

"Gosh, Eliza, that would be great. Are you sure?" It was as if Eliza had read Alice's mind.

"If you're asking me am I up to it, probably not! But I won't be doing the entertaining. If I get tired I will just go to bed."

"That sounds like a plan," Hugo said. "I could help Alice organise the food and maybe a few games and maybe Cassandra would help or one or two of the other tenants if they're here on the day."

"At least the girls are rehearsing after school every day this week so I have until five to get my work done. I'll put together some party food without any bother." Alice was delighted. "Eliza, I know the girls will be thrilled. Thank you so much."

"Think nothing of it. I'm off for a rest now. See you later."

"Take a nice long rest. We can bring you a tray up to your room later if you don't want to get up," said Alice.

"Thank you, Alice," said Eliza with a smile and left.

Alice turned to Hugo. "How many do you think we could ask to the party?"

"I suppose all the girls in the dance. It wouldn't be fair to leave anybody out but some of them will have other plans in any case."

"Fine. There's a lot of adult food in the freezer and we can do some quick finger food on the morning."

"Does it take long to prepare kiddy treats? It's a while since I had anything to do with that."

"It's fairly uncomplicated and maybe Cassandra could help – if I tell her what to do. She says she can't boil an egg but I'd say she could if she tried."

"Did I hear my name being taken in vain?" Cassandra was standing in the kitchen doorway, looking at them quizzically.

"Yes, we were just saying that with your culinary skills we should throw a big party on Saint Patrick's Day and you could be chief cook," Hugo said, his face straight.

There was a momentary look of panic on Cassandra's face and both Hugo and Alice laughed.

"Relax, Cassandra!" said Alice. "We're thinking of having a kiddies' party after the parade for all the dancers and their parents and probably some of their siblings as well and I was wondering could you help with the food if I told you what to do?"

"I thought you had already offered Eliza the job of scullery maid," Cassandra said in mock disdain.

"Yes, but you could be a stand-in until she's better," Alice said.

"Well, I hope you don't regret saying that but I'm sure I can do it as long as the instructions are clear."

"That's settled then," Alice said and Cassandra knew that she had been roped into something for which she was completely unprepared.

When Alice told the girls about the party that evening they were beside themselves with excitement. They had not had friends home since before Christmas and they had never had that many. In Lady Gregory Court there had been so many rules that often their friends' visits weren't much fun. But this time there was going to be lots of party food, parents could come and Hugo said he would organise games.

They set about designing invitations on the computer and printed them out to be taken into school the next morning. They wouldn't know for certain until the day after how many would accept the invitation. Alice knew that she had to organise the

party with military precision, because she couldn't afford to
neglect her work for the hotel at this crucial time in her budding
career.

Cassandra appeared in the kitchen soon after nine the next
morning and they got started. Alice had already prepared some
of the novelties for the children and asked Cassandra to time
them and, when they were ready, to take them out of the oven
and decorate them. Cassandra felt that she could do this with
ease and was delighted with having something to occupy her
time. They worked together all day and at the end of it they had
several dishes prepared for the party and Alice was also making
good progress with her hotel food.

"Is Nicola coming to the party?" Cassandra asked as she put
the Smartie eyes on the gingerbread men.

"I never thought of her. I'll ring her now."

"I'd love to come," Nicola said in answer to the call, "but
Séamus and I will be in Donegal for a hill-walking trip for the
long weekend."

"Sounds nice," Alice said. "Enjoy yourselves! I hope it stays
fine for you."

"That's what they say in Cork when they're expecting lousy
weather," Nicola laughed.

"That's a no then," Cassandra said with grin when Alice put
down the phone.

They got back to work. It was tough going but they methodically
got through it, working first on the items which could be kept in
the fridge without spoiling.

"I'm going to sell my apartment," Cassandra said out of the
blue. It was the first time she had said it to anybody except the
auctioneer.

"Snap!" Alice grinned. "Great minds think alike. I'm selling
mine too!"

"Well, isn't that interesting!" Cassandra mused. "I wonder
would it be a good idea if we put them up for sale together."

"We could ask an auctioneer," Alice said. "You know, I haven't been back to the apartment since the eviction and I don't know how I will feel."

"Well, I've decided not to go back to mine until after it has been decorated. I'm not sure how I will organise that yet."

"I think there are a lot of options," Alice said thoughtfully. "Let's get this party out of the way first but we may be able to work together and it might be to both our benefits."

With that the girls arrived home, all news about who was coming to the party and who was not.

Alice and Cassandra cleared up the kitchen and Alice put the finishing touches to the casserole she was making for Hugo and Eliza's dinner and put it in the oven. As she went up the stairs to her own apartment with the girls her mind was in a whirl. The possibilities were endless. She realised that she was happy and excited for the first time since Jack had organised her eviction. Cassandra was rather less upbeat but she too could see the potential for co-operation with Alice and making the sale of the apartments a joint venture.

Alice and Cassandra worked together flat out on the Wednesday. Alice was delighted at how much Cassandra, who claimed to be able to burn water, was able to help her. When they were not organising the logistics of getting Alice's order to the hotel and the food arranged for the party, they were mulling over the possibilities for their future. They had both decided to trade down – rather than downsizing. In fact Alice thought she would go for a bigger place but would probably get it cheaper if she moved out a bit towards Moycullen, though Cassandra thought that Moycullen was expensive enough as well.

"Not as expensive as Taylors Hill," Alice said and Cassandra had to agree.

While Alice was collecting the children from their final rehearsal and delivering her order to the hotel Cassandra remained in the kitchen decorating the novelty foods for the kids. She was particularly proud of putting the liquorice wheels on an enormously long chocolate-train cake and filling the carriages with assorted sweets just like a train the girls had seen in an illustration and which they thought would be cool. There were hedgehog cakes and rabbit cakes and all sorts of other novelties. Grace thought that some of the goodies were a bit babyish but Alice assured her that these were for the smaller ones and sophisticated young ladies like herself could have the adult food.

"But I hope we can have some cake," Grace said, wondering if perhaps she had shot herself in the foot in her effort to appear grown-up.

"Of course you can," Alice said and kissed her gently on the forehead.

Chapter 39

Saint Patrick's Day dawned cold and bright. The girls were beside themselves with excitement. They were to be in the Cathedral Square at twelve noon.

The whole household except for Cassandra went to Mass at ten.

Orla wondered if they could skip it. "Given the day that's in it," she said.

"I don't think so," Hugo said. "After all, aren't we celebrating the fact that Saint Patrick brought Christianity to Ireland?"

"Can we wear our outfits?"

"No," Alice said. "You will wear your ordinary clothes and we'll come back here and you can get dressed."

She and Cassandra had been up early to prepare more food for the afternoon's festivities. Cassandra did skip the Mass, seeing no point in going just for appearances, and continued the work while the others were out. She made enormous cauldrons of soup, following Alice's instructions to a tee.

"The adults will be delighted with that, having stood immobile for at least an hour while they wait to gaze proudly on their little darlings," Alice said with a grin.

"Yes, won't they?" Orla said, completely unaware that it might be a bit of an ordeal for at least some of the adults.

Alice worried that the girls might be cold in their light clothes but they were so restless it was unlikely.

"We can dance while we are waiting to start," Grace said and that was what they did.

As she gazed across the One Man's Pass on Sliabh League in Glencolmcille on that bitterly cold March day, a Saint Patrick's Day parade in Galway seemed like a very attractive option to Nicola. But there was no going back. They had climbed the mountain in conditions that had been far from ideal. The leader said that the fog would clear but they were not convinced. He decided that they should have their lunch before they crossed the notorious pass so they sat down on nearby rocks and opened their lunch boxes. These were no Chablis and smoked-salmon type of lunch boxes which are *de rigueur* on walking tours in France, or so they were told by another walker. They were what they could get at the local supermarket and which they cobbled together at their hostel accommodation. But there was an atmosphere of camaraderie, much improved by the flasks of hot coffee which their leader had warned them the day before were to contain nothing that might turn them into Irish Coffee or Russian Coffee. To be honest they were so cold that the quality of the lunches was irrelevant. They shared hot drinks and passed around chocolate before they tackled the pass.

"Are you glad you came?" Séamus asked Nicola.

"I'll tell you if I get across the pass," she smiled. "If I don't, you will have the pleasure of informing my parents."

"You'll do it okay – and you'll be delighted you did."

As they were talking the mist cleared to reveal a breathtaking view of the bay. One Man's Pass lay before them, a path running along a ridge with the summit of the mountain rising at its end. An almost sheer drop on both sides of the ridge was also revealed, so any sharp intake of breath had little to do with the beauty of the view and more to do with fright.

"This walk is about ten minutes long," their guide said. "Watch your footing. The path along the ridge is about a metre wide but you must go in single file and don't stop or take photos while you are on the pass. Gusts of wind can prove dangerous so we're lucky it is relatively calm today."

"Well, that really makes me feel better!" Nicola muttered to Séamus. "You go first!"

"Right! It's easy really. I've done it several times."

"It will be good to have you ahead of me. It will give me courage."

The pass was such that nobody could hurry in any case and it was indeed a very beautiful scene. One by one they got to the other side. Nicola sighed in relief and Séamus gave her a bear hug when she got there.

"Wow! I never thought I'd be able to do that," Nicola laughed.

"Of course you could!"

They had a lovely weekend and they were pleased they had the opportunity to spend so much time together away from what had undoubtedly been a very stressful time for both of them.

The parade was superb, an enthralling mix of art and commerce and afterwards there were about six green-clad *síogs* and some of their siblings dancing around the front garden at The Coven. Hugo had arranged an old-fashioned treasure hunt in the garden and there was Musical Chairs in the sitting room and Pass the Parcel when the weather got too cold to remain outdoors.

"It reminds me of when I was a child," Cassandra mused. "I didn't think they played these sorts of games any more."

"They probably don't," Hugo grinned. "But they are the only ones I know how to organise."

"The kids are getting a great kick out of it," Cassandra said over the loud laughter, shrieks and general mayhem which had taken over The Coven.

The parents appeared to be having fun as well.

"It's always such an anticlimax after the parade," one dad said. "So many people just go for a drink but you can't do that when you have children. It was so nice of you to invite us."

"It's our pleasure," Eliza assured him. "We are really enjoying ourselves."

All of the adults helped with the clearing up and by six everybody who wasn't resident was gone.

"I think we should all take it really easy for the weekend," Alice said and everybody agreed.

When Alice and the girls went up to their apartment they watched a favourite DVD and then the girls began to prepare for bed.

Alice switched on the news as she began to tidy up the room – she was exhausted and decided she'd have an early night.

"Oh, look!" exclaimed Grace, coming back into the room. "There's Uncle Jack!"

Alice glanced at the screen just in time to see Jack Madden presenting the President of the United States with a Waterford Crystal bowl of shamrock.

Chapter 40

Alice and Cassandra did a lot of thinking over the weekend. They saw hardly anything of each other but they were thinking about their options. On Sunday afternoon Cassandra dropped into Alice's apartment for coffee.

"I was thinking we could go and have a look at the apartments together this week," said Alice as she put coffee cups on the table, "and then decide what we should do. I don't know what condition Jack left mine in. I suspect that whatever plans he had for it came to a halt when we got the injunction."

"Probably," Cassandra said. "I'd say he'd see it as throwing good money after bad."

"What day would suit you?"

"Alice, I told you last week that I don't think I can go back. Not now anyway!"

"Of course you can," Alice said brightly. "If I can do it, so can you."

"Alice, Nicola and I weren't completely truthful when we told you I was assaulted in the street. The fact is a man tried to murder me in my apartment – and then when he didn't succeed he vandalised my apartment in the most appalling way. I don't wish to belittle what happened to you but compared to that I think your life is a picnic."

Alice was dumbstruck.

"I was lucky in that I had no life-threatening injuries. But that creep said that I had made enemies in high places and he had been paid to make sure that I was silenced. That gave him carte blanche and I think he is a psychopath and he would have enjoyed killing me."

Alice, who had been pouring coffee, had to sit down.

"Why did nobody tell me this until now? You told me that it was horrendous but not the bit about enemies in high places nor the other things he said – not even that it occurred in your apartment!"

"Because you had enough to worry about! It wouldn't have helped at all to scare you more than you were already scared."

"I can't believe I was so naïve."

"I can't believe that you have matured so much in six months. But I can't go back to the apartment yet."

"You know what? We'll ring Nicola and see what she thinks we should do next. She has a clear head and she will surely have some ideas. Hugo and Eliza will have enough to do this week. It's Eliza's last week of radiotherapy but they say that she will be tired for some time to come."

"I'll ring Nicola tomorrow," Cassandra said. "And maybe meet her for lunch and if she can do it we can all meet up later in the week. What do you think?"

"Good idea," Alice agreed. "And Cassandra?"

"What?"

"I'm sorry. I've been so wrapped up in my own problems I didn't really take in the seriousness of yours. And to think that this all happened to you because of me!"

"Think nothing of it. I can't say it was a good thing but maybe it was the push I needed to get out of this dangerous game. We'll talk again, after I've spoken to Nicola."

On the Tuesday after Saint Patrick's Day Cassandra called Nicola and arranged to meet her for lunch. They met in a café near the Health Centre because Nicola was up to her eyes and had only half an hour to spare.

"What can I do for you?" Nicola said.

"Actually both Alice and I have decided to sell our apartments but we suspect neither is in a condition to be sold at present."

"Well, yours certainly isn't. How do you intend to deal with it?"

"That's exactly it. I just can't bring myself to go back."

"I don't blame you. It's in an awful state. It shook me and it wasn't even my apartment."

"Alice feels she wants to view hers and see if it is in need of redecoration, which it probably is. But I just can't."

"Why don't I go with Alice and we can report back to you? I think it would be good for Alice to face up to this. It will be part of the moving-on process. I'll ring her and we can arrange a time."

"Thanks, Nicola. I owe you one."

"Not at all. I'm glad to help."

Nicola didn't tell Cassandra but she fully intended to inform Chief Superintendent Tom McEvoy before she or anyone else went anywhere near that apartment block.

He responded in his usual generous fashion when she contacted him. "I'll be happy to accompany you and Alice."

"That will be great," Nicola said. "What day would be okay for you?"

"We'll do it in the evening," Tom replied. "Because, strictly speaking, it's not part of our work any more or at least it's not mine and we could spend more time then."

"Great. How about eight on Thursday?"

"That's fine with me."

"Great. I'll phone Alice. We can all meet at my apartment and go down in my car. The doorman already has the reg of that."

"Okay. See you then."

Tom McEvoy put his phone back in his pocket and was glad Nicola had rung him. He had a problem of his own which he didn't know how to deal with and he hoped that Nicola with her training might be able to make some suggestions.

Alice arrived at seven on Thursday evening as Nicola had suggested they have a light bite together before they went to look at the apartments. Nicola noticed that Alice was not as jaunty about the visit as she had been, now that it was imminent.

Nicola produced two Spanish omelettes with side salad in double quick time and was quite pleased with the result.

"Not up to your standard," she laughed, "but not bad for an amateur!"

"It's great," Alice assured her. "Just what I needed! I could do with a stiff drink as well but I suppose that's not a good idea."

"No, it's not," Nicola said, rather more sternly than she intended. "But you'll be fine. The anticipation is always worse than the actual event."

"I suppose so," Alice agreed and with that the door bell rang. It was Tom.

"We'll be right down," said Nicola.

They drove in virtual silence to Taylors Hill – a trip which, at that time of the evening, took less than ten minutes. When they drove in the gates Nicola could sense the tension in Alice. She sat straight up in the front seat and didn't look left or right even though she hadn't been inside these gates for nearly six months. The gardens were immaculate as usual. Alice used to watch with interest as the various snowdrops, crocuses, tulips or daffodils began to peep above the surface but this evening she just stared straight ahead.

They pressed the code into the key pad to gain entry and the glass doors parted to let them into the foyer. Alice was delighted to note that the usual doorman wasn't there. She wasn't sure if there was anything significant in that fact or whether it was just a coincidence. They went straight to the lift and the man at the desk only very briefly took his eyes off the security monitor to glance at them but he showed no interest in who they were and which apartment they were visiting.

They took the lift to the second floor and when they got out Alice paused.

"We'll look at Cassandra's place first," she whispered.

Nicola and Tom looked at each other.

"No," Nicola said. "You should look at your own first and then Cassandra's. It will work better that way." Nicola was thinking that if Alice got very upset on seeing the vandalism in Cassandra's apartment she would be already in a vulnerable state when she went to see her own.

"I'd say Nicola is right," Tom interjected gently. "Don't worry, we'll be with you. Do you want me to open the door?"

Alice looked at him and then at Nicola.

"No! I can do it," she said and took out the new key which Gerard Murphy had acquired and put it in the lock.

None of them had seen this apartment since it has been gutted so they didn't know what to expect. Inside they found an empty shell. Everything was gone, the furniture, the personal affects, the floor coverings, the white goods, everything except the drapes, which along with the paintwork looked shabby in this stark environment. Even the lampshades were gone but the bulbs were still in the sockets. When Alice turned on the lights the stark shabby look was accentuated.

"It's like a barn," Alice said in dismay. "A bleak barn! It so doesn't look like the home I had here for so many years." There was a crack in her voice but she didn't cry.

"In some ways it's good that it's so bare because you have a blank canvas," Nicola said, trying to put a positive gloss on it. "When you decide what to do you can just go ahead and do it. There will be no deciding what to keep and what to remove."

"You're right," Alice said doubtfully.

She looked at Tom McEvoy as if looking for an opinion but he just looked back at her. In all of his career he had only rarely come across a case as bizarre as this.

"We'll go into Cassandra's apartment now," Nicola went on. "You will both have to brace yourselves for this."

"Do you really think it is a good idea for Alice to look at

that?" Tom said. "What you described to me sounded horrendous." He was concerned that Alice, who he still viewed as a little fragile, might find it too much.

But before Nicola could reply Alice spoke up. "No. I said to Cassandra that I would look at it and would tell her about it and then she could decide what to do. I can do this. I've done a lot of things over the last few months I wouldn't have thought possible or probable."

"Okay," Nicola said and she took out Cassandra's keys and opened the door.

Alice gasped at the sight that met her eyes. "My God. What kind of pervert did this?" Her voice was barely audible.

"It's pretty gross," Tom agreed, going around the apartment, opening doors, avoiding gooey substances on the floor and furnishings, picking up a few pieces of jewellery that Nicola and Séamus had missed during their first visit.

Alice began to wander around the apartment, taking it all in, but Nicola just stood there. The fact that it was her second time seeing this did not make it easier. This was just evil. The thug that did this should be locked up.

"I wonder will Cassandra make a formal complaint?" Tom mused as if he were reading Nicola's mind.

"I don't know. I suppose you'd better ask her. I know she had come across him before through her work but she hadn't brought him back to her apartment because she was afraid of him. She recognised him and he recognised her when he came to attack her but she thinks he didn't know until he arrived at the apartment that she was his target."

"There's no doubt he did the vandalising as well, given what he wrote," Tom mused.

"I suppose so," Nicola agreed and she noticed that Alice was just standing staring.

"Compared to my apartment this is just evil," she said eventually.

"I think there is one thing in common," Nicola said. "If I were Cassandra I wouldn't try and salvage anything else. I'd just gut the place and start again."

"Good idea," Alice said. "And then she could decide if she

should just refurbish or if she should furnish it as well for the sale. I will have to make that decision as well. I'm not sure. I need to think about this."

"Do you think you have seen all you need to see?" Tom asked.

"Too much," Alice said. "But I have enough to think about and I can answer Cassandra's questions. I think I'd like to go home now." In her heart she was glad that Lady Gregory Court would never be home again. Her life had changed out of all recognition in six months.

Alice said nothing at all as Nicola drove her back to The Coven. She thanked Nicola, said goodbye to Tom and slowly went up the steps to the front door.

The girls ran to greet her when she went into Eliza and Hugo's kitchen.

"Eliza gave us a lovely dinner, as good as yours," Orla said.

"That's because your mum cooked it before she went! I just served it." Eliza laughed.

"And she let us have two helpings of dessert," Orla continued, determined to give Eliza credit for something good.

"Guilty as charged," Eliza agreed. "But it's a one-off. I promise."

"Thanks, Eliza, and you too, Hugo," Alice said. "You've been great. I'll take these two upstairs and then, if you don't mind, I'd like to come down again and tell you about the apartments."

"Grand," Hugo said. "Don't rush. We'll probably be up for some time. Night, girls."

The girls said their goodnights and bounded up the stairs. Their relentless cheerfulness never failed to surprise Alice. She was delighted at how adaptable they were. She wondered if she had been so accepting when she was a child. But then again nothing quite so exciting had happened to her during her near idyllic childhood in rural County Mayo.

Cassandra came into the kitchen while Alice was upstairs. She looked relaxed and Eliza and Hugo were pleased.

"Do you know, I really don't think I want to talk to Alice tonight," Cassandra told them. "I feel so relaxed I'm afraid that if I hear what she has to say I might get upset and not be able to sleep. I'm going to make myself a cup of camomile and have an early night. Tell Alice to call me in the morning and if she has time we could walk the Prom or something."

"We will, Cassandra," Eliza said. She was worried about Cassandra. She wasn't as tough as she let on and she was definitely not as assertive as she had been before the assault.

"I'm glad that's over," Nicola said to Tom as they drove back to her apartment from The Coven.

"Yes, it can't have been easy for her," he replied. "But she seemed to handle it well."

"Considering all that has happened to her over the last six months she has really dealt with it remarkably well. She is some woman and when I met her first I thought she was completely naïve."

"She seems like a nice young woman. I find it hard to believe that someone as nice as her could be taken in by a sleazebag like Jack Madden."

"Do you?" Nicola asked. "I'd say very few people think of Jack Madden as a sleazebag. I never would have thought that he had any big secrets before I met Alice. In fact, I thought she was stark raving mad when she told me the story initially. Why do you not like Jack Madden? You're probably the first person I have met that had negative feelings about him even before this. I thought everybody liked him."

"I never trusted him. Maybe it's the guard in me but I am always suspicious of people who are too perfect and Jack Madden was one of them."

"Well, you were right and I think that both Alice and Hugo are very lucky that you are so astute."

"Thank you very much. But maybe I'm not so astute when it comes to my own life."

Nicola looked at him, stunned. She was hoping that this man whom she hardly knew was not going to show her the skeletons in his family cupboard.

"None of us is perfect!" she laughed, hoping that would put an end to that particular discussion.

When Alice came back down to the kitchen Hugo made them all hot chocolate and they indulged in some leftover desserts. Alice told them what she had seen that evening. Even though they already knew some of the story, Hugo and Eliza were shocked. They were glad that Cassandra had decided not to visit at this stage and they were amazed at how well Alice had taken what she saw.

"I can't get over how ruthless that thug was. I also can't get over the fact that Jack set Cassandra up for this. Do you think he really intended to kill her?" Alice was long past the stage when she thought he was a nice person but it still shocked her that he might be capable of murder. It was a possibility she couldn't ignore.

"I don't think there is anything to be gained from speculating," Hugo answered calmly. "We will never know for certain and it might be best from all of our points of view to give him the benefit of the doubt, though he probably doesn't deserve it."

"God, there's no end to it!" Alice sighed. "Still, maybe we'll enjoy the redecoration."

She finished her hot chocolate and went upstairs. When she turned on the TV Jack Madden was on, in a political debate regarding the constitutional protection of the dwelling.

They were drawing up outside Nicola's apartment when Tom McEvoy asked, "Do you mind if I come in for coffee?"

Nicola's head spun around to look at him and he saw the shock in her face.

"I'm not propositioning you," he laughed.

"I never thought you were," she replied but she could hear a level of hysteria in her own voice.

"I have a problem, which I thought, as a social worker, you might have some experience of."

"I thought gardaí never had problems and in any case my expertise is in child protection so I don't know if I can help."

"Well, this is definitely not child protection but you might be able to point me in the right direction. It's not the type of thing I would tell everybody, but I need to tell someone."

Nicola's heart sank. If he was having an affair she didn't want to know – though he seemed too nice. Maybe his wife was having an affair. What would she do? She decided that she had to let him talk – mainly because she didn't know how to turn him down. She regretted, not for the first time, that the days were gone when people just went to confession when they did something wrong and that was the end of it.

"Right, come on up. I'll make you a coffee."

"Thanks," he said and followed her up the stairs in silence.

"Well," Nicola asked as she poured the coffee, "what is so awful that you can't discuss it with your friends or family? I bet it's not as bad as you think."

"Maybe not. In fact I'm hoping that as soon as I articulate it, it won't seem that bad, but I don't know where to begin."

"Try the beginning and be assured that even though you are not a client I will apply client confidentiality to what you tell me. Fire away."

"It's my wife, Helen," Tom said. "I have just discovered that she owes more in credit-card debts than is left on our mortgage. Just when I began to feel that we could relax about money I discovered letters in a drawer from various credit-card companies demanding payment."

"That was a bit of a shock," said Nicola, feeling a bit relieved that he hadn't disclosed something worse. "What did she say?"

"Nothing really! She said it wasn't a problem. She said she had it under control. But she hadn't."

"What did she spend it on?"

"I'm not exactly sure. I've never actually seen the bills. There is no evidence in the house. Just the demands."

"Did you ask her?"

"Yes, but she said clothes and things. I don't see anything in the house that could amount to that."

"Don't ye have a joint account?"

"Yes, but about ten years ago she went back to work as a school secretary and opened an account of her own. I didn't think anything of it. Effectively, I thought she was entitled to her own salary – she had looked after the children for many years and indeed continued to take the lead role in that, even after she went back to work."

"And did she make any financial contribution to the household?"

"A bit but nothing organised. She would treat the children or maybe pay to redecorate a room or get something special that maybe we didn't need urgently. As I said, it meant that she didn't have to watch money any more and in a way neither did I."

"So! Do you know what happened? When did she start overspending?"

"I really don't know. All I know is that she owes in the region of €35,000 – and that's only the demands I saw. I'm really not sure what to do."

"And you're asking my advice?"

"Yes. Where do I go from here?"

"It looks like some sort of an addiction to me but there is usually some evidence around the house and you say there isn't."

"No. I don't see any evidence."

"Could she be a gambler? Or an addict of some sort? Or is she perhaps supporting someone who is? Does she have a family member who is an addict? Or is it likely she's having an affair?"

"I don't think any of those situations arise. I'd say I would have spotted any of those. It's the sort of thing I see a bit in my work. I'd recognise the signs. What do you think I should do?"

"You have a right to know the extent of her debts because in this country if she can't pay them off it will fall to you because she is your wife, so I would start there. When you find out exactly how much she owes and how much she has in the bank you can start to deal with it. It may not be as bad as you think but the fact that she is getting demand letters means that at least some of her creditors are not happy."

"And then what do I do?"

"That depends on what you find out. Come back and talk to me when you find out the extent of the problem and in the meantime I will talk to a friend of mine who is an expert on addictions."

Tom McEvoy finished his coffee and slowly descended the stairs, wondering how he was going to approach his wife on this very sticky subject.

Chapter 41

The following morning when Alice came back from the school Cassandra was waiting for her on the steps.

"Have you time to take a walk?" she asked. "I thought we'd do the Prom."

"Give me half an hour to prepare a casserole for Hugo and Eliza and then I'll be with you. I've loads to tell you. I'd say we'd need to wear something warm today. It was breezy when I was coming back."

They used Cassandra's car for the first time since the assault. Cassandra just approached it with a business-like air and Alice followed her. They didn't turn on the radio as they drove the fifteen-minute trip to the Prom.

"The disadvantage of the Prom is that you always meet people you know," Alice smiled.

"Yes, but we can ignore them today," Cassandra said grimly. "We've other fish to fry. Tell me all. All the gory details!"

"The good thing was that the usual doorman wasn't there and the new guy had no interest in us so we went up to the apartments unimpeded."

"What state were they in?"

"Mine was completely gutted and yours was totally ruined."

"What do you mean by ruined?"

There was no easy way to say it so Alice opted for blunt. She knew Cassandra well enough to know that she would want to hear exactly what Alice had found.

"I mean vandalised, destroyed, unliveable."

"What kind of destroyed?"

"Clothes shredded, carpets and walls spray-painted, lipstick and make-up ground into the floors. Curtains shredded. The beds slashed. Expletives written on surfaces. Everything strewn around the place."

"Don't go easy on the details," Cassandra grinned, knowing that Alice hadn't.

"You asked!"

"I know and somehow, now that it is said, I don't feel so bad. I was hoping this would be how I would feel. What do you think I should do?"

"I don't know," Alice replied. "But I was thinking that I will probably get the advice of an interior decorator and decide if I should just have my place painted and maybe put in some new drapes and carpets or if I should go for a complete refurbishment. I thought you could do the same."

"There'll be more work in mine," Cassandra said. "It will have to be gutted first and then done up."

"If you need any money I could lend you some. I got the €30,000 from Jack and I am working now so I can get a loan if needs be until I sell the apartment."

"Alice, you are so kind – probably too kind for your own good. But I don't need any loans thanks. I have quite a bit of money saved."

"Great. We could get a decorator together and do a deal. It might be cheaper that way and it might be good to sell them together. We could offer them to some of the multinationals for visiting staff from overseas. They're in a great location and of very high quality."

"Aren't you becoming quite the businesswoman?" Cassandra laughed. "That sounds like a plan but we might discuss it with

Nicola, Eliza and Hugo first – just to get their views. What do you think?"

"Good idea. Will we have a coffee before we go back?"

"Okay. Let's live dangerously and have cheesecake as well."

"Don't you think we have been doing enough dangerous living over the past months to last us a lifetime?"

Laughing, they went into CoCo's and picked a table from where they could see the sea.

Once Cassandra had made up her mind she decided to forge ahead. She looked up the *Golden Pages* and found a house-clearing company from Limerick and decided to go with them. She didn't want to get someone she was likely to bump into on the streets of Galway when she had changed her way of life. She rang up and got an estimate which was well within her reach. The man said he could come to Galway the following week and she arranged to meet him and give him his instructions. He said he would probably be finished in a day or two and she was pleased with that.

Alice, in the meantime, was looking up Daft.ie to see what price they could expect. She also bought interior-design magazines to get some idea of what they should do with the interiors of the apartments. They were both anxious to speed up the process. They were hoping that they would have the apartments sold before summer and would be in a position to look for alternative accommodation and start their new life when the city was at its best. They still had no clear idea of what they were going to do in the future but they knew that the first step was to sell the apartments.

Eliza had finished her radiotherapy and Hugo was insisting that she continue to take lots of rest. Easter was approaching and Lizzie and the boys were expected so Eliza and Hugo were full of anticipation.

Chapter 42

Tom had taken Nicola's advice and informed his wife that he was entitled to see her bank statements and her credit-card accounts since he might be legally liable for them if she was not able to pay. She was not happy. She had shredded her statements, as if destroying the evidence even from herself, but eventually allowed him to see the demands. To his dismay there were more demands than he had seen before and she owed at least €37,000. And her bank account was empty. Her net salary was €1,500 per month. He was dumbstruck.

"How did you spend €37,000 and have nothing to show for it?" he asked. "And how do you propose to pay it back?"

"It just crept up and I can pay it back," she replied in a small voice because both of them knew that paying it back would take years even if she didn't spend her salary on another thing and there was no added interest. Tom didn't know what to do. When he looked at their savings accounts he noted that there had been a €6,000 withdrawal about which he knew nothing from one of them. When he questioned his wife about it she said that one of the credit-card companies had threatened her with court.

"It's my money as well as yours," she said and of course that was true but she hadn't told him that she was withdrawing it and

288

that was the problem. He found himself being glad that it was only
€6,000 that she had withdrawn. Again he looked around the house.
He loved his home and he knew that this was mainly due to Helen's
good taste and her attention to detail but try as he might he couldn't
see what had cost them more than €40,000, not to mention
anything else for which she had paid. And Helen continued to
maintain that she didn't know how the situation had arisen.

When next Tom spoke to Nicola she had some advice for him.

"You should try and get her to consolidate the bills into one
loan and arrange a payment plan with the bank."

"I could pay it all off from our savings," he replied. "Wouldn't
that be wiser?"

"Only if there is a real reason for her running up the bills in
the first place but, if she has some sort of addiction, and I suspect
she has though I have no idea what it is, paying her bills would
only be facilitating it."

"I can't think what sort of addiction it would be. If it is drink
or drugs there would be some signs of it around the house and I
honestly can't see it."

"It's really odd." Nicola felt a gambling addiction was the
most likely option. She could be gambling on the internet and
there would be no evidence of it other than credit-card bills,
which Helen had destroyed in any case.

"Nicola, could I ask you a favour?"

"Yes?" She was dreading what might come next.

"Would you come to our house and have a look? Maybe you
will see something that I haven't."

"I don't know, Tom. I'd feel I was invading your privacy and
more particularly your wife's."

"I'm asking you. I'm begging you. We could go some morning
when Helen is at work."

"It's not ethical. I really couldn't."

"It's not ethical to help out a friend?" He was beginning to
sound desperate and didn't realise that Nicola didn't see him as
a friend and fully expected to lose contact with him as soon as
all this business with the apartments was over.

"Okay – but I don't like it. I feel like I am spying on your wife and I don't even know her."

"Look, at this stage I feel I don't know her either and I don't know where else to turn. Maybe you will see something I haven't been able to see. If I knew where the money was going maybe I would understand it."

They eventually agreed to meet at ten the following Tuesday and Tom would drive Nicola to his home.

The following Tuesday was also the day Cassandra was to meet the apartment-clearing company. She decided that she would meet them in a café and give them the key.

"I want you to clear up everything. Take everything including carpets and curtains. I believe that it is in an awful state and there is graffiti on the walls. So if you can't wash that off, just paint over it. I don't want to see it."

"If you don't mind me saying so, you sound a bit paranoid." The man had never got instructions such as these.

"When you see the apartment you will understand."

"Will I?" he asked, bemused.

She decided that the man needed some explanation for her behaviour but the whole truth wasn't a good idea. "I had a stalker and he destroyed my apartment and assaulted me and I am now afraid to go back."

"Sorry. I shouldn't have made that remark."

"Don't worry. I will pay you half the agreed price now in cash and will pay the rest tomorrow when one of my friends has inspected the apartment for me."

"That's fine," the man said, thinking to himself that life gets stranger by the minute.

Nicola and Tom drove out to Moycullen in near silence. Nicola wasn't comfortable at all with what she was doing but she could see that Tom was desperate. The house was a bungalow on a site which looked to be about an acre. The gardens were beautifully kept. She could see that the McEvoys were very house-proud.

Tom opened the door and stood aside to let her in. Nicola walked in without enthusiasm. In the hall the first thing she noticed was a Pauline Bewick painting. That by itself would explain a few thousand. She said nothing at first. She went into the sitting room. It was tastefully decorated with modern furnishings but it had a minimalist look. There was very little there that looked like it cost a lot though there were a few ornaments and a number of paintings which Nicola couldn't value. There was potential there but she wasn't sure. In the dining room there was a Louis le Broquay but she wasn't sure if it was an original.

When she went into the dining room she gasped.

"What's up?" Tom asked.

"That painting over there – do you know who painted it?"

"No, I think Helen got it about a year or so ago at some local exhibition."

"I know the artist," Nicola said. "That painting cost about €1,500." It was the last painting Jonathan had sold as far as she knew.

"But that isn't enough to explain €40,000."

"No, but if Helen is into good art that would go a fair way towards explaining it."

"This is the problem – I really don't take much notice of what Helen buys. She is the one with the good taste."

"Very good, by the look of it. You said she claimed she spent it on clothes. Should I look in her wardrobe?"

"I wouldn't have thought there was much there, though we do have a walk-in wardrobe which is full."

"Let's have a look."

Nicola gasped audibly when she walked into the wardrobe.

"What's the matter?" Tom asked, puzzled.

"Where does your wife shop?"

"Everywhere. Galway, Dublin and very occasionally she goes to London with friends."

"Do you ever go with her?"

"No. I hate shopping. Why do you ask?"

"Because this explains everything! She likes expensive things."

"Doesn't everyone?" he grinned.

"Yes, but most people on regular salaries wouldn't have the money to buy as many designer items as are in this room. The paintings downstairs are also likely to have been very expensive, running into thousands per piece of work, but I'm no art expert so I'm not sure. But I do watch enough TV to know that most of your wife's clothes are designer. There's a Gucci bag, Miu Miu sandals, a Versace dress."

"And you're saying that this explains the credit-card bills?"

"Yes, given her salary, these clothes are way beyond her means as are the paintings downstairs. Now you have to decide what to do about it."

"What can I do?"

"I think you have to confront her. Then you should come to an agreement regarding what to do about it. I can't help you with that."

"Well, you've been a great help to me. I'm not sure how to proceed from here but it's a start."

"Now you can do me a favour. Well, Cassandra actually!"

"Okay. What do you want me to do?"

"I said you and I would look at her apartment after the cleaner has finished tomorrow evening and that I will then pay him the second half of the fee."

"Okay. We'll meet tomorrow at five."

Nicola was beginning to see why Tom McEvoy might regard her as a friend. Like herself, he had gone above and beyond the call of duty regarding this case.

When they visited Cassandra's apartment the following evening it had been completely stripped – even more so than Alice's. The only evidence of the destruction that had occurred there was some fresh paint over the parts where obscenities had been painted. Nicola paid the man and they left.

"All they have to do now is get the apartments redecorated and put them on the market," Nicola said.

"Tell me, do they have a decorator?" Tom asked.

"I don't know. Why do you ask?"

"Because my daughter and son-in-law have just set up an interior-design business and I'd say they might be interested."

"I'll tell Alice and Cassandra," Nicola said. "They can get back to you. Have you spoken to Helen yet?"

"No, I decided to wait till the weekend when we will both be home."

"Best of luck. I hope it works out well."

"Me too." Tom McEvoy had never meant something so much in all his life.

Alice and Cassandra talked into the night. Nicola had rung Cassandra as soon as she got home to report on the apartments. She also told her about Tom McEvoy's daughter's business.

"It might save us a lot of time and trouble," Cassandra mused. "To have someone on tap!"

Alice had agreed.

They decided, initially at least, to just paint the walls of the apartments, erect blinds and varnish and polish the newly exposed wood floors.

"The buyers could then decide what they want to do regarding furnishings etc," Cassandra said.

"Should we put them up for sale together? I was thinking of putting them up on Daft."

"I don't see why not. We could show them ourselves and if we only had one customer they could decide which one they want."

"Or, as I said, if we're lucky we could get a corporate buyer who needed apartments for staff transferring overseas or just for visiting executives."

"Ever the optimist, Alice!" Cassandra grinned. "That's what I love about you."

"We could start looking around for suitable places to buy."

"Are we talking about getting places close to each other? In the same estate maybe?"

"I don't know. Are we?"

"I suppose we could see what happens."

"I would need a place with the potential for a commercial kitchen and planning permission to carry out a business."

"And I only need a small unit – but it would be great if we could live close together – after all, we got on great when we lived next door!"

The women howled with laughter, given that hardly two words had passed between them in the twelve years they had lived in Lady Gregory Court.

The next few weeks were spent in a whirl of activity for Alice and Cassandra. They employed Tom McEvoy's daughter Sinéad and her husband Will to refurbish the apartments. They were delighted to get the work, not least because the clients were known to Sinéad's father.

"You can't be too careful in a recession," Will said. "We know so many tradespeople who have done the work and not got paid."

"You need have no fear of that here," Alice assured him. "We need the work done fast and as long as you can stay within budget we will pay you on the spot."

They got to work immediately. They painted one apartment while they sanded and varnished the floors in the other and vice versa. Alice was thinking that if they were good she might use them to do her new place as well – in particular the kitchen area. But she would have to find it first.

"If we sell them unfurnished you could offer your services to the buyers and, if not, we might need you to furnish them in order to make a sale. Either way, this may not be the end of it – hopefully," Cassandra told them.

"We'll put the apartments up on Daft while they're being decorated," Alice said to Cassandra, "and see if we get any bites. If not, we can just give them to an auctioneer when the decoration is complete."

"I envy you," Cassandra said one day. "You have a plan. I don't know where I am going to go from here."

"It's clear to me that I will need an assistant in order to set myself up as a caterer. Why don't you work with me for while until you decide what you want to do for the rest of your life?"

"Do you think you'd have the work?" Cassandra asked doubtfully.

"We'll just have to wait and see but I still have the hotel work and I could do with a hand at that if I take on anything else there. They want me to do some more speciality cooking for them for small functions but I have put them off until we are organised here."

Chapter 43

Cassandra had heard from Luke. He could come to Galway the week before Easter. They decided on Wednesday. Cassandra said she would be delighted to meet him though in fact she was not looking forward to the end of the relationship.

They met in the foyer of the Merrick and Cassandra was glad that all evidence of the assault had disappeared. They stood there awkwardly, just looking at each other.

"It's funny that we don't seem to have much to say. We never had that problem before." Cassandra leant towards him and gave him a peck on the cheek.

"Oh, I have lots to say," Luke replied. "I just don't know where to start."

"Why don't you fire away so? We can order tea – or would you rather go for a walk?"

"We'll have tea and we can walk later."

They sat and ordered.

"How have you been?" he said. "I'm nearly afraid to ask."

"Well, it's been strange but I'm fine now."

She told him as much as she could about what had happened and also told him that she would be selling her apartment and moving elsewhere. She noticed a look of alarm cross Luke's face and wondered what that meant.

"I'll be staying in Galway and I'm hoping to find work. There is a possibility I'll get some work helping a friend setting up a business but it's early days yet so I'm not sure if it will work."

"Is there any possibility we could continue to meet?" Luke asked apprehensively. "As friends, even?"

"I'd love that," Cassandra said. "I need all the friends I can get and sure aren't you literally my lifesaver?"

"I'm not sure about that," Luke grinned.

"Oh, I have no doubt about it. If you hadn't come in when you did I would be dead."

"Gosh, I never saw myself as a hero," Luke grinned.

"Well, you should, and not just because of saving me," Cassandra answered.

They finished their tea then walked down to the Claddagh and looked at the sea.

In Easter week, just as things were particularly hectic, Alice got a letter from her mother asking her to come and visit with the girls on Easter Sunday. When she got the letter she had to sit down. She had really enjoyed her mother's Christmas visit but she had expected more notice of an invitation to visit her whole family. This was an opportunity she couldn't pass up. At least she hadn't any big function to prepare for but she was still cooking for Hugo and Eliza and fully expected to be cooking the meals for the Easter holiday.

As she returned to The Coven, having taken the girls to school, she realised that even though she was still doing a lot of cooking, she and Hugo and Eliza had hardly sat down together since the decorating had begun at Lady Gregory Court. She and Cassandra had been too busy for any of the usual chatting.

Hugo was making coffee when she went into the kitchen. She looked at Eliza carefully for the first time in weeks and noted that she was looking more like her old self. Her hair had started to grow and quite suited her short though it appeared to have a different quality than before her illness. Her eyebrows had grown again and her gorgeous eyelashes and she was no longer as pale as she had been.

"Myself and the girls have been invited home to my parents' place for Easter Sunday," she said.

"That's wonderful," Hugo said and Eliza nodded delightedly.

"I am so scared. The girls really liked my mother and sister but my father is more austere and less approachable."

"Don't worry. It will be fine. They are offering you an olive branch. Take it." Eliza was thinking that it was not long ago when Lizzie probably had similar misgivings. "Families are meant to make up their differences and your parents must feel ready to do that now. Don't worry. All girls love their granddads."

"I was going to do lunch here on Sunday," Alice said.

"Never mind that! We can do it ourselves and we'll have Lizzie to help," Hugo assured her.

"I could do some soups and snacks and things for the freezer and you could do the main meal yourselves," Alice suggested.

"We can manage fine," he said. "You should just concentrate on yourself and the girls and your family reunion. Don't worry. It will work out. Look at how well it did for us."

"Could I borrow the car?" Alice asked. "It will be just for the day. I don't think my mother had the courage to suggest longer for the first visit. I'd say she was right."

"Of course," Hugo said. "We can use the jeep if needs be."

"Thanks a million," Alice said and she wondered how she would tell the girls that they would be visiting their granddad for the very first time.

Cassandra had done all the work on finding out about what they could expect to get for the apartments. The plan was to sell the apartments and buy in a nice but less upmarket area and hopefully Alice would have enough money left over to set herself up in business. She could live on her maintenance for a while and she could probably continue to work for the hotel until things picked up.

Cassandra still had no great plan, other than to help Alice out, but she would have money left and she wouldn't need to come to any earth-shattering decisions until she was good and ready. She had a few ideas but nothing concrete and she needed time to research them.

She looked at the houses around the west side of the city. For some reason she was hoping that they would find a place near The Coven. She hoped that she wasn't developing a sort of dependency but she couldn't see herself going back to the kind of insular life she had lived up until the time of the assault. She wanted to keep the friendships she had developed over the last six months and she hoped that the feeling was mutual. She found a nice new estate on the Moycullen Road which still had a number of houses unsold. Looking at the prices she felt that they would be suitable for herself and Alice but Alice was so busy she hadn't time to look at them. In any case, until they got an offer on their own places they couldn't really do anything about moving on. Both women were really grateful for The Coven. Without it they would have been scouting around for rented places which almost inevitably wouldn't have been up to the standard of where they were living now. Cassandra was enjoying the search while Alice could only think of the visit to Mayo on Easter Sunday.

Chapter 44

Alice asked the girls to dress in their best clothes.

"What's so special about today?" Orla wanted to know.

"We're going to see Nana and Granddad."

"Oh, brill!" Orla said. "Can I wear my new jeans or should I wear a dress? I've really really always wanted a Nana and Granddad. It will be just brill!"

"I think it will," Alice said though she was very apprehensive about the meeting. "Maybe you should go with the dress. It's sort of an occasion. You are their first grandchildren but you have two cousins who are two and five. A boy and a girl!"

"Will we be meeting them?"

"I think so – if your uncle is around. He is working the farm and as far as I know he lives in a house on the land, so hopefully we will see him." Alice was by no means sure. Her brother Brian hadn't been in touch since she left home though he must have known that he could contact her by getting her address or email from their sister. But he had been very young when she left – about fourteen – so that was probably the explanation.

The girls got into the car with their usual enthusiasm but Eliza and Hugo noticed with sympathy just how apprehensive Alice was. Lizzie and the boys had arrived on Good Friday and would be staying till Monday and Eliza had planned an Easter Egg hunt in the garden on Sunday afternoon. She regretted that Alice's girls wouldn't be around for it but they had their own grandparents and it was only natural that if bridges could be built it was best that they spend the day with them.

The drive to Mayo would have been beautiful if Alice had not been so nervous. The girls were in great form and Alice was glad of that. The village hadn't changed much in the thirteen years since she had been there, though there was a Supervalu where Browne's used to be and the petrol station had been modernised and also sold hot food. There was also a large hotel at the edge of the village which hadn't been there before. Alice wondered who came on holidays to Ballydubh. It wasn't exactly a hub of activity. They drove through the village and about a mile out the other end and turned off the main road to the farmhouse. Alice was so nervous she could barely breathe. It was almost twelve thirty. Her parents would be home from eleven Mass and would have got the papers. Her mother usually served the dinner on the dot of one.

When they drew to a halt in the farmyard the girls jumped out of the car but suddenly went quiet and stood beside Alice – not rushing ahead of her as they usually did when they were out.

They walked slowly towards the door.

Alice braced herself and rang the bell.

Margaret opened the door and Grace excitedly thrust the box of chocolates they had brought for her into her hands. Alice thought her mother looked relaxed and softer somehow. She bent down and kissed both girls on the cheek and gave Alice a quick hug before leading the way into the kitchen.

Alice was shocked when she saw her father. He had aged so much. The effects of the stroke were visible in that the left side of his face had drooped and he stood up with difficulty and with the aid of a stick.

"Hello, Dad," Alice said.

Liam O'Brien dropped the stick on the floor and held out his arms – his left one falling to his side immediately. Alice walked over to him and held him. She tried not to cry but couldn't stop herself and before long all the adults in the room were weeping gently.

"Why is everyone crying?" Orla asked.

"Because we are happy," Liam said. "Which of my grand-daughters are you?"

"I'm Orla and this is my sister Grace," Orla replied formally. "I never cry when I'm happy."

That remark broke the ice and immediately everyone was laughing through the tears.

"I'm sorry, Dad," Alice said, while her mother busied herself with serving the dinner.

"So am I," he said. "I should have been more understanding."

"But you were right. He wasn't the man I thought he was."

Just then her mother asked the girls to help her with the table, which they did with great enthusiasm. She didn't want too many questions about why Granddad wasn't understanding and why Alice thought he was right. They were too young to understand all that had gone on thirteen years ago and she wanted them to enjoy the day.

Dinner was a cheerful affair. The girls regaled their new-found grandfather with tales of their dance in the parade on Saint Patrick's Day. They described their costumes and offered to put on a performance after lunch.

"Granddad might be tired," Alice laughed. "Maybe the next time."

"No, I am not," her father insisted. "I'm only sorry I didn't see the original performance."

Alice knew then that, though progress might be slower than she would like, the bridge had been built and things would be good in the future.

During lunch she told them her plans regarding the sale of the apartment and setting herself up as a caterer. She was now in a position to fill in the blanks which had been there when her mother visited at Christmas. The girls told them about The Coven and their life there and about Hugo and Eliza and Alice thought she saw a sad look flicker over her mother's face but ignored it. Her mother hadn't been around for the last thirteen years but they could make up for lost time. Margaret had always deferred to her husband and though his heart was in the right place she could see why her having an affair with Jack Madden would have been a huge embarrassment to him. Now, if she had been married to him that would have been a different matter!

Her brother Brian arrived early in the afternoon with his wife Ann and their children, Paul aged five and Emily aged two. Brian hugged her awkwardly and Ann shook her hand but they both relaxed when talking to Grace and Orla who came into their own playing with their cousins and chatting with an aunt and uncle they didn't know they had. Alice realised for the first time how much the girls had missed through having no extended family on either side. She was really angry with herself and more particularly with Jack Madden for the weird way she had lived for all those years. She was also sad that she had seen nothing wrong with it. But there was still a lot of living to do and they could make up for lost time.

Brian took the girls and the smaller children out onto the farm and showed them the lambs and let them feed them. They went and watched the cows being milked in the milking parlour and they were amazed. They had never seen a cow being milked before.

"Not sure I ever liked milk," Orla said loftily though until now she had never before expressed that thought.

Their granny kept hens and a few ducks so they looked to see if the hens or ducks had laid. It was all new for city children and they thought it was one large adventure playground.

While the girls were out with their uncle, Alice had a chance to speak to her parents frankly – Ann had followed Brian out to make sure that the boys were behaving.

"I suppose, if I had thought about it, I should have known that you had my best interests at heart," she said. "Looking at it now, if either of my girls took up with a much older married man I would be really distraught."

"We were," her father said truthfully but not harshly.

"I thought you were just trying to control my life and I suppose the fact that you didn't know a thing until I told you I was pregnant didn't help."

"Well, it's over now and we have two beautiful granddaughters," her mother said before her father had a chance to answer.

"And I think I was not very clever putting so much store in a politician," Liam said. "Maybe I should have spotted that he wasn't to be trusted."

"They were different times, Dad. Everybody trusted politicians. I gave him my life. How stupid is that!"

"Well, guess who won't be getting any votes from this household come the next election?" Brian had come in at the tail-end of the conversation and joined in with enthusiasm.

"I'd say he didn't get any votes here for the past twelve years," Alice said and she knew she was right.

"Uncle Brian said we can come for a week or two during our summer holidays," Orla informed them when she came back in, her shoes muddy from the farmyard. "I'll need wellingtons," she said, as if it was all arranged.

Alice looked at her father. She was not sure if he was ready to present his two older grandchildren to the village.

"That would be great," he said, smiling as if he meant it.

As they drove back to The Coven Alice was content. She intended to work hard on strengthening the bonds between the children and their new relatives. She wanted them to know who her family was, given that they wouldn't know who their father's family was for a long time to come – if ever. In any case, that branch of their family wasn't exactly anything to be proud of.

Chapter 45

Things moved faster than Cassandra and Alice had anticipated. On Easter Tuesday there were several replies to their advertisement on Daft.ie and that week they made appointments with all the interested parties to view the apartments. Cassandra had been visiting show houses in the area over the previous few weeks so when it came to actually showing their own apartments she felt up to the challenge. Her apartment now bore virtually no resemblance to what she remembered and Alice's was almost identical. Effectively they were like show houses without the furniture. So they both went together to the viewings.

There were two American companies interested in both the apartments and they had several individual buyers interested in buying one or the other. They showed to the individual buyers first, to test the market. There was good interest but none of them were interested in paying the asking price. They were clearly looking for a bargain and while Cassandra and Alice felt that their apartments were a bargain they weren't as good a bargain as the buyers wanted. Eventually one offered close to the asking price of €400,000 for Cassandra's apartment which was good indicator that they could get it so they said they would get back to him. He was a bit vague about how he would raise the finance, so they didn't jump at the offer and decided not to worry about it for the moment.

On the Friday of the week after Easter they showed both the apartments to a HR executive from each of the American companies. One immediately said that they were too small because they wanted to use them for families coming to Ireland. Their policy was to provide accommodation for the first six months so that the family had plenty time to look at the housing situation in Galway and buy or rent at their leisure. They felt that the apartments were too executive and not suitable for children.

"I raised two girls here," Alice said, hoping that she might sway them.

"One family coming here shortly has two teenagers, one boy and one girl, and I'm not sure this is big enough. These apartments are more suitable to childless couples. But, depending on what else is on the market, we might be interested in taking one of them and finding a larger apartment or house at another location."

Alice and Cassandra were disappointed but it was early days and to have such interest in the first week was a good sign. The reaction of the second company executive was less certain. She walked around both apartments several times as if measuring it with her paces. She *hmmm*ed and sighed a lot and looked out the windows, tested the showers and door handles and said very little.

"I had hoped they would be furnished," she said.

"We decided to leave them unfurnished so that the buyer could put their own stamp on them," said Cassandra, "but if you like we can arrange for them to be furnished, if we can come to an agreement on a price. Alternatively, we know a small interior-designing company that would do it at a very good price."

"I'll think about it. I'll try and get back to you by this day next week."

"Thank you. In the meantime we will continue to show it to other interested parties," Cassandra said with great warmth and she crossed her fingers behind her back, hoping that there would be other interested parties.

Alice spent the week on tenterhooks. Cassandra was much calmer. She showed Alice the estate on the Moycullen Road with three or four houses of varying sizes unsold. There was also a small commercial unit which the developer obviously envisaged as a shop but Cassandra thought that Alice could use it for a kitchen. Alice wasn't sure. She liked the area and the houses and she was delighted that Cassandra was considering buying there but she felt that the commercial unit was a step too far. She put her eye on one of the larger houses – four bedrooms – which was not quite complete. Downstairs it had a kitchen, dining room, sitting room and study.

"I could make the kitchen into my work kitchen and the study our own kitchen," she said. "I should talk to Sinéad and Will and see what they advise."

"Hold your horses," Cassandra laughed. "We have to sell our own places first."

"But it's an idea, isn't it?" Alice said. "I like it here. I certainly would consider buying here. What about you?"

"Well, I brought you here. I like it as well but we'd better not jump the gun."

They showed the apartments to three other viewers the following week but it looked like nothing concrete was going to come of those viewings.

"We can always give them to an auctioneer if we don't sell them soon," Cassandra said. "After all, there must be some knack in selling houses, otherwise nobody would employ someone to do it for them."

Then at precisely nine o'clock on Friday morning Cassandra received a call on her mobile from the woman from the American company.

"We are interested in the apartments," she said. "But we are offering thirty-five K below the asking price."

"I'll have to consult with Alice. She's taking her children to school at the moment and we're showing two other people after that. We'll call you back before lunchtime." The bit about showing it to others was a piece of fiction but Cassandra felt justified.

She rang Alice with the news.

Alice was delighted. "We weren't really expecting the asking price anyway," she said. "I think we should take it."

"I'm tempted to try and bump it up another five or ten grand for each apartment. I'd say they can afford it and we have had a bit of interest." Cassandra was a much more hardnosed businesswoman than Alice.

"But what if they don't bite? We'll have lost the opportunity and selling to a company would be much better than to an individual. They'll have the money so we won't have to wait."

"I think we should give it a shot. They may be expecting it. I'll try five."

"I hope you're right." Alice was doubtful.

"If I'm not we can let them have it at the price they're offering. One way or another I think we have a sale. We won't ring them until near one."

Alice's stomach was in a knot as she drove back to The Coven. She had an appointment that afternoon to look at vans. She would need a suitable one for carrying the food from her home to the customers. Hugo and Eliza had told her that she could continue to use their car if she needed it but she felt that she should at least look into buying her own and customising it a bit. An acquaintance of Cassandra's who had a small restaurant and did home deliveries was going to advise her.

She couldn't be alone that morning. She went into the big kitchen and was glad to find Hugo and Eliza there chatting.

"We have an offer. I'm scared."

"Don't be," Hugo said. "It will be okay."

Cassandra came in full of confidence.

"I suppose Alice told you our news," she beamed. "I'm going to try and bump up the price a bit but if they don't go for it we'll accept their offer anyway."

"I think you're right," Hugo said. "I'd be surprised if what they offered you is their final offer."

Alice was relieved to hear him say that. Hugo was so calm she relaxed a bit – but not much.

Cassandra rang the company at a quarter to one and asked to be put through to HR.

"We are interested in your offer but it isn't the only one we have had. If you were prepared to raise it by €10,000 per apartment we would be prepared to give it to you for a quick sale."

There was more *hmm*ing and sighing on the other end of the line and eventually the woman said, "Five thousand. That's my final offer."

"Done," said Cassandra and they agreed to email each other with the names of their solicitors.

When Cassandra put down the phone there was silence initially then they all spoke excitedly together.

Alice immediately rang Séamus and was disappointed to hear that, now she was a woman of means she was no longer eligible for Legal Aid, but he recommended a friend so she was sorted.

"That's great, Séamus. I hope he can get working on this right away. We want a quick sale."

"God, you're a fast worker when you get going!"

"You ain't seen nothing yet!" Alice said and the others were looking at her open-mouthed when she put down the phone.

Alice and Cassandra spent the next few weeks in a flurry of activity. Alice had to be more careful with her money, given that she needed larger accommodation and her costs in setting up her kitchen would put a large hole in the money from the apartment. Now it was Cassandra who was offering to lend her money if she needed it.

"I think I can manage," she said, "but I will need your help to set up the business and if you still have nothing decided about your own future you would be an ideal person to help me out with the day-to-day stuff, until you do decide."

They decided on the houses on the Moycullen Road. Alice opted not to go for the commercial unit and enquired if she needed planning permission to run her business from her house. She did but was assured that there would be no hitches since her business wouldn't involve extra traffic to the estate and the unit would be suitably designed. She would need Sinéad and Will for that and they agreed also to get her a person to do up the drawings to apply for the planning permission.

The developer nearly bit off their hands when they said that they were interested in the houses and they persuaded him to reduce the price by a few thousand in each case. A cash buyer was unusual in the current situation and he certainly didn't want to lose these sales.

Alice continued to work for the hotel but was anxious to start her new business before she left The Coven to see what she could expect.

"I'll help with the website," Cassandra said. "I have a bit of experience of that from my old life."

"That would be great. Do you know a designer?"

"Not one we could use for this," Cassandra laughed, "but I'd say if we put a notice in the IT Department of the University we could get a student who could do it for a good price."

"Great idea," Alice said.

"We can use my hosting company. They are quite good and not expensive. I have a contact there."

Alice took the girls to see their new home. It was just a shell when they saw it but she let them choose their rooms and she said they could choose their curtains, bed linen and floor coverings if they wished. They liked the place but she could see that they were apprehensive about the move.

"Will we still see Eliza and Hugo?" Grace asked.

"Yes, of course. We'll invite them over and we can still go and visit."

"You can choose your furniture as well if you like but you'll need a bit of advice from Sinéad," she told them and soon they were chattering about colours and designs. Alice was glad that they were both too old for Barney. She wasn't sure she could deal with being confronted by a purple dinosaur every morning when she called them for school.

Cassandra went about her business quietly. She arranged for a student to visit Alice to speak about the website. When he came they all thought he was about sixteen but he was in third year in university so he must have been at least twenty. He and Alice arranged that she would cook some sample dishes and he would get a photographer to take pictures. Alice was also to prepare some sample menus and a tentative price list and he would do the rest. He was as cool as a cucumber and was prepared to work fast.

"Thank you for giving us priority," she said as she said goodbye to him at the door. "I really want to get this up and running within the next few weeks. Is it complicated?"

"A piece of cake, if you'll pardon the pun," he answered with a grin and he put his laptop in his rucksack, jumped on his bike and cycled off.

Alice felt old for the first time in her life. Her barrister and her web designer both looked like they were just out of school but she supposed that this view was influenced by the fact the she had spent thirteen years of her life in a relationship with a man who was old enough to be her father.

The sale and purchase of the apartments and houses went through without a glitch.

"There are some advantages to doing business in a recession," Cassandra said chirpily.

There was a small problem with the planning permission for the kitchen but the town planner had not fully understood that customers would not be coming to the premises other than to view the menus and make arrangements and that in general Alice would be taking the products off site. There would be no added traffic, no big delivery vans and no pollution since Alice would be using natural gas as her main source of energy.

Sinéad and Will were great, taking all of the work out of doing the decorating. Alice arranged for the girls to go shopping with Sinéad and, while letting them make their own choices, she advised them about what would look nice. Alice was delighted and the girls came back to The Coven full of information about what their new rooms would look like.

Precisely seven weeks after Easter, Alice, Grace, Orla and Cassandra were ready to move out of The Coven. No moving vans were required because they had come to The Coven in the clothes they stood up in and very little else and in the intervening five or six months they had not accumulated much. They were all sad to be leaving but had always known that The Coven was a temporary arrangement. Eliza and Hugo were particularly sad to see them go but this was a success story for The Coven. It was an added bonus that they had all become firm friends and they knew that they would continue to be part of each other's lives for some time to come. Nonetheless there were tears shed the day they moved into Butterfly Grove.

Eliza and Hugo said that they would have a party in four weeks to celebrate the move. Four weeks would give them all plenty of time to adapt to their new situation. They would invite Nicola to the party as well – after all, even though they had hardly seen her since before Saint Patrick's Day she was very much part of their lives and without her they might never have met.

Chapter 46

The days that followed the move were strange for Alice. She had never lived in an estate before and she felt sort of exposed. It was a nice house but when she went out her front door she was immediately confronted with one of the neighbours. They were friendly in a superficial sort of way in that they saluted her but in a way that didn't invite further conversation. There were plusses and minuses in that for her. She was used to not telling her business to her neighbours and if they didn't speak to her that would be easy, but she felt that this was an opportunity for the girls to lead a normal life and she wanted them to befriend the neighbours' children. But she soon relaxed when Grace found that several girls in her class were living nearby and suddenly had friends to play with and places to go after school. Orla was a bit slower to make friends but it looked as if she would before long.

Alice was there less than a week when she got her first call in response to her website. She was beside herself with excitement. It was a small charity gig. They wanted her to provide finger food for an afternoon event which would have approximately a hundred guests. The function was four days away.

"It's quite short notice," she had said to the customer.

"I'll be honest," the woman said apologetically. "The usual caterer was double-booked and didn't realise it until today."

"I'll do it," Alice said without hesitation. "It's quite a small job anyway so it won't be difficult." She was not going to let on that she had never catered for a hundred people before, if you discounted the desserts for the hotel. The woman chose from the sample menu from the website and asked if Alice could also provide the wine.

"I'll speak to my wine merchant," she replied and asked what wines the customer required.

"Whatever you recommend will be fine," the customer replied and Alice put down the phone as soon as she could before she went into a panic.

She rang Cassandra and asked for her help.

"They've asked me to provide the wine as well!" she wailed. "And the woman said whatever wines I recommend."

"I'll talk to James," Cassandra said calmly as if James had been a lifelong friend rather than an ex-paying client. "He will recommend whatever is appropriate and he has contacts here that he can put me in touch with. You just get the ingredients for the menu and get to work."

Alice set to work making tartlets with Gruyère and spinach, frittatas, classic prawns, smoked trout, and tiny fruit baskets for dessert. James recommended and supplied the wine for the event and gave it to her at a good price, provided she would agree to have him as her wine merchant in the future.

On the morning of the party Cassandra came to Alice's early and they worked together on last-minute preparation and presentation. At two they had the van loaded and were ready to go to the venue.

There were many familiar faces there, mainly women, and the head count was exactly one hundred. Alice and Cassandra served the food with some help from the organiser and her committee. It was like a big party though Alice understood that tickets were in the region of €50. A local poet read from her work and the conversation was lively. There was a string quartet

playing in the background to add to the atmosphere. In general
it was a very successful event and Alice made sure to leave her
card in conspicuous places on the tables. She was paid by cheque
before she left and resolved to lodge it in her newly opened work
bank account the very next day.

About a week after the charity event Alice got two calls in the
one day. They were both a result of handing out cards at the
charity event, one a lunch in a private house for ten people and
the other was a surprise 50th birthday party at which there
would be about seventy-five guests. The functions were about a
week apart. Alice had to do desserts at the hotel for a function
in the same week as the lunch but the week of the 50th birthday
was free and she decided to keep it that way. This was the
biggest function she had done for which she would provide the
whole meal from start to finish and she decided that it would be
best if she had no distractions. In fact, in the interim, she turned
down two small projects just so that she could concentrate on
the party.

She knew that she would have to plan meticulously. She was
delighted she had Cassandra because the choice of wines for the
charity event had been perfect and that was where she really
didn't have any expertise. She invited both customers to Butterfly
Grove to discuss the menu. The woman who wanted the lunch
asked her if she could come to her home and bring some sample
menus with her and the other customer agreed to come to Alice's
premises.

The lunch was a simple affair and Alice assured the customer
that they would provide the perfect wines and the customer was
happy to let her do so. The other woman was much more
particular. She walked starchily into Alice's kitchen and looked
around.

"Well, you're very well set up," she said as if she was
surprised.

"We aim to please. But, tell me, why did you choose us?"
Alice asked. She was curious about why a woman for whom

money appeared to be no object and who obviously had local connections would choose a company whose name wasn't known to her.

"Well, you did a very good job at the charity event last week and in any case my brother-in-law is very well known and I don't want it getting around that his 50th birthday is about to happen. There is a danger it might be gate-crashed by every freeloader and wannabe that ever walked the streets of Galway."

"So, by using an unknown and not telling me who the person is, you feel you can avoid that?" Alice was amused at the cloak and dagger approach.

"Exactly! You're clever as well as being an excellent cook."

Alice accepted the compliment gracefully and she was glad that her premises was so well kitted out.

"So on the day, how will we arrange it?" Alice asked. "Will you blindfold me and take me there and keep me in a darkened room?"

"Not quite that clandestine. I'll tell you where the party is on the morning. It's a few miles outside Spiddal on the Connemara side. There's a fairly large kitchen in the house, a large dining room and a large sitting room so it should be easy enough to set up."

Alice was beginning to get a bit nervous so without giving it much thought she said, "I usually ask for fifty per cent up front and fifty per cent on the night of the event." If this was some sort of trick or a possible scam she didn't want to be out of pocket.

"Of course," the woman said without hesitation, beginning to write a cheque. "Do you want me to include fifty per cent of the wine as well?"

"No," Alice said. "That will be fine. I won't be able to price the wine until I speak to my wine merchant. I'll ring you about that, to run his proposed selection by you, and let you know the cost within a week."

She was relieved that she had asked for the advance and glad that the woman didn't seem to think it odd.

The lunch party was a week away and the birthday party was

the following week. It was the day before Eliza and Hugo had invited them for the farewell dinner. It would be nice to be back in the cocoon-like atmosphere of The Coven after such a big event. Alice started to plan. Cassandra came over and they discussed how they would organise things.

The lunch was first and it was fairly simple. The customer had chosen a light consommé for a starter, with melon for the two vegetarians she was expecting. The main course would be chicken in sherry sauce with mushrooms and croutons served in a bed of rice with a side salad. For the vegetarians she chose a light potato-and-onion frittata and the client was insistent on the Fruity Fish Cake, which was on the website, for dessert. This was large cake in the shape of a fish, covered with Greek yoghurt and then decorated with a variety of fruits. Alice was amused as she had made this many times for children's parties and it made a very colourful and attractive centrepiece but she hadn't expected to be serving it to adults. However, it would serve at least twelve and she could add some homemade ice cream if required.

They decided that Alice would do all the cooking and under her instructions Cassandra would do the presentation and the serving if necessary.

Idly they wondered who they would be serving at the party the following week.

"I hear Sting spends a lot of time in Connemara," Cassandra said. "But I'd say he's more than fifty."

"Yes. And so does Angelica Huston but I don't think she has a man in her life. But, then again, what would I know?"

They pondered a bit, considering Gabriel Byrne whose sister they knew lived in Galway though it was not the woman they were dealing with, whose name was Maureen Roche, and anyway he was over fifty as well.

"Brendan Gleeson?" Cassandra wondered.

"No way! He's a Dub," Alice laughed. "Though I suppose he could have a holiday home in Spiddal. But he's too old as well. We'll just have to wait and see."

The lunch party was a great success and not a great deal of

hard work. In fact they felt quite relaxed at the end of it all. They handed out their cards and Alice went back home to prepare some of the desserts for a function she had at the hotel the following night.

"On Monday we will start thinking about the party," she said to Cassandra and she spent the weekend concentrating on the girls, taking them to the pool and shopping and cooking their favourite food.

At nine o'clock on the Monday morning Maureen Roche rang Alice.

"My sister decided to go for a buffet in the end," she said.

She had been adamant up until now that it would be a sit-down meal and they had even agreed the menu.

"I think that's wise," Alice said calmly. "No matter how big the house, seating seventy-five people around a table for a formal dinner, even in relays, would be difficult. This way we can have occasional tables dotted around the sitting and dining rooms and guests can eat as they please. I will provide a few hot items and I'll do a really nice potato soup which always goes down well. Though we'll have to provide some seating at tables for those who go for that. Would you like to come over again and we'll make a final decision?"

"Very well. I'll be there at ten."

"Don't rush yourself," Alice whispered to no one in particular after she had put down the phone.

They spent two hours finalising the menu and Maureen ordered a crate of champagne along with a crate each of Joel Delaunay Touraine Sauvignon Blanc 2009 and Château de Frances 2007.

"Do you want some dessert wines – Tokaji perhaps? What about aperitifs or spirits?"

"No thanks. There is plenty of that at the house and we have ordered a barrel of Guinness. What party would be complete without Guinness!"

"Do you need us to bring silverware or glasses?" Alice asked.

"Not at all! My sister is used to entertaining," Maureen replied starchily as if it was stupid question.

Alice was glad when she was gone. She now had a handle on what the client wanted and felt she could do it. Maureen had said she would ring on Friday morning and give her instructions on how to get to the venue.

"We would like you to be there at around 5 p.m.," she said. "People will start coming at around seven and the Birthday Boy is expected to arrive at eight."

Alice thought it prudent not to remind her that it was a long time since this guy was boy. Some people were so sensitive about age.

She rang Eliza and asked if she and Hugo could pick up the girls on Friday and take them to The Coven.

"They could stay overnight, if you like," Eliza said. "We'd so enjoy having them."

"Thank you so much," Alice replied. "It seems ages since we spoke. Cassandra and I are really looking forward to the party on Saturday. It will be great meeting up with Nicola again as well."

"We'll keep the girls on Saturday as well and you can all stay over. God knows we have the room!" Eliza continued.

"Sounds great to me," Alice said, "but you'll have to ask the others yourself."

On Thursday Alice spent the day cooking joints of meat for the cold plates. She also did desserts and starters which could be done in advance. She got as much out of the way as possible because she didn't want to be rushed the following day in case anything went wrong at the last minute. She had the feeling this would be her most important event yet and she could get a lot of business out of it if it worked out well.

She took the girls to school on the day of the party and when she got back Cassandra was already waiting for her. They got to work, with Cassandra following Alice's instructions, and everything worked wonderfully. Alice began to relax. They had most of the food prepared when the phone rang.

"The address is Áit an Iolair, Spiddal. It is a large stone house west of Spiddal. You drive straight through the village, take the first turn right and it's about a mile up the road on the right. Once you take the correct turn you can't miss it."

"We'll be there at five," Alice assured her and put down the phone.

"So where is it?" asked Cassandra.

"It's just about a mile west of Spiddal."

"Great. We're all set then. Except for the question of what to wear."

They had discussed this earlier without reaching a conclusion.

"Well, I think we should dress as if we were guests and be ready to serve the food and drinks if they need us," Alice said. "Given that it is a house party, they will probably do a bit of serving themselves but with seventy-five guests – all of whom will certainly arrive if Maureen is to be believed – they'll almost certainly need help."

"Agreed. But I wonder if he has children?" Cassandra mused. "They could help. I've been to parties where the children of the house made very good waiters and were very enthusiastic. And if he's fifty they would at least be teenagers and could be a great help."

"We'll just have to wait and see," Alice said.

She would wear her cream linen dress, which was smart but casual and was one of her favourites. She expected to be outshone in the elegance stakes by Cassandra but that didn't bother her.

At five o'clock sharp Alice and Cassandra drove into Áit an Iolair. They drove around to the back door and rang the bell.

The door was opened by a young woman, a girl really, who was faintly familiar to Alice.

"Alice?" the girl asked tentatively.

"Yes." Alice was startled. "How did you know my name?"

Without answering the girl turned around and shouted over her shoulder.

"Mum, I think it's Alice!"

"Who is Alice?" a more mature woman's voice came from within.

320

The girl opened the door wider to let Alice and Cassandra in and led the way to the kitchen.

There, standing waiting for them, was Rosemary Madden.

Alice was afraid her knees were going to buckle.

"Alice! How lovely to see you!"

Rosemary came over to her, removed the trays she was carrying, laid them on the table and then hugged her.

"You disappeared so quickly," she said. "The children missed you terribly. Didn't you, Caoimhe?"

"We did. You were my favourite au pair."

Suddenly the penny dropped for Cassandra who had been looking on, not having a clue what was happening. Quickly she took charge of the situation.

"Hello, Mrs Madden. I'm Cassandra Grey, Alice's partner," she said, extending her hand. "How lovely that you know each other and what a surprise but I'm afraid we need to get to work if this party is to be ready for seven o'clock. Is there somewhere we can change as soon as we have prepared the food?"

"Of course," Rosemary Madden replied. "There is a small bathroom off the hall where you can change and freshen up. Have a shower if you like. Alice, we must talk later!"

"Of course," Alice replied and she was surprised that the words came out at all.

Cassandra addressed the girl. "Caoimhe, if your mum hasn't given you jobs, can you come out to the car with Alice and me and we'll bring in the rest of our things?"

"Of course," Caoimhe replied.

Cassandra practically had to guide Alice out the door. She looked as if she had seen a ghost.

When everything was in the kitchen and they were alone again, Alice said, "I can't do this."

"Of course you can," Cassandra said. "You have to. If you don't go ahead with this, apart from the fact that Rosemary will smell a rat immediately, your reputation will be on the floor."

Cassandra was horrified to see that Alice was shaking but she went on.

"This is your opportunity to get a name for yourself among the people who would use your service and if you let Rosemary Madden down that will be the end of you. Now buck up and tell me what to do."

Alice looked at the table laden with food. She had prepared almost all of it herself and the buffet would be cold even though she had also prepared a large casserole of beef stroganoff in case someone asked for a hot meal.

"Ask Rosemary where she keeps the tableware and we will start to set it out on the tables," she said.

Cassandra did as she was told and they set to work. Rosemary Madden was flitting in and out, instructing her housekeeper on which rooms to prepare for guests who were staying over, arranging flowers, and trying to get the children, the boy Ruairi in particular, to take a shower.

"I should have come down yesterday," she laughed. "But if I had Jack would have wondered why, so I didn't come down till today and now there's so much to be done."

"It will be fine," Cassandra said cheerfully. "We'll get the food ready and you don't have to think about that, though we may borrow your beautiful children to help with the service if you don't mind."

"No," Rosemary said. "That will be fine. And Alice, we really must chat later. I'd love to hear all about what you've been doing since we last met."

"Sure," Alice said. Her voice sounded normal even though she could hear her heart pounding in her chest. "But later! I really need to concentrate on making your party a great success for now."

"Great," Rosemary said and she swept from the room.

"Just brazen it out," Cassandra said under her breath as soon as Rosemary was gone. "It's all we can do now."

"I know you're right," Alice said. "If I can carry this off I'll be ready for anything, though I dread to think of his reaction when he sees me."

"He won't be pleased but it's not in his interest to reveal

anything. It would be the end of him. If I know him he will behave as if everything is normal. He's a smooth operator."

"Don't I know it," Alice sighed.

They worked hard and were ready and changed by seven. Cassandra helped Alice with her make-up because Alice still hadn't managed to stop her hands shaking though she cooked and prepared like the professional she was. They asked Caoimhe and Ruairi to serve drinks and canapés to the first of the guests.

"Be sure and bring back any empty plates, glasses and serving dishes," Cassandra instructed them. "We don't want dishes piling up out there. If you need help come back to us and we will give you a hand."

"Great," Ruairi said. "Do we get paid for this?" He was grinning but half in earnest. At fifteen he'd take money from anyone. He was obviously a chip off the old block.

"Of course you will," Alice said without thinking. She would give them €15 each at the end of the night.

There was a low buzz of conversation in the next room which was getting louder as time went on.

Caoimhe came in at one stage.

"Cassandra, we need a hand," she said urgently.

"You stay here and if you're needed I will come and get you," Cassandra said to Alice before picking up a tray of drinks and walking elegantly into the dining room.

At about seven forty-five there was an exodus to the door as the Taoiseach's Mercedes swept into the drive.

Alice stood in the kitchen, aware that things had quietened down in the other room. Then she could hear clapping from the front garden and somebody started up "Happy Birthday" and everybody joined in.

Cassandra remained in the dining room, aware that at least one of the guests had been a client. She felt a bit like Alice must have felt but again she realised that this man would have no interest in outing her because in doing that he would be outing himself. But she had to take several deep breaths to regain her composure.

She started to open the champagne. Rosemary had said that they would do the toast immediately Jack arrived. Alice helped but went back into the kitchen when she became aware that the guests were coming back into the house.

When all the glasses were full Rosemary Madden raised her glass.

"Happy Birthday, Jack!" she said.

"Happy Birthday, Taoiseach!" the gathered friends joined in the toast with fervour.

"Jack, guess who is catering the party?" Rosemary said to her husband.

Cassandra held her breath. She had remained out of the Taoiseach's line of vision so she was sure that Alice would be a complete surprise to him.

"I've no idea," he said.

"Hold on," Rosemary said. "I'll get her."

Rosemary went into the kitchen.

"Alice, come and wish Jack well! He'll be so surprised!"

Alice didn't have an option. She could hear the guests singing "Happy Birthday" again in the next room. Delightedly Rosemary rejoined the party with Alice in tow.

"*It's Alice!*" said Rosemary with a flourish.

"Happy Birthday, Taoiseach," Alice said.

Jack Madden didn't miss a blink.

"Thank you, Alice," he said smoothly. "It's lovely to see you again."

Alice noticed that there was a slight nervous twitch just over his left cheekbone. She had seen this only once before when it appeared as if his transfers wouldn't be enough to bring his running mate into the Dáil but it was so faint that only somebody who knew him well would notice it.

Rosemary Madden also noticed it and wondered what on earth could be the cause of it on such a happy occasion.

"I had better get back to work," Alice said.

"We'll talk later," he said and again only Alice noticed the menace in his voice.

"Of course," she said and left the room.

Cassandra came into the kitchen immediately.

"Well, you pulled that off well."

"I know. I think he was more scared than me."

"He has more to lose now," Cassandra said. "You have the capacity to destroy his career."

"I know but I wouldn't unless he does something truly dreadful," Alice said doubtfully.

"We'll forget the fact that he took a contract out on me," Cassandra said wryly. "If he tops that you can go for him."

Alice wasn't sure if she was serious or not but Ruairi had come into the kitchen to get more drinks and said that there were some dishes in the dining room that needed to be cleared so Alice gave him a tray of drinks and both herself and Cassandra cleared away and replenished the serving dishes.

At just before midnight, when things were winding down, Jack Madden came into the kitchen. Alice looked at Cassandra and then at Jack and waited for him to speak.

"What do you think you are doing?" he hissed.

"Catering your party," Alice said calmly.

"Don't be smart with me," Jack answered. "How the hell did you get the job?"

"Your sister-in-law hired me."

"You should have turned it down."

"Why? She didn't even let me know who the Birthday Boy was. As you now know it is a surprise party. I'm clever but I'm not a mind-reader."

"You can't expect me to believe that."

"I don't care if you do or not. It's the truth."

Jack Madden had opened his mouth to answer when his wife appeared in the doorway.

"Isn't it great, Jack? Alice catering our party!"

"Very nice," he answered through clenched teeth.

"You must come over for lunch tomorrow," Rosemary continued. "Bring Cassandra of course."

"I'm afraid I can't, Rosemary. I already have a lunch

appointment." Alice was delighted with how quickly the excuse came to her.

"Well, some time during the summer," Rosemary insisted. "We'll be spending quite some time here as usual."

"That would be nice," Alice replied, thinking up several excuses she could produce when the actual invitation arrived.

"Jack, they want you to sing a song," Rosemary said, taking her husband playfully by the hand and leading him back into the party.

Through the open door Alice and Cassandra could soon hear him singing "Rosemary, I Love You!".

"Well, that takes the biscuit! We just have to witness this," Cassandra said and they opened the kitchen door and stood in the doorway, watching the Taoiseach while he finished the song.

Rosemary too was watching her husband proudly though again she noticed the twitch above his cheekbone and wondered.

"It's enough to make you want to emigrate," Cassandra said when the song was over. "I think we're nearly finished here. I'll find Ruairi and Caoimhe before we leave."

She went and found the teenagers and gave each of them €15, as Alice had suggested and with which they seemed quite pleased, though Caoimhe was a bit reluctant to take it.

"I'd say he's a stingy old skinflint. The kids were delighted with the money," Cassandra said to Alice as they got into the car.

"Why wouldn't he be, with two families to keep?" Alice said and they burst out laughing. "I can't believe I got through that without a hitch."

"Not only that but several people asked me for your card," Cassandra said. "This could be the start of something great."

"I couldn't have done it without you," Alice said.

"You could have but I loved it and will be happy to help out for the foreseeable future."

"Great. Will we meet up in the morning for a walk? Eliza and Hugo said they would keep the girls all day."

"Better still, I have a guest pass for the gym. Why don't we have a swim and go to the Jacuzzi? It's very relaxing. And I have something to tell you."

"Tell me now. I'm curious." Alice wondered what it could be.

"No, it can wait."

"I won't let you out of the car until you tell me! Kiddy-proof locks are great," Alice grinned.

"Okay! Remember Luke, the guy who saved my life the time I was assaulted?"

"Isn't he also the guy you are in love with?" Cassandra had recently told her about him. "Yes, I remember, but of course I never met him."

"When he was a client I wasn't in a position to introduce him to anyone but I met him once since I left Lady Gregory Court and he's coming over next week to spend a few days."

"Are you happy about that?"

"Very. I'll tell you the whole story tomorrow. See you then."

Alice let herself into the house, pondering Cassandra's news. She put all the equipment into the kitchen and decided to wash and tidy them away in the morning. As she got undressed for bed she realised that she had never in her life slept totally alone in any house until this night.

The girls raced down the steps of The Coven when Cassandra's car drove up.

"Mum, Mum! We had a great time!" cried Orla. "Eliza took us on a butterfly hunt!"

"That sounds like fun," Alice said. "What did you find?"

"We saw eight different species of butterfly and Eliza says there are more. We're going to do it again later in the summer."

Nicola arrived just then and Hugo asked the girls to help set the table.

"Well, tell us. Who was the party for?" Eliza asked.

The girls were dashing in and out, getting cutlery and napkins.

"Remember I told you that I was an au pair when I was eighteen? It was the man of the house."

Hugo had just come into the room and there was a pause.

"His wife welcomed her as if she was one of the family," Cassandra grinned.

"He was a bit less enthusiastic but could you blame him?" Alice said.

"How on earth did you keep your composure?" Nicola asked.

"With great difficulty – but I did it."

Hugo was standing at the sideboard, with his back to them pouring champagne. His shoulders were shaking with mirth.

"Hugo! What are you laughing at?" Orla asked crossly. She never wanted to be left out of the fun.

"Nothing really," Hugo replied and he proposed a toast.

"To Alice!"

"To Alice!" everybody replied.

"Why's everyone toasting you?" Grace asked, puzzled.

"Because I'm just brill!" Alice laughed.

Orla looked around at the circle of smiling adults as if they weren't very bright.

"Grace and I always knew that," she said.